# Run With You

## KANDICE MICHELLE YOUNG

# Contents

# Chapter 1

*D*anielle

"Are we going to talk about it?" Sebastian asks.

"There's nothing to say," I reply, the roaring in my head matching that of the engine as we lift off the tarmac.

"It's been over a week, princess."

Tuning him out, I stare across the private plane at the sight of Geoff's solemn body. His head is leaning against the glass, eyes covered in shades. He appears to be sleeping, but I know him well enough to know better. Geoffrey Taylor is grieving. He's broken, a jigsaw puzzle scattered over the floor, and it's up to me to put those pieces back together again. Waiting for our steward to give the okay, I unfasten my seatbelt and go to him.

Sebastian's charcoal-colored eyes stare at me as I take the seat next to my best friend, but he doesn't say anything. He's knows better after the stunt he pulled. The only thing that could make me killing my stepfather, and him covering up the murder worse would be him telling her.

*Alana.*

The bitch from girlfriends past that always seems to know just how to weasel her way back in. I know part of Sebastian's logic in making her my alibi was in that she's lied about a murder once before. Sebastian killed someone to protect her. Knowing the lengths he went to for her safety hurts more than the knowledge of their child ever did. No matter what Sebastian claims, he once loved her. If she knew that, I'd lose him.

She has proven that her feelings for him will never stop. She's done countless things to break us up, and now she has received the biggest secret I've ever had. Shuddering at the thought of how she'll use that secret against me, I take Geoff's hand.

"You okay?"

"Sunshine and fucking rainbows," he says sarcastically, pulling away from me.

"Okay, I admit, it was a stupid question," I reply, grabbing his hand again. "What can I do for you, G? Is there anything?"

"Go back to your boyfriend while you still have the chance," he says, turning from me completely this time.

Defensively, I grab his shoulder. "What's that supposed to mean?"

"It means that you should go make puppy eyes at Mister Big while you still can. You never know when the bastard that used to be your stepfather is going to show up intending to kill him. Now, go the fuck away and leave me the hell alone."

His icy words cut through me like a sword, and I glance up at Sebastian. Geoff's partner, Jon, was gunned down in an alley just days ago. It was a message from Walt to me, and I guess you can say it worked. I never knew the days I spent with my ex-boyfriend, Kyle, teaching me how to shoot a gun would end in my killing Walter. Having the skill was supposed to make me feel safe.

I don't feel safe, though. I'm terrified, deeply aggrieved by what I'm capable of. Geoff is the one person I would normally tell something like this to. I haven't been able to, however, because he's been staying with his parents since the incident. I've tried going to see him, but he's always refused my visits. He blames this all on me. I can't say that he's wrong. Jon got caught in the crossfires of my war. The guilt of it all has been consuming me daily.

"I'll give you space if that's what you need, but I will not give up on you. Geoffrey Taylor, you are my rock and I'll be damned if I see you turned to sand."

Squeezing his shoulder gently, I stand. He places his hand over mine.

"I'm sorry, baby girl." Taking his sunglasses off, he looks up at me. "It's not your fault. I just need someone to be mad at. It doesn't do any good to be mad at the guy who did it, since he's dead. As far as Walter goes, no one has seen any sign of him since, so…"

Swallowing my confession, I smile at him. "So that leaves me. It's okay, I understand."

"You shouldn't have to," he says, patting the leather seat next to him for me to sit back down. "This is why I've been avoiding you."

"G, you know we're going to get through this."

Shaking his head, he asks, "How?"

"Well…" I pause, to keep myself from burdening him with what I've done. I hate having this secret between us. "I don't know the answer to that. I just know that we will. We always do."

"We've never had to face something this big," he says, looking out the window again.

"Maybe not, but we have loads of practice in the art of overcoming."

"Yeah," he whispers. "I think I'm going to get some sleep before we land. I'm going straight to Jon's apartment to clear out his things."

"Are you sure you don't want me to go with you?" I ask.

He shakes his head but doesn't speak. I know I've lost him. Fat, salty, tears fall from my eyes as I leave him with his pain, cross the plane, and resume my seat next to Sebastian. Sebastian places his arm around me, and I lean into his chest. I've never been so angry with anyone in my life, and yet, I can't help but need him.

"We don't have to talk about it now, but we do, eventually, have to stop pretending like there isn't a giant elephant in the room," he says, kissing the top of my head.

Not knowing what exactly to say, I simply nod. He's right in that we must talk about it, but I'm terrified of how the conversation is going to go. A part of me was lying to Geoff when I said we would get through this. I'm not sure that we can, and I truly doubt we'll be ever be normal again if we do.

****

My old bedroom seems smaller post-apocalypse. The quilt that my grandmother sewed for me doesn't bring the same comfort, and the walls box in on me, creating an unbearable suffocating feeling. *I have to get out of here.* The logical place to go would be to Sebastian's house in Malibu. I don't want to be logical, though. I want to be reckless. Determined, I pick up my phone and call the one person who I know will let me do that without going too far.

"What's up, sexy?" Kyle's raspy voice asks.

"Were you still sleeping? It's ten in the morning."

"Says the vampire."

"Touché. Feel like going out?"

"Sure, when?" He asks.

"Now. I've gotta get out of here," I blurt.

"Restless?"

"Reckless."

"Got it. Can you give me thirty?"

"Yeah, it will probably take you at least that long to get here, anyway. Do you still hang with that guy at the trapeze school?"

"Will? Yeah, why?"

"Can you call him?"

"I'll do it now."

"Thank you," I say, sincerely.

Not bothering with hair and makeup, I throw on a pair of shorts and leave a note for my dad. His dating is still weird for me. He spent the night at Bernadette's. I presume it was because he thought Sebastian would want to stay here with me. In all fairness, he did, but I just couldn't have him around. I'm so mad at him that every time I look at him, I want to scream. Screaming right now won't help anything. I must stay composed for Geoff's sake.

He didn't come back here last night. I had to call him three times before he finally answered and told me he was okay. Ordinarily, I wouldn't have believed him, but thanks to Sebastian's security detail, I know he slept at Jon's. Everything has changed so quickly for both of us. One of us will crack under this pressure, I know it. The question is, who will be first?

Shivering despite the sunny day, I open the front door and step out onto the sidewalk. Kyle is just pulling up in his jeep. Smiling, he walks over to me. He's wearing a pair of khaki cargo shorts that stop just below the knee, showing off his tautly toned calves, and a t-shirt with ripped sleeves that hugs his fit upper-body in all the right places. Fighting the attraction I feel for him, I look into his soft blue eyes.

"Thanks for saving me... *again*," I say.

Laughing, he takes my hand. "There's no need, sexy. I'll always have your back."

"I know," I say, hugging him. His scent is so familiar to me. Almost too familiar. It reminds me of other times in which I felt helpless. Times in which I was desperate to escape the nightmare by any means possible. Pulling away, I rub my wrists. Kyle notices, and takes both my hands in his.

"So, Trapeze School. I called, and they are pretty booked today, with it being Saturday."

"Oh," I say, feeling disappointed.

"However, he said he could work us in if we get there before one. I figure if we leave now, we should be able to make it."

"Sounds great. Do you think he'd let us do it together?"

"I'm sure I can work something out," he says with a wink.

****

The trapeze school is on the Santa Monica pier. It's a little gem Kyle discovered after watching the episode of *Sex and the City,* where Carrie has to write the article about flying on the trapeze. I made the mistake of telling him I would love to do it. Kyle did a little research on Google and two days later, we were in the air. For a while, it was a weekly thing. There's something about flying through the air that gives you an innate sense of freedom. I love it because it gives me that deadly rush of adrenaline I need without the usual deadly risks I take.

Taking my hand, Kyle helps me from the Jeep. I revel in the salty air against my skin and the sand rushing over my flip-flops as I walk. The waves crash in on the shore, and I close my eyes for a minute to take it all in. These are my stomping grounds, and I've more than missed them. Doctor Johnson once told me I can't run away from myself. Until now, I hadn't known I'd been trying.

I took the internship in New York for many reasons. At the time, it was easy to tell myself that Walt and my past weren't one of them. When Nonna asked, I told her it was because I needed to get out there on my own and see what the world really had in store for me. When my dad drilled me about it, I assured him it was purely for professional reasons. Doctor Johnson had seen right through me, though. She'd told me from the start that I was trying to escape myself instead of improving. I remember the heated argument we had over it and how I swore she was wrong. Turns out, I was just in denial. New York was a good fit for me in the beginning, but I'm not so sure that's true anymore. Just like every other part of my life, it's been tainted by the broken past I've been given.

We walk along the boardwalk and turn straight into the small front office. Will, an instructor that we met our first day here, is at the desk waiting on us. Will has blond hair, a Californian tan, and stands about five feet two inches. When he sees us, he flashes a friendly smile in our direction, showing his gold tooth. It's not the kind of thing you would usually see on someone who looks like him, and I always catch myself staring.

"My favorite couple," he says, coming from behind the desk. "It's been a long time. I think about you guys every time that song plays on the radio."

"Too long," I say, blushing and bending down to hug him.

Taking two clipboards from the desk, he says, "Just sign the waivers, and we'll get you flying."

"Awesome," I say, taking them from him and handing one to Kyle.

I fill out the form so quickly that I'm not sure anyone will be able to read my chicken scratch. Knowing better than to keep me waiting when I'm already feeling antsy, Kyle does the same and hands his form back to Will. It takes a few minutes to make sure everything is sound, but then he leads us through the door that takes us to the trapeze area.

We strap on harnesses, dip our hands into the large bucket of talc powder, and coat them thoroughly. Will takes us to the trapeze, and we climb the platforms. That Kyle and I used to take classes here works to our advantage, as we won't need instructors to fly with us and will be allowed to do our own stunts under their supervision. Waiting for me at the top of my platform is a petite blonde that's been working here since the facility opened. Smiling, she welcomes me back and helps me get into position.

From across the net, Kyle takes his position. Giving me a thumbs up as he grabs the bar, he jumps. I watch him swing, and my body suddenly feels alive again. This is exactly what I needed. Staring out at the place where the ocean meets the horizon, I pull the bar eye level.

"Ready," the blonde, says.

My heart pounding with anticipation, I bend my knees.

"Hop."

Legs working on their own accord, I take a bunny hop forward. The suspension of the bar catches me, and I'm flying. Ignoring the burning sensation in my abs, I swing my legs up and tuck them over the bar. Surprisingly, it all comes back to me as naturally as I've just done it yesterday. I swing toward Kyle, and he smiles at me. The dreamy dimple on the corner of his mouth, showing brightly, he mouths, "Ready."

"Yes," I say, as I swing away from him again.

I watch as he lowers his arms. Holding mine out to him, I close my eyes. *Kyle will catch me. He always catches me.* The wind rushes past my ears, and I feel loose hair from my ponytail slap my cheeks. Kyle's hands grab my forearms, and I know the time has come. Wrapping my fingers on his arms, I allow my legs to slide off the bar. Weightlessly, I dangle from him as we swing through the air. His eyes shining, he looks down at me.

"I love you, sexy," he says, unable to help himself.

I smile. As much as I know it shouldn't, hearing him say it brings me comfort. If Alana uses my secret to keep me away from Sebastian, at least I'll always have Kyle. Who knows, maybe I'll even learn to love him.

"You have to let go now," he instructs.

Closing my eyes, I release my grip on his arms. His fingers brush across my skin as I begin free falling. Feeling the sting of the wind against my skin, I think about what would happen if the net decided to snap. Landing softly, my weightless body bounces up slightly and falls back down again. Relief mixes with the disappointment I feel, and I roll off the net so that Kyle can come down.

I'm alive, although I have no idea what that means.

# Chapter 2

*S*ebastian

"Get off me!" My skin crawls at the feel of his sticky skin against my thighs as he lines himself up to me. My ass clenches reflexively, and my stomach curls. Looking up, I meet my mother's eyes.

"Please," I beg, "Help me."

Closing her eyes, she shakes her head and whispers, "It will all be over soon."

My flesh rips at the impact. "No," I scream, shards of pain shooting up my spine and down my legs. Salty tears stream down my face as I look back up at my mother. "Is it worth this?"

Ignoring me, she turns and walks out the door. Still trembling, I look up again and into the brightest green eyes I've ever known.

*Princess.* She's here. She came for me.

"It's okay," she says, extending a shaking hand in my direction. "Just grab ahold."

My fingers brush against hers just long enough for the pain to stop. Her expression turning cold and callous, she rips her hand away from mine.

"How could you?" She spits.

"Princess, don't. Please—"

"Save it, Sebastian! We're done."

Helpless, I watch as she turns and walks away.

*I'm alone, always alone.*

\*\*\*\*

Hot beads of water pound against my face, doing nothing to soothe me. Shamefully, I reach down and grip my cock in my hand.

She awakened this beast. She opened the doors to this darkness and then she ran again.

For over a week, I've been trying to make this right. She needs to understand that I had to tell Alana. She needed someone other than me who could back her up. The detective would never believe me alone. I saw it on his face. *He remembers me.*

She won't talk to me, though. She won't even consider it. I wanted to stay with her last night, and she told me she needed to be alone. She's not alone. She's in Santa Monica with the fucking guitarist.

*I must do something about him.*

My soapy hand glides across my cock with ease, my brain not even processing the steps to get me there.

Damn her, and her need to run. It's one thing when she's running away from me. It's something else entirely when she's running to him.

Tension builds as I stroke myself closer to the edge, my cock jumping slightly under the pressure.

I knew better than to love her. We are too damaged individually to ever be whole together.

Tossing my head back, I come in thick, heavy spurts. The swell of my cock shrinking in my hand as the pressure releases. Lowering my head in shame, I watch the evidence swirl around the drain and disappear. Sticking my face in the stream of hot water, I sob.

*She makes me weak. I swore I would never be weak again.*

Grabbing my towel from the hook, I step out and dry off. There is one way to fix this. She has to talk to me. Wrapping my towel around my waist, I dial her number. Pacing, I listen as the phone rings its maximum number of times before going to voicemail.

"Fuck!" I scream, launching the phone across the room.

It hits the wall with a hard smack, and I know instinctively that I've cracked my screen. Throwing on a pair of jeans and a t-shirt, I grab my motorcycle keys and storm into the garage.

If she doesn't want to talk, then I'll just have to make her.

\*\*\*\*

The lights are off when I pull up to her father's house in Santa Monica, but *that* car is in the driveway. I will replace it one day, regardless of the sentiments she feels toward it. Her safety is the most important thing. Someday, she'll understand that.

Climbing from my bike, I walk to the door and ring the bell. Ordinarily, I would refrain out of respect for her father, but he works nights. Even if he were home, Danielle has already told me he's a heavy sleeper. I wait several minutes before ringing it again. Unless *he's* in there with her, she'll get up and answer, eventually. On the third try, the door finally opens.

Peering up at me through sleepy eyes, she says, "What do you want, Sebastian?"

I look down at the perfectly plush lips that make up the entrance to that smart mouth. *I'd love to fuck her face until I can't withstand it any longer.* There's getting head, and then there's getting head from Danielle Stevens. Crossing her arms over her plump chest, she leans against the door frame. I scan my eyes down her body and over the exposed flesh of her long legs. My cock twitches as I imagine the various things I could do to her.

Drumming her fingers on her elbow, she glares at me with those Jezebel eyes, and repeats, "I asked what you're doing here."

Shifting my weight to allow more room in my jeans, I say, "We're going to talk."

Throwing her hands in the air, she sighs and curses me in Italian. Her hot-headed temper is one of the many things I love about her. Following her into the living room, I take a seat on the coffee table in front of her. She lies down and pulls a throw blanket from the back of the couch, covering the luscious legs that I can't stop envisioning around my head. Ordinarily, I would chastise her for trying to cover herself from me, but for tonight's purposes, it is probably a good idea.

"Stop shutting yourself off from me," I begin.

"Oh, if that isn't the pot calling the kettle black," she says, rolling her eyes and turning her head away from me.

Dropping to my knees, I take her face in my hands. "Princess, when we are fighting, I can't function."

"Then maybe you should have thought about that before you told her what I did," she snaps.

"I had to tell Alana what happened that night, Danielle," I say, biting back my exasperation and running my hand through my hair. "Why can't you understand that?"

"What I understand, Sebastian, is that you gave her more ammunition for her arsenal."

"She wouldn't use this against you, Danielle."

"How do you know that, or is it just one more thing you 'just know'? I have to tell you, hotshot, I've never met anyone with instincts like yours. If only we could all be so lucky."

Her sarcasm stings more than I care to admit. The truth is, I do have a rather unique gift when it comes to people. I can read them within the first thirty seconds. It's a skill I picked up trying to survive as a young child while living on the street. With Danielle, it was no different. The instant her eyes met mine, I knew she had the power to break down the barriers I'd worked so carefully to build. I saw her soul, which had been blackened by the things others inflicted on her, and I instantly recognized it because mine is the same.

Propping my head in my hand, I lean forward. "You are acting like a child again, Danielle. I did it to protect you. End of discussion."

"No, Sebastian, it's not the end of the fucking discussion. Did you not get the memo? Tomorrow, I am going with my best friend to bury the love of his life. Jon was everything that Geoff had ever known to be real about love. He was his version of what you are to me. Now, he's gone. Not only do I have to put on a supportive face and get Geoff through this, I also must keep this massive secret from him. I killed someone, and I can't even tell my best friend about it. Geoff can't know, but the woman who hates me more than anyone has ever hated me in my life does. Why can't you understand what I'm going through? Kyle understands it. Why can't you?"

"You told the guitar player," I say, feeling the anger bubbling in my stomach.

"His name is Kyle, and yes. I told him at dinner tonight. I had to tell someone."

"No, you didn't," I growl, towering over her. "For fuck's sake, Danielle, the more people who know about this, the harder it is to control. Do you not get that?"

Not backing down, she stands in front of me. I can see the fury in her emerald eyes as she focuses them intently on my own.

"What I get, Sebastian, is that this is my life. I'm the one who did it. I'm the one it's eating alive at night. You told Alana. Of all the people in the world, you picked her to trust. I'm allowed to confide in someone I trust, too. Kyle is my choice. I wish I could have told him everything about that night, but I couldn't. I tried, but something stopped me every single time. So instead, I made up an excuse. I told him that I'm on edge, because you shared secrets from my past with your ex-girlfriend. That doesn't change anything, though. I. Killed. Walter. Sebastian, the sooner we stop pretending like I didn't, the better off we will all be."

*"You what?"*

Peering behind me, I see her roommate standing at the other side of the room wearing only pajama pants.

"It's true, G," she whispers, going to him.

No longer able to hide my annoyance with her constant need to make a bigger mess of things, I turn to them.

"Great, now the fucking drama queen knows too," I say, storming out of the house and slamming the door behind me.

# *Chapter 3*

*D*<sup>anielle</sup>

"You going to get that?" Geoff asks, glaring at my ringing phone.

Sighing, I hit the shady button. "Nope."

"Fifth time, baby girl."

"Today's not about him," I reply, taking Geoff's hand in mine. "Are you ready for this?"

"Honestly? I am. I just want to get it over with and figure out what's next. Does that make me terrible?"

"No," I reply. "It makes you normal. I can't imagine what you're going through, but I can remember feeling that way when my mom died. I didn't want to deal with the people or the ceremony of it all. It doesn't make you a bad person, Geoff. It makes you someone who loved Jon too much to pretend like any of this matters."

Teary-eyed, he glances up at me.

"It doesn't. None of it matters one bit. He's gone. Nothing will bring him back and nothing will make it hurt less. *Nothing*," I say.

"I won't get high," he says, squeezing my hand.

Smiling at the relief I feel in my chest, I squeeze his hand in return. "You feel like it, though, don't you?"

Looking away, he lifts a shaking hand to his face to wipe the tears away. "More than I ever have."

"We'll get through this, G. I don't know how, but together we will."

13

"It's me and you against the world, baby girl," he says, attempting to smile.

"Always."

My phone vibrates against the nightstand again, and he pulls me into a much-needed embrace.

"We'll get through that too," he whispers. "There's no going back from what you did. I can't even process it right now, but I know you'll find a way to live with it. It's the only choice."

My chest feeling heavy, I nod. It wasn't easy for him to wrap his head around the fact that I murdered Walt, but I can tell he's trying to come to terms with it. At the very least, he understands my motivation behind it. I wish I could say that it brought me some sort of relief to open up to him about it, but that's not the case. If anything, I feel even more burdened. Post argument, Sebastian's words ring through my mind.

*The more people that know, the harder this thing will be to control.*

Geoff isn't just anyone, though. He's the only one in New York that will have my back one hundred and ten percent. He also has his own personal reasons for wanting Walter banished from the face of the earth. I still can't believe I watched Jon bleed to death. God knows I tried to save him. It just wasn't enough.

I wish I would've never gotten them into that party that night. Had I not, they would've been tucked away safely at Sebastian's, and Geoff would still have the love of his life. *Walter had to die.* Too many people have been hurt because of his sick obsession with ruining me. My mom, Jon... the cycle wouldn't have stopped until he'd taken out Sebastian and Geoff, too. Shuddering, I will my mind to stop racing. My phone rings again and I take a deep breath.

"You kids ready to go?" My dad asks, knocking on my doorframe.

Glancing at Geoff, I nod my head. The sooner we get this over with, the sooner he can start healing. I'm just glad my dad has agreed to be there with us.

****

Funerals are dark. Even in southern California, where the sun seems to always be shining, they have a way of suffocating all the life out of the air. Jon's is no different. In fact, in many ways, it's worse. Despite the beautiful day and the palm trees lining the property's edge, all I can see is the empty grave in front of me. In just a few moments, they will lower Jon's coffin, and that will be the end. Or, perhaps, it will be the beginning.

One phase of our lives, the one in which Jon was always standing at the ready with a comforting smile, will be over. A new one, a darker one, will begin. We'll be left alone with the loss. There will be nothing to distract us. Until this point, I don't think Geoff's been focusing on it. The absenteeism, maybe, but not the loss. He hasn't really considered what that all means. When he does, it's going to break him.

Noticing the crowd around me standing, I look around. The sound of the minister's voice has been nothing but extra noise in my head until this point. I completely missed the cue. Mirroring them, I stand and focus in on him as I watch Jon's coffin slowly descend.

"Dust thou art, and unto dust shalt thou return," he says.

Slowly, the coffin inches to its ultimate resting place. Weeping, Jon's parents approach. His mother throws a rose in the dark hole, and I watch in horror as his father pulls her away. Two women I haven't met yet rush to her side and help him. Heartbroken, I clasp Geoff's hands. Guiding him to the vase, I lift two American Beauties and hand one to him.

His body tenses more with each step. Helplessly, I wrap my arm around his, and do the best I can to urge him along. Stopping just shy of the grave, he turns to me.

"I can't do this, Dani," he says, tears streaming down his cheeks.

Hand fisted in the fabric of his suit, I wrap my arms around him.

"You jump, I jump, Jack," I reply, quoting one of our favorite lines from the movie *Titanic*.

Burrowed against my neck, he whispers, "He was twenty-four. We had everything in front of us."

"I know, hunny. I know," I say, stroking his hair.

"How could anyone destroy something so beautiful?" He asks.

Consumed by guilt, I feel my knees weakening under his weight. My stomach churns at the image of the light leaving Jon's beautiful blue-green eyes, and I swallow the thick bile in my throat.

"I don't know," I answer, hoarsely. "I don't know how Walter could do anything he ever did." My eyes blur with tears. I look around and notice that all eyes are on us. "We have to go," I say. "Just get through this part, and I'll get you to the car."

"Okay," he says, nodding.

We take two steps before I feel his body shaking with heavy sobs.

"G," I say, turning to him.

My words catch in my throat when I look up into his angst-filled face. *I caused this. It's my fault.* Not being able to withstand the guilt any longer, I feel the pressure of my own tears in my chest. Turning my attention to the seated area once more, I find my father's face. I'm wearing sunglasses, but it doesn't stop him from seeing that I need him.

He reaches us just as the world spins faster than I knew it could. Feeling myself falling, I reach out for him. I feel Geoff's weight next to me, but I can't focus on him. My chest feels like it will explode, and I scramble to find him. Our hands meet, and I notice that his is cold.

"You get him," Sebastian's voice says. "I've got her."

Looking up, I see the hazy outline of his frame. The sun behind him casts his shadow over me.

"Sebastian," I gasp, breathlessly.

"It's okay, princess," he whispers, nuzzling against my neck as he lifts me from the ground. "I've got you. Always."

# Chapter 4

S ebastian

I know she wanted me to stay away after the fight we had last night, but I couldn't. Instinctively, I knew she'd need me, and I'll be damned if I don't pull through for her a second time. I missed the mark when Jon died. I'd been with Alana handling the mess I made without even trying. Danielle can never know the real reason I left her at that club that night. She may stay pissed at me for the rest of our lives, but at least she'll be protected from my past. Feeling her stir in my arms, I tighten my grip.

"We're almost at the car, princess, just hold on," I say, delicately.

As soon as I saw the signs of a panic attack on her face, I took off running. I'd been hiding near the trees a few gravesites over. Some may call that crazy, stalkerish even. I say it's necessary. Danielle Stevens may pretend to be tough and unaffected by the things she's survived. I know differently, however. The horrors she carries with her have a way of catching up to you.

She thinks the worst is behind her. What she doesn't realize is that killing her stepfather was only the beginning. It's going to get darker, much darker, before she finally sees light again. She'll be stronger when it's all said and done, but I will not let this destroy her. She won't become tainted. Not like I was.

"Geoff," she whispers, looking behind us.

I glance over my shoulder and catch the sight of her father helping Geoffrey Taylor into his pickup truck.

"He's fine. Your dad has him."

"I should be with him," she says, fighting to get out of my arms.

My grip tightens even more.

"You will, princess. Just let me get you to the car, and Thomas will drive us straight to your father's."

"He needs me," she says, writhing harder.

"Danielle, listen to me. Geoff will be waiting for you when we get back to the house. You just had a panic attack. Let *me* take care of *you* for a few minutes."

"Okay," she agrees, unenthusiastically.

I know I've only won because she's too tired to fight, but right now I can accept that. Thomas opens the door for us, and I place Danielle inside.

"We're going to Santa Barbara," I tell him, sliding in next to her.

Taking a bottle of water from the car's mini fridge, I untwist the cap and hold it to her lips. "Here. Drink this."

Swallowing a few small sips, she takes her sunglasses off and looks at me. "Got anything stronger?"

Her eyes are swollen and bloodshot from crying. In a perfect world, I could make sure nothing ever caused water to spill from those pools of emerald again. The world isn't perfect, though. I learned that lesson when I was young.

"You need to catch your breath, princess. Alcohol won't help with that," I say, pulling her against me.

"Vodka helps everything," she contradicts.

Running her hair through my fingers, I place my lips on her forehead. "I'm sorry."

"Sebastian," she says, looking up at me. "I don't want to think about it anymore. I don't want to talk about it. I just want to move on. I did what I needed to, and you did the same. Can we just leave it back there, behind us, where it belongs?"

"We can ignore it for today," I tell her, truthfully. "However, we both know that this is too big for us to run away from it forever."

Nodding, she nuzzles back against my chest. "Yeah, still, it would be nice, wouldn't it?"

"Yes, Danielle. It would be perfect. I would give anything not to have to watch you breaking like this."

Waiting, I watch the scenery change as we hit the freeway. I'm not sure where she is, but it doesn't matter. Wherever the location, I'll be there with her for however long she needs.

"Thank you, Sebastian," she whispers, breaking the silence.

"For?" I ask, looking down at her.

Sitting upright, she turns her body to face mine. "Being here."

"Danielle, when you need me, I'll be there."

I never wanted to be this person for anyone before. If she were anyone else, I would've run a long time ago. I have enough baggage on my own. The last thing I should do is take on someone else's. Danielle makes it impossible to leave, though. She fills me so completely that even brief separations make it seem like I'm missing a piece of my soul.

****

"How is she?" Her father asks me as I emerge from the room.

"She's not great, but she'll get there," I tell him.

Even to my own ears, it sounds like words of comfort, but I know the truth behind my statement. Danielle will be back at one-hundred percent again. I'll destroy whatever I must to make it happen.

"Thanks for bringing her home. I would see you out, but I think I should get in there."

"Actually," I begin.

Curiously looking at me, he stops. "Yes."

"I was planning on staying here. I don't want to leave her right now."

"Oh." Sizing me up, he brings his thumb and forefinger to his chin. "Do you remember what I said to you when we had dinner at Mother's?"

"Yes, sir."

"I told you about Danielle's troubled past, and the fragile state of her emotions."

"Correct."

"Well, she's slipping. I don't know what the hell is happening in New York, but it's not the place for her."

"I'm not disagreeing with you, but things will change when we get back. I can assure you."

Arms crossed, he narrows his threatening gaze at me. "Can you? You've already given me your assurances once, and the next thing I knew, my daughter was being placed in a coma to protect her from brain damage."

"Those were special circumstances."

"Special circumstances like when she held her friend's dying body in the alley outside of one of *your* nightclubs?"

"That was not my doing."

"No, it wasn't. However, Sebastian, since you've come into Dani's life, she's not been the best version of herself. I sent her to New York, a happy, functioning adult with a bright future ahead of her. You've brought her back to me, a decaying fifteen-year-old that's seconds from her ultimate break."

Forcing myself to keep my temper at bay, I say, "With all due respect, Mister Lettiere, Danielle is an adult. You can't make her choices for her. She chose me. I gave her the chance to walk away, and she stayed. I realize that I've made mistakes, and I would be lying if I said I would never make another one. Here's the one thing I know, though. I love your daughter. I will always love her. No matter what she faces, no matter how bad she breaks, I will be there to help get her through it. I will never give up on her, because I know she'd never give up on me."

"But, son," he says, sincerely. "Sometimes loving means letting her go. I've been in your shoes. Danielle is everything her mother once was. I fought to keep her, and in the end, I almost destroyed us both. It certainly destroyed Dani. Everything she's ever had to go through... that's on me. If I wouldn't have pushed, her mother would've never left. Dani would've been safe if I would've just loved her mother enough to let her go. You know the history there. Are you really willing to see Danielle pick up where her mother left off?"

Looking at him, I realize he isn't trying to keep me from her because of his own experiences with Danielle's mother and step-father. His reluctance has never really been about me at all. His fears are about Danielle's experiences with her mother. It's about the fact that she found her mother that day. It's about the fact that the seed has been planted, and he's a father terrified of losing his daughter.

"Mister Lettiere," I say, placing my hand in my pocket. "I can assure you, I don't want to lose her either. Certainly not like that. Danielle isn't her mother, though. I know you know it's true. When you were in New York, you described her to me as a survivor. There's more to her than that. Danielle doesn't just survive. She fights. She thrives. She overcomes whatever this world throws at her. I know she can do it on her own. And I know she can do it even easier with your help as well. All I'm asking of you is that you let her do it with mine, too. I'm part of this team now. If you just let me do what I need to, I promise you'll discover that I'm a pretty valuable asset."

The bathroom door opens, and Geoff steps into the hallway. "Sorry, I was just going to the couch. I didn't realize anyone was out here," he says.

"You're fine, son," Giovanni says, placing a hand on his shoulder. "Did the shower help?"

"I guess," Geoffrey says, untruthfully. "I'll leave you guys to it."

"Giovanni," I say, keeping my voice low. "You have your hands full here. Without Danielle, he has no one. At least she has me. Let me focus on her so you can focus on him. You know it's what she'd want."

Exhaling, he looks from Danielle's bedroom door and into the living room where Geoff is lying on the couch with his back turned to face us.

"Fine," he says, giving in. "I'll allow you to stay, but consider my question."

"I will," I reply. "So long as you consider mine as well."

"I can assure you, I haven't stopped. It's been on my mind every day since you asked it. I can't say yes right now, but if you get her through this, it will certainly move you a few steps closer."

****

I'm awakened by the sound of Danielle's screams. *The nightmares.* I can fix everything, except the nightmares. "It's okay, princess," I say, stroking her hair. "I'm here."

"Sebastian," she whispers, strangling on her own tears.

"I'm right here." Arm around her waist, I sit up and fold her body over mine. "Walt or Jon?"

Tangled hair matted to her sweat-slickened skin, she looks up at me with the wounded eyes of someone who's seen too much evil in their lifetime. "Both," she says. "They're one and the same at this point."

"It doesn't happen overnight, princess."

Nuzzling against me, she says, "I just wish I could forget about it."

"Maybe I can help with that," I reply, rolling her to her back.

"I'm not exactly in the mood, Sebastian," she says, looking up at me.

"Relax, princess. I'm not starting anything." I roll to my side and pull her against me. "I only want to use my body to shield you from everything that you're afraid of."

"Okay," she whispers, pressing her back against me and wrapping her hand in mine. "Can I make a request?"

"Of course," I reply, softly kissing her ear.

"Can we leave before Sunday Dinner?"

Strumming my hand over her hair, I take a few minutes to contemplate her wish. "Are you sure?" I ask, trying not to sound alarmed.

"I'm not up for it," she replies. "And I don't think G will be. I'd rather just take the jet back early and focus on picking up the pieces."

"Okay," I respond. "Get some rest. I'll handle it."

She drifts to sleep shortly after. I, on the other hand, lay awake in the dark listening to her shallow breathing. Kissing her hair again, I whisper, "I will fix this for you, princess. Even if it kills me. That's my promise to you."

# Chapter 5

*D*<sup>anielle</sup>
"So, remember how jealous I was over your life?" Piper asks.

"Yeah," I say, not sure where she's headed.

"I've decided you can keep it," she says. "How do you handle having all this shit thrown at you at once?"

"Practice, I guess," I reply, easing behind my desk.

It's Monday. I'm back at work and hopefully on my way back to normal. It feels like my entire world has been turned upside down since the moment Sebastian came into my life. I'm not centered. I haven't been for weeks now. It has to change. I don't know how, but it must.

"Seriously though," she says, handing me a cup of coffee and leaning against my desk. "How are you feeling?"

Burning my tongue, I set the paper cup on my desk and fan my mouth. "Oh. You know."

"You could've taken some extra time off, you know. I'm sure Paul would've understood."

"Maybe," I say. "My bank account, however, wouldn't've been so understanding."

"Been there," she says, making her way to her own desk. "If you need me to pick up some slack for a while, I get it."

"It's okay. I'm better when I have something else to focus on."

23

"You're sure?"

Nodding, I say, "Yeah."

In truth, I've been dying to get back to work since I left Friday. When I'm working, it's easy for me to not think about Jon, Walt, Alana, Sebastian's daughter, or any of it. Sipping my coffee with care, I study the calendar for any new bookings. My heart pounds when I see it. *Lickwid*. I'm not ready to go back there. Not now, maybe never.

My mouth feeling dry, I turn to Piper. "When did Sebastian book us for an event at Lickwid?"

"Umm... Friday, I think. Didn't he tell you?"

"No. No, he didn't."

Fury bubbling in my gut, I open my email.

*To: Sebastian Black*

*Don't be an ass. Cancel the event now.*

Pressing send, I focus my attention on a brief for a new client. My cell phone vibrates against my ribs. I'd forgotten I tucked it into my jacket pocket instead of my bag. Paranoia prevented me from doing so. If Geoff needed me throughout the day, I would be there. This isn't Geoff, though. It's Sebastian. I don't even have to check to know it. Rolling my eyes, I pull it out of my pocket and slide my finger across the screen to open the text.

*I'm not cancelling an event that's been on my calendar for months. You won't be working it.*

Not even sure where the anger's coming from, I growl and type back: *How can you possibly say that? Paul hasn't even made it to the office for our staff meeting yet. I wouldn't have known anything about it had I not checked the calendar this morning.*

I don't even have time to place my phone on the desk before it vibrates again.

*I requested you don't.*

Rage. All I feel is rage.

*Sebastian, we've already had this fight. You won't interfere with my career. I won't allow it.*

*No, but I am going to protect you. You're not ready to go back there, and I'm going to make sure it doesn't happen.*

He's right about me not being ready, but it doesn't stop the exasperation I feel toward him.

*That's not your choice to make, Sebastian. I have work to do. I'll see you later.*

I store my phone back in my pocket just in time to see Paul coming through the door. He smiles sympathetically at me as he approaches my desk. Wanting nothing more than to feel normal, I smile back and say, "Good morning."

"Nice to have you back, Stevens. You're sure you don't need a few more days?"

"I'll do better with a distraction," I reply, fearing what that distraction will be.

"I knew I liked you for a reason," he says, patting my shoulder. "Staff meeting in ten. Can you go get the conference room set up?"

"I'm on it."

****

It turns out Paul agreed with Sebastian. It would be perfect that he's on board if not for the fact that in keeping me from working Friday's event, I'm forced to work tonight at Pure Sugar instead. Chill bumps on my skin, I stand at the entrance. They weren't kidding when they said the temperatures would shift drastically in August.

The sidewalk is packed with people desperate to get in. I watch them chatting excitedly with one another, and wonder if I'll ever feel that way again. At one time, club hopping was a way of life. Now, it just seems silly to even consider. Feeling out of my element, I go over the guest list once more. Sebastian called us in on this event to bring some positive PR to his entertainment empire. The least I can do is help him meet his goal, especially considering that the reason behind the bad press is my fault.

*If only I wouldn't have worked that night.*

I'm pulled from my thoughts by the toxic smell of a big-chested blonde wearing too much perfume. She smiles at me through thick red lipstick and informs me that there are three in her party. Checking my clipboard quickly, I step aside and let them in.

Tonight's live band is from New Jersey. Their music is loud, their fans even louder. I've only been here an hour, and I already want nothing more than to go home and crawl into bed with Sebastian. Three more groups come and go before anything truly interesting happens. I'm just checking the time on my smartphone when the loud boom of what sounds like a gunshot rings through the night. Screaming, I throw myself to the ground. Heart-racing, I dart my head left and right, frantically scanning the area.

*I can't believe this is happening again.*

Shaking, I look up to see the hand of Bill, the bouncer. "Dani, you okay?" He asks.

"Yeah," I say, allowing him to help me to my feet.

"It was just a car backfiring," he whispers.

25

Feeling the flush of humiliation in my cheeks, I bury my face in my clipboard as we let a few more people through.

*Will I ever be normal again?*

It's not long before Piper is coming to get me. Smiling knowingly, she says, "Paul thinks you'll do better at working the crowd than me."

"Really? I thought you were getting the hang of it."

"I am, but I'm not you."

"You're sweet, and you're lying. This is about the car backfiring, isn't it?"

"It just appears you could use a break, is all," she answers.

I appreciate having a job where the people truly care for one another. However, I hate being the freak in the group. This job was supposed to be about becoming something more than that. It was supposed to prove that my damage wasn't debilitating. If only it were really that easy.

I hand her my clipboard and walk through the heavy metal door. Nostrils burnt by the thick clouds of smoke, I blink my watering eyes and make my way to the bar. Ordering a water, I scan the room. I'm not sure where Paul is. He's also handling press for the band and several other clubs tonight, so it could be several places. Looking over my shoulder, I watch the bodies jumping up and down in time with the bass.

*If I ever feel that carefree again, it will be a miracle.*

"Your drink, miss," I hear.

I turn around to see a vodka and cranberry sitting in front of me. Not wanting to cause a scene, I politely push it back toward him.

"I didn't order this," I reply. "I'm actually part of the press team. No alcohol for me."

"It's on the house," he replies, nodding his head toward the back of the room. "Mister Black said it's your preferred drink."

Spinning around, I see Sebastian standing against the back wall. Shaking my head, I cup the drink in my hand and reply, "Thank you."

Sebastian smiles a mischievous smile as I approach, and I feel myself softening.

"Paul didn't request that I come inside, did he?" I ask.

Pulling me against him, he says, "I saw everything from the street camera. Are you okay?"

"I'm fine. I can't drink this, though."

"I'll handle Princeton," he says, clasping the straw and bringing it to my lips. "Come into my office for a sec?"

"Sure."

Instantly feeling safer, I place my hand in his. He leads me down a narrow hallway and into a grungy office. I look around at the cement walls and road signs. *This isn't Sebastian.* Pulling a face, I sit on his lap.

"I haven't had the chance to decorate yet," he says, running his hand down my spine.

"I didn't say a word."

"You didn't have to." He laughs. "Maybe that can be your next project."

"I think I'll have my hands full with the renovation," I reply.

"Yeah, about that," he says, kissing my collarbone and nuzzling into my neck. "I spoke with my contractor today. We can meet with him as early as next week."

Checking my fingernails, I let the words sink in for a few minutes. I'm not sure Geoff will be ready in a week. I still haven't had the chance to discuss any of this with him. He went straight back to his parent's house when we came home yesterday, and I haven't heard from him since.

"Tell him, Danielle," Sebastian says.

"I just don't want to overwhelm him," I say, sighing. "You're used to moving at warp speed, hotshot, but Geoff needs time to process things."

"Are you sure it's about giving him time and not you stalling because you're still expecting the worst?"

*Damn him for knowing me like he does.*

"It's a little of both," I say, honestly.

"Danielle," he begins, cupping my head in his hands. "We've handled it. Please stop worrying about it."

I lay my head on his shoulder, allowing his scent to soothe me. "I'll feel better after our therapy session tomorrow."

"You know you can't talk to the therapist about this, right?"

"I know," I say, reluctantly.

It was silly of me to ever expect to be able to talk to anyone about the fact that I committed murder. That would be the easy way out, and I never get to take the easy way out. Instead, I'm stuck with the guilt and the constant paranoia.

"You can talk to me about it, though," he says, lifting my chin.

"Thank you," I reply, closing my eyes and bringing my lips to his.

He strengthens our embrace, pulling my blouse free of my jeans and placing his hands on my bare back. "What do you say we get out of here?" He asks.

"Deal," I reply, smiling at him.

# Chapter 6

S ebastian

"Sebastian, what are we doing here?" She asks as we pull into the parking garage at Windom Tower.

"We're coping," I reply, casually.

"Not that I'm complaining," she responds. "But what can you possibly have to cope with?"

Cupping her neck, I pull her lips to mine. Sometimes nonverbal communication is the best communication. She willingly accepts the kiss, running the tip of her tongue over my lips and sending shock waves directly to my dick. No one has ever affected me like Danielle does. No one ever will.

"Don't worry, I have my own shit to handle," I say, climbing from the car and taking her hand.

It feels as though the elevator takes forever to climb to the penthouse I purchased just after I finally started seeing some profit from my first nightclub. Until then, I'd had to be careful with my sexual escapades. Windom allowed me the freedom I needed to finally let go. It was more than a safe house for my fantasies. It was a breakthrough. I learned how to control myself. How to give the aggression over to someone else without taking it too far. That's the reason behind the time limits.

Six weeks. Not a minute longer. Just enough time for them to leave without feeling used, never enough time for me to feel anything at all. Until Danielle. I knew it when she walked into the lobby that day. Six weeks will never be enough time with her. I need a lifetime, and even then, I fear it just won't be enough.

She's proven to be more difficult than I had expected. Her scars run just as deeply as mine, but her methods of coping aren't as contained. We're a tornado hovering on top of a volcano, and I know she's on the verge of forcing me to erupt. One day she'll learn to submit to me without question. Today isn't that day, however. Today, I'll turn the reins over to her because she needs control and I'll teach her how to get it.

I glance over at her as the car climbs higher. She's doing that thing she does when she shuts out her surroundings to cope with the elevator. The first time I saw her do it, I instinctively wanted to make it stop. Nothing should cause her fear, nothing should hurt her. If I have my way, nothing ever will again. Clasping her hand, I step in front of her and bring my palm to her cheek. She opens her eyes, focusing those glimmering emerald irises on me, and stirring something deep inside of me that only she can.

"I love you, Danielle," I say, pressing my mouth flush against hers.

Her hands thrust into my hair, hungrily pawing at me as she holds my tongue hostage with hers. My dick screams with warm heat, and I'm suddenly desperate for more. Bringing a hand to her breast, I sigh as my cock swells and my balls constrict. She gives me a knowing smile and reaches her hand to my trousers. Tossing my head back, I try to fight the flush in my cheeks as her fingers grip around me.

Her focus is on my cock, but I feel her everywhere. Dropping to her knees, she wraps her lips around me. Closing my eyes, I throw my head back in anticipation. Her lips close over me, and her tongue cups the bottom of my head, resting snuggly against me like a warm blanket.

Breathing in a sharp breath, I lace my fingers in her hair and look down. She gazes up at me with hungry eyes, and I know she won't let up anytime soon. Hallowing her perfect jaws, she descends the length of my cock. My head brushes against her tonsils, and I feel myself stiffening even more.

*Fuck, I'm putty in her hands.*

Losing all restraint, I rock my hips, fucking her face slowly. Slickened from her saliva, every nerve I have tingles as I thrust inside of her. She pulls her head back, focusing just on my tip as she runs her hand along my shaft in time with each bob.

"Fuck," I growl, knowing I'm on the verge of letting go.

Pulling her hair, I attempt to force her to release me. She's relentless, however, and it only causes her to work harder. My balls grow heavy with my arousal, and I know I'll come soon. She cups them in her hands, milking me as she sucks me into oblivion. Cock twitching, I throw my head back and roar as I expel into her mouth.

"You're so fucking good at that, princess," I reply, feeling the final sting of release.

Smiling, she licks me clean and kisses my cheek. "You can pay me back later," she says with a wink.

Her hand in mine, I lead her into the foyer. "Drink?"

"Not really," she replies. "I had other things in mind."

"Oh, did you now?" I ask, raising my eyebrows.

Her smile steals my breath as she moves in front of me. "Meet me in the fantasy room?"

"I thought this whole excursion was my plan," I say playfully.

Pressing up on her tiptoes, she brings her lips to my cheek and whispers, "Maybe I've taken over."

"Give it your best shot," I encourage, striding to the living room and sitting on the couch.

"Office," she chastises. "I don't want you seeing anything."

"As you wish," I reply, kissing her softly and wandering down the hall.

Truth be told, I need to spend some time in my office, anyway. I really do have my own personal shit storm brewing, and the more time I must focus on it, the better things will be. Sitting at my desk, I take my phone from my pocket and scroll through my missed calls and messages.

*Alana.* Every fucking last message is Alana.

Fighting the temptation to hit something, I scroll to her name and hit send. Dread seeps from every single one of my pores as I wait for her to answer.

"Thank God," she says, frantically. "I've been calling and texting. Where have you been?"

Fingers on the bridge of my nose, I glace at the door. "I'm with Danielle, so make this quick."

"Oh," she replies, an iciness in her voice.

"This is your last warning, Alana. Danielle is in my life. It will never change. Get over it. What was so fucking important that you couldn't wait for a return phone call but sought attention by blowing up my phone?"

"Sebastian," she says, a tinge of hurt in her voice.

"Save it and get to the point, or I'm hanging up."

"You've become so cruel since you broke the rules for her."

"No, Alana. I've become a better man since Danielle became mine. As such, I refuse to entertain the notions of anyone who wants to hurt her."

"Honestly, Sebastian. If I planned to hurt her, would I be covering for her with the police?"

Reaching the point of exasperation, I growl, "We both know why you're doing that, Alana. Now get on with it already."

"You're so moody these days," she replies. "Fine. I just wanted to let you know we got her back. You were right. She was exactly where you said she would be."

"Thank you," I reply, feeling a mild bit of tension leave. "Tell her I'll come by sometime tomorrow. Was that all?"

"Sebastian," she says, cautiously. "She's in terrible shape. This is probably the worst I've seen her."

"Just keep her there. No matter what it takes."

The door opens, and I look up to see my perfect princess smiling at me. She's wearing a genie costume that consists of a gold bra, a see-through purple skirt with slits on each side, and no panties beneath. My cock instantly jolts at the sight, and my voice catches in my throat.

Voice filled with arousal, I rasp, "I have to go. I'll see you tomorrow."

"Once upon a time you had the same reaction to me," she says.

"Tomorrow," I say again, hanging up the phone.

My dick feels painfully constricted against my jeans as I turn to truly appreciate her in all her glory.

"Who was that?" She asks.

"No one," I reply. "I just had some—"

"I know. I know. You just had some business to take care of," she says with a quick roll of her eyes. "I've heard it all before."

"Princess—"

"It's fine, hotshot. *I'm* fine," she says, twirling her skirt, and offering me a glimpse at her voluptuous backside. "Are you ready to play?"

"I was born ready," I reply, approaching her.

"Good," she says, turning on her heel and looking back at me. "Follow me."

She has transfigured the fantasy room into an Arabian Nights fairytale. I don't know how she accomplished it in so little time, but she did. Orange curtains form a tent around the bed and there are jeweled toned pillows scattered across it. The room is aglow with candlelight, and a tray of exotic fruits rests next to a bottle of Krug Brut Vintage that I suspect she selected more out of convenience than anything.

"So," she says, taking my hand and leading me into the room. "I know you brought me here for sexual healing and all of that, but I would much rather prefer playing it a different way."

"And what way would that be, princess?" I ask, climbing onto the bed and pulling her onto my lap.

"Well," she begins, stroking her fingers over my girth. Her touch is painful in the most pleasant way, and my head aches as blood swells into my tip. "I think it's time we got back to the basics. When you first brought me here, it was under the impression that I would submit to you. I'm not promising that I'll give up my will forever, but tonight, your wish is my command."

I watch as she backs away, twirling in a carefree way that sends her skirt in a swirl of purple fabric around her and offers me the benefit of seeing her freshly waxed pussy. Quickly glancing around, I'm suddenly full of inspiration.

"You're sure?" I ask.

"I'm positive," she replies, certainly.

"Okay. Lay down."

An excited smile fills her lips as she comes to the bed and positions herself on the mattress. I make my way to my prized treasure chest and pull out a blindfold and two scarves. She's given me everything else I could ever need without even knowing it.

"I'm going to blindfold you and tie you up," I warn, remembering the need to openly communicate my intentions with her.

"Okay," she says, wiggling her body against the mattress excitedly.

I can smell the sweet nectar of her arousal, and it adds to the hunger rooted deep inside of me. Lifting her head, I slide the blindfold over her eyes. My lips inches from hers, I hover over her for a few minutes. Nipples peaked, her breath grows heavier.

*I love watching everything I'm feeling mirrored in her body.*

Parting her plush mouth with my tongue, I kiss her as though I'll never have the chance again. Lifting her hips, she grinds her sweet pussy against me. Even through my jeans, I can feel the puddle resting between her legs. My cock jumps at the contact, painfully rubbing against the denim I'm still wearing, and I growl in frustration.

Pressing her hips to the bed, I roll over her and free my dick by removing the pants and tossing them sloppily on the floor. I lift a scarf from the bed and grab her wrist roughly, pinning her to the headboard. She moans at the feel of my hands on her skin, and it excites me even more.

Tying her off, I repeat the process with the other wrist and take a moment to reflect on her gorgeous body splayed out before me. Everything about her screams sex from the rounded hills of her chest to the toned legs attached to her plump ass. *She is Helena of Troy, and she's all mine.*

"This will be warm," I say, lifting a candle and holding it over her. "If it's too much—"

"I'll safe word. I promise," she says, her chest rising and falling heavily.

I smile. It takes a lot for her to trust me. I'm more aware of that now. I should've understood in the beginning, but it was hard for me to see past my own insecurities. It's just as hard for me to trust her. She has the most fragile pieces of me, and there are times I fear her intentions. These are the moments we get past all the things that threaten to keep us apart. This is our common ground.

Tipping the candle slightly, I watch the first few drops of wax fall onto her breasts. She gasps and arches her back as her body adjusts to the unfamiliar sensation. *Pure erotica.* I must fight the desire to grab my cock and jerk off as I watch the color rising in her cheeks and listen to the sounds of her breath. Hovering over her, I run the wax down her breastbone and onto her flat torso.

"Sebastian," she whimpers, writhing against the mattress and clenching her thighs together.

The sound of my name coming from her lips turns me on even more, and my balls ache as my dick grows harder. Beating myself against her hip to bring a small sense of relief, I spread her legs. The waistband of her costume snaps easily at my touch, leaving her raw before me. Grunt escaping me, I toss the shredded fabric to the floor.

"Your pussy is perfect, princess," I say, running my fingers over her slickened folds.

She moans again, and I watch, awestricken, as her muscles tighten. Never have I had a woman as greedy as her before. Dripping the candle over her stomach again, I slide two fingers inside of her.

"Oh," she cries, welcoming me.

Fingers curved, I find the spot that only well-trained men can and bury the pads of my touch there. She tosses her legs flush against the mattress and arches her back once more. Engrossed by how responsive she is, I pour the final pool of wax over her breasts and blow out the candle.

"Sebastian," she begs, as I continue working her.

"In time, princess," I reply, wanting to sink balls deep inside of her just as badly as she wants me to.

"Please," she whines, as tremors spread from her hips and down her thighs.

"Come for me, princess," I command. "Then you can have me. I promise."

She responds instantly, tossing her head back and arching from the mattress as she floods my fingers. Continuing to tease her G-spot, I refuse to let up until her shaking subsides. Panting heavily, she tosses her head from side to side as I drain her of everything she offers. Before she's had time to fully recover, I climb onto of her and drive my cock inside. She clenches at me hungrily, the softness of her lips threatening to force my undoing before I've even gotten started.

"Fuck! You're so wet," I growl, as she sucks me in.

"Yes," she cries, as I sink myself deep inside and withdraw again.

I wait for her to stop clenching for me and repeat the process again. Within minutes she's on the verge again, and I'm relieved because I'm right there with her. My cock fills to the point of no longer being able to stand it, and I speed my pace as I chase the orgasm. She locks her legs over mine as I slam against her walls.

"You've destroyed me," I say, spasms engulfing my dick. "I'll never be the same."

I come in heavy spurts, filling her with my seed and bringing her down with me. Panting, I fall on top of her.

"Never. Ever," I whisper.

"Well then, I guess it's a good thing I'll love you always," she replies.

****

"So, I'll see you tonight," Danielle says, sweetly, staring up at me with hungry eyes.

"I wouldn't miss it," I say, pulling her into me.

"Is everything okay, hotshot?" She asks, stroking her finger over my chest and fueling my fire even more.

"Fine," I reply, inhaling her scent. These are the moments I want embedded in my brain until my dying breath. "Why do you ask?"

"You just seem a little off. Is it therapy? Things didn't exactly end well last time."

Tensing, I push the memory of being so close to the man my mother felt so indebted to that she gave him me as payment from my brain. "That was different. We'll be seeing someone new this time."

"It's okay to be nervous you know," she says, looking at me once again. "I am."

Pressing my lips to hers, I use the friction of my tongue to say everything I want to, but don't quite know how. Even though my father is a therapist, the very idea of therapy makes me uncomfortable. It's the whole vulnerability thing. I don't like letting people in, especially not in the places I know therapists aim to go. It's important to Danielle, however, so that makes it a priority for me. Besides, it's not the therapist that has me on edge. It's the other important appointment I have today.

"You'd better get in there or you'll be late," I say, releasing her.

"We wouldn't want that," she replies. "I've already missed way too much work as it is."

"So, go," I encourage. "I'll see you after."

"I love you," she says, stepping onto the sidewalk and turning to me with an expectant glance.

"And I you," I reply.

I watch as she walks into the building, waiting for her to get safely inside before tapping on the privacy glass. Cringing, I settle in as Thomas eases the car out onto the street and we cruise toward the rehab facility. I've never liked these visits, but lately they've gotten worse. She's been trying to get out since she saw the photo of me and Danielle outside of my hotel. The very thought of my life moving on without her in it, sending her spiraling back to wonderland. Now I have to clean up the mess, protect her from the consequences.

*Even though she didn't protect me.*

"Not much longer, Mister Black," Thomas says, lowering the glass as we cross the bridge into Brooklyn.

After all these years, he knows just the right time to pull me back from my thoughts. We've been making this trip at least once a month since college, just after I learned she was still alive. I'm not sure if it says more about me or her that I'd hoped she wasn't. Sometimes I still do. It would be easier that way.

"I'll be ready, sir," he replies, closing the door and propping against the town car.

Breathing in the crisp morning air, I button my jacket and stride through the glass doors of the renovated apartment complex. Ironically, she's the very reason I started this program — with the help of my father, of course — and now she's in jeopardy of being kicked out. This was supposed to stop the cycle once and for all.

I saw too much before I was even twelve years old. It's because of her I know firsthand what it looks like when an addict cannot get their life together yet again. I can pretend that I don't remember how living that way feels. I can even suggest that these burn scars on my chest aren't from her lit cigarettes. If only I didn't still see the glowing red embers every time I close eyes. That's the reason the Black House started. I thought it was important to give these women — mothers and daughters — a chance to reclaim their identities without the pressures they faced on the street.

Black House is a halfway house of sorts. It's a place rehabilitated addicts with nowhere else to go can come while they learn marketable skills and attempt to acclimate themselves into the real world. The residents of Black House receive meals, housing, job training, and outpatient therapy at no cost for their first few weeks. Once they've successfully procured a job, they gradually begin paying rent and utilities, graduating to meal plans, and eventually leaving to start a fresh life in the real world. It took my father and me countless days of pouring our souls into the project to get it up and running.

He'd been more than supportive every step of the way. Unfortunately, she's not been as receptive as we'd hoped. Thanks to the carefully thought out treatment procedures implemented and overseen by my father, combined with the financial planning seminars ran by Alana, the program has had a much higher success rate than others of its kind. Not with her, however. *Never with her.* She has nothing to gain by getting well.

"Mister Black," the receptionist greets me, as I approach the desk for my visitor's badge. "I wasn't aware we were due for an audit. Ms. Sinclair didn't mention anything, and I'm afraid she's stepped out of the office for a meeting."

Of all my charities, Black House is the one I insist on attending to myself. When she wasn't here, the only time they saw me was on days when I came by to make sure things were running as smoothly as the reports on my desk suggested.

"I'm here for more personal reasons," I reply, all the while wondering what meeting Alana could've had so early in the morning.

"Of course," she says, smiling. "You can go straight back. She'll be happy to see you. They say she had a rough night."

"Thank you," I respond, signing my name on the visitor's list.

"Mister Black, you own the building and God knows you supply most of the expenses for this place out of pocket. You don't have to go through the formality of signing in."

"It helps me to keep my personal and professional life separate. Just because the lines sometimes get blurry doesn't mean that I can't take small measures to remind myself."

I can tell I've puzzled her by her expression, but I don't feel as though I owe any members of my staff an explanation as to why I do anything. It's only because today is a personal visit that I'm able to keep myself from berating her. Once again, another example as to why it's so important, especially here, for me to sometimes remind myself when I'm wearing my boss' hat and when I'm just Sebastian. The second appears to be sleeping as I turn the corner and enter the one-bedroom studio without knocking. Given the updates I received throughout the night, I know it would be pointless to do so.

"Isabelle?" I ask, softly.

"Bashie, is that you?" She questions, turning toward the door and flinching as the hall lights reflect in her eyes.

"It's me," I reply, stepping into the room and closing the door.

"Bashie, oh my Bashie! I told them you would come," she exclaims, struggling to get out of bed.

"Lay back down," I say, gently, helping her back into her bed. "You need your rest."

Covering her up, I pull a dining room chair next to the bed and sit at her side.

"What happened, Isabelle? I was just here three weeks ago, and things were going well."

"You left me, Bashie," she says, pathetically.

Even with my conditioned containment, it's hard for me not to feel sorry for her as I look down at her pale, frail frame. Walking to the kitchen to fix her a glass of water, I say, "I told you it would be a few weeks before I made it back. Did you forget?"

"Lauren came, but you didn't."

"Lauren's been here without me?" I ask, turning the lamp on and handing her the glass.

Her nose is stained red with dried blood, and her eyes have the wicked glaze of someone who is coming down off their high. She squints past the light in her effort to focus in on me. Swallowing, I place a shaking hand on hers to steady her as she brings the glass to her lips.

"Yes. Lauren, Alana, and Richard. But not you." She looks up at me sadly. "Why?"

"I had things to take care of. You know I'm busy."

"You were with that girl, weren't you? The one you say can't see me."

"I didn't come here to argue, Isabelle. I came to help you."

"Help me?" She asks. "You always help me, but then you leave again. Why do you leave me, Bashie? Why?"

Exhaling, I look down at my watch and fix the cuffs of my jacket. "Isabelle—"

"You used to call me mommy," she says, cutting me off. "Remember that?"

Shivering, I stand and tuck my hands in my pockets. Of course, I remember my years with my birth mother. I also remember how she sold me in order to get the money for her next fix. How I cleaned up the vomit after another night of her binge drinking when I was only six. *The way her words cut through me just as much as the leather on my back when she beat me with the belt and told me I was her biggest mistake.* Tears welling in my eyes, I shake my head. This is why I had to take some time away from her. She brings up too much pain. Pain that I, in turn, relinquish onto Danielle and my princess doesn't deserve that.

"Yes, Isabelle, I do. I also remember why I stopped. Anyway, I didn't come here to talk about that. I came here to take you on a trip."

"A trip?" She asks, straining to set the glass on the bedside table. "Is Lauren coming too?"

"No, Lauren has school. She'll catch up to us later, though. How's that sound?"

"Will you call me mommy when we get there?" she asks.

"I'll consider it," I lie, swallowing the panic in my voice at the thought of ever using that word again.

"I should get dressed first. If my Bashie is taking me somewhere, then I know it must be nice."

"It's very nice, Isabelle," I reply, telling a half-truth.

My father's clinic in Connecticut is nicer than most, but it's still a true rehab facility. It designed for the advanced treatment of addicts, not to be a spa for them to escape to. "In fact, I think we might even stay there for a few days. Do you think you can pack a suitcase?"

Nodding her head, she smiles at me, and I feel a nauseating rush of guilt engulfs me. I hate doing this to her, time and time again. It's one thing to pull back from seeing her for a week or two. It's something else entirely to watch her believe that she'll ever have the kind of relationship with me and Lauren that she dreams of having.

"I'll be right back," I reply. "I have to clear a few extra days with your doctor first."

"I'll be ready when you get back," she says, pulling some tattered clothes from her dresser.

Apparently, it's time for me to purchase a new wardrobe for her again as well.

Closing the door, I walk to Doctor Thorpe's office to sign the transfer papers. As hard as this is for me, it's going to be at least ten times harder on Lauren. She, at least, still believes there's a chance we can save our mother. I gave up long ago. Taking my phone from my pocket, I send her a quick text asking if she can meet when school dismisses.

*I have a swim meet. Can we do dinner instead?*

Dinner with my sister would mean cancelling not only on my mother but also on Danielle. I haven't told her I have another sister yet. I'm not sure why I hid Lauren from her, except that it's something I've grown accustomed to. Apart from my father and Alana, no one in my inner sanctum knows about her. I learned about her identity shortly after I found Isabelle. Lauren was eight, and they were living at a women's shelter here in the city at the time.

I made it my life's mission to ensure that Lauren didn't have the life I had at Isabelle's hand. With the help of my father and one of his colleagues, I got custody of her. I was in college at the time, and beyond fucked up over Alana and what I believed was a secret abortion. My father suggested I hire a nanny to help take care of her, so I did. To keep things hidden from Jewels, Katie, and my mother; we put Lauren up in an apartment with her nanny at her side. That was eight years ago, and she's been there ever since. I spend as much time with her as I can, but since Danielle walked into my life, that hasn't been as much as I'd like. That must change, but there's only one way to do that.

*I already have dinner plans. Can we do breakfast instead?*

*Danielle?*

Shaking my head with a smile on my face, I reply: *Yes.*

*Should've guessed. Are you bringing her to breakfast or are you still terrified I'll embarrass you?*

*You could never embarrass me, little sister, and yes, I think I'll have her join us. How about seven-thirty at my place?*

*Sounds great. I gotta go. Love you.*

Breakfast will clear up one of the many complications in my life. Now, I just need to get Isabelle to Connecticut to clear up another one. Taking a deep breath, I turn the handle to her doctor's office and announce my presence.

# Chapter 7

D anielle

"You have the opera tonight, right?" Piper asks as she logs out of the company mainframe.

"Yeah. What's up?"

"Oh nothing," she sighs. "Except that I just found out I'll be there as well."

"Really? I didn't know we were covering it."

"We aren't," she replies, holding the door open for me.

"So, it's a date then?" I ask, thankful that I'm feeling genuine excitement for something for a change. "Like an actual date."

Nodding her head as the smile spreads across her face, she squeals, "Yes!"

"Oh-Em-Gee! Do you know, like, what you're going to wear and stuff?"

"I don't have a clue. What are you wearing?"

"Well... I really didn't have any idea what to wear, so I texted pics of two outfits to Sebastian's sisters this morning. They each picked something different. Now I'm thinking I'll just let the housekeeper decide," I laugh.

"You guys have a freaking housekeeper? What's next?"

"It's not *you guys*. It's Sebastian," I say shyly, holding the door open for her.

I haven't thought anymore about moving in with Sebastian since we last discussed it. For one thing, I know Geoff will never go for the offer to live in the penthouse next to us, and I'm not ready to leave him just yet. For another, I'm not sure how I can move in with him now. Walter's death turned my world topsy-turvy, and it's selfish of me to just expect Sebastian to continue living in the middle of my mess.

"I don't really have anything that says opera," she says. "I mean, I did a quick search to see what one usually wears to an event like this, and I came up short handed."

"I think it depends on the seats," I offer.

"Right, so where are yours? Maybe we'll be sitting close enough to entertain each other."

Stifling my giggle, I shrug. "I'm not sure. Sebastian's family is the primary benefactor, so I'm sure there's some sort of special section we have to sit in or something."

"Of course, there is," she says, rolling her eyes as we step onto the sidewalk and Sean opens the door to the black town car for me. "Well, maybe we can meet up during intermission."

"If not, I'll certainly see you during the schmoozing time afterward," I reply, with a hint of disgust in my voice. "I'm quickly learning that at least one hour of boredom comes along with the territory of being on the arm of a powerful man at a high society event."

"Great tip," she says, waving. "I have much to learn from you, Yoda. I'll catch you later."

"Absolutely! Text me if you need someone to run your outfit options by," I say, sliding in next to Sebastian.

"You know I will," she replies, turning on her heel and heading toward the subway.

"Good day, princess?" Sebastian asks, lowering his phone and taking my hand in his.

"Better than yesterday," I answer, leaning into him for a kiss.

He takes my cue. Kissing me softly, yet so intensely that it spreads warmth over every inch of my skin, and I pant breathlessly when he pulls away.

"I'm glad," he says, turning his attention back to his phone. "I just have a few more things to wrap up and then I'm all yours."

"So, you've had a busy day," I say, swinging my legs over his and pulling at my skirt to keep some sense of modesty.

"No busier than usual," he replies, typing a message on his phone.

"Really? I called earlier to see if I had left my phone charger in the car. Robin said you weren't in yet."

"That doesn't mean it was anything out of the ordinary, princess. I had a few important meetings," he says, storing his phone in his jacket pocket. "Did you find the charger?"

"No, I guess I forgot to grab it," I reply, trying to ignore the feeling in my gut that tells me he's once again hiding something from me. "It's not like me to lose things."

"You've been under a lot of stress, princess," he says, gently running his thumb over my calf muscle. "Don't let it get to you."

"Yeah," I reply, exhaling, and leaning against the window. "So, are you ready for this?"

"As ready as I'm going to be," he says, avoiding my gaze.

"Talk to me, hotshot. You seem off."

Running his free hand through his hair, he exhales and says, "I'm fine, Danielle. I promise. It's just been a long day and while I'm used to long days, we are also in for a long night. We have to get ready and head to The Met pretty much as soon as we get home if we're going to make it on time."

"Why did you schedule the appointment for today if you already had these plans?"

Turning to me with a gentle gaze, he replies, "Because I knew how important it was to you. I want to be the man you need me to be, Danielle."

"You already are," I answer, leaning forward and stroking his face with my hand.

"If that were true, then you wouldn't need this."

"I need this for reasons that have nothing to do with you," I reply honestly. "Just as you need it for reasons that have nothing to do with me, whether you want to admit it or not."

"The problem is neither of us can discuss the things that we really need therapy for with anyone except each other."

"And apparently, Alana," I say, unable to help myself.

He takes a deep inhale and begins, "Danielle—"

"Save it," I reply, shortly. "We're here."

****

Doctor Tanowitz is a small-framed woman with brown hair that's light enough it teeters on the edge of honey-blonde, and eyes in a brilliant shade of blue. She wears an oversized sweater that hangs awkwardly off her thin shoulders, jeans, and high heels that are chipped at the toe. Her pink lipstick has rubbed off on her tooth, and it's the only thing I can see when she smiles. Pushing her thick-framed glasses up her nose, she says, "So, Dani, what I'm hearing from you is that despite Sebastian's masterful communication skills in a boardroom, you struggle to get him to open up to you. Is that correct?"

"It's one of the many things, yes. Another issue is his baby momma drama, for lack of a better explanation. If Sebastian had his way, I would never speak to my ex again, regardless of the fact that my job depends on me maintaining communication with him. With Alana, though, he's allowed to divulge not only his own secrets, but mine as well. And I'm supposed to be okay with that," I reply, glancing over at Sebastian, whose shoulders and jawline both tense as I turn the conversation onto yet another issue he refused to mention when it was his turn to share.

"And Alana is the 'baby momma'?" Doctor Tanowitz asks, almost making me laugh.

"Yes, but it's not like they are raising their child together or anything. She had an open adoption, and he didn't even know anything about it," I blurt before I can stop myself.

Sebastian turns an icy gaze in my direction, and I feel myself shrinking. I know mentioning his daughter was probably overstepping my boundaries, but I didn't even realize how much it was bothering me until now. Doctor Tanowitz must notice because she makes a clucking noise with her throat before jotting some notes down on her tablet and turning her attention back to Sebastian.

"So how does Alana play a part in your life if it's not in joint parenting?"

"It's complicated," he replies nonchalantly.

"Everything is complicated with him," I say, exasperated. "Mysterious phone calls in the middle of the night, this lovechild, meetings that keep him out of the office until well past noon..."

"I just don't see a point in telling someone every single detail of my day," he says to Doctor Tanowitz instead of directly to me.

"I'm not asking you to tell me every detail," I hiss. "*Some* details would be nice, though."

"Not when it comes to Alana," he growls.

"And why is that?" Doctor Tanowitz questions, jumping straight to the heart of it.

"It just isn't," he replies. "Let's move on."

"Actually," Doctor Tanowitz says, using her stylus to tap her tablet screen. "I'm afraid that's all the time we have for today. What I would like to do is see you each individually for the next week. I believe there are some important underlying factors to your relationship that we will best be able to work through separately first and then together in order to bring you where you need to go. Danielle, I would like to start with you. What's a good day?"

We schedule our appointments, despite everything in Sebastian's body betraying his calm composure about the process, and exit the office. I'm not sure what exactly I was expecting from him, but I had hoped for a little more. That he became so defensive regarding my mention of Alana is enough for me to know that there was more to his morning meeting than he's letting on.

*He was with her.*

Stopping, he pushes the call button for the elevator and takes out his phone.

"I think I'll take the stairs," I say, watching the stoic expression on his face as he replies to his text.

Not bothering to respond, he grabs my arm and pulls me in with him.

"What's with you?" I ask, jerking my hand away as the doors close and my panic sets in.

"What's with me?" He mocks with a snicker. "You're the one who felt the need to give a complete stranger an all-access pass to the most private parts of my life."

Shamefully staring at the floor, I say, "I'm sorry I brought up your daughter. I don't know why. It just sort of came out, but you could've at least addressed it."

"No, I couldn't," he replies. "She has nothing to do with the problems we're having."

"I'm not one hundred percent sure that's true, Sebastian. You told me Alana was a part of your life because of your daughter, but then you ran to her with my secret. And now you're quick to jump to her defenses in our counseling session. It just feels like I'm missing so many important parts to the story, and I can't help but wonder if they are all about your daughter or if it's about something else."

"Let's begin with your secret," he says, pulling me from the elevator, through the lobby, and onto the sidewalk.

"I don't have any secrets," I snap as soon as Sean has closed the door. "Apparently, everything that goes on in this relationship is between you, me, and Alana. So, what's the point in even trying to keep anything private? Talk about an all access passes."

"For weeks now, I've been trying to have this conversation," Sebastian says, dropping two ice cubes in a glass tumbler, and pouring scotch in on top. "You've refused, but clearly it's something that needs to be discussed. So, now we will."

"I don't—"

"No!" He barks, effectively silencing me. "You want to talk about it. What you don't want to do is *fight* about it. That's the reason you chose this particular time to bring it up. You knew I would refrain from making a scene in the middle of the therapist's office. I will finally explain to you exactly what I told Alana about your situation and you will listen.

Then you will apologize and if there's enough time left after, I will fuck your frustratingly beautiful face until I'm no longer furious with you."

Crossing my arms, I glare at him. "If you think I'm sucking anything after the way you just talked to me, then you've got another thing coming."

"We'll see about that," he replies with a delicious smirk. "Now, as for Alana, she knows exactly two things about that night. The first is that you were in trouble, and I needed to help you. The second is that *my* actions required the need for her to be *my* alibi, and since I didn't want you to be associated with what *I* had done, *I* needed her to cover for you as well."

The smirk on his face and the simmering heat in his eyes giving his amusement away, he crosses his calf over his knee and watches me. Dumbfounded, I stare back as the car glides through the crowded street.

"I believe this is what chess players effectively call, check, princess."

"I wouldn't know. I've never been a fan of chess," I say, recovering some of my sarcasm. "So, what you're expecting me to believe is that Alana knows nothing about Walter's death?"

"That's correct, but *now* Geoffrey does. It would appear that the damage control now lies with you and not me. So..." Grinning wickedly, he leans back and spreads his legs. "I believe there's still plenty of time."

*Oh, I don't think so.*

"Not so fast, hotshot. What exactly was her reaction to all of this?"

"She agreed. Why wouldn't she?"

"Because it's *me*, and she's intent on destroying me!"

"She's intent on getting you as far away from me as possible. That doesn't mean that she hopes to destroy you."

"Then what exactly does it mean?" I challenge.

"She wants to break us up again, Danielle. That doesn't mean she's out to harm you."

Rolling my eyes, I say, "Sure, because the first break up was nothing but rainbows and unicorns."

"What have I told you about rolling your eyes at me?" He asks, grabbing my wrists, and pulling me to him before I can do anything to fight him off.

Adrenaline courses through my veins at his touch. My body betraying me, I struggle against him, the throb of my pulse thumping against his thumbs. Using one arm to wrap my hands behind my back, he grips my hip and lifts me onto his lap. Sex slickened; I exhale and give up on the fight.

"As I have already stated, I have handled everything with Walter." His teeth gently graze the thin skin on my neck, and my stomach tightens as my nipples peek through my blouse. "You're uneasy because you don't know everything, but the less you know, the better it will be. On this, you'll just have to trust me."

"It's not just about Walt," I gasp, as he traces his tongue over my collarbone in rhythmically, slow circles. "I feel like I don't know anything about you at all. You have so many secrets."

"I know, princess," he says, kissing me softly on the lips. "That is going to change, I promise."

"When?" I pant, trying hard to stay focused as his hand glides across my stomach and up toward my breast.

"Soon," he whispers, kneading my nipple with his fingers. "I've already arranged to show you another side of me as early as breakfast tomorrow."

"Why wait till then?"

"Because I have other plans for the evening," he says, sliding me down his shaft. "And they begin with your lips wrapped around my throbbing dick."

"Oh, that's too bad," I say, smiling mischievously at him as the car comes to rest in the parking garage. "We wouldn't want to be late for Virginia and Richard Senior."

"No," he says, grabbing his swollen cock through his trousers and repositioning himself. "We wouldn't want that at all."

****

My dress is simple enough. Floor-length, cinched at the waist, with a long v cut down the center of my chest. I've paired it with a pair of glittery black peep toes and my mother's pearls. Even though I look like I'm in my element, I'm not. I've never been to an opera a day in my life, and I'm not looking forward to seeing any of the Blacks again after the last encounter I had with them.

It turns out Sebastian's grandparents are an absolute nightmare. No wonder why Sebastian and his siblings drink so heavily to cope with being around them. It's the only way to survive. Knowing that I'll have to be face to face with Richard Black Senior and his wife, Virginia, has me on edge. Right on cue, Sebastian approaches me with a vodka and cranberry in hand.

"Almost ready, princess?" He asks.

Within twenty minutes, he not only showered and shaved, but managed to also look dapper in a fitted-gray suit and black tie.

Smiling at his reflection in the mirror, I ask, "Do I have to be?"

"Afraid so," he says, turning me to face him and bringing the glass to my lips.

I take it from him and look into his eyes, captivated by the smoldering heat that awaits me there.

"So, how long is this thing?"

"Roughly four and a half hours with intermission," he says, placing his hand on my back and luring me out of the bathroom.

"Wow, that's long."

Smirking, he lifts my diamond bracelet from the bed and clasps it over my wrist. His fingers run over the platinum encrusted handcuff ring I wear as a symbol of my bond to him. "I think you'll be pleasantly surprised," he says.

"How are you so cool, calm, and collected about this?" I ask, studying him suspiciously. "The last time we saw your grandparents, you were on the verge of unravelling."

"Because," he begins, handing me my clutch. "This little family outing is actually the one night that my grandparents are too preoccupied to dish out insults. And, the production is typically top notch. Plus, it's for a noble cause."

Sebastian's parents support many charities, but this one is near to both of our hearts. It's a fundraiser for Sebastian's nonprofit organization, Blackstone Adoption Foundation, which he started alongside his parents and the case manager that helped them start Sebastian's adoption. The organization works to help children in foster care escape the system by giving more families access to private adoptions. I only spent a weekend in foster care, but it was long enough for me to realize how great the need for parents like Richard and Emmalyn Black is.

"If you say so," I reply, as we step into the elevator.

Sebastian clasps my hand in his, stroking his thumb over mine, and I look up at him.

Smiling down at me, he says, "I love you, Danielle Stevens. Regardless of what my grandparents might have to say about that, it's not going to change."

Smile plastered on my face, I cup his cheek in my hand. "I love you too, Sebastian Black, and I couldn't care less what they have to say about it. I'm not a quitter, so they'll just have to get used to me."

"There's the fiery Italian I've grown to know and love," he says, bending down and kissing me softly.

My toes curl as his tongue grazes over mine. Breathlessly, I sink against him, offering my body to him to do with as he pleases. He spins me against the wall, pressing his hips flush against mine. Gasping, I revel in the feel of his hands on me as he runs his palms over my body. My nipples harden, painfully pressing against the fabric of my bra.

"You have me by the balls, princess," he growls against my neck. "I haven't forgotten what you owe me."

Grinning wickedly, I slide my hand over his crotch. "Well, I'll happily pay up if you just turn this elevator around and take me back upstairs."

"Fuck," he hisses. "If not for the fact that we are already running behind, I would march you back up and fuck you into oblivion."

"I'm holding you to that," I say with a wink, as the door opens to the parking garage.

By the time we arrive at the opera, I'm so turned on that I feel as though I could spontaneously combust. Sebastian has been relentless with his smooth strokes and salacious kisses in various areas of my body. It makes me even more reluctant to get out of the car. Despite what Sebastian says, I can't imagine Virginia Black having anything but an insatiable need to make everyone around her miserable.

Leaning into me as the doors open, he whispers, "Ignore the cameras and act natural."

Taking a deep breath, I step onto the sidewalk. It happens in a blink. Ears ringing, I try to make out at least one voice in the venomous crowd of media. Sebastian's grip on my hand tightens as he navigates us through the chaos.

"Miss Stevens, we understand you were an eyewitness to the shooting at Lickwid a few weeks ago? Care to comment."

"Mister Black, it's only been a matter of weeks since the shooting at one of your nightclubs. Should patrons be worried about tonight's festivities?"

"Miss Stevens..."

"Mister Black..."

*What a fucking nightmare!*

Trembling, I dig my nails into Sebastian's hand. He pulls me into him, wrapping his arms around me and shielding me from the cluster. Dizzied by the sounds and lights, I gasp for air. Reminding myself to breathe, I turn my head into Sebastian's chest, focusing on his scent and stealing my strength from him.

"No comment," he growls at a pushy reporter who jabs her microphone at me, nearly knocking me in the head.

Somewhere nearby, I hear Cyrus and Sean doing their best to contain them as we approach the strikingly artistic façade of the building. Sebastian runs his hands over my shoulder as we walk into the low-lit room. Looking up, I glance around at the curved staircases and red carpeting before turning to face him.

"Is this the way it's going to be now?" I choke, my eyes blurring with tears.

"It'll pass over, princess," he assures, escorting me through a roped off VIP entrance.

"I hope so," I whisper, accepting a glass of sparkling champagne from a penguin-suited waiter.

Despite everything that just happened, it's game time. Sebastian's grandparents will be lurking around somewhere, and I'm not about to let them see me rattled. Feeling slightly intimidated, I walk hand-in-hand with him as he maneuvers through all the beautiful people. We're stopped a few times along with the way, and I sip my champagne while Sebastian mingles. I never dreamed of living my life as arm candy. Frankly I hate it, but it gives me the chance to people watch and take in the dramatic architecture.

Real New Yorkers are probably so used to seeing it that they're unimpressed. However, I'm not a real New Yorker. Every nook and cranny of the building is breathtaking and I'm quite happy to lose myself in it for a little while. Julie, Sebastian's younger sister, is the first to notice us when we finally make it to the entrance for the Grand Tier. Smiling, she elbows their older sister, Katie, who releases her fiancé, Brad's, hand, and wraps her arms around Sebastian's neck, kissing each of his cheeks.

"It's absolute madness outside," she says. "Did it take you guys long to get in?"

"It wasn't too bad," Sebastian replies.

Avoiding her gaze, I sip my champagne and turn my attention to Julie. "Only a few more weeks until term resumes, I guess that means we'll be seeing less of you."

"I wouldn't count on it," she says. "I'll still be around for family things, and there's Katie's wedding, of course."

"I would still like to get together in a more casual environment when you have the chance. Maybe we can start doing dinners or something when you're home."

"What's that?" Sebastian asks.

"Julie and I were just plotting against you," I tease.

"Oh, I want in on that," Katie mocks. "I have years of hell to make up for. Do you have any idea what an annoying little shit this guy could be?"

I laugh. "I'd love to hear these stories."

"No. You wouldn't," Sebastian says, glaring at his sister.

Katie shrugs and tosses back the rest of her champagne, setting the flute down on a silver tray that's been placed just outside the door. "Are you joining us for Labor Day?" she asks me.

"Labor Day?"

"Honestly, son, don't you tell her anything?" Emmalyn asks, finally tearing herself away to join us and pulling me into an embrace. "It's lovely to see you again, Dani."

I look at her, apprehensively. "It's nice to see you too, Emmalyn. I'm sorry about last time."

"It's water under the bridge, my dear. If I had a dime for every time I've wanted to tell that troll of a woman where to stick it, we wouldn't need to have this fundraiser. I only wish I had half the guts you do." She winks. "Speaking of... Mom, you remember Danielle."

Sebastian's grandmother sizes me up but says nothing. Griping Sebastian's hand, I stand firm.

"Of course," Virginia says at last, forcing herself to smile. "How could I forget? Now that the remaining members of our party have found us, perhaps we should take our seats. The show will start soon."

"You go ahead, I'll be a minute," Emmalyn says politely. "I need to run to the ladies. Danielle, do you care to join me? It'll be awhile before intermission."

"Umm... sure," I say, handing my champagne flute off to Sebastian. "I guess we'll see you in there."

"Don't take too long," he says, giving me a quick peck on the lips.

"For God's sake," Julie says, pulling me away from him. "It's only the restroom. No need to pretend like the world is ending."

"No kidding. I've never seen you so whipped, bro." Katie laughs, looping my arm through hers.

"Girls, behave yourselves," Emmalyn scolds, doing a poor job of hiding her smile.

There's a glimmer of amusement in Sebastian's eyes as his lips curl into that infamous heart-stopping smirk, and he shakes his head. I watch over my shoulder as he walks through the door with his father and grandparents.

"It's nice to see him happy," Katie says, bringing my attention back to our group.

"Ditto," Julie replies. "So, Hamptons. Labor Day. Are you coming?"

"Julie, surely you can put together a more articulate sentence than that after all the money your father and I have devoted to your education," Emmalyn mocks. "Danielle, I think what my daughter was meaning to say was would you like to be a guest at our home in the Hamptons on Labor Day weekend? It's a family tradition. I can't believe Sebastian hasn't told you."

"Oh, umm... I have to work an event that weekend. That's probably why he didn't mention it."

"Can you get out of it?" Julie asks.

"Probably not. I've missed way too much work as it is. Honestly, it's a wonder they haven't fired me with everything that's going on."

"That's actually what I wanted to ask you about," Emmalyn says, her voice filled with motherly compassion. "How are you holding up? Do you need anything? I can only imagine how traumatic the entire ordeal has been for you."

"I'm okay," I reply, smiling at her genuine concern. "It hasn't been easy, but I'm falling back into a routine. That always helps."

"If you need anything," she says, extending her hand to the stall that's just become available.

"I'll let you know, I promise."

Sebastian and the rest of his family are seated front row center. We get to them just in time for the lights to go dim. "Turn your phone off," Sebastian whispers, leaning into me and handing me a pair of gold opera spectacles.

I reach into my clutch and power my phone off, then turn to him. "Why didn't you tell me about your family's big weekend?"

"Because I'm not sure I'm going this year."

"What? Why not?" I whisper just as the prelude plays.

"There's just too much going on right now," he says, pointing to the stage where the curtain is rising.

Unconvinced, I lift the glasses to my face and settle against my seat. Sebastian is unconventional in many ways, but skipping out on the family he adores isn't one of them. Something else is going on.

****

I don't need to use the restroom again during intermission, but I do so anyway. Mainly, because it keeps me away from Virginia Black and Richard Senior. They've been nice enough throughout the evening. I'm not naïve enough to presume they've reconsidered their opinion of me, though. I know this only because they have their public faces on. A few months with Sebastian are all it's taken for me to learn that Manhattan's elite is very good at keeping their personal drama separate from their public reality. Realizing I've spent fifteen minutes hiding out in here, I wash my hands and make my way to The Grand Tier Restaurant for the dinner portion of our evening.

*Halftime. You can do this.*

"Don't you think I'm trying," I hear, stopping dead in my tracks at the sound of Alana's voice.

"Try harder," Richard Senior snaps.

Heart-racing, I tuck myself behind a row of fichus trees as I attempt to figure out what they're talking about. It can't be anything good.

"He will not end up with that tramp. I won't allow it," he bites.

"I don't want him with her any more than you do," she replies. "You haven't seen what he's like now. There's no reasoning with him."

"You were given a very powerful gift, my pet. Use it."

"I can't," she says, fearfully.

Sickening waves of nausea plow through my stomach. He's talking about the coverup. He must be. It's the only thing Alana could possibly use against Sebastian. If he knows, it means Virginia probably knows as well, and it will only be a matter of time before the news spreads.

*I have to get out of here.*

Turning on my heel, I race down the corridor and take the stairs in stride. Cyrus grabs hold of me as I'm nearing the exit, and I nearly clobber him with my clutch before I realize who he is.

"What's wrong, Miss Stevens?" He asks, scanning the room.

"Nothing," I reply, breathlessly. "I just need some air."

54

Unconvinced, he glances down at me for a few minutes and says, "Here, let me escort you out."

The cool night air does little to suffice the panic I feel inside.

*Richard Sr. knows what I did to Walt.*

I look out toward Broadway. I'd never make it there and hail a taxi. The lingering press hounds would swarm me long before I got one. "Can you get me to the parking garage?" I ask, turning to Cyrus.

"Sure," he says. "Come with me."

Sean is sitting idly inside the car when Cyrus opens the door for me. Jumping, he turns his attention from his smart phone to the back seat. "Dani? What are you doing here?" He asks, a look of concern registering on his face.

Attempting to shut the door, Cyrus says, "I'm going to get the boss."

I block him by sticking my hand against the window. "Please don't."

They exchange a knowing look, and I know it's hopeless. Sighing, I throw my back against the seat. The one-night Sebastian lets loose, and I've gone and blown it. He'd be better off without me. I know it, and he knows it. Yet, he still sticks by me through all my damage. Maybe it's because he's damaged, too. Maybe it's because he really does love me enough that it doesn't matter.

Whatever the reason, I have a nagging feeling in the pit of my stomach that tells me Sebastian Black would be much better off without me. Attempting to clear my thoughts, I close my eyes and focus on my breathing. The door opens so abruptly that it shakes the car, and I snap my head up in time to see Sebastian climbing in next to me.

"Are you unwell, princess?" he asks.

"It's nothing," I reply, turning in the seat to face him. "You should go back in with your family. I'll be fine."

"Danielle," he begins, running his hand over my cheek. "You're my priority. If something's wrong, they'll understand."

"Really, Richard Senior and Virginia will understand?" I ask, arching my eyebrow at him.

"Okay, maybe they won't get it, but I can assure you the members of my family who aren't insane will."

Laughing, I shove his shoulder. "I'm being serious, Sebastian."

"So am I, Danielle. Whatever it is, you come first. I don't care what my Gran and Gramps think about it. Tell me what's going on and let's fix it."

"Like I said, it's nothing. I just heard your grandfather and Alana talking about me. It's stupid now that I think about it. I completely overreacted."

"I doubt that," he says, reassuringly. "It's no secret to anyone that Richard Senior is a conniving snake, and we both know Alana's opinion of you at this point. What did they say, exactly?"

"Sebastian—"

"Tell me, Danielle," he growls.

Startled, I stare at him.

"I'm sorry," he says, exhaling and taking my hands. "Please tell me, what has you so upset?"

"He said something along the lines of use your weapon against her. Meaning me. Alana only has one weapon against me, Sebastian. If he knows—"

"He doesn't," he replies definitively.

"How do you know?"

"For one thing, if he knew, he wouldn't be sitting on it. Richard Sr. wants nothing more than to destroy me and prove that I'm nothing but the street rat he's always believed me to be. If he had that kind of leverage, he would use it."

I nod, feeling sad for him. I can't imagine not having a loving relationship with Nonna and Nonno. Although he puts up a brave face, I know this must be painful for Sebastian.

"And the other thing?"

Inhaling, he brings his fingers to the bridge of his nose and I already know what he's going to say.

"You still trust her," I snap.

"Danielle, calm down. I know you don't trust Alana. I respect your feelings for her, but believe me, whatever she's plotting against you, it has nothing to do with what happened the night of the shooting at Lickwid."

"I can't trust her, Sebastian. Not unless you want to tell me why I should?"

"I can't do that, Danielle. When the timing is right, you will know everything. I promise. You don't have to trust Alana, but can you trust me? I have handled this."

Sinking my body against the seat, I stare into his stormy gray eyes. If only trust was that easy, and I could just give it willingly whenever I so choose. Trust needs to be earned, however, and Sebastian's given me plenty of reasons not to trust him. We're trying to move past all of them, though, and the only way for us to do that is for me to try and believe him when he says it's taken care of.

"Okay," I agree.

"Good," he says, leaning in and kissing me. "Now come on. We'll make it just in time for the curtain."

# Chapter 8

*S*ebastian

*More brown nosing.*

If only I could get away from these ass-kissers and get back to Danielle. At least she appears to be happy. *That smile.* It's one of the many things that I love about her. Unfortunately, I've hardly seen it for weeks. Tonight, however, she shines like the princess I've always known she is.

Sure, we had a minor hiccup with the conversation she overheard between my grandfather and Alana — a conversation in which I fully intend to address — but once all was said and done, she truly enjoyed herself. I've always quite enjoyed watching first time patrons at an opera. In many instances, they've provided me with more entertainment than the actual show.

Whether they are clueless about when to clap and how loudly, or they try to leave during the curtain call, there's no short list of etiquette faux pas that first timers make. Not my Danielle. She was the very picture of perfection. She doesn't believe she belongs in this world, but she's proving herself more with each day. It's time they all see it. My grandparents, my brand advisors, and especially Alana.

Seeing the top of her red head through the crowd, I excuse myself. She's been careful not to approach me since the final bow, and I don't think it's purely coincidental. Taking the opposite staircase, I head her off at the velvet ropes.

"A word," I say, placing my hand on her bicep and pulling her out the door.

"The nerve," she snaps, wrestling away from me. "What exactly do you think gives you the right to accost me on my way out of an event?"

"Save it, Alana. I know you were talking to Richard Sr. about Danielle earlier this evening. What have you told him?"

"Oh, is that what this is?" She asks with an air of amusement in her tone. "Your precious *princess* overheard your grandfather telling me he much prefers the sight of me on your arm, and it hurt her feelings."

"*Alana,*" I caution. "It's been a long day and I'm in no mood to play your games. What are you and my depraved grandfather plotting?"

Gently stroking my face with her thumb, she says, "That's right. How did she handle it once you got there?"

"It devastated her," I reply, slapping her hand away. "And you, of all people, already knew she would be. Don't try to distract me. We can discuss the details of Isabelle's treatment at our scheduled time in the morning."

"You made me the head of Black House for a reason—"

"I made you the head of Black House because you were the only person on this planet, except for my father, who knew my secret, and that was due solely to your own snooping, not to my willingness to share. Regardless, that will change soon and, as such, so will your position at the company."

"So, you're going to continue with this façade of giving my place in your life to your whore?"

"Shut your mouth, Alana," I roar, grabbing her arm without thinking. "Danielle has done nothing to deserve your insults. If anyone is the whore, I believe I'm looking at her. As for your place in my life, you don't have one."

Jerking her arm free, she says, "Mind your tongue, *Sebastian Hayes*. I know secrets that can bring even you to your knees."

"Make no mistake, Alana, those secrets are the only things keeping me tied to you, and there will come a time when I'm the one that blows them wide open."

"Oh, I have a feeling you're wrong about that," she says, snidely turning her head to the glass doors.

I follow her gaze, feeling as though someone has punched me in my stomach as I watch the smile fade from Danielle's face. Within seconds Richard Senior. is turning his back and walking away, leaving her standing alone. She quickly looks around before checking her phone, baring her teeth, and then bolting for the door.

*Why does she always do this?*

Pulling my phone from my jacket pocket, I hit the speed dial and bark, "Bring the car around." Elbowing my way through the blockade of people at the bottom of the stairs, I place my hand on her shoulder. "What are you doing, princess?"

"Leaving," she replies, coldly.

Spinning her around to face me, I reply, "Why? Because I was with Alana?"

"I didn't even know that's where you were."

"What was my grandfather discussing with you?"

"Oh, you know... just my subservience and the fact that I'll never be good enough for a Black. *Even a fake one.* I swear, Sebastian, I love you, but I cannot stand your grandparents. If I would've stayed in there..."

Suppressing the urge to laugh, I pull her to my chest, "Shh... don't let them get under your skin. They won't beat us unless you let them."

"I just don't know how you deal with it. They claim to be better than you, but they aren't. Except for Walt, they are the worst people I've ever met."

"They're all bark, Danielle. Once you understand that, they really don't have any ground to stand on."

"He certainly seems to think that he has something. The way he stood there in his smugness telling me to get out now before I go down with you... look at this." She hands me her phone.

I stare at the six-figure deposit into her account. "This is from him?"

"Of course it is! I either take the money and run, or he reveals whatever secret he has on me. I could've slapped him. I would've if not for the fact that I didn't want to cause a scene and have it reflect poorly on you."

"I appreciate that, and I'll handle this," I say, looking up to see that the car is waiting on the street. "Why don't we get out of here and get Richard Ser. out of your head?"

"I thought you would never ask," she replies, with a smile.

# Chapter 9

*D**anielle*

"Danielle, are you okay in there?" Sebastian asks, shaking the locked doorknob.

"I'm fine," I say, staring into the mirror and breathing deeply.

*It will pass.*

I repeat the phrase to myself until it becomes white noise in my brain. Pressure builds inside of me, and I pace the floor.

*Don't give in. Just breathe.*

Clenching my fists at my sides, I try to shake off the angst that I'm feeling. *It's too much.* This life is simply too much to take. It's now much easier for me to understand why my mom made the choice to end her own life. No matter how hard I've fought to end it, I'm still that scared fourteen-year-old who just learned that her step-father's spawn had died inside of her. *He's dead. It's not supposed to hurt anymore.* Except I'm the one that killed him and in many ways that only makes it hurt worse.

Guilt.

I'm drowning in guilt.

Lifting my trembling hand to my cheek, I wipe at the tears I'm unaware I've been crying. Sebastian can't see me like this. He wants me to be strong. He expects it. I'm not supposed to let what I did to Walter get to me, but how can I not?

Eyes closed, I see the callous gleam in his stale brown eyes as he taunted me. *No!* I can't let myself go there. I'm going crazy. This is what the ultimate breaking point feels like. The pressure boils inside even more, and I know the eruption is dangerously near.

*Just breathe.*

Leaning against the wall, I press my palms to the cool tile to stabilize myself. If only I wouldn't have cut myself shaving. It was the sight of my blood encircling the drain that triggered all of this. I thought I was cured. My life was supposed to go on like that of any other American without a self-mutilation addiction. *Then why am I struggling right now?*

I knew the pressure of this would break one of us. There's no way that so many damaged people could deal with such a momentous truth and come out unscathed. I had selfishly hoped that I wouldn't be the one to crumble. Honestly, I expected it to be Sebastian. Between Geoff, him, and myself, he's the one that has the biggest load to carry. Foolishly, I've been preparing myself for his fall for weeks.

He'll never fall, however, he's too controlled. The exact opposite of me. He doesn't wear his emotions on the cuff of his sleeve for the world to see. I do, and suppressing them is killing me. Sliding down the wall, I twist my shaking hands in knots as I stare at Sebastian's straight-edged razor on the counter across the room.

*I can do this. I'm strong enough.*

My chest heaves as Walter's voice fills my head. *You're weak.* I'm not. I'm stronger than he ever thought I could be. *You're nothing.* That isn't true. Sebastian loves me. I must matter for him to think so. Except he loves Alana too, and she's far more than I'll ever be. Even his grandparents think so.

Richard Sr. made that clear when he confronted me last night. He'd told me all about how Sebastian Black could never marry a nameless invalid like me. Despite my indignation at his rudeness, by the time he'd finished, I couldn't help but feel like he was right. Then the deposit came through my bank account, along with his threat. "If you're looking to profit from this romance, consider your mission achieved. Take the money and get out now. Otherwise, I'll be forced to tell the world what I know."

I don't know what Richard Black Sr. thinks he has on me. Whatever it is, it's bound to have a ripple effect on Sebastian's life as well. I've already caused him enough stress. Can I really risk yet another one of my crazy past demons coming back to haunt us both? Then there's Alana. Her message has always been clear. She has a power over Sebastian that I never will, and that conversation I overhead last night proves that she's not the only one who knows it. Despite the love I have for him, maybe Richard Sr. is right and I'm only delaying the inevitable. Sebastian's return to Alana Sinclair.

"Princess, you have five more minutes, and then I'm coming in."

His words echo through the silence, and still they feel as though they are miles away. *There's only one way out of this. It's pointless to fight it.* Raising my hands to my arms, I squeeze as hard as I can, pressing my quaking fingers to my skin and sinking my nails in. The bite is quick, a sharp pain that's dangerously intense until the skin breaks. My body shakes uncontrollably as I force every ounce of angst I feel inside to come out of my fingertips. Then there's nothing. No pain. No pressure. Just a void deep inside of my chest that leaves me feeling worse.

Catching my breath, I pull myself off the floor and wrap the silk robe around me. Sebastian is standing on the other side of the door when I open it. Looking down at me with concerned eyes, he instinctively brings his hands to my arms. Concentrating on not wincing, I wrap my arms around his waist.

"You okay?" He asks, pulling me tightly against him.

"Yeah, I just cut myself shaving," I answer, poking my ankle out for him to see.

"Were you bleeding out or something?" He jokes. "You were in there for much longer than the standard 'cut myself shaving' injury requires."

"I had trouble with the band-aid." I shrug. "And I was embarrassed to show you."

"I find it impossible that anything would embarrass you after the compromising positions I had you in last night," he replies.

My pulse racing, I think back to the previous night at Windom and the various ways that Sebastian teased and tested my body until he finally allowed me my release. My thighs quiver at the thought and my nipples peak expectantly. I've never responded to anyone the way I do him. It's as though my body was made for his and on some instinctual level, I know it.

"Maybe you should compromise me more now." I take his hand, pulling him toward the bed.

"Oh, I would love to," he replies, his voice low and throaty. "However, it will have to wait. We have a breakfast guest."

"We do?" Confusion washes over me as I try to remember breakfast plans. "Is it Geoff? I know he said we might hang later, but it's not like him to just drop in."

"No, it's actually someone pretty important to *me*. Get dressed, and I'll introduce the two of you."

"Umm... okay..." I reply apprehensively.

I've already met all the Blacks, Sebastian's assistant, and Alana. He never really speaks about any of his friends, but I've also had the privilege of meeting the dynamic brother and sister duo, Ernesto and Francisca, whom Sebastian helped get established in the restaurant industry. I'm not sure who could be so important that he's waited this long to introduce us. Waiting until he's gone, I pull my robe down from my arms and check the skin. My nails have left small marks, and I'm already bruising.

*It's a long sleeves kind of day.*

Treading to the closet, I select a pair of jeans and a black top with fitted sleeves that cuff at the elbow. To dress it up, I wear my diamond encrusted whip necklace Sebastian gave me to remind me he has the power to tame me, and a pair of platinum bangles. Because I both hate doing my hair and don't want to keep Sebastian's guest waiting, I simply pin back my bangs and leave my natural waves. A quick touch of make-up, and I'm ready to go.

The first thing I see when I walk into the formal dining room is long brown hair resting on the shoulders of a young girl in a crimson and navy school uniform. Noticing me, Sebastian turns his attention from her to me and smiles.

"There you are, princess," he says, raising to his feet and pulling me flush against his side. "This is Lauren. Lauren, this is Danielle."

"Oh. Em. Gee! She's even prettier in person," Lauren responds, sticking her hand out for me to shake. "I'm so excited that I'm finally getting to meet you."

Finally, face to face with her, I notice her shockingly gray eyes. The same shade as Sebastian's. It's not a color you see often, and I can't help but wonder what their connection is. She has other features of his as well, like the copper-color to her skin and the way her lips curl when she smiles. She could easily pass for his daughter, if not for the fact that she's developed enough to be at least sixteen.

"It's nice to meet you too," I reply, sweetly, despite not having the slightest idea who she is.

"Come. Sit. Join us," Sebastian says, excitedly.

I can't help but smile at the childlike joy on his face. It's an expression I've only seen when he's interacting with Julie. Whoever this Lauren is, she has a privileged place in his heart. He pulls my chair out for me and I sit in it, grabbing my napkin and placing it in my lap.

"Lauren is my sister," he clarifies. "I've talked about you so much the past few months that she was thinking I had reason to be ashamed of her because she's yet to meet you."

*His sister.*

Room spinning, I try to process the news. The Blacks don't seem like the type to have a lovechild hidden in their closet, and they took Sebastian from his biological mother's care early in life. He has mentioned nothing about seeing her since, and I'm sure he would've. Is she his biological father's? We've never really talked about that part of his life before. It's possible.

Remembering my manners, I turn to Lauren and say, "I'm sure that's not true. I mean, look at you. What's there to be ashamed of?"

Except, it kind of is. Just when I think all his secrets are out in the open, more of Sebastian's skeletons come to light. Just how far do the lies go?

"She's a sweetheart," Lauren says, looking adoringly at Sebastian.

"That she is," he replies, squeezing my arms gently before returning to his seat.

My flesh stings from the feel of his touch on my delicate skin. I have my own secrets to worry about. Maybe I'll forgive him for his this time.

"So," I say, smiling. "Tell me all about yourself."

****

Nothing distracts me at work more than thoughts of Sebastian. Breakfast was amazing, despite the slight awkwardness I felt. It turns out that Lauren is sixteen, just like I suspected. Sebastian is her legal guardian and has been since she was eight. He was twenty at the time and found out about her when he went searching for his birth mother. Sebastian, of course, wanted to make sure his mother could never get custody of her again, and this is where it gets weird.

He did it all behind his family's back. Despite Emmalyn's prowess in family law, the Blacks have no clue that Lauren exists. I can't imagine why he'd want to keep her from them, but at least it sheds some light on why she would feel as though he were ashamed of her. I probably would too.

In any case, it sounds like he's done an amazing job of taking care of her. She lives in a penthouse here in the city under the care of a nanny. That part, I'm not crazy about, but Sebastian said he did it initially because he was still at Yale and too messed up to take care of her. By the time he somewhat had his shit together, she was comfortable where she was, and he didn't see a reason to uproot her.

She attends Chambers Institute, a private school that costs Sebastian more per semester than a full year at UCLA had cost me, and carries an almost perfect four-point-zero grade point average. In the early years, Sebastian had to spring for tutors to help her catch up, but around junior high she started standing on her own and has ever since. She's looking forward to cotillion, and even invited me to go shopping for a dress with her. I could tell Sebastian was a little hesitant for us to have an unsupervised bonding experience, but I never had siblings. I plan to soak up as much time with his as I can whether it's Julie, Katie, or now Lauren.

"Stevens, you okay?" Paul says, grabbing my attention.

"Yeah, sorry, just taking a breather."

"It's a crazy time of year, but things slow down some from here. Sure, you can handle it?"

"I'm good," I respond. "I just needed to take five, and I guess I got caught up in my own thoughts."

"Well, if you're sure," he replies. "You have that meeting with Burdens Bared in about ten minutes. Are you all set?"

*Shit. I didn't realize I'd been out of it for so long.*

"Yep, good to go," I lie. "I was just about to go set up the conference room."

"Great. I'll be out of the office for the rest of the afternoon." He glances over at Piper's empty desk. "In fact, I'm pretty sure you'll be on your own, but you can brief me in the morning."

"Sounds great," I answer, trying to look past the blatant obviousness of it all.

I thought my coworker dating my boss would get a little awkward. In reality, it's not them dating that bugs me. It's the fact that they make up lame scenarios to hide what's really going on with them.

"One last thing. As you know, I royally screwed up the schedule when you were gone. I might need you to oversee things at Pure Sugar tomorrow night, but we can discuss that in the morning as well. Just clear your schedule in case."

"No problem."

"I knew I could count on you," he says, walking to the door. "I'll see you tomorrow."

"See ya."

Kyle's never been the type to hold a grudge, thankfully, because my job would be exceptionally awkward if he were. As it is, the meeting goes precisely as planned, and I find myself alone with him in the conference room as he helps me clean up. I don't know what it is exactly, but just having him near brings me a sense of security that is unmatched by anyone else.

"Thanks," I say, holding the door open for him.

"No need, sexy," he replies, stroking his thumb over my arm. "You know I've always got you."

Wincing, I pull away from him and force a smile. "I know."

"What's that about?"

"I don't know what you're talking about," I lie, stepping out into the hall and toward my office.

"Danielle, either you tell me what's up, or I'll drag you back into that conference room and find out for myself."

"You respect me too much to ever do anything I didn't want you to, and it really is nothing. Just drop it, okay?"

Holding the door to my office open, he says, "Fat chance. You're forgetting how well I know you."

"Ky, I appreciate the concern, but please just let it go."

"You're doing it again, aren't you?"

Sighing, I sink into my desk chair and tap my mouse to bring my computer to life.

"Answer me, Dani," he demands, his voice screeching slightly.

Avoiding his gaze, I skim through my e-mail only half paying attention. He walks to my desk, spins my chair around, and bends over me, forcing me to look at him. Before I can do anything to stop him, he grabs my forearms and flips them over to expose my wrists. I watch his face change from concern to fury and back again, as he stares down at the semi-healed scratches.

"How long?" He asks.

Tugging my arms free, I reply, "Since everything happened with Jon."

"Fuck! That was weeks ago, Dani! Why didn't you come to me?"

"Shh... lower your voice," I hiss. "I didn't want to burden you with it."

Placing his hands on my face, he says, "You're never a burden, sexy. I thought you knew that."

"I used to, but then I found you with her. As if that wasn't complicated enough, you came back, and I chose Sebastian. Now, I just... it just felt weird."

"I know I could've handled all of that better, but c'mon. You can't possibly tell me you wouldn't be just as pissed if you found out he'd been fucking you while harboring feelings for that Alana chick. Especially if things would've been reversed, and I was the one who left you because I *thought* you'd had a momentary lapse of judgment and fell back into bed with your ex. Again, I put emphasis on the word *thought*."

Feeling the resentment in his words, I lower my head. Maybe Kyle knows how to hold a grudge after all. What hurts more is the overwhelming sense that Sebastian is doing exactly that, sleeping with me, all while loving her.

Stroking his thumb over my chin, he says, "I'm sorry. None of that even matters. What matters is getting you better. Is this the extent of it, or has it already gotten worse?"

"I'm not cutting yet, if that's what you mean." I sigh and wrap my arms around myself to chase the chill away. "I had a close call this morning, though. That's why I winced when you touched me. I had to bruise my arms to keep from doing something worse."

Using his thumb, he dabs at the tears spilling over the corners of my eyes and smiles. "I'm taking you to lunch. Name your place."

"You don't have to do that, Ky. I'm sure you have other things to do."

"Nope. I'm wide open in a foreign city. Show me a hidden gem."

"Well..." Feeling myself perk up a little, I suggest, "There is a really great smoothie shop just around the corner. They serve wraps, panini, and things like that too."

"Smoothie shop it is," he replies, pulling me to my feet. "Lead the way."

# Chapter 10

*S*ebastian

"Robin, see if you can find some space in my schedule for an impromptu meeting with the lead guitarist from Burdens Bared this afternoon," I speak into my intercom.

I thought I'd gotten the point across when I approached him after his show the night my team received photos of him with his hands all over my princess's body. *Apparently not.* I just received intel. He was escorting Danielle to her favorite smoothie shop. It's three o'clock in the afternoon, and she's far too busy to take time off to spend with him. I made sure of it. I may live in the middle of a PR nightmare after Jon's murder, but I don't need all these extra promotions to be successful.

I have thousands of nightclubs and other entities around the world. If one fails, I'll survive. Failure would give my grandfather ammunition in his arsenal against me, though, and I refuse to let that happen. Richard Black, Sr. will never see me fail. Not if I have anything to say about it.

His personal vendetta against me started when I was young. Too much partying, too many wild antics. I was tarnish on the Black family name, one that he felt the need to polish. I didn't make it easy for him then, and I certainly wouldn't do so now. It's eating me alive that I haven't gotten to the bottom of the conversation Danielle overheard between him and Alana. My team will find something, though.

*They always find it.*

"I can push your conference call with Martin Media Group from five to six, but that means you probably won't make dinner with Dani."

*Fuck! I can't cancel on the woman I love, but I also can't be around her until I sort out this shit with Marcum.*

"Do it," I growl.

Preparing myself for the fallout, I pull my phone out and send her a text. I can't call. Calling would mean I would have to pretend I don't know the company she's choosing to keep, and I can't do that. Not right now. Not when my whole life is in ruins.

*I can't make dinner tonight, princess. I'll make it up to you. Can you see if Geoffrey is available?*

Now, I just have to wait for her date with the guitarist to end before calling him. If I do it while they're together, he'll tell her. I refuse to give him anything he can use to drive a wedge between us. Kyle Marcum is a weed in the beautiful garden I'm planting with Danielle, and I will dispose of him.

Smirking at my inevitable triumph, I read her text. *Um... I guess. Everything okay?*

*Everything's fine, princess. A meeting just got pushed.*

It's a half truth, but if she's choosing to sneak around with the damned guitarist again, it's the only truth she deserves.

*Okay. I'll text him. You don't care if we just stay in the penthouse, do you? He hasn't been in the mood for nightlife lately.*

My ability to care or not care is yet to be determined. If she is indeed restarting her affair, I'll be in no mood to see her, let alone the drama queen she calls a best friend. However, if my meeting with him is successful, I'll be much less tense by the time I get out of this place tonight. *There are no ifs.* Things will go exactly the way I want them to this evening.

*Go ahead. Order takeout. Just let me know where and I'll cover it.*

*No, you won't, but thank you. I'll see you when you get home. Xx*

Despite the fury I feel with her, my cock surges at the thought of her full, perfect lips on mine. *Damn her.* She is both my blessing and my curse. Loving her will be the death of me.

"Mister Black," my assistant's voice calls, bringing me out of my trance. "Your three o'clock is still waiting in the lobby."

Shit! Of course, Huang Cho is still waiting for me to call him back for our meeting. He might need me more than I need him, but his company would still be a welcomed addition

70

to my portfolio, and I've just committed one of the biggest faux pas one can when dealing with a Chinese businessman.

"Bring him back."

****

By the time five o'clock comes, I'm ready for a hot shower and a cool scotch. I have one more fire to put out before I can head home, though. *Kyle Marcum.* The very thought of his name brings fury to my gut. He'd feigned surprise when I'd called him up to arrange the meeting, but he didn't decline. He may be a punk with a tiny brain, but he's bold. I give him points for that, even if I can't understand what Danielle sees in him.

"Mister Black, Kyle Marcum is here to see you," Robin's voice rings in my ear.

Standing, I fasten the buttons of my jacket and push the intercom. "Send him in."

Seconds later, she opens the door and escorts the guitarist into my territory. In this room I am king and it's my right to eat peasants like Kyle Marcum for breakfast. Showing no sign of weakness, he looks me directly in the eyes and shakes my hand before taking a seat.

"So, I'm assuming this is about Danielle," he says, cutting straight to the point.

"I thought I made myself clear the last time we spoke," I reply, loosening my jacket and sitting in my ergonomic office chair.

"Oh, you mean the time that you ambushed me backstage at a nightclub I had no idea you owned, and threw a few cheap shots? Sorry, I guess I didn't get the message."

"You're walking a fine line, Marcum," I say, my composure threatening to break as adrenaline courses through my veins. "You would do well to heed my first warning. I will crush you if you continue to pursue what belongs to me."

Snickering, he says, "Danielle doesn't belong to anyone. She's a gift. One you seem to continually take for granted. I get it. To you, she's some trophy that can be thrown on a shelf and forgotten, but doing so will come back to bite you in the ass."

"What are you going on about?" I ask, unimpressed by his attempt at intimidation.

"Do you even realize what she's doing behind closed doors? You don't know her like I know her, Black."

"I know her better than you ever will, Marcum. Bow out gracefully and keep this from becoming ugly. We both know she doesn't need any added stress."

"That's just it. It's already uglier than you could've ever prepared for. You're the one who's going to back off, Black," he says, leaning forward and resting his elbows on my desk. "You'll release her or else I will be the one destroying you."

Unable to contain my laughter, I ask, "Really? And how exactly do you expect to do that?"

For the first time, he doesn't appear to be trying too hard. Taking out his phone, he leans back in his seat and says, "Check your phone in about three seconds."

I lift my smartphone from the desk and wait while he fidgets with his. Almost instantly, a video of me backstage at my club, Cloak, pops up on my screen. My eyes are filled with fire as I approach him, grabbing his shoulder and turning him to face me. We exchange various insults before I launch at him. My fists working in time with my legs like the well-oiled machine I've become. It isn't security footage. I had my team take care of that.

"I guess you didn't see Brett filming some behind-the-scenes stuff," he says, smugly. "I'm thinking you don't want Danielle to see that."

"If you think some amateur footage from a bar fight is enough to keep me away from her, you don't know who you're dealing with, Marcum," I growl. "I've made my requests known. Stay the fuck away, or I will bring your house down around you."

Calmly standing, he walks to the door and says, "You underestimate me, Black. May the best man win."

I don't give him time to close the door before sending a message to Thomas. The guitarist doesn't know what kind of war he just started. The best man will win alright.

# Chapter 11

*D*anielle

"Chinese or Moroccan?" Geoff asks.

"Hm... Indian."

"Leave it to you, baby girl."

"What?" I ask, grabbing the takeout menu from the drawer.

"Always having to have everything your own way."

"Is there another way?"

"Depends on who you ask," he says sarcastically. "So, what are you thinking?"

"Tandoori buffet, vegetable biryani, and naan."

"Works for me. You call. I'll go see if I can find something on cable."

"He has Netflix now."

"What? Mister I'm Too Important for TV subscribed to Netflix for you? It must be genuine love."

"Shut up and find us something to watch," I say, rolling my eyes as I call in our order.

Geoff has already made himself comfortable on the couch in front of the movie *Hitch* by the time I come in carrying a bottle of sparkling water and two glasses. Taking them from me, he pours while I nuzzle down beside him.

"I don't know about you, but I thought we could use some humor after the shitty past couple of months," he says, handing me a glass.

Taking a sip, I nod my head. "Agreed. So, how are you? I miss coming home to you every day."

"Back at ya, baby girl. I've actually been thinking about this living situation of ours."

"Oh?" I ask, the rhythm of my heart increasing as my nervousness builds.

"Yeah. What would you say to me talking to my dad about selling our apartment and then us getting a place in the village?"

"Well…"

"I mean, I know my mother will probably freak out about it, but it's not an outer borough, so she can at least take some comfort in that. And I know it's a pretty steep hike to work, but tons of people travel twenty to thirty minutes to get to work. Plus, it's more our kind of people. I don't know about you, but I'm over the stuffed shirts and dogs in purses."

"Wow, you sure know how to sell a place." I laugh. "Sure you didn't major in real estate?"

He laughs. "Seriously, though. What do you think?"

"Hmm… well, I'd love to live with you again and I'd happily agree to let your dad sell the apartment. But the village is out of range of everything we know. Your family and Sebastian all live on the Upper East Side. Work is on the West Side. I can understand your need for a change of scenery, but we're just getting settled."

"I thought you might say that. Air go a second offer," he counters. "What would you say to Chelsea?"

"Chelsea. Hmm… how about this? Why don't you talk to your dad, and meet with the real estate agent and we can look at some places and then decide?" I ask, praying I know him well enough to know that he'll hate them all and be more open to moving to this building.

"You're being weird. What's up? Oh, God!" A look of horror comes over his face. "Don't tell me Mister Big asked you to move in here."

"No," I say too quickly. "I mean, not just me. He owns the penthouse next door too, and it's yours if you want it."

"That's not exactly us living together again." He crosses his arms and glares at me. "And I don't need anyone's spare apartment. Seriously? Who in the absolute fuck just has an extra apartment in their back pocket?"

"We wouldn't be in the same apartment anymore, no, but we would be in the same building. It would be a total Apartment Twenty situation, and Sebastian isn't trying to give you a handout. He's offering to lease the apartment to you. In essence, he would be your landlord."

"As funny as *F.R.I.E.N.D.S.* is, thanks, but no thanks," he says, crossly.

"G—"

I'm interrupted by the sound of the elevator doors opening. The delivery guy must be here.

"Hold that thought," I say, getting up to pay him.

Geoff is in the kitchen waiting with plates and silverware in tow when I walk in to set the food on the counter.

"So, listen," he says. "I get what you were attempting to do with the offer, and I can even understand that you want to move in with your boyfriend. I mean, you and Mister Big have gotten pretty serious. Sure, it's happening super fast, but let's face it... I was about to marry a guy I'd only been dating for a little over a month."

Feeling the stabbing pains of guilt in my chest, I place my hand on his.

He forces a smile and continues, "My point is... I don't want to keep you from doing what's best for your relationship. But, I don't want to lose you either and there's no way I'm going to agree to some reverse *Three's Company* living arrangement. It was cool when we needed to do it to keep you safe, but that just isn't the case anymore."

"You'll never lose me, hunny," I assure him, loading both of our plates with the aromatic food. "You and me... we're lifers. Me moving in with Sebastian won't change that."

Sliding his plate across the counter and picking up his fork, he replies, "I'm not just talking about physically, Dani."

I know exactly what he's getting at. "G, I'm just as worried about you as you are about me, but like I've said before... we will get through this together. If you can stay sober, I can stay the course with my issues as well."

"I want to believe that, but you have to admit... there's been some *distance* between us the past few weeks. I mean, you cut your hair and didn't even tell me about it."

"I was wondering if you were ever going to say anything about that," I tease, running my hand through my shorter tresses. "As far as the distance... G, I've tried reaching out to you. You pushed me away. What else could I do?"

"Push back," he demands. "Any other time, that's what you would've done."

Stuffing a large hunk of garlic naan in my mouth, I say, "True, but I've had my own shit going on too. I knew you blamed me for what happened to Jon, and to be honest, it was easier for me to let you hate me than for me to face the truth that it's my fault."

"No, it's not," he says, rounding the counter and placing his arms around me. "I blamed you. But, I know you would've done anything to stop it if you could've. And you were there for me when no one else was. I wouldn't have made it through that funeral without you. I know I've done a shitty job at being there for you. But you *killed* someone, baby girl. I don't know what to do with that."

"Well, that makes two of us," I say, breaking free of him.

"I know you said Mister Big has people on it, but what if..."

"That's something I worry about every day." Fighting back the tears, I look up at him.

"I knew there was more going on," he says, pulling at my chin. "What's up?"

Sighing, I pull my arm free of my shirt and show him my bruises. "I've been self-harming again."

Saying it out loud never gets any easier, but it's the first step to recovery.

"Baby girl!" He pauses, staring at my arms while he tries to collect himself. "I don't know what the hell you're going through, but I know addiction. You helped me through mine, and I'm going to get you through yours."

This is why it's comforting to have Geoff on my side, and why I'll never give up on our friendship. He understands that my destructive behavior is the same as his, only with a different poison. Geoff gets high on narcotics and sometimes booze, whereas for me the adrenaline comes from seeing the drops of blood spill from my flesh. Other than Kyle, who held my hand through my cutting when it first became a problem, Geoff is the only person I've ever really been completely comfortable talking about it with. Even with my therapist, I was always reserved.

"Just don't tell Sebastian," I say, looking at him desperately. "I'm not sure he can handle it."

Another thing I love about him. He doesn't question me. He just hugs me again and says, "It's not my truth to tell."

Sighing my relief, I look up at him. "Tonight wasn't supposed to be about any of this. I guess that just means I owe you a second date. Somewhere out of the house next time?"

"I'll be pretty crazy with being the *Taylor Tragedy* and all, but how does the Monday I get back from the Hamptons work for you?"

"I can't think of anything I'm doing."

"Good," he says, excitement shining in his eyes for the first time since Jon's death. "I found the perfect location for the photo shoot and I've booked it for that day."

"You're still doing it?" I ask, remembering his fantastic opportunity to be a photographer for Fashion Week. A move like this will catapult his career if all goes well. First, we have to get him the gig. "I thought that maybe you'd decided against it when you didn't mention it again."

"No such luck, baby girl. Prep your pucker because you're going to be my ticket to the big leagues. No more shooting look books for wannabe designers. This is my chance at real fashion photo journalism."

"I'm so glad you're getting back to it," I say, taking hold of his hand.

"It's what he would have wanted," he replies.

**\*\*\*\***

"How are you?" My dad asks.

I can see the frown lines on his forehead. Perhaps Skype wasn't the best idea.

"I'm okay, daddy," I answer, trying not to worry him. "How are you? How is Bernadette?"

"She's good, but you're avoiding my question. Are you doing okay with carrying such a large load at work?"

"Everything is fine. I promise. I didn't Skype you to talk about work. I miss you."

"I miss you too, angel-girl. You're still at Sebastian's, I see."

"I am. Please don't start with that either."

"I just want to see you happy, kid. Is that so bad of me?"

Running my hand over my face, I take a minute to decide how to answer. My father has every right to be overprotective, and I don't want to upset him more by fighting with him. However, I'm an adult and there are some things in my life that I can't run to my daddy with anymore. This is one of those things.

"I understand that you're worried, daddy. I just don't want you to waste all your energy on me. My friend died, and it sucked, but it's not the first time I've dealt with something hard. It's better for me to keep busy. We both know how restless I can get when things are too quiet. It's good for me to have a little chaos. I promise."

The door to the bedroom opens, and Sebastian sticks his head in. Glancing up at him, I smile and hold up one finger, instructing him to be silent for a minute. Leaning against the doorframe, he nods his understanding.

"I have to go, daddy. Ti amo. Don't worry. Okay?"

"Impossible," he replies. "Be careful. Ti amo."

Sebastian joins me on the bed as I'm closing my laptop, and I sit up to talk to him. There's a mysterious heat in his eyes, almost as though his desires are mixing with the darkness buried inside of him. The threat of it brings chills to my bones and I glance away.

Taking my hand in his, he says, "Did you have a pleasant visit with Geoff?"

"It was good. Not what either of us expected, but exactly what we both needed. I told him about moving in here."

"I'll have the lease agreement drawn up tomorrow," he presumes.

"Not so fast," I reply, balling my knees to my chest and resting my chin on them. "It's exactly like I expected."

"He didn't take it well."

"Not at first, but he gets it. He won't be moving in, though, so you can do whatever you'd like with the other apartment."

"I'm sorry," he responds, taking his shoes off and bringing his feet up on the bed. "How about I leave it vacant for a while, just in case?"

"I'm telling you, he's not caving. The part of my life in which Geoff and I were roommates is over."

"And the part where you and I are taking our relationship to the next level is just beginning."

Closing his eyes, he breathes deeply, presumably trying to cover up the tension that developed in his muscles as he said the words. It's noticeable, however, and my heart speeds up just a little. *Maybe The Village or Chelsea wouldn't be so bad.* If he's having doubts, there's a good reason for it. Sebastian Black is nothing if not sure of the decisions he's made.

"I have to ask you something," he says, his voice overtaken with nerves.

*This is going to be bad.*

The beautiful gray of his eyes isn't the usual stormy smolder that drives me mad, instead what I see behind his gaze is fear. Feeling my anxiety rising, I twist my hands in my lap. "Umm... okay..."

"What were you doing with Kyle Marcum this afternoon?"

Trying not to laugh, I take a deep breath and allow the relief to wash over me. Of everything I was expecting it to be, I never expected this. This I can deal with.

"The band had a meeting," I begin. "Paul stepped out of the office for the afternoon and Piper called in at lunch, leaving me to have to work through lunch to pick up the slack. Kyle offered to take me to lunch so that we could talk, and he could check up on me. The last time we've really had the chance to talk was the day before the funeral."

His face doesn't change as he stares back at me. I'd hoped that would help to put him at ease, but I should've known better. *I cheated, and in Sebastian's world, my indiscretions will never fade.*

"Is that all?" He finally asks.

Nodding my head, I pull myself on top of him. "I swear to you. It was purely platonic."

Relief visibly washing over him, he pulls my lips to his. The greediness of his kiss builds a ravenousness hunger in my body, and I thrust my hands into his hair, deepening our embrace. Breaking free, he rolls me onto my back and positions himself over me.

"I had a feeling he was only trying to get under my skin."

"Excuse me?" I ask. "When did you see Kyle?"

"At our meeting this afternoon. We had some common interests to discuss."

"Sebastian, the only interest you share with Kyle is me."

"Precisely."

"So, you're telling me you called Kyle into your office to try to strong-arm him into staying away from me?" I say indignantly.

"Those are your words, princess. I would use the word persuade."

"Get off me," I growl, shoving at his chest.

He grabs my wrists and pins me to the bed. My pulse racing, I struggle against him. The last place I want to be right now is trapped underneath Sebastian when he has his possessive, domineering hat on, for all the wrong reasons.

"Surely, you understand where I'm coming from. The guitarist—"

"You know his name," I interrupt.

"As I was saying, *the guitarist* seems to believe that he has an innate connection with you that I never will," he continues, glaring at me as if he's daring me to interrupt him again. "Given the carelessness of your recent actions, I would almost agree with him. Then

I find out that you had lunch with him today and once again divulged parts of yourself that are apparently only accessible by him..."

"Windom!" I scream, forcing him to release me, and jumping off the bed. "Are you kidding me? Did I or did I not just have breakfast with the sister I never knew you had until this morning? You're angry because I have secrets, but yours just get bigger and bigger."

"And you're the only person I've ever told any of that to, Danielle!" He roars. "My own mother doesn't know! Do you think it's been easy keeping such an enormous secret for the past decade?"

"Oh, but you haven't been keeping it by yourself. Have you? No, you've had your *precious* Alana at your side. Be careful, Sebastian. You'd hate to say something in the heat of the moment that could have dramatic consequences later."

Lunging at me, he wraps his hands around my arms and squeezes. Pain shoots through my bruised flesh, and I wince away from him.

"Let me go," I say weakly, tears welling in my eyes.

"Fuck!" He growls, releasing me and moving to the other side of the room. "Why do you bring this out of me? I'm going fucking crazy with you."

"Then maybe we shouldn't be together," I quip, heading straight for the door.

He jumps in front of it, slamming it shut, and softly says, "That's not what I meant, Danielle. No one has ever made me lose control like you do. The more I try not to hurt you, the more I do. I don't know how to love someone this much. I'm always getting it wrong, and I don't know how to change it."

"You're not always getting it wrong," I say, taking his hand in my own. "And you didn't hurt me. Scared me a little, but you didn't hurt me."

"I saw the look in your eyes."

"That wasn't about you." Closing my eyes, I breathe as deeply as I can, mustering up the courage to come forward with him. "Do you really want to know what Kyle and I were talking about at lunch?"

Stroking my hair off my face, he nods. Speechless, I stare into his fear-stricken eyes. I've always thought he was the one with the power in this relationship, but I'm coming to realize that it's a two-way street. I can do just as much damage to him as he is to me.

"Okay," I say, taking off my long-sleeved t-shirt and throwing it on the floor.

I can hear the breath whistling past Sebastian's teeth, and I know he thinks his biggest fear is about to be realized.

"Not that," I assure him again, turning my right arm toward him. "See this bruise?"

"Yes," he replies angrily. "Did he do this to you?"

"No!" Exhaling, I turn so the left arm is showing. "Kyle would never hurt me, Sebastian. I know you don't like him, but you can always rest assured that I am safe when I'm with Kyle."

"Unlike when you're with me," he mumbles, barely loud enough for me to hear it.

"That's not what I meant," I quickly respond.

Forcing himself to straighten, he says, "Just finish what you were trying to say. Please."

"Okay... Kyle didn't do it, but I did. This morning," I clarify. "When I was in the bathroom for so long."

Turning my wrists over to face him, I add, "And the other night when I was in the shower with the door locked, I was doing this. When you grabbed my arms, I wasn't wincing because you hurt me. I was wincing because I hurt myself, and the pain I felt from you touching the scratches and bruises was a reminder of that."

"Princess," he says, breathlessly, pulling me to him. "Why?"

Shrugging, I take the time to allow his scent to soothe me before responding, "Old habits die hard, I suppose. I don't expect you to understand."

"What does that mean?"

"You may have your moments, hotshot, but you'd never do anything this crazy," I say, looking up at him.

Pulling away from me, he tears his shirt open and places my hand on one of the scars on his arm. My fingers trail over the rough skin of the now familiar mark. Most of his scars are obvious burns. This one... this one. I've always wondered where he got it. It was undoubtedly from one of the sickos his mother sold him to when he was a child.

Creeped out by the thought, I swallow. "What's the message I'm supposed to take from this?" I ask, bringing my hand to his, and looping our fingers together.

"You once asked me where I got that scar," he says, his eyes never leaving mine. "Here's your answer. Every single time I was sent to a client's bedroom, my mom would light a cigarette and use it to burn me. She said the pain from the burn would block out any pain I was about to feel. It never worked."

"Crying was against the rules. If any of them saw me crying, it only got worse. But, the pain, the anger... I didn't know how to deal with it. I had to find some way to get it out. I loved my mother, Danielle. Despite what she did to me, there was no denying that maternal-child bond. I wanted to believe her, but the more cigarettes she lit… the more trips into that room… I knew. I knew there was no way to stop the pain unless I stopped it myself. So, I grabbed a kitchen knife on my way back to my room one night. That's how I got this."

"Sebastian," I breathe.

Smiling a sad smile, he brings his hand to the bruise on my arm and pulls mine to the scar on his.

"My scars. Your scars. Our scars. They're the same, princess."

I don't know how to respond, so I just kiss him. His hands pull at my thighs, lifting me from the floor. Refusing to break our kiss, I wrap my arms and legs around him, surrendering to his will. He carries me to the bed and gently lies me down.

"I intend to take this slow. I want to make love to you, Danielle. Can you let me do that?"

Chills spreading over my body from his words, I nod my head.

"Yes," I say, breathlessly. "I'd love nothing more."

He lowers his head to mine and kisses me again, a perfect, sensual, slow kiss that reverberates in the depths of my core. His breath heavy with desire, he runs his hands over my stomach and under my shirt. His thumb and index finger find my aching nipple and work it in slow, rhythmic circles. Feeling the throb of my dampened sex, I part my legs and arch my back from the bed. A breathy moan passes my lips before I can stop it.

Taking his cues from me, Sebastian lifts my shirt over my head. The heat from his tongue sends shivers of ecstasy through me as he rolls it over my collarbone. Throwing my head back, I revel in the feel of his hands on me, grazing over every inch of my skin. Each movement is slow, concise, perfect.

He lowers his head to my chest, taking my nipple into his mouth. My sex clenches with need as he rolls his tongue over it, encircling me and drawing it into his mouth. Panting, I run my hands through his hair, the hunger inside of me reaching an insatiable point. He doesn't stop his sweet torment, rather takes his time. Kissing, caressing, and licking all the folds of my chest and torso before finally paying attention to my greedy sex. Lowering his hand to my cleft, he parts my lips and growls a feral growl that only makes me more desperate to have him.

"You're soaked, princess," he says, his voice low and leaden with desire. "I can't wait to taste you."

"Please," I beg, thrusting my hips toward him.

"Greedy, perfect, and all mine," he replies before accepting my request.

His tongue teases my swollen clit with the expertise of a skilled artisan. Tears leak from my eyes as I try not to give in. I don't want to come just as badly as I do. Always knowing how to read my body, Sebastian slides his fingers inside of me, hooking them into my G-spot.

"Sebastian," I pant, tossing my head back as the pressure builds in my core.

"Just let go, princess," he coaxes.

Unable to control myself any further, I arch my hips. My sex floods and pools over his fingers. He continues milking me, refusing to give in until I've completely finished. Legs shaking, I thrust my hands into his hair, trying to pull him away. He closes his lips, suckling my clit into his mouth, and it starts all over again. Thrashing my head from side to side, I beg for him to stop, but he's relentless in his pursuits.

Breathing heavily, I lie on the bed, feeling completely spent. Standing, Sebastian frees his swollen cock and lowers himself on top of me. "I'm going to sink balls deep inside of you and live there for days," he says, his need clear in the tone of his voice.

"Oh God," I cry in response, my sex throbbing again as the anticipation washes over me.

Parting my thighs, he lowers into me. His girth stretches me, filling me to capacity. Hands placed on my hips, he slowly inches inside of me, his head just barely nipping my sweet spot before he pulls out again. I thrust my hips upward, feeling empty without him. His thrust growing ever more aggressive, he rocks into me, taking me to the height of ecstasy and back again. Desperate for the rush of release, I grind my hips against him.

"Fuck," he growls, intently focusing his gaze on me as his pace quickens.

The fullness of his head pounds against my G-spot, and I clench around him, gripping him as though my life depends on it. Legs shaking, I sink my nails into his back.

"I'm going to come," I scream.

Chasing his own orgasm, he growls in response. It starts at my toes and moves its way to my head, a life altering mind blowing orgasm like nothing I've ever felt before. My head spinning from the sheer amazement of it all, I lock my eyes in his. Lowering his head, he smashes his lips flush against mine. With a moan into my mouth, he comes in quick, hard bursts. My sex pulsates greedily, drinking him in. Breathing heavily, he collapses on top of me, stroking the hair from my face as he kisses my neck.

"On second thought," he pants. "Let's go to the Hamptons this weekend. I think we could both do with a little time out of the city."

"Well," I say, smartly. "I was already going to be in the Hamptons this weekend since we have a full agenda there at work, but I'll accept your offer, anyway."

Laughing, he kisses my nose and says, "I love you, you know that?"

"Not as much as I love you," I reply, smiling at him.

# Chapter 12

Sebastian

The sound of my phone vibrating on the nightstand pulls me from my sleep. For a minute, I can't figure out why it's so hard to move, and then I realize Danielle is lying on my chest. Her arms are wrapped around my waist, and her leg tossed over mine. Deciding to let it go to voicemail, I stroke my fingers through the brown locks of her hair. The early morning sun peeking through the curtains gives me just enough light to clearly see her supple ass poking from under the twisted sheet.

*I'm the luckiest man alive.*

It's hard to imagine her being in enough pain to hurt herself. Nothing was ever supposed to hit her so hard again. I knew the death of her stepfather would have consequences. I can remember them from when I was in her shoes after protecting Alana. I'd give almost anything to go back to that night. One wrong decision, one momentary loss of control, and my fate was sealed forever.

*Danielle can never know the rest of the story.*

I'll never be able to survive again without her. Hating myself for continuing to keep my secrets from her, I bring my lips to her forehead, kissing her gently.

"You're more than a princess. You're the oxygen my blood has been missing for so long," I whisper.

Stirring, she opens her eyes and strains to focus on me. "What time is it?"

"Shh... it's five-thirty, princess," I reply, soothing my hand over her face. "Go back to sleep. I was just going to grab a workout, then I have a few things to get done in my office. I'll be back after with breakfast."

"Mmmm... chocolate chip pancakes," she says, barely coherent, as she grabs my pillow and almost immediately falls back to sleep.

Laughing, I arrange the blankets to protect her from the chill before walking to my attached master bath and preparing for a full session with my trainer. Typically, I only see him on Tuesdays and Saturdays, but ever since I saw that picture of Danielle with her legs wrapped around the guitarist's waist, I've been booking extra sessions. It's necessary. Alana may have been able to reel me back in that night, but I could've easily snapped his neck when he sat across from me yesterday.

Pulling on a pair of boxing shorts, I text Bernice with Danielle's request, then go to the foyer to greet Omari "O" Jones. I started working out with Omari as soon as I moved to the city full time. He's a retired professional MMA fighter who took on the art as a hobby in order to cope with his life as a fatherless African American teen in Harlem. O's hobby quickly grew into a career that earned him well over thirty million dollars, making him one of the richest men in his profession.

Despite his wealth, Omari moved from Harlem to Brooklyn, where he opened up his first gym. Now, thanks to some intervention on my part, he owns eleven within the city and dozens of others across the nation. Still, he refuses to move to Manhattan. "Brooklyn keeps me humble," he always says. Ordinarily, we meet at the gym a few blocks over, but since Danielle's revelation last night, I'm paying him extra to come here so that I can stay close.

As usual, O is prompt. Standing in my foyer, I realize just how intimidating he must be to the average person. His legs are covered in breakaway pants, and he's wearing a hooded sweatshirt to keep the chill from his arms, but there's no denying the sheer mass that is Omari.

"Sup, man," he says, clapping his hand in mine and pulling me into a bro hug. "You ready for that ass whoopin'?"

"Ha, you wish," I joke, clapping him on the back and pulling away. "I'll meet you in the gym. Just going to grab some water."

"Pussy," he says, smiling

"We'll see who's the one crying like a bitch when it's all over," I say, heading toward the kitchen.

Trash talk is part of the experience with O. If it were anyone else, I might take it more seriously. Grabbing a jug of water from the fridge, I head to my in-house gym. Omari has already changed into his boxing shorts, allowing the ripped muscles of his arms, back, legs, and torso to shine.

It's not those that I notice, though. It's the scars on his shoulders, proof that despite our different backgrounds, O and I are the same. It's the reason I trust him so much. Growing up with an abusive addict for a mother gives him a vantage point of me that almost no one else can see. Our abuse might not have been the same, but the hate was. He saw through me on the first day I walked into his gym and hasn't stopped since.

"Let's see you get that skirt up," he says, barely giving me time to set my water down.

"I never seem to have any problems with that," I smart back.

I lie across the foam roller on the floor and begin sliding my hips to roll my butt to my heels and back up again. Warm-ups like this help to condition me not only for my more intense sparring session later in the workout but also for my bedroom marathons.

"World's greatest," Omari calls, not giving me time to break.

By the time we reach the end of our seven-stretch workout, I'm loose in all the right places and ready to ease the tension I've felt since I saw those bruises on my Danielle's arms. I can't, though, not yet. Omari takes me through a series of reps that focus on my core and response times, before finally ending our warm up with some isometrics. By the time we've finished, I've already had a full-body workout by most people's standards, but I can't give in yet. We still have another hour to go.

"Get some water," O yells.

Our water break only lasts a few minutes and then I'm gloved, padded, and ready to go. Moving some of my equipment around, O lays down a mat.

"It ain't pretty, but it'll do," he says. "You ready?"

"Readier than you'll ever be."

"You talk a lot of trash, kid, but let's see if you know how to use those feet."

In the beginning, I was afraid to let go when sparring. O later informed me that was my first tell. He knew I had something inside of me, because I was so afraid of losing control. Although my agreements helped me to gain control sexually, it was Omari who taught me how to keep my composure, even when I wasn't in the bedroom. I owe a big part of my ability to be the powerhouse I am today to him.

*And I hope he'll be able to fix me again once Danielle's done with me.*

Shaking off the thought, I psych myself up for what's going to be one of our most brutal sessions yet.

"Damn," Omari begins, thirty minutes into our session. "Whose ass are you thinking about kicking today? I've never seen you so on fire."

Swallowing a gulp of water, I shrug and say, "It's nothing."

"It's your woman. Isn't it?"

Fighting the swell of my dick, I think about Danielle lying naked in my bed, only yards away. Getting my hands on her right now is the last thing I need to do. My impulses are all over the place. I want to protect and punish her all at the same time.

"I knew it," he says, pride written all over his face. "So, when do I get to meet her?"

"The fifth of never, if I'm lucky," I say, wiping my face with a towel.

"Oh, come on now. I'm not that bad. Am I?"

"That's debatable," I reply. "Are we gonna do this or what?"

"What's wrong, Black? You worried you won't get what you paid for?"

"With you I rarely do," I reply, walking back to the mat.

Another half hour passes more quickly than I'd hoped and still O hardly gets a hit in otherwise. Of course, I know it would be different if it were an actual fight, but even I know my form is always better when I have something to be pissed at, and right now I have plenty. Sitting on a bench, I guzzle water and wipe the sweat from my brow as O packs up.

"Are you headed to the Hamptons with the rest of the crazies?" He asks, casually.

"It appears so. Any chance I can drag you along?" I offer, already knowing his answer.

"Not a chance in hell. The only thing worse than the rich food is the rich attitudes you have to endure to eat it. I'm much more comfortable on the Jersey Shore, where the beer is cheap, and the women are cheaper," he replies, laughing.

Shaking my head, I say, "As you wish."

Truth be told, I'm not one for the Labor Day Weekend parties with the social elite either. I do it for my parents and my sisters. Family time with the Blacks is everything I once thought was mythological in this world. Labor Day in the Hamptons is our version of family time on steroids. It pleases me to be a part of the private moments of the weekend.

Although, I always must leave half my heart in the city to attend. It destroys me that I have to leave Lauren behind on her long weekend from school, but I have no other choice. I can't mix the two worlds. No matter how much my baby sister would love it.

"There you are, hotshot," Danielle says, her voice pulling me back. "Come back to bed. I'm getting lonely."

"Damn!" O exclaims, before I even have the chance to look up at her.

Standing in the doorway in nothing but the shirt I ripped off myself last night and a pair of black lace boy shorts is Aphrodite herself. The fabric, which is now missing several buttons, barely covered her breasts. The luscious rounds of her nipples are nearly visible through the thin satin. Dick hardening, I scan her from head to toe.

*I will punish her for this.*

"Oh my God," she says, grabbing at the shirt to pull it both down, and closed at the same time. Her cheeks turn the pleasant shade of pink they were the day I discovered her sex toy lying on the sidewalk. "I'm sorry. I didn't know you had company. I'll just... I'm so sorry."

"Oh, don't worry about it, hunny," O says, fighting the urge to make an off-color comment. "Get on in here."

Glaring at him, I stand and grab my robe from the hook by the door. Using it as a shield, I hold it out while she slips it on.

"Thank you," she whispers, tossing a hand through her messy hair, trying to tame it.

Leaning forward, I kiss her cheek and whisper, "Don't thank me yet."

She tenses slightly, and I know she's fighting the flood of anticipation pooling between her legs at my suggestion. I lead her into the room, fearing what Omari might say to her. I've grown very fond of the guy, but he wasn't born with a filter. It was something I constantly had to work past when we were in negotiations for his gym expansion.

"You must be Danielle," he says, holding his hand out to her. "Heard a lot about you."

"Oh, really?" She asks, eyeing me curiously.

"Well, no, but I know this guy well enough to know that means you must be something special."

"She is," I butt in, pulling her into me. "And I'm pretty sure you've been holding her hand long enough."

"Geez, Black, I've never seen your panties in such a wad. You've really got him pussy whipped, you know that? I'm O by the way. Omari, but you can call me O."

I glare at him for the out-of-place comment, but Danielle simply laughs and says, "It's nice to meet you, O. I'm Dani. So, you're Sebastian's trainer?"

"Trainer? Therapist? I guess they're the same thing, really. I know all this guy's dirty little secrets. You ever need some good dirt to hold over his head, you just come looking for me."

It's not true, O may know a lot about my personal life that most people don't, but it's nothing I haven't already told Danielle. The real secrets are locked away with the one person who has just as much to lose if they are spilled as I do. Still, the thought of Danielle and Omari getting cozy is enough to force my unease.

"Oh, really?" She asks, cutting her eyes up at me. "I might just have to take you up on that."

"Unfortunately, you'll have to wait for another time to do so, princess. Omari was just leaving."

"Princess. Isn't that sweet," he says, mockingly. "I'm actually wide open today, Black. Why don't you invite your old friend to stay for breakfast?"

"No can do. I have a meeting, and you have a gym partnership in danger of being dissolved," I joke.

There's no way I would ever dissolve my partnership with O. I value it too much. It's the same reason I continue paying him his fee as a personal trainer plus a healthy tip. He's good at what he does, and it shows.

"Maybe another time," Danielle says, almost too sweetly.

"I'll hold you to that," he says, lifting his large duffel bag from the floor.

"And I'll see you out," I reply, finally releasing my grip on Danielle's waist. "I have another meeting here in about ten minutes."

"How about I get dressed and go for my run? We can have breakfast when I get back."

"Sounds like a plan," I answer, kissing her forehead. "I'll see you in about an hour."

****

"Robin, bring me some aspirin," I speak into the intercom, rubbing my temples.

This is the appointment I've been dreading all day, and the one that there's absolutely no way to change.

"I'll be there in just a sec," she answers.

I pour myself a scotch and pace the distance to the panoramic window behind me. With the view, it feels as though I'm on top of the world. I remember the first time I looked out at the twinkling lights from this vantage. I felt like a king. However, at this moment, I still feel like the same kid that used to camp out on the sidewalks, looking up at buildings like the ones I own now, and telling myself that I'd be up here one day.

*Why do I let her do this to me?*

I shouldn't care. After everything she put me through, I should just let her die and be done with it. If it weren't for Lauren, then maybe I would. I just can't bear the thought of causing my beautiful sister anymore pain. She's already been through more than any of those prep school brats she's friends with will ever face in their lives. Keeping Isabelle safe is just another way to protect her. That's all.

"Your aspirin, sir," Robin says, interrupting my thoughts.

"Thank you," I reply coldly, walking to my desk and taking them from her.

She's silent, her head down, as she waits for me to finish. Maybe it's my current mood, or maybe it's the fact that Danielle is changing me. Either way, I look up at her and smile.

"Have I ever told you how much I appreciate the work that you do here?" I ask.

A confused look spreads over her face as she shakes her head and says, "No, sir."

"Well, I do. Thank you."

"You're... you're welcome," she says, unsure of what's happening. "Will you need anything else?"

"That's all."

Hearing her phone ring, she returns to her usual efficient self and asks, "Should I patch your father directly through, or would you like a few minutes first?"

"Give me another minute or two," I reply, loosening my tie and sinking into my chair.

"You got it, boss."

Cradling my head in my hands, I stare down at the blinking red light. My father is a patient man. He'll wait on hold all day if that's what it takes to get this family session over with. Bracing myself, I press the button to lock my office door and hit the speakerphone.

"Hello, Father," I say, finishing my scotch.

"I was beginning to wonder about you, son," he says, a comforting tone in his voice. "Rough day?"

"Not until recently," I reply, honestly. "How has she been?"

"Well..."

The length of his pause tells me everything I need to know.

"How do you think we should proceed?"

"Truthfully — and please don't shut me out here — I think she's never going to find a reason to fight the addiction until she knows that you've forgiven her."

"You can't ask me to do that," I snap.

"You're right," he begins, calmly. "As your father, I can't. Frankly, as the man who witnessed those nightmares first hand, I don't want to. You don't know how hard it is for me to treat the woman responsible for the darkness that threatens to destroy my son. Every day is a battle to not force her to tell me the things you won't. I do it, however, because I love you, son, and you asked me to care for her."

Eyes closed, I breathe deeply. I've never been able to adjust to hearing the words *I love you* coming from my father's lips. I don't think I ever will.

"As her therapist," he continues, "I have to ask you to. My focus in this office has to be on her treatment, and repairing her relationship with you is a vital component to that."

"She has no relationship with me," I growl, my body trembling from my rage. "She never did. I was nothing but extra baggage for her to carry around. She should be glad that you saved me. She got what she wanted."

"I can see this is a conversation we need to table for now," he says, backing down. "Are you ready to begin?"

"Let's just get it over with," I reply, counting down the minutes until I can put this behind me and fall into Danielle's arms again.

"Take a few seconds to calm down," he encourages. "I'll be right back. I have to bring her in."

Pouring myself another scotch, I twist my head to fight the tension building in my neck. The very fact that my father would suggest that I give Isabelle the chance at a relationship with me has every rigid muscle in my body clenching with fury. It was he who told me I had to keep her and Lauren a secret from my mother and sisters to begin with. "They can never know," he'd said.

When I'd asked why, his only response had been, "That's just the way it has to be."

I was desperate to get her off the streets and into a facility and move Lauren into a stable living environment. I would've agreed to anything at that moment. Now, I regret that decision. Not for Isabelle's sake, though, but for Danielle's. My secrets are hurting her more than they've ever hurt me, and I can't stand to watch her breaking.

In my meeting with my security team this morning, we discussed closing the gaps between her and us at all times. She'll fight me on it, of this I'm certain, but it won't matter. Isabelle's recovery may be out of my hands, but Danielle's safety is fully under my control. I'll hire the fucking Swiss Guard if that's what it takes.

"Sebastian, are you there?" My father asks.

Draining my glass, I reply, "I'm here."

"Great. Let's get started. Isabelle, would you like to say hello?"

"Bashie?" she asks, with the childlike innocence in her voice that I've learned to loathe.

There is nothing innocent about Isabelle Hayes

"I'm here, Isabelle. How are you today?"

"I miss you. Richard says you get a long weekend this weekend. Are you coming to see me?"

"I have other obligations this weekend."

"Oh," she replies, her voice shaking.

"Isabelle, does Sebastian's response to your request upset you?" My father asks, softly.

Chest constricted, I listen to the silence, wishing I could be anywhere but here.

"He can't see your head nodding," he encourages. "Why don't you try telling him how you feel?"

"I'm... I'm upset," she blubbers.

"I'm sorry if I hurt your feelings, Isabelle, but I have a busy life. You know that. Lauren will be there on Saturday, though. So at least you'll get to see her."

"I don't need Lauren, Bashie. I need you. Just like I needed you when you were little. Remember how you used to sing to me?"

Fighting the swell of emotions in my chest, I roll up the sleeves of my shirt.

"Isabelle, what you need is to get better. There will be plenty of time for me to come see you when you're back at Black House."

"But you don't come and see me there. You say you will, but you never do. It's lonely there, Bashie. I need you."

*She wants to guilt me about her loneliness. Where was she when I was alone and fighting men much bigger and stronger than me as they got what they were paying for?*

Shuddering at the thought, I fill another glass and drain it in one gulp.

"Sebastian," my father begins, cautiously. "Did you hear what Isabelle said?"

"I did."

"And what would you like to add?" He asks.

"What do you want from me, Isabelle?"

"I want to be part of your life," she replies confidently.

"You are a part of my life."

"No," she begins, taking a deep breath. "I want to be a *real* part of your life. I want to meet the girl in the picture. Lauren said she was nice. I want to meet her."

Of course, my baby sister would have mentioned Danielle to my birthmother. As much as I love her, I sometimes forget just how naïve she can be when it comes to Isabelle. Despite everything we've both been through at the hands of the woman who brought us into this world, Lauren truly believes things can change. She thinks we'll all somehow be a family on the other side of this storm.

"That will not happen. Danielle is off limits."

"But why?" She demands. "You already keep the rest of them away from me. Why do you need to keep her from me, too?"

"*They* are my family, Isabelle. You can call it what it is, and I'm not explaining myself to you. Danielle is off limits. End of discussion."

"*I'm* your family, Bashie," she says, a hint of tears in her voice again.

"No!" I roar. "You're the woman who... Argh! Isabelle, you aren't my mother. You haven't been my mother for a long time. I know you think we can somehow go back to the way things were, but I don't want to go back. I never want to be that helpless again. You were a horrible mother. I'm just glad I saved Lauren from you before you completely destroyed her, too!"

"Bashie," she barely whispers.

"Okay," my dad starts, trying to smooth things over. "I think that's enough for today. I'll be in touch next week with a progress report, son... Sebastian. Thank you for your time."

The line goes dead, and I grip the arms of my chair, desperately trying to catch my breath. There's only one thing that will make this better. *Danielle.* I must get to her. Even though I'll only be able to watch her on the monitors until she's finished her work, I'll at least be able to take comfort in the fact that she's close.

"Robin," I say, pressing the intercom.

"Yes?"

"Can you have all of my calls forwarded to my cell? I'll be in my office at Pure Sugar if anyone desperately needs me."

# Chapter 13

Danielle

Another lonely night at Pure Sugar. There are hundreds of people lining up at the door to get in and yet, I barely register a single face. Once again, I struggle with the reality of the fact that I used to be one of those cheerful people. *Will I ever be happy again?* Looking up, I meet the eyes of Detective West. Adding another tally mark to my clipboard, I give the signal for the bodyguard to undo the velvet ropes. He waits patiently as the overly dressed brunette and her blonde-headed friend pass.

His oily hair sticks to his forehead, and he wipes the sweat from his brow with a handkerchief as he says, "Miss Stevens, fancy meeting you here."

"Some might say the same about you, Detective West," I reply. "Are you a fan of The Ravens?"

"The who?" He asks.

"Tonight's band," I reply.

"Oh, afraid I've never heard of them. I'm actually meeting someone."

"I see," I say, checking the tally unnecessarily. With it being the Wednesday before Labor Day, most of our A-listers and socialites are saving their appearances for the weekend. Nodding to the bouncer, I say, "Well, don't let me keep you…"

"Actually," he begins. "Since I've got you here, I wonder if I might have a word with you."

"Um… sure," I reply, stepping away from the ropes for a minute despite the outcry of a few impatient club goers behind him.

"I've been meaning to follow up with you," he begins. "Have you heard from Mister Smith since we last talked?"

"Afraid not," I reply, looking back at the small crowd.

"Interesting," he says, running his hands over the stubble on his fat face. "It's not like him to go missing for such extended periods of time, is it?"

"Detective, given that you've read my file from Napa, you're already aware that I haven't had regular contact with my stepfather for several years. I'm not capable of providing information about his habits."

"Are you not the least bit concerned?"

Running my hand through my hair, I look at him. He's trying to bait me. It's obvious the police have taken their investigation in another direction.

Planting my feet firmly on the concrete, I reply, "The only thing I'm concerned about when it comes to Walter Smith is that he's out there, somewhere, lurking in the shadows again. No matter how unwelcomed his emails or other various threats may have been, at least I knew to be on guard. Now, it's hard to determine whether he's truly gone or if this is, like I've said before, just another one of his games."

"Well, you should know that I don't think it's a game at all. In fact, I think someone got their hands on him. Do you know of anyone who would have an incentive to do so?"

Checking the crowd again, I shrug and say, "Given Walt's character, he probably made lots of enemies. When I lived with him, he was trying to expand his winery around the world. If he was indeed successful in that, then there's no telling who he crossed to make it happen."

"Great minds think alike," he replies. "I was actually thinking the same thing. Do you want to know my theory as to who finally put a stop to him?"

"If you feel you should share it," I say, trying hard not to show any sign of panic.

"I believe it was Sebastian Black," he says, looking at me in a curious sort of way.

"You think Sebastian had something to do with Walt's disappearance?" I say, my voice wavering, despite my desperately trying to play it cool.

"I do," he replies, with no further explanation. "Has he done anything that you would consider off kilter these past few weeks?"

"You don't have to answer that, Danielle," Sebastian's voice booms from behind me.

Turning my head, I see his chiseled jaw set in a firm scowl as he approaches from one of the club's fire exits.

"She doesn't have to answer a damn thing you say without a lawyer present," Sebastian growls, pulling his arm around me. "Unless you'd like to lose your badge, I suggest you either provide me with a warrant, or you leave the premises. This is police harassment, and I'm not the type to stand for it."

"Relax, Black," Detective West replies, throwing his hands up defensively. "Running in to Danielle was purely coincidental. I'm meeting a friend inside."

"Then you won't mind at all if Danielle comes with me, and lets you get on with your evening," Sebastian says shortly.

"Not at all," Detective West responds, a twinkle in his eye. "I'll be seeing you around."

Sebastian spins me around and presses my head to his chest as Detective West goes inside the club. Bending low, he whispers, "Not a word until we are in my office with the door closed."

"The door," I say, as he drags me back toward the fire exit.

"Piper's covering it for the rest of the night. Just trust me, princess."

He leads me down the dark hallway to his newly redecorated office and offers me a seat on a leather sofa.

"Drink?" He asks, pouring himself a scotch.

"No," I reply. "And from the smell of you, you don't need one either. What the hell is going on, Sebastian?"

Ignoring me, he drains his drink, walks to the couch, and takes a seat next to me.

"I'm being investigated for Walt's disappearance."

"You're what?" I ask, my heart rate escalating.

"Relax, princess," he says, stroking his hand through my hair. "You're safe. They won't come after you."

Trying hard to contain the anger gnawing at my gut, I say, "You honestly think this is about self-preservation? I'm worried about you, hotshot. If you don't know me well enough to know that, then I don't know what we've been doing these past few months."

"Dammit, Danielle," he roars. "I'm trying to protect you! If you can't understand that, then I'm the one who doesn't know what we've been doing."

"I don't need protection, Sebastian. What I need is you. We are a team. When are you going to realize that?"

"And every team needs a captain, princess. I've been in this world for a lot longer than you. I know more about how it works."

"Is that what you think? What happened to 'your scars, my scars, our scars'? We *are* the same, Sebastian. That darkness inside of you, it's inside of me too. The only thing that makes you better at handling it than me is that you've learned how. So, teach me."

"Teaching you means taming you. I don't want to destroy you, princess," he says, pouring another scotch.

Enraged, I stand and grab it from him. "You think this isn't destroying me? You think I enjoy worrying about what's going on with the investigation into Walt's," I look around and lower my voice, "*disappearance*. Do you think I'm happy about watching over my shoulder to see if the police are coming for me? Or that I'm thrilled at seeing the man I love drown his sorrows instead of talking to me?"

"No, Sebastian. The only way we're going to get through this is if you let me be a part of it. I know you're worried about me. I'm worried about myself! But I will not get over this unless you let me face it. Stop hiding things from me."

"You want me to stop hiding things from you, Danielle," he says, cutting his burning gaze at me. "Sit down. Shut up and listen. You made the dumbest mistake of your life that night, and I'm not talking about the moment you pulled the trigger. It started long before that. As soon as you left the hospital."

"It took all of ten minutes for Thomas to check the pings on your phone. He saw you were in the penthouse, and we followed you. By the time we got there, your dress was on the floor, and the drawer beside the bed was empty. It took me one look at my desk to figure out where you were headed, but it would've taken the police even last time to track your next move."

"So, Thomas and I left immediately and headed in your direction. I called Walt's phone that night, Danielle. I knew yours was still on, and I had no other choice. Just in case something went wrong, I had to have all the fingers pointing in my direction to save you from your own self-destruction. They have no reason to suspect you of anything, because they're certain that it was me."

Staring at him in disbelief, I take a sip from the scotch glass I'm still holding. It burns my throat as it makes its way down, and I can almost swear it's going to come back up just as painfully. Taking a deep breath, I say, "But you told Detective West that I was with you that night."

"I told him you left the hospital to come to me while I was meeting with Alana. And today, with my lawyer present, I told him I dropped the two of you off at the penthouse, and then I went to discuss some things with Walt because I suspected he was at fault for the scene at the club. Then, I went to the club to assess the damages. Alana has also given her statement. I'm assuming Detective West will be in touch with you soon for yours."

"Sebastian, I won't let you go down for this."

"I'm not going to," he replies confidently.

"You don't know that," I argue. "I don't think you're taking this seriously."

He's on his feet faster than I have time to process it. His hand reaches behind me and cups my neck, his other pinning my arm above my head as he lowers me to the couch. Helplessly, I drop the glass, spilling his scotch on the floor. Scorching heat burns from his gray-black irises straight into my green ones. I reach for him, but he grabs my free hand and pins me to the couch. His body rigid, he hovers over me. The smell of scotch seeping from his pores teases my senses, and I cringe at the nausea it inflicts upon me. Pulse racing, I struggle to break free, but his grip only tightens.

"You want to be a team. Fine, we're a team, but I'm calling the shots in this, Danielle. You will follow my lead. You will tell the detectives exactly what they need to hear. You stayed in the penthouse with Alana. You went to bed, and she waited with you until I returned. When you saw either of us again, it was daylight, and we called Geoff to check in with him. Do you understand that?"

Fighting for breath, I shake my head. "I can't let you do this, Sebastian."

"Dammit, Danielle," he says, punching the couch and standing.

Gasping for breath, I struggle to regain my composure. The only way around this is for me to turn myself in. Our scars might be the same, my pain might be his too, but my mess is no one's but my own. He's not going to prison for me.

"If you can't accept my decision, then you leave me with no other choice," I say, turning toward the door.

"You're not going anywhere except with me," he says, grabbing me and flinging the door back.

****

The car rushes through the streets as quickly as any car can in New York. Heart racing, I glance over at Sebastian. His posture is perfectly poised, his face stoic except for the familiar smolder of his eyes.

*I am fucked.*

We come to a stop inside the Windom parking garage. Swallowing the lump in my throat, I thank Thomas for opening the door. Sebastian steps out behind me, turning to him and saying, "You're off duty for the rest of the night."

Gripping my arm just hard enough to remind me he's in control, he leads me to the elevator. The silence between us speaks volumes as we wait for the car to come. Trembling, I step inside.

"Sebastian," I whisper.

"Eventually, you will stop running, princess. For both our sakes, I hope it's sooner rather than later."

Heat rises to my cheeks. Ripping my arm free, I move against the wall.

"Eventually, you'll learn to let me do what's best for me," I reply. "For both our sakes, I hope it's sooner rather than later."

"If you knew what was best, it wouldn't be an issue."

Snorting, I glare at him. "I am not a child, Sebastian."

"Then stop acting like one, Danielle."

Growling, I turn my back to him.

"Case in point," he says, coldly.

"I hate you," I quip, turning to face him again.

"Prove it," he replies, closing in on me.

"Get away from me, Sebastian," I say, pushing against him.

Lowering his lips to my ear, he whispers, "Make me."

Brazen, he grabs my wrists and pins them to the wall. The heat of his tongue melts my flesh as he licks his way down to my barely covered chest. Panting, I fight to free myself. His grip tightens, and he shakes me slightly.

Teeth clenched, I growl. "Get off me, Sebastian."

His smoldering gray eyes meet mine. "No."

The doors open, and I feel a sense of relief flooding over me. Taking my hand, Sebastian leads me through the apartment to the marble island in the kitchen. I glare at him as he pours a glass of vodka and places it on the counter in front of me.

"Drink this. I'll be back."

And just like that, he's gone. Gulping at the smooth liquor, I fight the urge to follow him. Sebastian is both the brightest and most idiotic man that I've ever met. Him not realizing that his involvement with me is going to be his downfall is proof of that. Fueling my rage with alcohol, I pour another glass. Sebastian comes behind me, takes the glass from my hand, and places it on the counter. Desperate to see some semblance of understanding in his eyes, I take his hand in mine.

"You have to let me go, Sebastian," I say, bravely.

"No, I don't," he replies, pulling me into him.

His hands cup my face, and his lips collide with mine. Breathlessly, I allow his tongue to meet mine and drink him in.

"Come on," he says, pulling away.

Reluctantly, I follow him to the fantasy room.

"Sit," he commands. I stare at the wooden backed chair. It's the same one I handcuffed him to, on what feels like an eternity ago.

"Did you even hear me?" My words are rushed and impatient as the sound of my frantic heart beats into my eardrums.

"I heard you, princess," he answers, gesturing to the chair once again. "Now sit."

"Sebastian, now is not the time to play. You're going to fucking jail. I knew I should've turned myself in. If I had, this would have never landed on you."

My breath faster than it's ever been before, I pace the room. Sebastian walks to the chest beside the closet and pulls out a long strand of pearl colored plastic beads. His arm is around my middle before I have the chance to back away. Annoyed by his persistence, I try to wriggle free. Swooping me over his shoulder, he carries me to the chair and gently sets me down.

"I'm not in the mood," I say, attempting to stand again.

He presses down on my shoulders, forcing me back to my seat, and sticks his knee between my thighs. I gasp as he threads my wrist through the beads, looping them around me several times, then lacing them through the chair, and continuing with my other wrist. He keeps threading the pearls around the chair and around my body until I'm sitting with my ankles tied together. My wrists are pulled together so my palms touch, and then restrained against the bareness of my thighs.

"Let me go," I scream.

He runs his hand over my hair, smoothing it behind my ear. "You're not getting out unless you use your safe word or calm down. The choice is yours."

*I refuse to admit weakness. It's exactly what he wants me to do.*

"That's what I thought," he says, the corner of his mouth turning. "When I return, you should be cooled down enough to trust me. I will handle the detective, Danielle. You'll see."

Horror overcomes me as I watch him approach the door.

"Sebastian!" I call out after him.

He turns to face me. "You can scream all you need to. Just remember, the room is soundproof."

With that, he's gone. I stare at the purple coated door. My anger rising to the surface again, I struggle against my binds, wincing when I feel the burn of the plastic against my still-healing scratches. Bucking my back against the chair, I attempt to use my full weight to break the beads, but they only grow tighter.

"This isn't funny, Sebastian!" I yell, struggling against the beads again. "Get your ass back here and untie me!"

# Chapter 14

*S*ebastian

"Did you prep her?" William Rush, my attorney, asks.

Fighting the desire growing in my gut, I glance at the security monitor, at the image of Danielle struggling against her restraints.

"She'll be ready to go by morning," I reply.

"I'll wait for your word," he responds, ending the call.

Taking another sip of my water, I imagine all the ways I'll punish her before this evening is over. *Once for her destructiveness, once for her rebellion, and once as a reminder of who is in charge.* She struggles against her restraints once more, yelling into the void of the soundproof room, and a smile spreads across my lips.

Grabbing my throbbing cock, I sit back in my chair to enjoy the show. Her fresh hair cut eases my need to pull it back, a habit I've been trying to break since my one amateur mistake with Alana. Looking down at my distressed jeans, I think about how many other play habits I adapted during those two weeks. She needed to believe everything was going to work out after what happened that night all those years ago. I needed to figure out a way to get control of the monster inside of me.

She was the first, but Danielle would be the last. Contemplating how to erase her from this part of my life forever, I tug at the worn denim. It was Alana that suggested I wear them. Something about the untamed way they made me look. So much of that early experimentation with her has become a part of who I am. I've learned things along the way, become a proper master to my toys, but Alana is still in the details. She always has been.

Glancing at the screen again, I revel in the sight of my princess's voluptuous body slumping in defeat. *She's ready.* But am I? Danielle once asked if I still love Alana. The question is simple to answer. I never have, I never could. What I feel for her is something different entirely. It's respect. I loathe her for keeping our daughter a secret, but I also respect her for her ability to see the darkest parts of me and not run away.

Even Danielle isn't capable of that. I've never known love like I do now that my princess is in my life, but I've also never known fear this great either. She's the only person who has ever had the capacity to destroy me. She isn't strong enough to be with me, and I'm not strong enough to release her. I must release one of them, though.

Walking into the kitchen, I finish my water and grab a bottle for Danielle. She's most likely parched after all those hours of screaming. I check the time. It's already one in the morning. I'm exhausted, and I know she is, too. But we will not go to bed until we've finalized this once and for all. Danielle will trust me with everything she has by the time the sun rises. I will make sure of it.

Stopping by my dresser, I change into a pair of low hanging sweats. *In order for her to trust me, she has to have every part of me. I'm ready for that now.* It will take time for all these walls to come down, but if she can trust me, she'll be patient with me and getting Alana's ghost out of our lives will help with that.

The door opens almost automatically once I punch her birthday into the keypad. Turning her head slowly, she looks up at me. Her sun-kissed face is streaked with mascara from her tears, and the somberness in her eyes pulls at something deep inside of my chest. I can't give into that emotion now, though. She must become the submissive she was born to be. She must learn how to let others take care of her. It's imperative that she learn how to trust me again.

"Here," I say, approaching her slowly and lifting the water bottle to her lips. "Drink this."

"Just go away," she croaks.

"No. I have left you alone with your thoughts long enough. It's time we settle this now."

Rolling her eyes, she parts those tantalizingly pink lips and allows me to put the bottle to her mouth. I wait patiently as she quenches her thirst, begging myself to gain control while I still can. *Why does she do this to me?* She's an enchantress, and I'll forever be locked in her spell.

"Does this mean you're going to untie me now?" She asks.

Leaning back, I reply, "That depends. Are you going to trust me now?"

"Sebastian, I'm tired. I just want to go to bed."

"I take that as a no."

My muscles tight with fear, I walk to the chest I keep much of my darker objects in. I grab the steel knife I once used to free her from some of her inhibitions and stroll back to her. Heaving her chest with her heavy breaths, she whispers, "What's that for this time?"

Holding the blade between my fingers, I stare down at her. "What's it going to take for you to have faith in me, Danielle? How many hours do we need to spend revisiting the same issues before you know that I will not disappoint you again?"

"I have faith in you," she replies, her eyes scanning over the knife to my body and back again.

"Then why were you planning on running? *Again.*"

Fighting against her restraints to resituate, she looks away from me and sighs. "Because, Sebastian. I can't let you destroy everything you've worked for to protect me."

Lightly pressing the blade to her cheek, I turn her face to meet mine again.

"Princess, you are the only thing I need in this life. If you're my downfall, then so be it," I say, tucking the knife between the beads and her thigh, and jerking upward.

White pearls fly across the room, hitting the wooden floor in haphazard patterns. Breaking free, she rubs her wrists. I try to ignore the stabbing pain in my chest as I realize why. The friction of the beads has reopened some of her scratches. I bend low and scoop her into my arms, carrying her across the room, and laying her down gently.

"Stay here. I'll be right back."

The very thought of her scars threatens to break my composure as I grab the first aid kit from the bathroom. *Get yourself together, Black.* Every nerve in my body quaking, I walk over to her. "Let me see your hands, princess."

"It's fine, Sebastian," she says, holding them out to me. "The beads just got too tight."

"You must learn to stop fighting," I say, kissing each of her wrists softly.

Cringing from the burn of the antiseptic on her broken skin, she quips, "Or you could learn to stop persisting."

Ignoring her, I finish tending to her wounds. She watches me, but never speaks. I can tell she wants to fight, but it's clear that I've successfully won the battle.

"How's that?" I question.

"Good. Thank you."

Nodding, I stand and walk to the chest of drawers for a bottle of massage oil.

"Take off your clothes and lay down," I command.

"You're going to massage me?"

"Yes."

Stepping out of her dress, she says, "I have to say, that's the last thing I was expecting."

"This is only the beginning," I reply, tucking her hair over her shoulder.

She shivers under my touch, and I can't help but smile. Popping the cap on the warm oil, I pour a generous amount on my hands and lower them to her back. Her body is rigid with tension, the proof of her struggle written deep in the recesses of her muscles. My cock throbs painfully against the constraint of my pants as I carefully rub my hands over the smooth curvature of her ass. I continue working my way over her until at last she feels loose and completely prepared for me.

Freeing my aching dick from its prison, I hover over her as I dig through the drawers in the bedframe. My skin prickling with anticipation, I take the silk blindfold and secure it over her eyes. As if she shares my very desire, she holds her hands out to help me place them in the leather cuffs and does the same with her beautifully toned legs as I slide her ankles into their cuffs as well. Taking advantage of her lack of vision, I slide my tongue up her body in search of her lips. Her kiss is needy, the weight of the day driving her lips to mine with a violent passion that sends all the blood I have directly to my aching cockhead.

Stroking myself lightly, I push the button on my remote and lower the custom bar from the ceiling. Her head snaps back at the sound of the chains rattling, her face both curious and concerned.

"What's that?" She asks.

I watch the hills of her breasts rising and falling in time with her rapid breath. Stroking her hair with my hand, I bring my lips to her ear and whisper, "Just trust me, princess."

Exhale audible, she nods her head and melts into my touch. Carefully lifting her limbs, I position the cuffs on the hooks until she's hogtied and suspended before me. Fighting the urge to simply take her now, I press the button to lift her. The custom harness gives a slight jolt, and she lets out a quiet scream.

Her voice trembling, she asks, "What are you doing to me?"

"I'm suspending you, princess," I reply, calmly. "If you're in the air, you have no choice but to depend on me to do what's best for us both."

"Sebastian..."

"You have your safe word," I remind her.

"Okay," she replies, exhaling.

I slowly lift her, my cock growing even more painfully stiff with each gasp or whine. Positioning myself in front of her, I part her lips with my purple head. "Suck," I command.

Rolling her tongue along the vein on the underside of my shaft, she takes me into her mouth. Hallowing her jaws, she sucks me as though she has a savage hunger only I can fill. The sheer force of her greed sends desperate surges of juice through my cock. Gripping her head, I steady myself. I fuck her mouth at a slow, rhythmic pace, savoring the lavish feel of her tongue on my skin. She moans, and I push myself deeper, grazing across her tonsils and withdrawing again.

"Fuck," I growl, watching my dick twitch.

Panting, she rolls her tongue over her lips. The sight of her helpless and desperate for more resonates in my depths, stirring up cravings I'd long since suppressed. Using the remote, I lift her a few more inches. Her body tenses with the motion, but she doesn't speak. She simply goes with it, waiting for her next instruction.

*Good girl.*

Sliding beneath her, I carefully roll my thumbs and index fingers over her nipples, kneading and twisting her in preparation. I pull slightly, and she cries out joyfully, the pleasure overtaking her. I pick up the plastic nipple clamps. I'll eventually work her up the metal ones with clitoral clamps attached, but for now it's not about whether the sight of her wearing them is aesthetically pleasing or not. It's about stretching her further than she's ever been before and letting her know I will always be there to hold her up.

Her back arches when I position the first clip. "Sebastian," she squeals, the rose pink of her bud turning slightly purple with the pinch.

I give her a minute to adjust before clamping the other nipple and turning to position my head beneath her plush pussy. Lowering her once again, I place my hands over her hips and use my position to lift my mouth between her folds. Cock aching for attention, I take in the smell of her arousal. I part her lips with my fingertips and bury my tongue in her warmth.

"Oh, Sebastian," she squeals, her legs shaking from the force of her impending orgasm.

Reaching my hand over the curve of her back, I bring my finger to the pucker of her ass. My chest tightening, I gently rub over her delicate nerve endings. She clenches, her body stilling at the realization of what's coming.

"Sebastian," she whispers.

"Safe word, princess," I remind her, teasing the delicate hole once again. "Use the safe word if you want me to stop."

Her breath quickening, she replies, "I don't."

*At last.*

Reeling in my victory, I lubricate my finger and slowly insert it inside of her. She clenches around me, and I still, allowing her the opportunity to adjust to the unfamiliar sensation. Until this moment, everyone who has touched her here, including me, has done so with malice.

I lost all rationale the night I abused her, and she ran out on me. I broke her trust, and in return, she broke mine. The best way for me to earn that back is to repair that damage. Carefully inching further, I watch her reaction.

Her breathing is rushed and impatient, an anxious crease lining her forehead. Bringing my lips to her clitoris again, I gently draw her into my mouth. She moans and releases some of the tension she's been carrying since I started. Slowly gliding my tongue over her, I gently pull out and push back in. She fights less this time, and I increase my rhythm.

Her head snaps up, and her ass tightens. I wait patiently for her to relax again. We carry on this routine until she's primed and ready. Her cheeks flush with arousal, she turns her head in my general direction and says, "Sebastian, don't stop."

"I've got you, princess," I assure her, clamping my lips over her clitoris again.

I feel her legs quiver and wrap my free hand around her lower back to help stabilize her. I press firmly on her walls, massaging her, and letting her know it's okay.

"Ah!" she screams, tossing her head back.

"Just let go," I coach.

In rushes of warmth, she comes undone. Her body shaking uncontrollably as the last of the sensations fades away. Impatiently, I raise the harness again. My cock purple with passion, I lift to my knees behind her. Gripping it, I line myself up with her, allowing the natural silk of her juices to slicken me.

She pulsates around me, willing me to give myself over to her. Taking her hips in my hands, I pull her into me. My head driving over the roughness of her G-spot. She cries out, and I thrust deep inside of her once more. My balls constrict with the pressure of my impending orgasm. Reaching around her, I stroke her clit with my fingers and pound into her as hard and fast as my legs will allow me to.

"Fuck me!" She yells, tossing her head back.

I wrap my hand in her hair and give it a tug. She moans for more, and I drive into her, stroking my fingertips over the lush swell of her core. Her body shakes again, and I feel my cock twitching with its first hint of release. Growling, I grip her hips again and chase my own orgasm.

Breathlessly, I rock into her, reveling in the feel of her sweet pussy as she comes. My cock erupts with violent force, and I throw my head back. She's mine for the taking, and I'm relentless in my pursuit, not easing up until I've given all I can.

Quickly lowering her, I undo the straps of the harness and release her from the nipple clamps. She pulls the blindfold off and squints at me through the dim light. "Well, that just happened," she says.

Smiling, I pull her against my shoulder. "Indeed, it did. How do you feel?"

"Confused," she answers, honestly.

"About?"

"I know everything about that was wrong, and yet, you somehow made it feel right. I didn't think I could ever trust you that much again, but you made sure I did."

"That was my goal," I say, running my hand along the smooth skin of her back. "I'll never hurt you again, Danielle, and I'll give no one else the opportunity to either."

"I believe you," she replies, bringing her lips to mine.

Her kiss is a breath of fresh air, and I welcome it gratefully. If she can manage to stay in this mindset, we'll get through this. However, something tells me it won't be that easy.

# Chapter 15

Danielle

In just a few hours, I'll be headed to the Hamptons. I can't deny the fact that I'm feeling a small tinge of excitement. Sebastian is to blame for that. I'm finally feeling free again. I don't know how, but I know he has everything under control. All I have to do is follow his lead and he'll get us both exactly where we were meant to be. I've spent the entire morning distracted by the erotic night we had.

If it would've been anyone else, I would've never been able to do half of the things I allowed myself to last night. With Sebastian, though, it didn't feel dangerous. After everything we've been through and all the ways we've broken each other, he still somehow makes the unnatural feel natural. He's everything I never knew I needed, and then some.

"Dani, Piper," Paul says, calling my attention back to the boardroom. "This will be the first Labor Day Weekend for both of you. It moves fast and gets crazy. If either of you have any hesitations, speak now."

I know this is Paul's way of giving me a scapegoat. I refuse to take it, however. It's time for life to get back to normal. I've decided it will happen, and so it will. Besides, I'll already be in the Hamptons with Sebastian and his family. It would just feel weird not helping the team while I'm there.

"I'm all in," I reply, smiling at him.

"Me too," Piper says, nodding.

"Good. So that just leaves assignments. Unfortunately, Kirsten's leg injury prevents her from joining us," he begins, passing around a stack of agendas I completed just yesterday. "So, Dani, you'll be taking over her events for the weekend."

"Me?" I ask, stunned.

"You up for it?" he replies, grinning.

"Of course! Thank you!"

"Great, so everyone spend the rest of the day memorizing your schedule and making sure you have the last details good to go. Once we get there, there's no turning back. I'll be in my office if you have questions."

We file from the conference room like a herd of cattle, everyone so anxious about the weekend ahead that we can't seem to get started fast enough. I've never experienced life in South Hampton, but even on the west coast we've heard rumors of the craziness that can happen on the Fourth of July and Labor Day weekends. It's not exactly that I'm excited to add anymore crazy to my life, but from a professional standpoint I am amped about the career experience I'll receive.

"So," I say, catching up with Piper. "Do you still want to catch a ride? I've heard terrible things about the Jitney."

"I think I'll take my chances," she says, angrily flinging the door to our office open.

"Um... okay then. You sure?"

"Yep," she replies, dropping the agenda on her desk and flopping into her chair.

"Alright, what's gotten into you?" I ask, walking over and propping myself on the corner of her desk.

"How do you do it?"

"Do?"

"I'm fucking him, and you're still getting ahead," she says, coldly.

"Piper, I didn't ask for this. If you want to run the events, you can. I'll go talk to him."

"Oh sure," she says, spinning her chair to face me. "Make me seem like a spoiled brat who didn't get her way. Go ahead, I bet you'd love that."

"Piper—"

"Save it," she snips. "I'm taking lunch. Just drop whatever assignments you have for me on my desk."

I watch, dumbfounded, as she storms from the room. Until this moment, Piper has always seemed genuinely okay with my seniority in New York, even though she spent years working for P.E.S. in Los Angeles. Something tells me that whatever is behind her sudden change of heart goes much deeper than the change to the weekend's agenda.

****

"Need some help, princess?" Sebastian asks, stepping into the bedroom.

Sighing, I look up from the mess of clothes I've scattered across the bed. He's wearing jeans and a t-shirt. Plopping down, I stare at the pile and say, "I just realized that all of my suitcases are at my apartment."

"This *is* your apartment now," he corrects, coming to me and pulling my head against his abdomen.

"You know what I mean."

"Yes, I do. And I've already thought about that." Bending down, he retrieves an expensive designer luggage set from under the bed. "That's why I had these picked up for you earlier."

"Thank you," I respond, neatly tucking my clothes for the weekend into the oval-shaped tote. "You didn't have to buy me anything new, though. If you were going to go through all this trouble, you should've just sent Sean to my apartment to get mine."

"Once again, this is your apartment now, Danielle. Don't make me remind you again," he says threateningly. "I wanted to buy you new suitcases considering that the only thing I've seen you travel with is a canvas duffel bag, and a tattered shell of what used to be a backpack. You deserve better."

"I like that duffel bag," I reply haughtily.

"It's not fit for world travel. And we will travel the world together, princess."

"Is that so?" I ask, stepping into the bathroom to pack my toiletries and makeup.

Coming behind me and wrapping his arms around my waist, he says, "Yes. But I'm assuming you have other things you'd like to get from your old place?"

Sinking into him, I close my eyes and try to focus on anything other than the memory of Walt standing in my living room. "I do." I whisper, "but..."

"Make a list of anything that's not in your room. I'll have Benson and Bernice handle it while we are away."

"Sebastian, I'm really not comfortable with that," I reply, turning and looping my arms over his shoulders. "I barely know either of them. It just feels weird to have them going through my personal space."

"I would send Thomas, but I've already sent him to Southampton to get a few things in order."

"It's okay. It's better if I do it myself. Besides, I need to face it. It's the only way I'm ever going to get past it."

Nodding, he responds, "In that case, we will do it together next week. Right now, though, we have Labor Day with the Blacks. Are you ready for family bonding?"

I stare at our reflection in the mirror. There's a rare sparkle in Sebastian's usually smoldering gray eyes. I'm not sure that I'm ready for any level of socializing, especially not something on the grand scale of one of Emmalyn Black's parties. However, the childlike innocence of his excitement is enough reason for me to try.

"I think so," I reply.

"Good," he says, playfully kissing the top of my head. "Just remember, you play on my team now. My team never loses."

"You're really into this whole weekend of family competition thing, aren't you?" I ask, smiling.

"If you think I'm bad, wait until you see Katie," he answers, winking.

****

"If you run into any trouble, Thomas is already at his station, and Rhodes is in the chopper waiting," Benson, Sebastian's second driver, informs us.

Fighting the swarm of butterflies in my stomach, I look at the metal shack in front of me. It's hard to see from this vantage point, but I can just barely make out the large propeller blades of the aircraft.

"Thank you, Benson," Sebastian says, dismissing him.

He reaches in the car, grabs the garment bag with my outfit for our P.E.S. event tonight, and places his hand on my back, ushering me forward.

"Sure, you don't want me to carry that?" I ask.

"I've got it," Sebastian replies, locking his fingers in mine. "Shall we?"

I nod.

"Nervous?" He asks.

"More excited than anything. When you said you preferred for me to ride with you, I just assumed you meant we'd be driving on the Long Island Expressway."

Laughing, he says, "What would've been the fun in that? Besides, the drive is a night-mare on a normal Friday. On a holiday weekend, it would be hell. The helicopter will be must faster."

Hair entangled around my face, we edge onto the tarmac. I squeeze Sebastian's hand a little tighter and toss my arm up to hold the wild strands from my face. The co-pilot opens the door for us, and I note that Cyrus, my bodyguard, is in the pilot's seat. I climb through, drop my handbag on the floor, and lean my head into the leather headrest. Sebastian follows suit, reaching all around himself, and fasting his seatbelt. I take his cue, careful to watch how he's doing it, and secure myself as well. Cyrus toys with various nobs and handles, and we whir into action.

Throwing my hands over my ears to drown out the whistling, I snap my head toward Sebastian. He laughs and pulls a set of headphones down from the ceiling. Wrinkling my nose at him, I take them and place them over my ears. His touch feels like silk as his hand slides up the bare skin of my thigh in response. Cyrus continues his careful maneuvering, and every ounce of my body comes alive with vibrations.

I watch through the cockpit of the windows as the shadow of the blades grows faster and faster until slowly we're hovering over the ground and edging out toward the water. Unlike an airplane, we don't climb high enough to be amid the clouds. Instead, we hang tight somewhere in between. The ride is comfortable, smooth, and evenly paced. Releasing the tension I've been carrying for weeks, I settle into my seat. I don't know what this weekend has in store for me, but I know the brief moments of R&R that I'll get are well deserved.

Forty-five minutes later, I'm waking up to a completely different world. We've landed on a helipad surrounded by bright green grass. Sebastian helps me from the helicopter, and escorts me to a waiting Mercedes. He climbs behind the steering wheel with a smile and leans in to kiss me.

"Sorry, I fell asleep," I say, placing my hand on his leg.

"Don't be," he replies. "You'll need it. Trust me."

"So how long until we get there?"

"It's about a ten-minute drive up to the main property."

"The main property?"

"Yeah, I bought this lot a few years after I had my parents' house built. Someday, I'll build my own place here. For now, it's just for the helipad."

"I didn't take you for the kind of guy who would build a house next to mommy's," I tease.

"Well, considering I built a smaller house on their property in order to have some privacy during these functions, I figured it was only fitting for me to expand the estate and build a larger one in order to do my own entertaining." He winks at the word, and I find myself no longer feeling playful.

A beautiful gate marks the entrance to the Black summer home. It opens with ease when Sebastian taps in the key code. We follow a paved drive, outlined on either side by gorgeous red oaks, to the main house. Wide-eyed, I stare up at the sandstone structure. If the exterior is this breathtaking, I can't fathom what the interior looks like. Sebastian has proven to me on more than one occasion that he only accepts the best, but when it comes to the vacation home he built for his parents, he truly outdid himself.

"Don't be intimidated, princess," Sebastian says, putting the car in park. "You have just as much right to be here as anyone else who's coming."

"Right," I reply, gawking at the Doric columns framing the door. "And who all is that going to be again?"

Gripping the back of my shirt in his hand, he presses into my back, urging me forward. "Alana will be with her family at their own estate this weekend, Danielle. She'll probably make an appearance on Sunday. As will her mother and father."

"Great," I sigh, rolling my eyes. "Three Sinclairs for the price of one. Happy vacation to me."

His amusement written on his face, he rings the doorbell. "Just don't think about it. I'm with *you*. I believe we've made that much clear."

Praying that he's right, I lean into him. Within seconds, a frantic maid is opening the door and taking my garment bag.

"You're moother and vather are on the patio," she says, her words heavy with a foreign tongue I can't quite place. "I'll place deese in the guest house."

"Danke, Magda," Sebastian replies, showing off his never-ending mastery of language by using the perfect German accent.

He leads me through a gorgeous sitting room filled with antique furniture that probably costs more than my father's entire house, and out a sliding glass door, which opens onto a breezy patio. Looking like the definition of elegance, Emmalyn Black sits on a padded wicker couch. Katie sits next to her, a thick binder filled with wedding details in hand. Across from them are Brad, Katie's fiancé, and Richard, Sebastian's father. The ladies may not notice us, as they are busy with what looks like a rather complex seating chart, but Richard does.

His eyes light up as he stands to hug his son. "The party has arrived," he says, clapping Sebastian on the back. "How was your flight, son?"

"It was as to be expected," Sebastian replies nonchalantly, releasing me to hug both his mother and sister.

"It's great to see you again, Dani," Richard says, pulling me into a hug. "Glad you could make it."

"Thanks for having me," I reply, still trying to adjust to the embrace.

"We would've insisted if you'd turned us down," Emmalyn says, taking my hands and air kissing each of my cheeks. "Maybe you can help us sort this wedding mess out. We could use someone with your expertise."

"I'd love to," I reply.

"Dani has enough work to do this weekend, Mother," Sebastian says, wrapping his arms around my waist and pulling me against him. "She's mine for the limited amount of time she actually has off."

"You never were any good at sharing," Emmalyn jokes, pulling me away from him and offering me the seat in the middle of the couch.

"Relax, hotshot." I look up at him and smile. "Whatever it is, I'm sure it won't take long."

"You don't know these two," he teases. "I need to find Thomas and make sure the team's all squared away. I'll see you when I'm done."

"I'll be here," I reply.

# Chapter 16

Sebastian

Truth be told, my mother distracting Danielle for a few hours is a blessing in disguise. I need to check in with William Rush and bring the rest of my team up to speed. The storm that's coming may very well be strong enough to bring my ship down. If that happens, Danielle is the priority. I need a plan in place, just in case.

It takes Rush longer than usual to answer the phone. When he does, the melancholy tone of his voice lets me know we don't have our desired results from this morning's interrogation.

"I'm going to give it to you straight. It's not good," he says.

"Was she not as ready as we'd hoped?"

Danielle met with Detective West at the apartment shortly after I left for work this morning. Based on the information I received from her security team, the meeting was short and cordial. West kept his filthy hands to himself, which was one of my greatest concerns. I'd done my job well. As far as I know, Danielle doesn't have any suspicions about our history. That doesn't mean I can forget it, though.

"She did great," Rush replies, reeling me back in. "Her answers were short. Precise, but not defensive. You'd think she's done this before."

"Then I don't see what the problem is."

"Well... I got the feeling they have more evidence than they're letting on. I don't have the slightest idea what it is, exactly, but I have some people working to find out."

Sinking down on the sofa, I say, "Keep me up to speed."

"I will. I just have one question. Considering everything that's happened, do you want me to hold off on our other plans?"

I rub the bridge of my nose as I contemplate my options. I've wanted this for too long to give up on it now. We're too close. However, I can't risk everything going to hell if this investigation doesn't go as I've planned.

"What's your advice?" I ask at last.

"Everything is ready to go. I could file it as early as today. The problem is that if things take a turn for the worst, Alana can then use the investigation to fight you. How confident are you she'll remain loyal?"

"I'll handle Alana. File the paperwork."

"You're sure?"

"I'm sure. She'll cooperate."

"Sebastian, if you have something on her you've failed to tell me, now's the time. Once I send these documents off to the judge, it's a done deal."

"It's nothing pertinent to the progress we've made. I just have reason to believe that she'll do as I ask."

"She's kept the kid from you this long, buddy. I'm taking my lawyer's hat off now. As someone who knows when you're about to fall to pieces, I'm here to help. I can't do that, though, unless you bring me in the loop."

"We both know I won't give you more information than you need to know. File the damned paperwork. Call me when you have developments in either matter. As far as going to pieces is concerned, name one time you've seen me crack under pressure."

"I'm just saying, Romeo. If you need backup, I'm here."

"I always hated that nickname," I reply.

"It was fitting. Just like Oberon was the perfect name for me. I think we can both agree that I have a magic touch."

Lips turned in a smirk, I reply, "You realize you got that name because of your failed attempts at being a trickster."

"No self-respecting bonesman would ever fail at anything."

"I hear ya. I need to update the team and get back to Danielle, as I'm sure you need to get back to Christina. We all know what a short leash she keeps on you."

"A short leash that's tied to the hand of a Kennedy. It will all be worth it in the end, and you'd better be one of the biggest contributions to my campaign."

"I'm afraid I can't support having you in any public office," I joke. "I know too many of your secrets."

"As I do you," he quips. "Bribery can be a powerful thing. I'll be in touch as soon as I know something. Martha's Vineyard waits."

We say our goodbyes, and I fix myself a scotch. William Rush and I were both tapped into a society so secret that only members know of its existence our senior year at Yale. Our fathers and our grandfathers before them were all members dating all the way back to the society's charter in the eighteen hundreds. For an entire year, I spent two nights a week locked away in a dimly lit room with Rush and thirteen other inductees. For hours, we would divulge the deepest secrets we had. We were supposed to anyway. Thankfully, an early childhood spent with Isabelle prepared me for the experience. The things they think they know about me could easily be turned up by any decent reporter. My darkest demons stayed where they always have, locked away in the deepest parts of my blackened soul.

I set my empty glass on the counter and move to the office where my team awaits. Danielle is convinced that this weekend would be the escape we've been needing. I promised her it would, but now I can't be sure.

****

"What time is it?" I ask, sleepily.

I'd come to the living room just after my meeting to wait for Danielle. The last thing I remember is the distant sound of the waves crashing against the shore as my eyelids grew heavy. I never nap. It's a testament to the estate I gifted my parents on their anniversary two years ago that I'm able to do so here.

"It's almost eight o'clock. I need to leave soon, but I wanted to do this first."

She tosses her legs over my waist and brings her lips to meet mine. I welcome the sensation, our tongues gliding in rhythm with each other. When she pulls away, I pull her flush against me, not yet ready to let go.

"Call in sick and let's do that again and again until the night fades into the morning."

Laughing, she says, "And what illness do you suggest I claim to have contracted in the last three hours?"

"Hmm... passion fever?"

"You're a cheese ball," she says, laughing as she pulls herself free. "But I love you."

"I love you too, princess. You'll be home around?"

"I have no idea. Late, that much I do know. I thought this place was supposed to be more relaxed than the city. Why would anyone schedule a party to start at ten at night?"

"Because they knew their guests would be on the expressway until seven at the earliest. Not everyone is lucky enough to date a guy who owns his own helicopter."

"Of course, because that's the only reason I'm with you," she teases.

"No, that's one of the side perks. The main reason you're with me is because I do this." In one swift motion, I lift her in my arms and stand. Turning us, I lower her to the couch and bring my hand under the hem of her dress while nibbling her collarbone."

She sighs and then says, "You're playful in the Hamptons."

"I'm horny in the Hamptons as well. Why don't you fix that?"

"Later," she replies, shoving me off with a smile. "I really should go. I don't know how long it takes to get from here to Bridgehampton."

It's hard to fight the fit of laughter bubbling up inside of me. Danielle has taken to this world so much more naturally than I did when I transitioned. It can be hard for me to remember that she's still new at all of this. There are small moments when I can see her insecurities about the glamour of it all, but for the most part, she's held her own.

"It's only about fifteen minutes, though traffic might slow you down today. The rest of the weekend should be smooth sailing," I inform her, tucking a flyaway strand of hair behind her ear.

"Walk me to the car?"

"If I have to," I say with a wink, pulling her from the couch.

I hold her steady while she slips on her shoes and notice for the first time the small oval picture frame peaking from under the couch. I must have dropped it when I fell asleep. I can only hope Danielle didn't take note of it.

****

"Hungry?" my mother asks when I step back into the main house. "Danielle didn't want to wake you earlier, but she made sure we kept a plate for you."

"Thanks," I reply. "I'll get it in a second."

"What'd you guys do all day?"

"Wedding planning mostly." She smiles and clasps my hand. "Danielle is a godsend."

"That she is, mother," I answer, turning toward the kitchen.

"Sebastian," she says, placing a gentle hand on my shoulder as I lean into the fridge. "What's wrong?"

"Nothing. It's Labor Day weekend. I'm here with my family, and everything will be perfect, as always."

"You're sure? You seem off. I mean, the last time I can remember you taking a nap, you had the flu."

Placing the plate on the counter, I hug her. I pull away, look down into her face, and say, "I'm fine, Mother. I just had a headache."

It's not a lie. I've been suffering from tension headaches almost daily since this whole mess started, but now they've grown to become unshakable. I can't tell Danielle about them, though. It would only cause her more worry, and that's what we've all been trying to avoid.

"Well, that's understandable. You have a lot going on. Just one more reason I'm glad Dani could convince you to come this weekend. We would've been lost without you. Now, heat your dinner and turn your phone off. It's time for charades."

"I'll be there in just a minute. I will not, however, turn my phone off. And you already know this."

"A mother can dream, can't she?" She asks.

"I hope you never stop. Someone has to dream big enough for the both of us."

She squeezes my shoulder. "You deserve happiness, Sebastian. Just remember that."

Maybe so, I have been to places my mother wouldn't dare go, however. I've seen things first hand that she only experiences through her various clients. Dreaming is something I forgot how to do long ago.

# Chapter 17

*D*anielle

"So, the last thing is the gate. Piper, do you think you can cover it?" I ask, turning my attention on her.

We're officially at the one-hour mark, meaning that guests will show up within the next thirty minutes. My clipboard shakes slightly from the nervous twinge of my hands. I'm still shocked that Paul has trusted me with such an enormous task. It's one thing when he leaves me alone at a nightclub in the city, but for him to give me Kristen's entire weekend worth of accounts... I just hope I don't screw things up.

"Whatev," she says, smacking her gum and rolling her eyes.

Hugging my clipboard to my chest and inhaling deeply, I reply, "Thanks."

Piper has had nothing but an attitude toward me since the incident at the office. I'm still not sure why she's taking it so personally. If the situation was reversed, and Sebastian had given her a significant job to do over me, I wouldn't be upset about it. I would accept it as a sign that he was trying to keep the line between personal and professional from becoming too blurred. I'm sure that's what Paul's intentions were as well, but I intend to make the most of it.

I dismiss my crew and head into the kitchen to check on the caterers. I've just finished when I feel the light, yet commanding, touch on my shoulder. Fighting my instinct to run, I turn and force myself to stay calm when I see Doctor Murray behind me.

Cocking his head to the side with a condescending smile, he says, "I didn't know you would be working this party, Danielle. Are you sure you're feeling up to it? You've missed our last few sessions."

"I'm doing just fine," I reply, skirting around him. "I've actually sought counseling elsewhere."

"Shame." He strokes his hand over a cleanly shaved chin and considers me. "May I ask why?"

"I just felt that we had different interests as far as my treatment was concerned."

He nods but doesn't reply.

"Well... I'd better go check on the DJ. I hope you enjoy yourself," I reply, my stomach growing tighter from the repressed anger.

This is the creep who hurt my Sebastian. One of them, at least. I wonder who the others were. Do they live in the city as well? I know the statute of limitations has most likely been exceeded, but maybe I can offer Sebastian retribution in other ways. Maybe I can give him his, like I got mine with Walt. The hair on my arms stands on end, and my veins fill with ice at the thought. What's wrong with me?

"Danielle, are you okay? You don't look so well," he says, reaching for me.

"I'm fine," I snap, avoiding his touch. "Just busy. If you'll excuse me."

"Wait. Don't you want your check?"

"My check?"

"Well, yes, my daughter Crystal is the one responsible for this event. I'm just covering the expense."

"Crystal O'Brien, is your daughter?"

"Last time I checked. I'm surprised she didn't mention it to you when you she hired the firm. I'm the one who suggested she go with P.E.S."

That explains a lot. I may not have been born in this world, but I learned enough in my own dealings with Walter to know that Doctor Murray is trying to smoke Sebastian out. *Why would he be concerned about him after all this time?*

"I wasn't the initial rep in charge of her account," I admit. "As far as the payment goes, save your check. We'll send you an invoice in the mail, and you'll have fourteen days to pay it after receipt."

"Very well," he says. "I guess you should go make my little girl happy. You only turn twenty-one once in a lifetime, after all."

"Indeed," I reply.

If Doctor Murray's daughter is twenty-one, that means she was already born when Sebastian was going through hell at her father's hands. Where was she, and does Sebastian know about her?

****

Around eleven, I decide to go check on Piper at the gate. The night has been so crazy that I haven't had the chance to touch base with her yet. I've also been waiting for the flow of traffic to slow down so that maybe we can talk. Hair on my neck standing on end, I sense that someone is following me. Heart racing, I turn to see Cyrus. He promised to be unobtrusive, and I must admit that he has been. The problem is; he's so good at it I sometimes forget he's there and panic sets in. I wonder if I'll ever stop looking over my shoulder now that Walt's gone.

Shaking off the sense of doom I'm feeling, I hold my head high and turn the corner leading to the main gate. I'm just approaching when I see her leaned against a post, talking on her cell phone. She stares up at the night sky and clenches her hand into a fist.

"I'm trying, okay! Is it my fault that he gives her a leg up every chance he gets? Clearly, he's got a soft spot for poor, damaged, Dani."

I freeze in the middle of the drive as I ponder who she's possibly talking to, and why they're talking about me.

"I said I'm on it!" She screams. "Stop harassing me. You'll get what you paid for."

"I'm trying, okay! Is it my fault that he gives her a leg up every chance he gets? Clearly, he's got a soft spot for poor, damaged, Dani."I freeze in the middle of the drive as I ponder who she's possibly talking to, and why they're talking about me."I said I'm on it!" She screams. "Stop harassing me. You'll get what you paid for."

"I wasn't. Not really... I mean... I may have been a venting a little, but you misunderstood—"

"Bullshit! I'm not an idiot, Piper. Who is paying you, and what do they want with me?"

"You're just a regular little eavesdropper, aren't you?" She asks, walking up the drive and getting in my face. "Looking for another way to usurp me with our boss?"

"What?" I ask, fighting to keep my voice even. "How could you even consider turning this around on me? I've done nothing to you, Piper. I've been in New York longer. I know the clients here better. It's that simple. I understand that you've worked for the company for longer, but you are the second assistant now. You accepted the demotion, because you wanted a chance to move through the ranks and thought it would be easier to do that if you could work more closely with Paul. I'm sorry it hasn't gone as you've planned it, but that's for you to discuss with your *boyfriend* during pillow talk time. I have nothing to do with it."

"You stupid bitch!" She screams, lunging at me. "You think this is about Paul? It goes so much deeper than that."

Cyrus is between us in a flash, using his body as a shield to block me from her. Limbs shaking; I take a deep breath, look at her rage-swollen face, and say, "I thought we were friends. I don't know what the hell your problem is, but I can assure of this one thing. You've crossed the wrong girl."

The gleam of headlights reflects on the metal bars of the gate as what's presumably a fashionably late guest arrives. Cyrus sets Piper down just as the car rolls to a stop beside us. Paul peeks out at us over the glass of the back window, and I swallow at the lump of guilt in my throat. "Why don't you both get in?" He asks.

Shamefully sliding into the seat across from him, I wait for my lecture. Piper practically throws herself into the seat next to him, slams the door, and crosses her arms.

"Anyone care to explain what I just came up on?" He begins.

"It was nothing," I reply, glancing at Piper. She turns her gaze out the window. "I'm sorry for the scene."

"Piper?" He asks, giving her the chance to respond.

Keeping her face turned away from us, she shrugs.

"Perhaps you should both clock out for the night. We can regroup tomorrow. Dani, do you have transportation, or should I call you a cab?"

"I have a driver, but I'm really okay. I mean, someone has to be here to oversee the cleanup crew."

"I'll handle it," he says, sternly. "Just go and get some rest. I'll call you in the morning, and we can discuss this further."

"If that's what you want," I reply, unable to hide my disappointment. "For what it's worth, I really am sorry for acting so unprofessionally."

Piper snorts, and Paul glances over at her again.

"We'll reconvene tomorrow. Let me take you back up to the house to meet your driver."

****

The lights at the main house are mostly out when we pull into the garage. I gather my shoes and clutch and wait for Sean to open the door. My head pounds as I pull myself out of the car and take off through the yard. Sean offers to escort me to the guest house, but I tell him I'll find my own way and walk barefoot through the grass.

The blades are already dampening with dew, and my feet quickly grow cold as I stumble toward the paved path that will lead me to Sebastian. The guest house is pitch black when I finally arrive, and I wonder if he's sleeping or if I should've checked for him in the main house. I find him in the bedroom, propped up in bed with his laptop. He looks up with a smile when I open the door and turns my side of the bed down for me.

Dropping my shoes, I climb in next to him, lay my head on his shoulder, and ask, "What 'cha working on?"

"Just keeping myself busy until you got here, princess," he replies, closing the laptop and stowing it inside the cabinet on the bedside table. He pulls me on top of him and runs his hands down the length of my back. "How was your night?"

"Ugh. I'd rather not talk about it."

"Anything I should know?"

I debate telling him about my encounter with Doctor Murray, and reply, "Piper unleashed on me, and I'm not sure why. Plus, I overheard her on the phone with someone and she was mentioning my name. It didn't sound good."

"Paul?"

"I don't think so. She said it was her parents, but we both know she's lying there. Whatever it was about, it sounded like she was working against me with someone."

"The team still has some intel from when you had me investigate her before. Want me to see what they know?"

"No, not yet at least. I'm supposed to call Paul tomorrow to discuss the whole thing more. I'm hoping she'll have a better explanation then."

"You're sure?"

"I am." I look at the worried expression on his face. "God, I'm sorry! This is supposed to be our time away from it all, and here I am throwing more fuel on an already blazing fire. I'm going to take a shower. When I come out, I promise I won't be a freak show. I'll just be a normal girl, loving a normal boy, and we can do whatever normal people do when they are on vacation in the Hamptons."

He squeezes my hips and replies, "Princess, we both know you're not a normal girl, and I'm certainly not a normal boy. As far as doing what normal people do that kind of takes the fun out of it doesn't it?"

I laugh, and climb off him. "I'll only be a minute."

# Chapter 18

*Sebastian*

The smell of bacon fills the air when I open my eyes. I roll over to find the sheets still imprinted with Danielle's shape. *What time is it?* It's rare that I sleep in past anyone, but it's especially rare when it happens with Danielle. My princess is not a woman who likes to concern herself with mornings. Pulling on a pair of boxers, I make my way into the kitchen. She's standing at the stove, naked from the hips down, her t-shirt barely reaching the mound of her ass. My cock twitches at the site, and she giggles.

"I thought we'd already discussed your stalkerish tendencies, hotshot," she says, turning to face me.

"Did we? I'm not sure I remember that," I tease, wrapping my hands around her and pulling her in for a kiss.

The taste of strawberries mixes with the sweetness of her lips, and I pull her feet off the floor to indulge further.

"Turkey bacon burns faster than regular bacon," she says, pulling away from me with a smile.

"We don't need either," I reply, holding her in place. "Virginia and Richard Senior will have plenty."

"Excuse me?" She questions, pushing herself free. "I didn't think we had to deal with them until tomorrow."

"Afraid not. I said they wouldn't be coming *here* until tomorrow." I reply, pouring a cup of coffee and turning off the stove's eye. "Today we go to them for family brunch, followed by the big game."

"Game?"

"Oh yeah, the Black Family football game. It's a tradition."

"Football. Really?" A look of disgust sweeps across her face. "I hate football."

"Just remember, you're on my team. I'll make sure you find it enjoyable," I reply, lightly tapping her backside.

"Oh, I'm sure you will," she retorts, firing the stove back up. "But if I'm going to be forced to play football, then you're going to skip out on family brunch."

"Cancel on Senior and Virginia? It's unprecedented."

"All the more reason for you to do it," she winks.

"You're diabolical. I've officially corrupted you," I reply, taking a seat at the island to watch her work.

"Well then, I guess it's a good thing I enjoy being corrupted," she replies, sticking her ass out and intently pivoting her hips.

"Keep that up, and you might talk yourself out of a football game too," I tease, parting my legs to allow room for my lengthening erection.

"Hmm... sounds like a challenge. I'm willing to accept."

****

We eat a breakfast of egg white omelets and turkey bacon, and then retire to the couch for the few quiet moments we have left. My attention is immediately drawn to the photo on the coffee table. I lift it and study it carefully.

"I found that under the couch," Danielle explains, settling in next to me. "Lauren's so little there. How did you get one of her so young?"

"How do you know it's Lauren?"

"The eyes," she says, glancing up at me. "They're gray, just like yours. The two of you are the only ones I've seen with that color."

"It's a genetic trait," I reply, thinking of the two other people I know besides Lauren and myself who have eyes in my same unique shade, one of whom is in this picture.

"Really? Do you know who you got it from?" She pries.

Not wanting to go down that road with her, I place the picture back on the coffee table and roll on top of her. "I do, but I would rather spend our time doing more interesting things than discussing the origin of my eye color."

"Won't they be looking for us?" She asks.

"Let them look," I reply, kissing her neck.

"Now who's corrupting whom?" She responds, spreading her legs.

She presses her lips to mine, and I dig my grip into the supple curve of her ass. There's a gentle cough in the distance, and I pull away. Looking over her shoulder, I see Thomas standing just inside the entryway.

"I'm sorry to disturb you, sir," he begins, "but it's important. It's about the list."

"List?" Danielle asks, sitting upright and scooting off me.

"It's nothing for you to be concerned about, princess," I assure her, sitting upright and adjusting myself. "I'll meet you in the office, Thomas. Give me five minutes."

He nods and exits without hesitation. Thomas's ability to take a direct order without question is the thing that I've always liked most about him. It's also why I didn't hesitate when he suggested a few of his comrades from the Army to help with my security.

"Sebastian," Danielle says, looking at me with a weary expression. "What aren't you telling me?"

"I promise it is nothing. Just some work stuff that I couldn't leave behind."

"I'm not buying that."

"Well, then." I tuck a strand of hair behind her ear and stroke her cheek with my thumb. "I guess you're just going to have to trust me. Why don't you get ready? I'll just be a quick sec and I'll do the same."

"Your grandparents and football," she says sarcastically. "The only thing better to do with my Saturday would be to stab myself in the eye with a spoon."

I laugh and pull her to the feet. "Surely, it won't be that bad."

Raising her eyebrow to challenge me, she says, "Sure. Just how many bottles of scotch have you stashed in the car for the trip?"

"Touché," I reply, kissing her forehead. "We'll get through it together."

Thomas doesn't waste any time, another quality I appreciate about him. He stands as soon as I open the door and waits for me to take my seat before finding his again.

"I'll make it brief," he begins. "You already know we had to increase surveillance on Ms. Stevens last night."

I nod, thinking about the phone call I received from Cyrus Rhodes shortly after Danielle left for work yesterday.

He lays a series of black and white photos on the desk in front of me and continues, "Three from the list. It can't be a coincidence."

"He's circling the wagons," I reply, looking down at the faces I thought I'd only see again in my nightmares.

"How do you want to proceed?"

"Do they know we're on to them?"

"There seems to be no evidence to suggest so."

"Let's keep it that way for now. I want to see how far they're going to take this. Don't let them get close. She's the priority. Always."

"Got it. Is she going back out there tonight?"

"I'm not sure, yet, but since we're on the topic, I might have another assignment for you."

"The girl?"

"What do we know?"

"I had the team back home re-open the investigation after she got confrontational with Ms. Stevens last night. We should know more soon."

"Good work, Thomas," I reply. "It'll be hard to find a quiet place to discuss anything once we reach my grandparents' estate, but I'll have my cell."

Nodding, he asks, "Should I get the car ready?"

"Give me half an hour."

****

Danielle is sitting on the bed wearing navy trousers and a ruffled yellow tank top that compliments her olive skin tone and plump breasts. Her hair is still damp and falls in curls around her face and over her shoulders. She's gazing at the floor with a look of uncertainty on her face.

"What's wrong?" I ask, approaching her cautiously.

"I didn't want to tell you this," she says, looking up at me. "Doctor Murray was at that party last night. It was for his daughter."

"I know," I answer, sitting next to her. "Rhodes called me. I had a feeling he would try to contact you once you stopped your sessions, so I've been having them watch."

She nods. "Oh."

"Why didn't you tell me last night?"

"I really wanted to leave the drama behind for the weekend. I realize he probably told her to hire us to get to you, but I thought that maybe, just maybe, we could have seventy-two hours without worrying about it."

I lay her head on my shoulder, and ask, "So what changed?"

She lifts her hand to expose the cell phone she's been gripping. "I just got off the phone with Paul."

"I take it the news wasn't good."

"He wants me to take the weekend off. He said we'll meet back up at the office on Tuesday."

"I see. Because of Piper?"

She turns toward me and brings her leg up onto the bed. "He said I deserved the break, but I know that's a lie. If anything, he's sick of me taking breaks. It's Piper for sure. I just don't know what I did to her."

"Any guesses?"

"Not really, but I think it all ties back to that phone call I heard her on last night. Do you think it had something to do with Doctor Murray? I mean, he would need someone inside the company to help him with his scheme, right? Just because I work there doesn't mean it was guaranteed that I would be there to handle his event, and I—"

"I understand why you would think that, princess, and I don't blame you for jumping to that conclusion. He doesn't work like that, though. From my dealings with Walt, I can only imagine why you would think that every predator chooses to openly assert their power. It's different with Murray, though. He's like a storm that sneaks up on a quiet afternoon. He prefers to brew in the distance and unleash his fury all at once."

"So, hiring Princeton Enterprise Solutions was part of the brewing?"

"I think so, but I don't think it goes any deeper than that. In any case, we're watching him, so you have nothing to worry about."

"What about his daughter?"

Tension creeps into my shoulders, and I stiffen. "What about her?"

"Do you think she has anything to do with it?"

"No, I do not," I reply, walking to the closet.

"But how can you be sure?" She asks, following me and leaning against the doorway.

"I just am."

"Wouldn't it do us some good just to investigate it, though?"

"Drop it, Danielle," I growl.

She turns and sulks to the living room without saying a word.

"Dammit!" I roar to myself, throwing my hands through my hair and following her. I find her on the couch, curled up with her tablet. "I'm sorry, princess."

She looks up at me with tearful eyes. "Why are you so protective of Crystal? Is there some kind of history there that I should know about?"

"What? No! There's nothing at all," I assure her. "I just don't like the idea of going after an innocent person just to get to their father. I know she has nothing to do with his plot to bring you down, because I don't even know her. She lived with her mother when I was staying with him. I didn't even know she existed until I found Lauren. I had a private investigator dig up everything he could on anyone my birth mother had contact with when I was looking for her."

"Oh. I guess that makes sense."

"So, we're okay?"

She puts the tablet on the couch arm and turns to me. Pulling me down next to her, she snuggles against me. "We're okay. I'm just on edge. I worked so hard to get that internship, and I got promoted so fast. I just don't want to do anything to screw it up, and if we're being honest, I put my job at risk from the beginning by getting involved with you."

"Your job has never been at risk. I've made that abundantly clear."

"I know, but still... you understand what I'm saying, don't you?"

"I do, but I also think you're overthinking things. Let's just make the most of the time off while we can. We're in the Hamptons, and we can officially act like it now that you don't have to work."

"Does that mean you'll put your work away too?"

I roll the idea around in my mind for several minutes, then look at her, and say, "I would love to, but right now is the worst possible time for me to do so."

"That's what I thought," she says, rolling her eyes. "You should probably get ready. We're already late enough, and I have plenty of emails I can thumb through to keep myself busy. Just because I'm not working on events doesn't mean I can't be useful."

****

"What took you so long?" Jewels asks, almost as soon as the car door opens. "She's been bitching for hours! I thought you said you were just going to skip brunch. She had enough to say about that, but this... what were you doing?"

"It's my fault," Danielle says, stepping out after me. "I got a bit of bad news from work, and we were trying to deal with it."

"Oh." Julie's entire mood changes as she hugs Danielle. "Is everything alright?"

"I hope so," Danielle replies, unsure of herself.

"Well, come on," Julie says. "I know it sucks, but we have to at least get through the game. After that, we get off the hook. Mom and Dad aren't as lucky." She giggles. "They have to deal with the dinner party."

"Dinner party?"

She knocks my hand off Danielle's elbow and loops her arm through. I shake my head and move to the other side, taking her hand in mine.

"Richard Sr. and Virginia host a dinner with all the old families in the area every Labor Day weekend," I inform her. "We're never asked to stay, thankfully. It's a time for them to brag about how perfect we all are, and how could they do that if I were here to show the world how much of a fuck up I really am."

Danielle winces and looks up at me.

"It's okay, princess," I reply, half-joking. "I've quite come to appreciate being the black sheep."

"You're not the black sheep," Jewels argues. "I wish you would stop doing that. Who cares what Gran thinks? If she was accurate, then I would be a man-hating lesbian with no future, because I've chosen to major in women's studies. She's a quack, and the reason Grandpa drinks like a fish."

She leads us to the backyard where everyone is already assembled. I can hear my Gran complaining about my tardiness the moment the gate opens. Coming up behind her, I place my hand on her shoulders and say, "I love you too, Gran."

Danielle covers her mouth with her hand to stifle her laughter and tucks her head in my shoulder.

"Don't give me that nonsense, boy," Gran replies. "When someone extends an invitation and you accept it, the polite thing to do is to arrive on time. Of course, if you were purebred, then you would know that."

"I'm sure I would," I reply, stepping back. "We're here now, though, and that's all that matters, isn't it?"

"The nerve—"

"Mrs. Black," Danielle begins. "Please don't be angry with Sebastian. It's my fault. I had some things to handle with work."

Gran looks at her with disgust written all over her face. "Yes, well, I should've known. Honestly, Emmalyn, why do you allow your children to run around with the lower class? Just think of the image it portrays."

"Okay!" my father exclaims, rising to his feet. "Who's ready for some football?"

Everyone except for Mother and Gran follows him out onto the lawn. Surprisingly, Grandfather is nowhere to be seen.

"Looks like I'll be heading up one team and you'll head up the other," Father says in my direction. "Flip to see who chooses?"

"Nah, you take it. You need all the help you can get," I reply.

"Suit yourself, son, but if I remember correctly, you were more of a lacrosse man yourself."

Danielle looks at me with a curious expression, and I shrug. "Our parents made us all pick at least one sport. I was apparently too aggressive for football."

"I didn't realize that was even possible," she responds.

"Yeah well." I shrug again and turn to my father. "So, who's it gonna be?"

"Katie," he says, assuredly.

"Danielle," I say, without hesitation.

"You sure you want me as your first choice?" She asks.

"Always," I reply, kissing her softly.

"I'm going to start making you put a quarter in a jar every time you do that," Katie teases.

"Good thing I have a lot of them," I reply, kissing Danielle again.

"We're going to go with Bradley," my father says, ignoring us.

"That leaves us with Julie," I reply.

"Gee, thanks," she says, as she strides over to us. "I feel so wanted."

"You're guaranteed to be better than me," Danielle tells her.

"She's actually very good," I reply. "Any other time, she would've my first choice. Katie is competitive, but cocky. There's also the fact that her wedding is only weeks away, and she's not about to risk breaking a nail."

"Good one," Jewels says.

"So, we're all set then," Father says. "What's your call, son?"

"I'll take heads."

"Heads it is," he replies, balancing the quarter on his thumb preparing to flip it.

"You weren't thinking of starting without us, now were you?" Richard Senior calls out, stepping onto the porch.

I look up and see a flow of red hair trailing behind him.

"What the hell is she doing here?" Danielle asks, before I can even wrap my mind around it.

"I'm not sure, princess, but I intend to find out." I wait for them to approach, and grab Alana by the elbow, pulling her away from everyone. "What the fuck are you doing?" I growl.

"Black Family Football, of course," she replies.

"This event is family only, Alana. Go home."

She looks over at Danielle and a mischievous glint forms in her eyes. "Family you say? Well, in that case, I'm sure I have more right to be here than she does."

"You and I have an agreement, Alana. I would advise you to remember it and tend to your own family today."

"But, darling," she begins, bringing her hand to my cheek, and lightly stroking it with her thumb. "*You* are *my* family. Your needs are my number one priority. After all, that's how we came to our *agreement* to begin with, isn't it?"

Revulsion courses through my veins, and I snatch her hand away. "I don't know what you think you'll accomplish by being here, but I'm only going to say this once. Fuck with Danielle today, and it will be the last thing you do. I'm not in the mood for your games, Alana. Do you understand?"

"Relax, darling," she says, yanking her arm free. "I'm not planning on doing anything to hurt your precious Danielle. I'm here because Richard Sr. asked me to be. It's as simple as that. Do you honestly think I want to play football on a Saturday that would've otherwise been spent on my father's sailboat drinking Mai tais? Besides, I've been here since brunch. You are the one who's just arrived. The way I see it, if anyone should be the one to leave, it's you and Danielle."

"You don't want to test me, Alana. If you try to force me to choose between you and her, she'll win every single time. If you'd like to keep things the way they are, you'll smile and be polite. Otherwise, I'll start working on the paperwork before you've even found your car."

"So touchy," she replies, patting my chest and stepping around me. "It really is unbecoming of you." Clasping Danielle's hands in hers and kissing both of her cheeks, she exclaims. "Danielle, how lovely to see you!"

Bemused, Danielle looks up at me. I shake my head and make my way to her. "Don't let her rattle you," I say, pulling her into a tight embrace. "You're on my team and my team—"

"Yeah, I know. Your team always wins. The problem, hotshot, is that she's apparently on your team too, and I don't know which one of us is the starter and who's doomed to play second string."

With that, she pulls away from me and takes her place next to Jewels. Alana looks at me and waves. Jaw flinching with tension, I walk over to them and begin dealing out instructions for the game. All the while, thinking about Danielle's words. She's the starter. She always will be. If she doesn't know that now, I'll make sure she soon never forgets.

# Chapter 19

D anielle

*Breathe in. Breathe out.* I feel like you could knock me over with a pin. *Why is Alana here? What is it that keeps her so close to Sebastian's grandfather?*

I was already dreading spending the evening with her tomorrow night. To have her not only show up here but to be wanted is killing me. My mind races with thoughts of my inferiority. Despite Sebastian's speech about being his first pick, it's becoming increasingly clear that things would have been different had Alana shown her presence sooner. I watch as he tosses the ball to her, just in time for her to score the game point.

*She's even good at football. I can't compete with this.*

"Good game," she says, joyfully skipping up to me. "With a bit more practice, you might just be able to keep up."

Glaring at her, I reply, "Yeah, well, I'm personally more of a basketball girl."

"Of course," she says, turning to stride away just in time for Sebastian to find me.

"What's that face about? We won!"

"Yep, *you* sure did," I reply, crossing my arms. "So, what happens now?"

"We say our goodbyes and go back to the house. Typically, I'll spend some time with Katie and Jewels, but we can do our own thing if you want."

"Is *she* coming?" I ask, tilting my head in Alana's direction.

He looks across the lawn where she hangs from his grandfather's arm, laughing in her annoying hyena voice, and cutting her eyes at us. Noticing that she has our attention, she smiles and waves Sebastian over. He nods and turns his attention back toward me.

"You have nothing to be jealous of, princess, and I can assure you that I knew nothing about this. I think the day went well, though, all things considered. Don't you?"

"Oh yeah, it was a gas alright," I reply. "You go see what they want. I'll do the polite thing and say goodbye to your grandmother. Then I'm heading to the car."

"Hey," he starts, affectionately squeezing my arm, "you sure you're okay?"

"Oh, I'm just perfect," I reply shortly. "I'll be in the car waiting."

"Danielle—"

"Not here, Sebastian. Not now. Just clear things up with your father and grandfather, and let's go."

I don't give him the chance to respond, knowing he'd never make a scene in front of his family. The family house in Northampton differs from Sebastian's parent's estate in Westhampton in many ways. For starters, it's not on the waterfront, and while it's still grand, it's much more modest. That is, of course, assuming you can call a million-dollar home modest. In any case, it's easier to navigate than the one I arrived at yesterday.

It only takes minutes for me to find the kitchen where Virginia barks orders at various members of what I can only assume to be a catering team while Emmalyn watches from a distance. She sees me first, and her blue eyes sparkle. "Heading out then?" She asks.

"Yes," I reply, stopping at the end of the bar. "We'll see you after you're done here?"

"Possibly," she answers. "The kids typically do their own thing on Saturday evening. Richard and I are never cool enough to be invited."

"I see. Well, I hope you enjoy your night."

"Oh, I'm sure it will be a blast," she replies, winking and placing her hand on my elbow to usher me forward. She turns her attention to Virginia and says, "Mom, the kids are leaving now."

"Right, well," she turns to me and pauses. I feel myself shrinking under the full force of her condemnation.

"Thank you for inviting me," I manage to say. "I had a lovely time."

"Humph. I didn't invite you, but I'm glad you amused yourself. Next time, perhaps you'll do us all the kind favor of arriving on time. Honestly—"

"Yes, well," Emmalyn interrupts, placing her hands on my shoulders to steady me. "I think I'll show Dani out. You don't need me, do you, Mom?"

"Need you? Of course, I don't need you. You wouldn't know how to throw a proper event if it came with an instruction manual."

"I suppose you're right," Emmalyn replies, smiling in a forced way that exposes too many of her teeth.

"How do you do that?" I ask once we're safely outside.

"Do what?"

"Pretend like it doesn't bother you."

"Oh, that." She shrugs. "After a while, you just stop listening to whatever it is she's rambling on about, nod your head in agreement, and move on. The longer you're with us, the easier it will become."

"That is assuming I'm with you any longer," I mumble.

"Why wouldn't you be, dear?"

Realizing that I've stuck my foot in my mouth, I reply, "It's nothing. Sorry, I didn't mean to say anything."

"Is this about Alana?"

"I'm just in a mood. I'll get over it."

"I would be in a mood too if I had someone as conniving as Richard Senior trying to sabotage my relationship."

"So, I'm not crazy?" I ask, wearily. "You see it too."

"Of course I see it, darling. Don't let it get to you. My son is over the moon for you." She smiles the warm smile of a mother who adores her child, and something twists inside of me. "Sebastian has never cared what his grandparents think of his choices. The harder they try to push him away from you, the harder he'll fall into your arms."

I smile, even though I'm not so sure she's right. I know Sebastian cares what Richard Senior thinks of him. He may not share it with the rest of the world, but I've seen the change in him. I've seen the silent cry for approval and echoed it with my own.

"You're such a sweet girl, Dani," she says, pulling me into a soft hug. "I'm so glad he found you."

"Me too," I whisper, all the while hoping he doesn't choose to lose me.

"I guess you're officially a Black now," Julie's voice interrupts. "Forget ever getting in a car again without mom throwing her arms around you."

"Oh, stop teasing," Emmalyn replies, placing her hands around both of her daughters at once. "Can I help it that I've been blessed with such beautiful, intelligent, and gifted children? Any mother would be just as proud."

"Indeed, dear sisters," Sebastian says, moving next to me. "You've given our parents loads to be thankful for."

Emmalyn quickly throws her arms around his neck and replies, "They're not the only ones." She lowers her voice to a whisper and continues, "You, son, are probably my biggest accomplishment of all."

He says nothing, but I can see some of the tension leave his shoulders as he places his arms around her and lightly squeezes. For the first time, I feel slightly guilty for leaving him to face Richard Sr. alone.

Emmalyn pulls away and repeats the process with Bradley. "Are you kids going out tonight?" She asks, releasing him.

"Actually," Katie begins, turning a mischievous gaze on Sebastian. "Our dear brother was just informing us he doesn't think Dani will feel up to it. Personally, I think he's just trying to save himself the embarrassment of a sibling bonding moment."

"I second that," Julie replies, nudging him playfully.

"I suggest you both change your tones before you find yourselves hitchhiking home," he threatens. There's a playful gleam in his eye, and he looks down to hide his smile. "I've already told you, Dani practically lives in nightclubs. She won't want to spend her time—"

"Actually," I interrupt. "Dani is right here, and she's perfectly capable of speaking on her own behalf."

"Uh-oh, bro," Julie teases. "You're in trouble now."

"I think a night out with your sisters sounds fabulous," I reply, tilting my head up at him. "Are you sure you have to come?"

"Watch it or you'll be walking with them," he replies. He presses his lips against my ear and whispers, "And that won't be your only punishment."

I feel the heat rising in my cheeks and turn away from him. Emmalyn's eyes meet mine, and she smiles.

My cheeks grow redder still, and I say, "You wouldn't put me on the side of the road, hotshot. I'm the best thing that's ever happened to you."

Feeling triumphant, I slide into the backseat. Julie slides in beside me. Laughing, she turns to me and says, "Thank you for loving him."

"It's not really anything to thank me for," I reply.

"You're changing him. I love my brother for everything he was, but there's something about the man he's becoming. It's like you've somehow shrunk the black hole inside of him."

"What are we talking about?" Katie asks, climbing in opposite us with Bradley close behind.

"Sebastian," Jewels replies, pulling a compact from her purse. "Dani's changing him, don't ya think?"

"Oh, most definitely." She looks at me. "I've never seen him like this before."

"Move over," Sebastian says, breaking up our conversation.

"What if I don't want to?" Julie challenges. "I think there's plenty of room next to Katie."

"Just enough room for you, little sister," he glares at her, "Up. Now."

"Geez. You're so territorial," she teases, moving to the seat next to her sister. "It's like when we were kids and you used to get super pissed when we went into your room. Remember that, Katie?"

Katie laughs and looks at Sebastian. "Like the time I caught you with that cheerleader and you completely flipped."

Even though I have absolutely no reason to be jealous, I can feel it creeping in. I know Sebastian has a past. He's been bluntly honest about that fact from the beginning, and it's not like I'm a saint by any means. Still, the idea of teenage Sebastian with some cheerleader only takes me back to what my Sebastian once told me. Alana was completely comfortable with his sexual exploits, as long as she was the one on his arm at the end of the night. After this afternoon's football game, I can't help but question if maybe I'm just another distraction.

****

"I think I'll change and spend some time by the pool. What time are we leaving?"

Sebastian catches me around the waist and pulls me to him. "Around eight, but I know far better things we can do with our time than go swimming." He cups my butt with his palm and adds, "Starting with where we left off this morning."

I tear his grip away and turn down the hallway. "I think I'd rather take my chances with the pool."

"What's with you?" He asks, following me into the bedroom.

143

"Nothing is wrong with me, Sebastian. I just want to be alone for a while. Is that such a terrible thing?" I grab my swimsuit and he clasps my wrist.

"It wouldn't be if not for the fact that you're only doing it to avoid being with me." He turns me around and places his hand on my cheek, searching me. "You've been acting odd since we left my grandparents. Did Richard Senior say something to you?"

"What? No! God, you really are clueless sometimes," I reply, jerking my arm free and storming to the bathroom.

The door opens without so much as a knock, just as I'm pulling my top over my head.

"Have you never heard of privacy?" I scold.

Laughing, he steps in and closes the door behind him. "Better?"

"You know what I meant."

"I do. I also know that you're being completely ridiculous." He reaches behind me and unclasps my bra, lightly brushing his fingers across my spine. No matter how hard I try to fight it, a shiver of pleasure runs through me, and he smirks. "Your body was made for me to admire, Danielle. We both know it."

"Stop," I say, helpless, as he kisses my neck and slides his hands over my hips.

"Is that what you really want?" He works the button of my linen pants with his fingers.

"Yes," I reply, pushing his hands away. "Sebastian, look at me."

Exhaling, he lifts his gaze from my breasts and stares into my eyes. The familiar burning heat of his lust rests in his irises, and it takes everything I have to keep myself from giving in. Closing my eyes, I inhale and force my voice to remain even.

"I can't keep doing this. I can't keep believing that you're sincere when you say I'm the only one for you, only to have it ripped apart when Alana shows up. She still wants Sebastian. And I *know* there's more to your story than just keeping her around for your daughter. If anything, that would make you trust her even less. I'm tired of you treating me like an idiot, and I'm losing respect for myself for letting you."

He runs his hands through his hair and sits on the edge of the tub. "How long is this going to continue driving a wall between us?"

"For as long as you allow it to," I reply, tying my bikini top and stepping out of my pants.

"Haven't I proven myself to you, Danielle? *You're* the one I love. *You're* the one I fight for. It's *you* I can't breathe without, princess. Not Alana. *You*. Always you."

"Except that it isn't." I pull on my swimsuit bottoms and turn to face him. "It's *her* when you need stolen moments at charity galas. *She* is the one you call when someone needs to cover for you. It's *her* when you want to win your family football game. It's me when you need a good fuck, or someone to freak out on every once in a while. But she's the one who saves you, and I don't know how I ever allowed myself to believe it would ever be anything otherwise."

"Do you honestly think you would be here with my family if you weren't the one for me, Danielle?"

"She's—"

Standing, he bellows, "Do you think I would've arranged for you to have breakfast with Lauren if all you were was a good fuck? Why do you keep dragging us back to this place? You wanna know all my truths? Then stop acting like a crazy person and let me give them to you on my own time. Stop pushing before you push too far. You want to know what Alana has that you don't? She knows when to shut the hell up."

Speechless, I stare at him, feeling the sting of tears in my eyes. His chest rises and falls with hard, rapid breaths. His nostrils flare and his eyes cut straight through me. I study him from the veiny lines in his biceps to the fists clenched at his sides. My heart pounds against my ribs and I try to catch my breath. I don't know what I fear more, losing him or staying.

"I'm yours, Sebastian," I say, after several moments of silence. "I'm yours completely. There's nothing left for anyone else. My biggest fear is that I'll never be able to say the same about you. She has a hold on you, and I honestly don't think you'll ever break it."

"I *am* breaking it," he replies. "I know you can't see that, princess, but I am. Alana is clinging on to the last threads she has, because she knows things are changing. She *knows*, Danielle, and so does the rest of the world. Why don't you?"

"I just don't want to have my heart broken again."

"Princess—"

"You guys in here?" Julie's voice rings through the house.

"Dammit!" Sebastian growls. "If I would've known it was going to be this hard to have a moment alone with you, we would've stayed in the fucking city."

"It's okay," I say, wiping tears from my eyes. "Go."

He comes to me and clasps my chin between his fingers. "I love you. I'm sorry my life's a fucking mess and you were thrown in the center of it. If I would've known I'd ever be able to have this, I would've done so many things differently. I'm trying to do them differently now. It's just going to take some time. Please don't give up on me, princess. I used to think fairytales were for fools. Now, the only thing I want to do is give you yours."

Julie knocks on the bedroom door and asks, "Anyone in there?"

He glances at the door, then turns his eyes back to me.

"Go," I repeat. "I'm fine. I know you're trying. I just wasn't expecting to see her today, and it set me off."

He leans down and kisses me. "You're sure?"

I nod and smile.

"I love you, princess."

"And I you," I say, winking.

I wait until I hear the click of the bedroom door closing before walking to the bed and taking my tablet off the nightstand. Today has been filled with all the wrong kind of surprises. I may not be able to do anything about Alana and her connection with Sebastian, but I can find out more about that party last night. As much as I want to believe Piper would never plot anything against me, I can't deny what I heard, and there's no way that party was just a coincidence.

I log into the company server and find Crystal O'Brien's file. To my shock and disappointment, there's absolutely nothing out of the ordinary, except for the fact that her mother, Priscilla O'Brien, paid the party in full. Deflating, I sign out of the system, lie back on the bed, and stare at the ceiling.

I'm completely lost in my own thoughts when Sebastian comes in and climbs next to me. Seeing him out of the corner of my eye, I jump and clasp my hand over my pounding heart.

"I didn't mean to scare you," he says, pushing my hair back from my face.

"It's okay. It wasn't your fault."

"What were you thinking about?"

"Work, mostly," I reply, honestly.

"Piper?" His fingers lazily trail around my navel.

I nod and lean my forehead against his.

"I thought we were leaving all of that behind us for the rest of the weekend?"

"I tried. I just can't get over that phone call. I mean, I know I haven't known her long, but I thought Piper was my friend."

"This is New York, princess. Friends become fauxs in the blink of an eye when success is at stake."

"I refuse to believe that's true."

He shrugs. "Believe what you want, but we both know the worst of mankind. Humans are nothing if not fatally flawed. So, let's say we take your mind off things for a bit."

"What'd you have in mind?"

He rolls off the bed and takes my hand in his. "Come on. I'll show you."

\*\*\*\*

Laughter bubbling inside of me, I look down at the Twister game sprawled across the living room floor. "This is your big idea, hotshot?"

"Yep. You might want to stretch first. I've been known to dominate this game."

"Of that I have no doubts," I reply, winking and slipping out of my shorts, "but I have my own special kind of secret weapons."

"That you do," he replies, scanning my body with lust-filled eyes.

"So, who's going to spin for us?"

"Ah, that's part of the fun. An added challenge," he answers, placing the spinner on the edge of the plastic mat. "Ready?"

Doing my best to imitate his stony stares, I narrow my eyes at him and turn my lips into a smirk. "I'm so gonna kick your ass."

He gives the plastic arrow a hard thump and pronounces, "Right hand, green."

I slam my hand down on the green circle at the edge of the mat closest to me and extend my left for the spinner. Sebastian taunts me by holding it in the air, just out of my reach.

"Oh, so you've got jokes," I say. "Fine. We don't need a spinner, anyway." I pause and analyze his position, intending to stretch him as far as I can. "Left leg, blue."

Extending his foot in my direction, he uses the opportunity to invade my side of the board. I wait for him to get in place and slide my leg so that I'm positioned in a partial backbend beneath him. Grinning, he looks down at me.

"Thanks for the view."

"You're shameless," I reply.

"Maybe so, but it doesn't make it any less true," he says, smirking mischievously. "Left hand yellow."

Rolling my eyes, I place my hand on the closest yellow circle, arching my back further and bringing my chest just under his face. He slowly licks the space between my breasts, and I quiver under the heat of my own pleasure.

"That's cheating," I whine. "Right leg, red."

There's no denying the sexual tension as we move forward with our game. His every move is more calculated, and mine more suggestive. We've twisted and turned in seemingly every way imaginable until I'm now facing away from him with my butt directly in his face. He laughs, and I'm caught off guard, giving him just enough time to sink his teeth into my barely covered flesh. Hand lifted from the mat, he slides my bikini bottoms down to expose my skin.

"You're breaking all the rules," I say, fighting the effects of his warm breath on my sensitive skin.

"I certainly hope so," he says, pulling at my hips and causing me to lose balance. "I win."

Propping up on my elbows, I roll over and look up at him. "No, you cheat, and I demand a rematch."

"Later," he growls, lowering himself on top of me and pressing his lips to mine.

His kiss ignites a fire inside of me that quickly grows too hot to control. The fever spreads through my body, causing my nipples to peak and my sex to slicken. I fist my hands into his hair, drawing him nearer.

Breaking our kiss, he hovers over me and stares into my eyes. "You're my sanctuary, princess."

I don't have time to respond before his lips are on me again, moving down my collarbone and onto my shoulder. Reaching under me, he lifts me from the floor and unties my top. "What about your sisters?" I ask.

"I took care of them," he says, tugging my bikini bottoms the rest of the way off my hips.

"And Thomas?"

"Handled. We won't be disturbed," he says, teasing my clit with his fingers.

"Thank God," I reply breathlessly, surrendering to his will.

"I know you're not fully primed," he begins, turning me on my side, "but I'm going to go crazy if I don't get in you soon."

"Just do it," I reply impatiently.

He inserts his fingers into me, drawing my juices from within as he positions himself on the floor behind me. Hand placed on my ankle, he lifts my leg in the air and rests my foot against his thigh.

I can't see him from my position, but I can feel the mat pulling under me as he aligns the head of his cock with my opening. My sex clenches greedily, willing him to enter. He growls and tilts his hips, sending the thickness of his shaft into me in one swift motion. Moaning, I rock my hips, feeling myself stretch to accommodate him.

"So tight," he says, his voice rough with need.

Swollen, dripping, ready... I throw my head back as he thrusts hard into me. "Oh, yes!" I cry, panting as the intensity of his pace grows.

Ever the master of torture, he slows, inching his way inside of me and pulling out again. Every veined ridge of his length rubbing against my clit, he grips his cock in hand and places it in me once more. Leg quivering, I bite my lip and fight the moan bubbling in my throat.

With one hand on my hip, he uses his other hand to grip my knee and raise my leg in the air. Swift and steady, he drills into me. His head milks my G-spot with each impalement, forcing an insatiable hunger to build in my belly. Heat radiating from his eyes, he lifts onto his knees, wedging himself deeper into me. Balls slapping against my ass, his fingers stroke my clit.

"You're going to make me fucking come!" I scream, feeling the plastic mat tear in my grip.

"That's the point, princess," he taunts, his breath quick.

Eyes rolled in the back of my sockets, I come undone. The orgasm explodes through me like a bomb through a quiet night. Body quaking, my sex convulses over him, willing him to finish. Relentless, he tosses my leg over his shoulder and continues his rapid pace. Relinquished inhibitions, I go limp beneath him as another orgasm picks up where the last left off.

Careful not to slip out of me, he lowers behind me once more, bringing my legs over his. Twitching cock thrusting deep inside of me, he throws his head back and roars. Intensified stare burning into mine, he grits his teeth and growls, "Fuck!"

Prisoner to his passion, I come once more, my sex convulsing wildly as he fills me with his seed. Breathless and spent, we collapse on the floor, mangled bits of plastic sticking to our skin. Ears filled with the sound of seagulls, I curl into him.

Lips planted on my forehead, he whispers, "I love you."

"Promise?"

"With all my heart."

Smile wide, I close my eyes and allow the sound of his breath to lull me to sleep.

# Chapter 20

*Sebastian*

"Almost ready, princess?"

"I just have to decide on a top." She comes out of the bathroom holding a blouse in each hand. "I didn't really bring anything for clubbing, except the clothes I was planning on wearing to my work events. Which one do you think?"

My eyes dart from the shirts to the feather-adorned skirt, which shows way too much leg, and back up. Some men are completely okay with their women wearing next to nothing in public. I am not one of those men. I take the sheer tank top she's holding and throw it on the bed.

"Definitely the long sleeves," I reply.

She laughs, tosses my choice on the bed, and goes for the other. "It'll be like a thousand degrees in the club."

I draw my eyes to the form fitting top which subtly hugs her firm breasts. "If you were going to disobey me, then why did you even bother asking?"

Bent low, she shakes her head and runs her fingers through my hair. My eyes find hers, and I'm sucked in by the sparkling emeralds looking back at me. "First, I asked for your opinion, so there are no orders to disobey. Second, you can punish me for it later. We have to go. Your sisters are waiting."

"I can give them a decent distraction again," I suggest, winking.

"Come on," she says, pulling me toward the door.

Bradley is alone with my parents in the den when we enter the house. This is unsurprising given my sisters and their tendency to evaluate every outfit no less than twenty times before changing and starting the process over again. Danielle and I take seats next to him, and my mother smiles warmly at us.

"Bradley and I were just discussing pre-wedding jitters. Any chance I'll be having the same discussion with you soon?"

"Mother, the least you could do is offer us drinks before making us uncomfortable."

Danielle fidgets next to me but doesn't make eye contact. I take hold of the hand she's been twisting in her lap. Not being able to read her is unsettling. Is she nervous because of the idea of marriage in general? Or is it marriage to me she fears?

"Just a suggestion," mother says with an amused smile.

"Yes, you seem to be full of suggestions lately," I reply, shaking my head.

From the first day my parents met Danielle, my mother has been very open about her approval. For the few weeks we were apart, she was constantly badgering me for more details about our breakup. The last time I saw my family this attached to someone, I was a boy. I think about everything that went wrong with Alana, and lean back, pulling Danielle in closely. Things will be different with her. We'll face all our demons together, and we will win.

The click-clacking of high heels on hardwood draws me out of my thoughts. I look up at my little sister — her arms, navel, back, and thighs all exposed in the piece of fabric she's attempting to pull off as a dress. Enraged, I walk over and turn her back toward the stairs.

"Change."

"What?" she asks, spinning around with an annoyed look on her face.

"I'm not leaving this house until you put some clothes on, Julie."

"Whatever." She rolls her eyes and walks to the drink cart. "If you think this is bad, just wait until you see what Katie's wearing."

"Katie has a fiancé to keep her in line," I begin, following her. "You still need your big brother to do so."

"Right, because you've expressed such fondness for the rules in the past." She rolls her eyes again and sits next to Danielle. "Hey Dani! You look great."

"Thanks," Danielle replies. "So, do you."

"Don't encourage her," I growl, resuming my seat. "I'm serious, Jewels. That outfit is nothing but trouble. You don't want the men you'll attract in it."

"Oh, don't sell me so short, brother," she teases. "I think every girl could use a little trouble now and then."

"Sebastian," Danielle starts, placing her hand on my thigh to soothe me. "I think Julie can take care of herself. Give her a little credit."

"Would you let your sister out of the house like that?" I snap.

"Well, considering that I've been known to dress *exactly* like that, then I would have to answer with yes," she chastises.

"This isn't southern California, Danielle. It's the fucking Hamptons. She looks like a tramp, and the whole town will agree."

"Sebastian," my mother says, assuredly. "Maybe you should take a breather before you end up taking this to a place that you don't want it to go."

I look from her, to Julie, and finally at Danielle, whose face bears the sting of my words. Nostrils flared, I take some time to regain control of my rapid breaths and address my sister. "I'm sorry, Jewels. I just don't want anyone taking advantage of you, and that outfit seems like an open invitation for them to do so."

"Because it makes me look like a common tramp?" She asks sarcastically. "One of these days, big brother, you will realize that I'm not the twelve-year-old little girl you caught getting kissed in the garden. If I want someone to take advantage of my body, I'm for damn sure going to let them. However, I choose to believe that as a woman I have earned the right to express my sexuality without having to fear misogynistic pigs thinking that my clothes give them free rein to take from me whatever they please. It's because of you and men like you that women are repressed now."

"And now you've gone and done it," my father says. "Sebastian, why don't you come with me? I'd like to discuss a few things."

One look at him and I know exactly what he's getting to. I squeeze Danielle's hand, pleading for her to look at me. "You okay?"

"I'm fine. It's fine. You were just being overprotective."

"You're sure?"

She nods. "Yeah. I'll be fine here. Just go have a chat with your dad."

Though I don't want to leave her, I follow my father to his study. I can hear my sister on her tangent for most of my walk down the hall. It's not the first time she's been on a tirade because of my protective instincts, and it most likely won't be the last. I know this world in ways Julie will never understand. I've seen how dark the desires of man can be.

My dad waits for me to walk through the door, then closes it behind us. I don't wait for him to offer before pouring myself a tumbler full of scotch.

"A little on edge this weekend, I see," he says, taking a seat behind his desk.

"Can you blame me?"

"No, I cannot." He rubs his temples as though he has a headache. "The reason I wanted to chat with you, actually. We haven't really had any time to discuss what happened the other day."

"If you're going to give me some bullshit lecture—"

"I don't want to lecture you, son, but I would like to help if you'll let me. Are you okay? To say you seemed irritated would be a gross understatement."

"I fine," I growl, knocking back my scotch and pouring another. "What were the other reasons behind this chat?"

Disappointment filled eyes cast downward, he inhales. "I've been on the phone with the clinic this afternoon."

"What'd she do now?"

"Have you spoken with Lauren at all this weekend?"

"No. I called yesterday, but her phone went to voicemail. I've been in contact with both her driver and her nanny, however."

"So, you're aware that she, too, had a visit with Isabelle that didn't go well."

"I knew she was visiting today. I didn't know of the outcome."

He nods solemnly. "Isabelle has been depressed since our phone session, Sebastian. She's not thinking clearly."

I snort. "Is she ever?"

Ignoring me, he continues, "She tried to get Lauren to take her home."

My jaw flexes with tension, and I narrow my eyes. Settling into a chair across from him, I take a gulp of the slow burning amber liquid.

"Lauren explained that, being a minor, she couldn't even if she wanted to. But Isabelle grew desperate. She insisted and when Lauren, again, told her she didn't have the authority, I'm afraid she grew violent."

Hands clutched on the armrests of my chair, I grit my teeth and ask, "Why am I just learning this now? Where's my sister?"

"Calm down," he says, looking up at the closed door. "We don't want them to overhear. She's with Alana at the Sinclair estate. I've already been in touch with her. She didn't want to bother you while you were having a weekend away with us and Danielle. To use her exact wording, she, 'didn't want to be a burden', but I couldn't keep you in the dark about it, son."

"How long?" I demand, jumping to my feet.

"About an hour."

"Dammit! You waited an hour — an entire fucking hour — before telling me."

"Sebastian, please calm down. I wanted the chance to speak with you first."

"Well, now we've spoken," I roar, heading for the door.

Well versed in dealing with my rage, he catches up with me in a flash. Placing his hand on my shoulder, he says, "Son, think about what it will say to Lauren if you show up in this state."

My chest tight, I grip the door handle.

My father pats my shoulder and says, "Just take a moment, son. The problem isn't Isabelle. The problem is her addiction."

"The problem is her selfishness," I retort.

"You have a good reason to be angry with her, but I think we can both agree that it's more important than ever that you visit her."

"You really think that's wise?" I snarl.

"Not today, no, but once you've had a few days to collect yourself."

"Why are you always defending her?"

"I'm not defending her, Sebastian. I'm treating her. There is a difference, even though you don't like to see it. I'm doing what you asked me to do when you knocked on my bedroom door all those years ago."

I quietly reflect on the night I found my mother at the last house I shared with her.

*She was sitting on the sidewalk, her limbs shaking from withdrawal. "Bashie," she'd said. "I knew you'd come back. I knew if I just kept returning, you'd come home."*

*I wasn't sure what I'd expected to find, a dead body perhaps, but seeing her alive and frail broke something inside of me. Alana offered her jacket to Isabelle for warmth. She'd taken one look up at her before vomiting all over the couture. Shamefully, I turned my back on them both and walked back to the car. From the window, I could see Alana holding Isabelle's hair back while she grew even more ill.*

*When Isabelle had finished, she helped her from the concrete and propped her up against the car. Sliding in next to me, she took hold of my hands and softly said, "I know you're only being nice to me because of everything that happened last week. I expect nothing else, but I'd like to help you get through this if you'll let me."*

"There's nothing for me to get through," I replied coldly, pulling my hand from hers. "Maybe you having an abortion was for the best. I would've been a horrible father. Just look at where I come from."

"Sebastian, I didn't do it because of you." She lifted a hand to my hair and slowly ran her fingers through it. "I did it for my own selfish reasons. You would've been a brilliant father, and someday you will have the chance again. But you broke my heart and the worst part about it was I knew that nothing I did could bring you back to me. Not even giving you a child. You would've loved our baby, but you never would've loved me."

"I told you from the beginning, Alana. I can't love. It's not part of me. At least now you can see why."

She pulled my fingers between hers again and said, "I do, but that doesn't change the fact that she needs our help." She turned her head to the window, where the sounds of Isabelle's retching came through the glass. "You've been so strong for me in the aftermath of everything I've gone through this year. You protected me from getting raped, for God's sake. The least I can do is see you through this, Sebastian. It's not enough to redeem me. You'll never forgive me, and I know that. But, like I told you once before, it doesn't mean I'll ever stop trying to earn your forgiveness."

"Bashie," Isabelle cried out, her voice weak with exhaustion.

"One step at a time," Alana suggested. "I'll stand by you until it's all over if you'll let me."

I didn't trust her to not break her promise. Still, to this day, I've waited for her to decide that dealing with all this drama would never be worth it when she could never have me. It will all change soon, though. Alana was right when she'd said I would never forgive her for hiding her pregnancy from me. That was when I'd believed she'd ended it. Now, I knew differently. Now, I knew that she'd kept our daughter a secret from me to have her all to herself.

That not only called for my unforgiveness, it forced my revenge. I think of the papers waiting for me in the city. Soon, Alana will no longer be a part of the team. I must learn how to handle this on my own. It's imperative to Lauren's safety that I do.

Turning to my father, I reply, "Call Robin and set it up. Cover for me with the girls. I'm going to check on Lauren."

He nods. "And Dani?"

"She doesn't need to know anything. I'll figure out a way to fill her in without giving away anything about Isabelle, but for now, just give her the same story you give Mother and the rest."

"You're sure that's for the best?" His stern look settles into my veins.

"What other choice do I have? Aside from the fact that she'll want to know more, she'll demand to be a part of this. Telling her also puts her in the position of lying to our entire family. I don't want to do that to her. She has enough shit to deal with."

"Okay, son, it's your call." He studies me for a few minutes then says, "I love you, Sebastian. I push for your sake, not hers. You know that, right?"

Looking away from him, I nod.

"The sooner Isabelle is sober, the sooner you can move into the next phase of your life. You can truly open yourself up to Danielle and experience everything that love offers."

"So, you've said," I whisper, voice straining. "I have to go."

He nods and pulls the door open.

****

"I'm outside," I say into the phone as the car approaches the closed gate.

"I'll buzz you through," Alana replies. "Come to the patio entrance. I'll wait for you there."

We hang up, and I watch the iron gates swing open. By now, I know Alana's family estate as well as my own. It's no secret that her parents were less than thrilled with the termination of our engagement. Though they've since learned how to be cordial, I try not to expose myself to them if I can help it. Alana is waiting on the balcony, as promised, when I make my way around the hedge. She takes me to the pool house, where I see my baby sister lying on the couch watching television.

Turning to me, Alana says, "She's okay. A little shaken, but I had Daddy look her over. There's no serious damage."

"You brought your *father* into this?" I hiss.

"Yes, I brought my father into this." She snaps. "What would you have me do, Sebastian? Should I have taken her to Southampton Hospital, and explained to them what happened? Or perhaps you'd rather I didn't give her any medical attention at all."

"Don't be condescending to me right now, Alana. It's not the time."

"Oh, I'm not being condescending at all, Sebastian. I'm genuinely requesting clarification on the matter. Your sister shows up at my doorstep bruised, crying, and shaking.

157

What she really wants is for her big brother to come and hold her. What she needs is for your lips to assure her that everything's okay. But she's afraid to even ask for it. She's afraid that it will cause problems for you with your family. So, instead, she begs me not to tell you and asks me to hide her. I felt sorry for her, Sebastian. Lauren isn't like you. You got a new mother when you left Isabelle. The closest thing she got was me. I'm sorry if you don't like that we're bonded, but that doesn't change the fact that we are. I love your sister, Sebastian. I love her like she's my own flesh and blood. It's why I agreed to..." She looks up at me and exhales. "It's why I agreed to everything, no matter how much it hurt. And tonight, it's the reason that I threw away eight years of keeping this secret in order to make sure that she was going to be okay. If you want to add that to your list of reasons to hate me, then go ahead. Just don't expect me to apologize for it, because I'm not sorry."

"Just open the door," I reply coldly.

Lauren's head lifts as soon as she hears the click. "Hey, bro," she says, forcing a smile. "I told them not to call you."

"They didn't," I reply, walking to her and kissing her forehead. "My father did. He got a call from the clinic. We'll discuss that not calling me bit at another time. What happened?"

She sits up to allow me room next to her. Lip tucked in her teeth, she flinches and turns her head to me. In the dim light peeking through the window, I can see the handprint on her swollen cheek.

"I went to see Mom. I know I told her I'd be coming this weekend, but she acted like I wasn't supposed to be there. She was crazed, Sebastian. All she kept asking me was where you were. When I told her you were with your family, she lost it. She started calling me stupid and telling me we were your family. She accused me of lying. She swore that we all lived together in that old house. That one she used to take me to all the time. Where we'd watch the family through the windows. Do you know it?"

"I do," I reply, solemnly, thinking of the last place I saw Isabelle before bringing her to my father. "I know it all too well."

"Okay then, you know she has some kind of sick obsession with that place. Anyway, I told her that we'd never lived there. That you found me at the shelter and brought me to live with a nice woman in an apartment in the city. Then she flipped out. She started screaming at me, begging me to get her out of there and take her home. She went on and on about how I owed her that much after everything she gave up for me. She kept telling me I was a mistake, and that if she'd never had me, she'd still have you. I tried to calm her down. I tried to explain that I didn't have a way to get her out, but she just kept yelling at me. That's when the staff came in. Before they could get her down, she slapped me. It's like she completely lost touch with reality, Sebastian. She's been bad before, but I've never seen her like that."

"Believe it or not, she's been worse. I know it had to be horrible for you to see, though. That's why I've been trying so hard to protect you from it."

"This isn't your fault," she says, hugging me. "You aren't responsible for her. I know you feel like it, but she made her choices. There's nothing you could've done to stop her. You're just as much a victim in all of this as me. The only difference is you had Doctor B. and all the rest of them."

"Yeah, well," I say, squeezing her a little more tightly. "You may not have a father or a big family to care for you, but you'll always have me."

"And me," Alana says, sitting on the other side of her.

I look over at her. This time, she has made a promise she won't be able to keep. In only a matter of days, she'll know that.

****

"How's our patient?" Alana whispers just before dawn.

"Finally, asleep," I reply, checking my phone. It's four in the morning. The last time I spoke to Danielle was just after two o'clock. I need to get home and explain things. "Can you handle things from here?"

"You're leaving?" She asks.

Hand on my stiff neck, I bend forward, kiss Lauren's cheek, and stand. "I have to get back."

"Back to *her*, you mean," she hisses, folding her arms. "*Your* sister has been through something tragic, and you're running back to your whore."

Hand wrapped around her arm, I drag her into the living room. "It's time for the territorial bullshit to stop, Alana. *I am not yours.* I'm hers. Everything I have belongs to Danielle. Why do you keep trying to draw water from an empty well? From the moment my lips met hers, I had nothing left to give you."

"That's not true," she replies, a wry smile forming on her lips. "Not true at all. I have things with you that Danielle will never have. At least not so long as I'm living. You think you hold all the power, Sebastian, but we made choices. Agreements were reached. As long as *our* contract is still legal and binding, I've got you by the balls and there's nothing you can do about it."

"Alana, sweetheart," I say, touching her face in mock affection and lowering my lips closer to her ear. "The truth is...you haven't had me by the balls in quite some time, and you never will again."

With that I turn and walk to my car.

# Chapter 21

Danielle

The sun comes in through the windows, waking me from my sleep with a blinding flash. Squinting, I roll over to see Sebastian lying next to me. He disappeared after his conversation with his father yesterday and never made it to any of the clubs afterward. The last time I talked to him it was going on three in the morning, and he texted to let me know he was still busy and didn't know how much longer it would take. Richard told us all that he had some urgent business to attend to in the city, but I don't believe that.

Slowly sliding out of bed, I walk to the bathroom to pee, wash my face, and brush my teeth. Whatever took Sebastian away from us last night, I'm betting it has nothing to do with work and everything to do with Alana. He's sitting upright when I open the door. A sleepy smile forms on his lips, and he reaches his arms out to me.

Climbing next to him, I swivel my hips and position myself so that I can rest my head on his chest and still face him. "What time did you get back?"

"Sometime around five."

"Hmm. Must've been a crazy night."

"You can say that," he replies, looping his fingers in my hair. "I need to tell you something, princess."

Heart in my stomach, I study him carefully. Worry lines have formed on his forehead. He has dark bags under his eyes, and a rough five o'clock shadow forming along his jaw. I run my hand over the stubble and smile as best as I can. "Go ahead."

"I wasn't in the city last night. I drove out to Alana's family property."

Spine curved with tension, I clamp my hands into fists to suppress the rush of anger I feel. "You did?" I ask, forcing my voice to stay even.

"I didn't go for her," he quickly assures me. "Lauren was there."

"Oh." Relaxing somewhat, I reply, "I thought she was staying in the city for the weekend."

"She was, but something happened. Someone hurt her. Someone she trusted."

Eyes wide, I stare at him expectantly, waiting for more of an explanation.

"It wasn't as bad as it could've been," he says, doing little in the way of offering me his assurances. "But it was still enough to rattle her."

I nod in understanding. "Of course. So, why did she go to Alana? Why not come to you?"

"Because coming here would've raised questions that don't need to be raised. Alana and Lauren are close, Danielle. It's not out of the ordinary for her to call Alana if she can't reach me."

"Oh..." I trail off, trying to come up with something else to say, but what is there? Yet again, Alana has wormed her way into parts of Sebastian's life that are unseen by the rest of the world.

He strokes my hair. "I put a lot of things in place before I knew you, princess. It's like I told you yesterday, if I would've known that I could have this," He waves his hand in the open air between us, "I would've made different choices, but just because Alana is a part of Lauren's life doesn't mean that *Alana and I* are a part of Lauren's life. It's never been like that, and it never will."

"You're sure?"

He laughs. "Not even the power of Lauren's puppy dog stare can convince me to walk that road again, princess. Relax."

"I'll try." Smiling, I sink against him. "So, she's okay then?"

"She will be," he answers, pulling my head back to his chest. "She asked about you."

"Oh, yeah?"

"Yeah, she was a little surprised by your absence, but I quickly explained the situation to her. I told her we might meet up before she heads back into the city."

"I'd like that," I reply, then sparked with curiosity, I ask, "So why didn't you take me with you?"

"Pardon me?"

"Why didn't you take me with you, hotshot? I mean, I can understand you lying to your parents and your sisters. You already told me they don't know about Lauren, but I do. Why wouldn't you come find me?"

"Because if I did, the lie wouldn't have stuck. What kind of business would I need to tend to — on a holiday weekend, no less — that would require you to go with me? They would've seen right through it."

"I suppose that makes sense." I'm not sure that he's telling me the whole truth, but he opened up to me without my having to pry, and I don't want to push my luck. "So, you'll never guess who we saw last night."

"Who?"

"Geoff and Gavin!"

"Gavin. That's Geoffrey's brother, correct? The one who accompanied you to the benefit."

"Yep. That's the one."

"And you didn't know they would be here?"

"I knew their family rented a place in the summer, but I didn't expect to see them. Geoff didn't say anything about it when I told him about our plans for the weekend. Apparently, he didn't decide to come out until the last minute."

"He probably didn't want to be alone in the city."

"That's what he said. In any case, I chastised him thoroughly for not telling me. After that, we made plans for all of us to head to the beach for a bit before your parent's thing tonight."

"All of us?"

"You, me, Geoff, Gavin, Julie, Katie, and Brad."

"I see. Well, I'm not too sure about spending the day with yet another one of your many suitors, but I guess there's no getting out of it now."

"Nope," I laugh. "Katie actually said she'd drag you kicking and screaming if she had to, as payback for bailing on us last night. And Julie said you'd better show up with diamonds in tow for the 'shitty remarks' you made before you bolted. Otherwise, I've been given strict orders not to forgive you."

"Hmm..." His gray eyes shine with mischief, and a shiver runs down my spine. "I don't have any diamonds on me, but I think I can do you one better."

163

He kisses me, and for a moment, the world stops spinning. I become completely lost in him. Overwhelmed by the desire he carries for me, I place my arms over his shoulders and raise my hips to straddle his lap. He runs his hands under the t-shirt I'm wearing and cups my ass. Giving into the hunger building in my core, I grind my pelvis against his growing erection.

"What time is this afternoon at the beach going down?"

"Around two," I pant. "Just enough time for us to spend a few hours in the sun and come home to get ready."

He bites my neck and pulls my legs out from under me. "Consider yourself busy until then."

I laugh and fall back, allowing him to take his position over me. He lifts my shirt over my naked breasts and teases and tastes his way down my body. His tongue lands on my clit with a lavish stroke that starts at the opening of my core, and slogs its way upward. I'm instantly desperate for more, fisting his hair in my hands and directing him back down again. Insatiable, he devours me with needy sucks on my most sensitive flesh. His tongue rolls over my clit again, and I toss my head back in response.

Always knowing what to do next, he inserts two fingers into me, hooking them on my G-spot and beckoning for me to come. My legs quake in response, my orgasm inching its way to release. He works with haste, greedily licking my swollen clit until the bottom falls out and I feel myself flood around his tongue. I throw my hands on the bed and arch my hips, letting out a soft moan as waves of orgasmic bliss wash over me.

"Mm…," he says, wiping his mouth clean with the back of his hand, "there's nothing I'd rather have for breakfast than your pussy."

Every move slow and calculated, he brings himself on top of me, lining his cock with the fleshy opening of my sex.

"I'd take sex with you for breakfast any day of the week, Mister Black," I reply, gasping as he stretches his way inside of me.

Like the sex god he is, he rolls his hips, driving his cock into me and filling me completely. I lift my arms, reaching for his back, but he grabs my hands and pins me flush against the bed. Trapped beneath him, I have no choice but to lie back and enjoy every delicious inch of him. He varies his speed, thrusting into me with carnal force just until he has me on the brink of another orgasm and slowing again.

"Please, Sebastian," I beg, unable to take the anticipation.

My sex throbs with need, and he smirks. "I'm nowhere near finished with you, Danielle."

He pulls out and commands me to sit up on my knees. Following his orders, I hunch over, expecting a fast-paced, doggy-styled thrill ride. To my astonishment, Sebastian sits on his knees, sliding me over him with ease. Placing his fingers on my clit, he lowers us until I'm sitting atop him. Using his toes to thrust, he drives into me, his cock grazing my G-spot. Fueled by the sensation, I grind against him. Reaching back, I place my arm around his neck. He wraps his other arm around my chest, cupping my breast in his hand and effectively holding me in place.

We move in sync with one another until I'm panting for breath, hanging on the verge of release. His cock swells and he throws his head back with an animalistic grunt. The sound reverberates in my core, sending me into an orgasmic orbit. My legs shake with release, and I scream, "I'm coming, Sebastian."

Hand on my throat, he pulls me against him and holds me in place until the very last of my climax fades away. Releasing me, he throws me forward. Placing his hands on my hips and rocking me against him in hard, fast motions that quickly build another orgasm in my core. Spent from emotion, tears leak from the corners of my eyes as I cry out again.

"Fuck," he roars, his cock twitching wildly as he spills his seed into me.

His pace increases still, his balls slamming against my clit as he drains himself into me. My legs give way to the pleasure, and I feel myself go limp. Wrapping his arm under me, he holds me in place as my body shakes and sex clenches, drinking him in. At last he lowers us to the bed, lying on his side and pulling me flush against him. My back sticks to his sweat covered chest as I try to catch my breath. We lay there quietly, wrapped in each other, until I feel his breathing even out. Smiling, I curl my fingers around his and close my eyes.

**** 

The venomous sound of Sebastian's phone ringing wakes me. He stirs beside me, but doesn't budge. Stretching, I crawl up the bed to the nightstand. Seeing Lauren's name on the screen, I answer with a sleepy, "Hello."

"Dani?" she asks, sounding confused.

"Yeah."

"I... um... is Sebastian with you?"

"He's right here," I reply, nudging him. "How are you feeling?"

"I'm okay. Sebastian wanted me to call him when I woke up, but if you guys are busy..."

"No, it's okay," I try, once again, to shake Sebastian awake. "We were just sleeping."

Laughing, she replies, "It's almost noon."

"I know. Strange right? Well, not really strange for me. I'm perfectly comfortable sleeping the day away, but it's odd for Sebastian." At last he opens his eyes. Covering the phone with my hand, I whisper, "Lauren's on the phone."

"Is he sick?" She asks, as Sebastian stretches and holds his hand out to me.

"Nah, he was just wiped after being out so late. He's awake now, just a sec."

I hand off the phone and head to the shower to give them some privacy. Halfway through my shampoo, Sebastian joins me. Smiling, he places a kiss on my forehead, and takes over rinsing out my shampoo-coved locks.

"You gave Lauren a good laugh," he says casually.

"How's that?" I question, wiping stray soap from my eyes.

"No one answers my phone except for me. She said she had to double check that she'd dialed the right number."

"Oh. I tried to wake you up, but you weren't budging."

"It's fine," he replies, running a generous portion of conditioner through my hair. "Just so long as you don't make a habit of it."

I can't deny the punch to the gut that his words deliver. "Umm... I wasn't planning on it. I saw Lauren's name and knew you didn't want to miss her."

He narrows his eyes to drive his point across. "I just want to be clear that my phone is off limits."

"What do you have to hide, Sebastian? I mean, I know I don't know all there is to know about you and I'm really trying not to push, but you seem to be making something huge out of nothing here. Your little sister was injured yesterday. I answered the phone to make sure you didn't miss her and chatted with her because I was concerned. What exactly did I do wrong?"

"Nothing," he replies, exhaling. "You did nothing. I just never know why my phone's ringing. That's all."

"Sure," I reply, shrugging. Clearly there's more to the story than this, but I already know better than to ask for it. "So, are we going to Alana's?"

"No. Alana is at her family's estate. I won't put you through that. Lauren's driver is taking her to one of the smaller cafes in town. We'll meet her there."

I nod. "Sounds good to me. I'm starving."

"I bet you are," he replies, winking

**** 

Lauren brightens up the otherwise mundane café with her bright blue tank and coral shorts. Her hair is down, and she wears a hat tilted just low enough to cast a shadow on her face. It's a trick I know all too well from the days of hiding my own bruises. Pretending not to notice, I smile and give her a hug. "Look at you being all cute," I say, perhaps a little too enthusiastically.

"I didn't really have much time to get my things together. I just grabbed whatever looked good and headed up here," she replies, glancing down at the table.

"I wish I could throw cute outfits together that fast," I reply, ordering coffee for both me and Sebastian, and taking a seat. "I'm kind of hopeless when it comes to the art of defining my look."

"Really?" She takes a sip of her orange juice. "You've looked fab every time I've ever seen you. Those paparazzi photos were all the rage with my friends."

"Well," I whisper, leaning in close as if it's a secret, "that's because I have a secret weapon."

"A personal shopper? She's not so secret. Sebastian sends her out for my clothes a few times a year as well."

I laugh. After seeing Sebastian's reaction to Julie's outfit last night, I have no doubt that he would try to exercise control over Lauren's wardrobe by having someone shop for her. Judging by the hemline on her shorts, I also know that it doesn't work.

"Actually, I was talking about my best friend. He's a fashion photographer, and he has a brilliant eye for what works."

"Really?" She leans forward, an excited smile showing on her face. "I love fashion! I'd love to model, but Sebastian refuses to let me. He's afraid the lifestyle might trigger some genetic predispositions or something."

I think about everything Sebastian's told me about his birthmother. "I can see that. It's a crazy world, but not all models buy into all that crap. You just have to remember to keep your head on your shoulders."

"Yeah," she replies, scanning the room. "Where is my brother, anyway?"

"Oh, he had an important call. He'll be a sec."

"Cool. So, you having fun?"

The sadness in her eyes tugs at my heartstrings, and I'm suddenly sparked with inspiration. "I am, but I know something that would be even more fun."

"What's that?"

"How about you and I have a girl's night on Friday?"

"Really?"

"Yeah! I'm sure I have to work late, but I doubt Sebastian would mind if you hung out at the penthouse for a while. We can get movies, pop some popcorn, and do manis and pedis. I'll even see if Geoff's available."

"Geoff?"

"The aforementioned best friend."

"Oh, that sounds like a lot of fun, actually. I'd love to! Tell you the truth, I've never stayed the night at Sebastian's before."

"Well, Sebastian's is now Dani's too. As co-inhabitant, I say it's about time we fix that."

"What are we fixing?" Sebastian asks, sitting next to me and giving Lauren's shoulder a squeeze.

"Dani invited me over for a sleepover," she replies, beaming.

"She did, did she?" Sebastian asks, sending a curious glance in my direction.

"She did," I confirm. "Friday."

"Actually," he begins. "Friday's not great. I've arranged to have your stuff brought over."

"Well, rearrange to have it brought on Saturday," I counter.

"It's okay," Lauren states, slumping her shoulders. "I know you guys are busy."

"We're not *that* busy," I suggest, cutting my eyes at Sebastian and turning back to her. "How about we clear Friday, have the stuff brought over on Saturday, and Lauren and I can hang out on Friday night? I'm going to be exhausted after work, anyway. The last thing I want to do is worry about a bunch of boxes. Plus, no one can move anything until I pack, and Geoff and I haven't even discussed a date to pack up yet."

"I didn't realize you needed him there to do this."

"I don't," I reply, "but I would *like* to have him there. It's a big deal. We've been living together for so long that I've forgotten what it's like to not have him down the hall. It doesn't feel right just packing up and pretending like those years never happened."

"So, a girl's night?" He sighs. "You're pretty set on this, aren't you?"

"Yep," I answer, taking a sip of my coffee.

"It would be nice," Lauren says, giving him what can only be described as puppy dog eyes.

A smile forming on his lips, he shakes his head and says, "I'll work something out, but if you two think you're kicking me out of my own house, you have another thing coming."

"You can stay, but I get to paint your toenails," I joke.

Lauren laughs. "Now that's something I *have* to see."

"Don't get your hopes up," Sebastian responds, squeezing my leg. "I'm comfortable in my masculinity, but that's stretching it a bit."

\*\*\*\*

I walk next to Sebastian, the warm, white sand squishing between my toes. So far, I'm positive that today is one of those days that will go down in the history book of my life as perfect. Brunch was delicious, but it was watching Sebastian with Lauren that really made the event.

I'm not sure it's possible to have Sebastian Black wrapped around one's little finger, but if it is, Lauren has succeeded. His primary focus was on taking care of her. The whole thing made me loathe Alana even more for keeping his daughter from him.

"There you guys are," Julie says, making me aware of the fact that we've finally caught up to our group. "Where'd you disappear to?"

"I took Danielle for a late breakfast," Sebastian replies nonchalantly.

"You know, brother," Katie starts, "I'm beginning to think you're embarrassed by us."

"You shouldn't think. You should already know," Sebastian teases, taking a seat on the blanket Julie's occupying and pulling me down between his legs.

Wrinkling her nose in frustration, Katie kicks a heap of sand his way.

"Watch the food!" Julie shrieks. "It took forever to fix all this."

"You cooked?" Sebastian asks.

"As a matter of fact, I did."

"Be glad you already ate," Katie jokes. "The rest of us may just need you to take us to the hospital to have the food poisoning treated."

"Hey!" Julie says, cutting her eyes in her sister's direction and pouting.

I don't have siblings, but at this moment, Julie has painted the picture of the stereotypical *baby of the family* perfectly, and I can't help but double over with laughter.

"It's not all bad, Jewels," Sebastian says, his tone comforting. "All else fails, we can give it to the seagulls and earn ourselves a little pest control."

"You're a dick," she replies, slugging him. "I want you all to know that this is going to be the best pesto you've ever eaten."

"Well, I think I'm still going to pass-o," Katie jokes, handing me a wine cooler. "Liquid diets are better for my wedding dress, anyway."

Sebastian digs in the cooler and exchanges my beverage for a bottle of water. "Suit yourself, Katie, but for the rest of us, I think it's a little early for day drinking."

I know why he's so sensitive about my alcohol intake. Given his past with his mother, and my recent behavior, I can't say that I blame him. Still, I don't like being treated like a child. Glaring at him, I rip the bottle from his hand to drive my point across without causing a scene. He doesn't show any sign of noticing my subtle hint, but a threatening haze clouds his eyes.

"Call it the hair of the dog, little brother. I don't know how you keep up with that one."

"Me! You're the one who kept ordering the shots." I smile in her direction. "I thought debutants weren't supposed to drink the heavy stuff."

"Oh, sweetie," she says, reaching forward and patting my head. "You have so much to learn."

I laugh and take a sip from my water bottle, choosing to ignore the smirk on Sebastian's lips.

"So, when are your friends getting here?"

"I'm not sure," I reply, taking my phone from my bag. "I thought they'd be here by now."

I check my messages, my heart sinking when I read the text from Geoff: *Not feeling it, baby girl. Sorry.*

"What's wrong?" Sebastian asks, strumming his thumb over my shoulder.

"I guess they aren't going to be able to make it," I answer, staring out at the turquoise water.

Lately, every step forward for Geoff leads to two steps back. I just wish he'd let me help him.

****

"It will be over before you know it," Sebastian assures me as he loops his tie into perfectly done knots.

"Surprisingly, this isn't about Alana." I swipe another brush full of powder across my nose and turn to him. "I can't stop thinking about Geoff. Sebastian, I'm worried about him."

"He's just processing." He steps behind me and pulls the zipper up on my champagne-colored beaded dress.

I turn to him and center his matching tie. "That's just it. Geoff doesn't process. He self-destructs. We're a lot alike in that department, and we've been dancing around each other for weeks. I just wish..."

"You just wish you could be like you used to?"

Nodding, I reply, "Yeah."

Careful not to smudge my makeup, he brushes my chin with his thumb. "That will never happen, princess. You know it won't. Every desperate action heals with a fresh scar. The scars may fade over time, but they'll always be there. You and I both know it. The best thing — the only thing — to do is embrace them. That moment of weakness was so much more than that, Danielle. It was a testament to your strength. You stared your demon in the face, and you destroyed him. It's the thing every victim wishes they could do, but only a few of us ever get the chance."

I lean against the counter, my legs no longer steady enough to support my weight, and fold my arms across my chest to block the sudden chill growing deep in my bones. "Still, if I could take that night back, I would."

"I know, and if I could switch places with you, I would." Taking my hands in his, he places his forehead to mine. "There's something you should know about that night, princess."

"What?" I barely manage, alarm bells ringing through every inch of my body as I watch the silent storm brewing in his eyes.

"Things were supposed to go differently. I was handling Walter. I don't know where it all broke down, but if anyone is to blame, it's me. When Alana showed up, I got distracted. He reached out to me earlier that day. They both did, actually."

"They?"

"Yes." He takes a deep breath. "Your friend Jon called my office several times that afternoon. I was having a hell of a day, and I just never had the chance to call him back. The team had him and Geoff under surveillance, so I knew they were safe. You were safe. I'd been checking on you regularly. I should've made him a priority, and I didn't. If anyone's to blame for all this—"

"Sebastian, no, don't take my mess and place it on your shoulders. Random chance. That's all it was. There's no way Jon would've had anything to do with Walt. He wasn't even the target, from what I understand. It was supposed to be Geoff. Walt did enough research to know where to hit me if he wanted to make it hurt. I don't know what Jon called you for that day, but it had nothing to do with this."

For a moment, he looks as though there's something else he needs to say. Then, shaking it off, he pulls me into him and plants his lips to mine. "I love you, Danielle. I just need you to know."

"I know, hotshot. You've proven yourself more than a few times today. And if you're lucky, I may just let you prove it a few more."

"Be careful what you wish for, princess. I'd hate to mess up that sexy look you've got going for yourself before you even have the chance to show it off." He winks and takes my hand, leading me to the party already in full swing on the lawn.

The moment we step under the canopy, I see Alana, smiling a toothy grin so fake it should be on a Crest commercial, walking directly for us.

"I'll get us drinks," I say, leaning into Sebastian.

"It'll only take a minute. I promise."

"I'm counting on it."

Thankfully, Julie has already found the bar by the time I get there, so I at least have a friendly face to talk to. She waves, excuses herself from the myriad of male attention she seems to have collected and meets me at the corner. "Thank God you showed up when you did!" She rolls her eyes dramatically. "I couldn't handle the Titan Triplets for another second."

I order a vodka and cranberry for myself and a scotch for Sebastian. "Titan Triplets?"

"Ugh, Bradley's brothers. All captains of industry, and all hoping to score their chance with Sebastian Black's remaining single sister."

"Ah." I nod, suddenly aware of why she's so annoyed. "Not interested in being anyone's meal ticket?'

"*Please*," she says, exhaling. "Have you met me?"

I laugh. "Well, as it turns out, you're saving me, too."

"Oh really? From what?"

"Alana."

"Bitch. At least you can rest assured that she'll be nowhere near us when we're in Vegas."

"At least there's that," I reply, clinking my glass against hers and taking a sip. "So, how is that whole Vegas bachelor/bachelorette party coming along away?"

"Pretty good. I've just about confirmed our whole itinerary."

"Well, if you need help, you know where to find me," I offer.

"Think you can convince Katie that penis cakes aren't trashy, they're necessary?"

"The only penis going anywhere near your mouth will be mine," Sebastian's desire laden voice whispers in my ear, sending chills of anticipation down my spine.

"Ditched the groupie already, bro?" Julie asks, setting her empty glass on the bar.

"Behave yourself, Jewels. We're at our parent's anniversary party."

"Me? I'm the good child," she replies, smiling mischievously.

"Even so." He knocks back the rest of his scotch and turns to me. "Dance with me?"

"No one is dancing," I reply.

Richard takes the microphone in hand and clears his throat. "Many of you know that Labor Day is a special time for our family. For years, we've been throwing the end-of-summer party here in the Hamptons. This year it happens to fall on the day I celebrate my love for this beautiful woman who decided to have me as a husband twenty-something years ago—"

"Thirty-two," Emmalyn interrupts, sending uproars of laughter through the crowd.

"Thank you, darling," Richard says, sweetly. "For some reason, I always block out those first ten."

She gives him a playfully stern look, and their guests break into a frenzy again. Smiling, I look up at Sebastian. He places his arm around my waist and pulls me against him.

"In any case," Richard continues, "this year we have many other things to celebrate. For starters, today is also the anniversary of the day our lives became much more interesting to say the least. All of you know we adopted our brilliant son, Sebastian. He's been everything I could've asked him to be and then some, and today also marks the anniversary of the day the courts made it all official. Happy Gotcha Day, son."

He raises his glass in our direction, and the rest of the audience follows suit. I watch Sebastian smile and lift his back in Richard's direction. Ordinarily, someone would show some semblance of pride after such a beautiful sentiment was made in their honor. Not Sebastian.

Though his smile is genuine, there's a cloud of disappointment in his eyes. A wrinkle in his forehead that says he doesn't feel worthy. My heart wrenching to take the pain away from him, I wish I could break down the barriers his birth mother created so that he could see just how much his actual parents love him.

"And," Richard begins again after a small sip of his champagne. "We also have the honor of giving away our amazing daughter Katherine's hand in marriage in just a few short weeks. Bradley, you may have won Katherine's heart, but you've thoroughly earned my blessing. We are so excited for the two of you and the journey you're about to begin." Beaming at each other, Katie and Brad nod their glasses in his direction. "Traditionally, Emmalyn and I would lead you all in the first dance of the evening at this time. However, I think it's only fitting that we let Katie and Brad do it just this once. What do you say?"

Everyone claps and Katie and Brad step into the center of the dance floor just in time for the band to play "So Close" from the *Enchanted* Soundtrack. Her bright smile lights up the night as Brad takes her hand and begins leading her in a waltz. Their eyes never leave each other's. It's as though we're all transformed into the moment with them. I lean my head against Sebastian's shoulder. Someday that could be us out there. Who knows? For now, this feels right. It's more than right, it's perfect. Until I see Alana coming in our direction again.

"I need to talk to you," she says to Sebastian. "*Now!*"

He doesn't move. "I've told you Alana. Anything you have to discuss with me can be said in front of Dani."

"I'm sure you don't want me to tell her this," Alana says.

"I'm not playing this game with you," Sebastian replies. "If you'll excuse us..." He turns and guides me toward the dance floor. His phone rings, and I release his hand so he can answer it. "It'll only take a minute," he promises.

I watch as he walks to the edge of the tent with the phone to his ear. He looks back at me, and I smile.

"I tried to warn him. Just remind him of that, will you?" Alana asks, coming beside me.

I sigh and turn to her. "You're pretty pathetic, Alana, you know that? Your scare tactics aren't going to work on me anymore."

"This is serious, Danielle. But if you don't believe me, just see for yourself." She waves her champagne glass in Sebastian's direction, and I turn to face him again.

His expression has changed into the cold, callous one I've come to associate with a threat. His eyes meet mine, and I know. Something is wrong.

# Chapter 22

S ebastian

"You're leaving, now?" Danielle asks, sitting on the bed and staring at me in disbelief.

"You can stay," I reply, ensuring that I have everything I need in my briefcase, "but I have to go back to the city."

"We're supposed to have one more day, Sebastian. Can't it wait until tomorrow?"

"I'm sorry. I wouldn't go if I didn't have to. You know that, right?"

"At least let me leave with you," she pouts.

"Rhodes will take you to be with Geoffrey and his family, or you can stay here." I sigh, ripped apart by having to deny her. If she comes with me, she'll insist on staying at my side, and I'm not ready to expose her to this part of my life. I never will be. "It'll probably take me all night. At least this way you can still have some company to talk to."

"What am I supposed to do in the morning, Sebastian?" Fuming, she jumps to her feet, the fiery Italian nature bred deep within her bones surfacing. "Am I just supposed to walk in and have breakfast with your family like it's not awkward without you? Lay by the pool all day and pretend like I belong here? I don't fit into this world, hotshot. Not without you."

Wrapping my arms around her waist, I pull her close to me. "I'm sorry, princess. I wish there was another way."

"Fuck that, Sebastian," she growls, pushing away from me. "There is another way. You just don't want to take it. Is it so damned hard to let me in? Just tell me what's wrong. You never know, I might understand. I might even be able to help."

"You can't help with this," I reply solemnly. "I wish you could, but you can't."

"That's bullshit. You'll never know what I'm capable of unless you let me try. I know you think I'm some fragile object, just waiting to break. And, I know that lately I've been all over the place emotionally, but I can handle your demons, Sebastian. I can handle them just as well as you handle mine."

She storms into the bathroom, slamming the door, and I do nothing to stop her. Ordinarily, I'd try to back her from the edge of the cliff she's now standing on, but tonight her anger works to my benefit. If she's pissed at me, she'll want nothing to do with me. If she wants nothing to do with me, she'll be safe. I gather my briefcase from the bed and walk to the bedroom door.

"I love you, princess," I say, hoping she'll understand some day.

****

The chopper ride back into the city is uneventful. The car ride away from the landing pad is a different story. White knuckles clutched over the fabric resting on my knees, I stare out the window as we head toward the cube-like two-story house on Quincy Avenue buried as far away from Manhattan as you can get in the Bronx without landing yourself in Queens. I bought it years ago, almost as soon as I had any money of my own to screw around with. My plan was to bulldoze it, and the ones next to it, and build a park in their place. Somewhere nice for kids from the neighborhood to escape the impending doom brewing at home.

I was successful with the first two units, but not that one. There hasn't been a day since I called the whole thing off I haven't regretted it. Not just because of the constant neighborhood complaints that lead to phone calls from city officials, but more so because of nights like these. Anytime Isabelle implodes, she goes to one of two places: the house on Quincy Avenue that I spent my early years, or the one we used to daydream in front of after we lost everything.

It's been almost a year since I've been forced to stare into the face of the devil himself. *A year is never long enough.* The car rolls to a stop in front of the rundown eighteen-hundred square foot home. Even in the black night, I can make out the broken front gate.

Swallowing a lump of hot bile rising in my throat, I clutch the handle. She's in there. I know it.

"Want me to go have a look?" Thomas asks, allowing me the privilege of losing my shit in private by keeping his eyes trained in front.

"I just need another minute," I reply, extending a shaky head forward and clutching a bottle of scotch as though it's the bag of blood my lifeless body has been waiting on.

"I'll scan the perimeter. Take all the time you need."

I nod, sloshing the amber liquid into a glass tumbler. With unsteady hands, I bring it to my mouth, closing my eyes as the slow burn makes its way down my esophagus. I can see Thomas's shadow moving toward the grassy patch where I used to play with my toy airplane. My lip quivers, and I knock back the rest of the scotch. My princess once said we can only get out of things if we go through them. I wonder how many times I'll have to go through this before I'm finally out.

*Inhale.*

*Exhale.*

It's now or never. I pull the silver handle and open the door. Thomas meets me, his face soft with an unspoken understanding. "All clear. I couldn't get a visual. My guess is she's upstairs."

"Probably," I answer, trying not to picture the pale blue paint that I once peeled off the wall, thinking it was candy.

"I'll cover you, just in case."

I nod and take an unstable step toward the door. The gate creaks when I pull it back, and my eyes automatically dart to the porch, expecting to see her standing there in her bathrobe, hair wild with a cigarette hanging from her lips. "Did you find any treasure, Bashie?" She used to ask.

I never found anything of value, but she'd always indulge me anyway, saying, "Oh, pretty. Mommy found some treasure, too." Then she'd show me the scraps of what her body was worth for the day. She'd get dressed, and we'd start our walk to the store around the corner. She'd grab a few bottles of booze, a fresh pack of smokes, and a snack for me, her little Bashie. That snack would serve as my dinner, and breakfast for the next day, before we'd start the process again.

Chest tight, I struggle for air as I wrap my hand around the doorknob. It opens with ease, a sure sign that someone's been here recently. I scan the room, noting the pile of blankets in the corner I huddled shivering on a particularly cold winter when our heat was out. They aren't Isabelle's, but no doubt belong to some other liar who threw their life away and tossed the hopes and dreams of their spawn right along with it.

The bottom step squeaks, and I still. There's a rustling noise upstairs, too big to be that of rats. Behind me, Thomas draws his gun. He places a hand on my shoulder, holding me in place as he skirts around me, carefully checking each corner as we step onto the landing and make our way past the small bathroom. I peak in just enough to see the same hexagonal shaped tile I used to curl up next to Isabelle's body on after particularly painful binges. The rustling returns and Thomas nods his head in the direction of the room I've been hoping we wouldn't have to see.

Pacing myself, I search for a way to avoid it. It's not too late to call the whole thing off. We could leave her here in the mess she's made for herself and forget all about her until something came up on the news. God knows she deserves it. Thomas places a hand on the doorknob and looks over at me. Forcing my lungs to expand, I nod.

Someone has replaced the pale blue with a soft yellow. The hardwood is now carpeted, but I still see everything as it was before. The dingy curtains with sailboats she hung for me. My bed in the corner, and the light from the lamp, just enough to make me feel safe. The closet Isabelle locked me in when she didn't want me to see the evil she was about to do. Shuddering, I chase away the memories that haunt the place.

Half-naked, Isabelle is slumped over in the corner, her pupils dilated. There's a syringe, cooker, and plastic lighter on the floor at her side. Her arm is tied off with a tourniquet, the bulging veins causing my stomach to flip. Suppressing the urge to turn and run, I lean down next to her. "Isabelle?"

Glassy eyes roll up to meet mine in response. "Bashie?"

"Where'd you get the money, Isabelle?"

She pulls the torn strap of her bra over her shoulder, only for it to slip back down again. "Just close your eyes, baby. It'll be over soon." Her eyes roll back into her sockets, and her head bobs lazily. Her fist opens, dropping a mini-bar sized bottle of gin. It rolls to a stop against the toe of my shoe, and I cringe.

"Isabelle? Isabelle, look at me." I shake her shoulders gently.

Straining against the haze trying to consume her, she lifts her lids.

"Where's the rest of it? Can you show me?"

She barely lifts a finger toward the closet, only inches away from us. "Just get inside, baby," she replies, her voice straining with each word. "It'll all be over soon."

Thomas crouches down, shining his flashlight into the darkness and retrieving a backpack, turns it upside down and gives it a firm shake. What appears to be an entire mini bar spills out, along with a bag full of white pills I can only assume to be Ambien, and an 8-Ball of cocaine.

"Jesus, Isabelle, what are you trying to do?" I look back over at her, noticing the uneven rhythm of her breaths. Slow but definitely not steady, with several seconds passing in between. "Thomas!"

Swinging into action, he kneels beside me, taking Isabelle's wrists in his hand and frowning. "We need to get as much of this out of her as we can. Do you want me to call an ambulance?"

"No, that will only draw attention, and then the cops will get involved. As seedy as cops are in Manhattan, they're even worse here. Do you think she'll make it to the hospital?"

Isabelle groans, a gurgle coming from her throat that sounds like she's aspirating.

"Help me get her on her side," I bark, knowing the sound all too well. It's a disgusting thing to watch someone choke on their own vomit. Something no one should ever have to witness, but that doesn't change the fact that I've seen it more times than I can count.

Thomas crouches beside me, helping me lay Isabell over without letting her fall on her back. With a gigantic lurch, she spews putrid smelling chunks, gagging and going for it again. Fighting my own desire to retch, I turn my head, doing the best I can to hold her steady.

"I love you, Bashie," she whispers, her head lulling to the side again once she's finished.

The hot sting of tears pulls at my pupils, and I grit my teeth to stop them from falling. I've shed enough tears for Isabelle to last a lifetime. I refuse to give her anymore.

"Sir, if we're going to that hospital, we need to go now. I'm not sure how much time she has, but I'd say it's not much."

Unable to form words past the knot in my throat, I nod my head. "Can you help me get her downstairs?" I'm too weak to give orders, the little boy inside of me forcing all his pain on me.

I hold Isabelle under the arms, doing the best I can to keep her steady, while Thomas holds her legs. In no time, we've got her into the car. Not having the strength to stay at her side, I belt her in and open the passenger door.

I know Thomas wants to say something. Over a decade of spending time with him has me aware that there's wisdom in those eyes. His respect for my position as his employer keeps him from doing so, though. It was different when he was on my parents' payroll. Thomas saw me for the fucked-up kid I've always been and took on the role of mentor.

Being assigned the role of my driver through my teenage rebellion, he's seen his fair share of my shit and then some. He's different from most of the people in my life, though. There's no judgement in his voice when he speaks to me. I never have to worry about disappointing him, because he doesn't have any expectations. And he never tries to get inside of my fucking head. I think that's what I admire most about Thomas. He never asks me what I'm thinking, or tries to push me into sharing my *feelings*. If I want to talk — which is rare — he listens. If not, he sits in the quiet with me until we reach the next stop.

He practices this artful silence as we cruise down the street to Bronx-Lebanon Hospital. It's not my first choice, but they can at least get her stabilized, so I can have her transferred to one of the private facilities in the city. As we pull up near the emergency entrance, I risk glancing through the open privacy window.

Gray skin moist with sweat, Isabelle's mostly lifeless body bobs in time with every bump. I search for signs of life in her hallowed eyes, but all I see is a cold, glassy stare. My heart thudding against my ribs, I try not to imagine the potential outcomes as I round the car, open the door, and sweep her into my arms like a protective father holding his newborn for the first time. Her arms and legs dangle helplessly toward the ground, causing alarm to flash across the face of the redheaded admissions clerk.

She gives me a clipboard containing tedious paperwork for me to fill out, which I quickly hand off to Thomas. Auburn top comes toward me with a wheelchair, informing me it'll be a few minutes before Isabelle can be triaged. Thrusting a wad of Benjamins toward her, I instruct her to find an open bed and get us in it.

Letting the silent understanding pass between us, she punches a code into the keypad on the wall and motions us through despite the groans from the busy waiting room. I grab the first doctor I can find — greasing his palm as well — and explain Isabelle's situation to him. The rest happens in a flash of CPR, crash carts, shouted orders, and the deafening sound of my own heart beating in my eardrums.

Guilt-ridden and filled with loathing, I watch in horror as Isabelle's body is prodded with tubes and injected with IVs. How can one hate something and still feel such an unbreakable attachment to it at the same time? Wishing she'd just die for all the pain she's caused Lauren and me, and already unable to forgive myself if she does, I lean against the wall and watch the blur of doctors and nurses at work.

Seconds pass, then minutes, and the only sign of life is the faint line of the cardiograph moving up and down at the slowest pace imaginable. Some fluffed up nurse with blonde hair and garlicky breath approaches me, instructing me to wait in the hall. I'm about to refuse, when I see Thomas's face in the doorway, his eyes understanding, his face telling me it's for the best. Sighing, I take my place next to him. Blondie has the nerve to shut the door in my face, leaving me fuming beneath the pale white light.

Still, Thomas doesn't utter a single word. My thoughts drift to Danielle, probably asleep on some couch inside of a beach house that's been inhabited by God knows who. Guilt plagues my chest as I think of the look on her face before she stormed off to the bathroom. One step forward, two steps back and it's all because of fucking Isabelle. Why can't I just let her go? Why do I feel the need to rescue someone who clearly doesn't want to be saved?

My throat tightens, my tongue sticking to the roof of my mouth as I try to swallow. I know why... *she's my mother*. No matter how strong the bond I have with Emmalyn Black is, it will never take away the numbness in my chest where Isabelle's love used to be.

She always had her issues, but she wasn't always a twisted bitch who'd sell her own son to get her next fix. Having run away from her own abusive parents at sixteen, Isabelle met a man who promised to help her establish herself in the city. Before long, he was grooming her to become the prostitute she'd forever remain. When his wife grew jealous of his attraction to Isabelle, she threw her out on the streets once again. Knowing nothing other than selling her body to get by, she quickly established a customer base. In the early days, her clients were a source of necessities. A meal for a blowjob here, a hotel room for the sick privilege of fucking her primed teenage body there.

Then she met Carlos, the man whose DNA I supposedly share. A pimp and drug lord from Columbia, he's the one that introduced her to the life we were forced to live long after he left. I don't have any memories of Carlos. No matter how hard I've tried to picture his face, I can't. All I know is that something broke inside Isabelle the day she last saw him. From that moment on, she moved solo. We worked our way around the city until landing in the Quincy house. I was five.

I remember Isabelle's excitement, the pure joy on her face that she could finally give me a home. I don't think she ever meant to keep living the lifestyle, but the bills never stopped coming and she had me to take care of. One of the girl's she knew from the street — a wild-eyed woman with a purple wig I used to call Aunt Lucy — gave her her first hit that I know of.

I asked what they were doing sticking dollars up their noses to which Isabelle replied, "It's candy, sweetheart."

"Can I try?" I'd asked her.

"This candy's for grownups," she'd replied, holding up the bag of white powder. "Never touch it."

I stared at her, a confused look on my face.

"Never touch it, Bashie!" She screamed. "Promise me!" Her hands flew to my shoulders, griping tight and shaking me. "Never! Promise, Bashie! Say you promise!"

Shaking my head clear of the wild look in her eyes, I turn my head to the sound of the door opening. "Mister Black," the doctor I introduced myself — and my deep wallet — to earlier calls. He approaches with that controlled, practiced look of concern in his eyes that I'm convinced is taught on the first day of med school. I can almost picture some bald guy whose entire life is wrapped up in what advancements he's made in the medical field smiling proudly as Doctor Greased Palm says, "We got her stabilized. I had to hook her up to oxygen to do some of the breathing for her, and we pumped her stomach so that should help sober her up. You didn't give anyone medical history when you brought her in. Before I can continue treating her, I'll need to know more about her case. Do you mind coming with me?"

I follow closely at his heels, unable to stop myself from peaking in at Isabelle along the way. She's still hooked to an array of monitors, her heart still beating slowly as a nurse stands close by, monitoring her vital signs. Another busies herself with changing out an IV bag full of what I can only assume is something to combat the dehydration typical of times like these.

"Why do you do this?" I whisper, my will no longer strong enough to keep a lone tear from sliding down my cheek as I follow the white coat into the doctor's lounge.

# Chapter 23

Danielle

My phone hums against the wooden nightstand. Shaking off the sleepy haze, I open my eyes, noting that Sebastian's side of the bed is still cold. Throat clenched with longing, I rub my hand over the still smooth sheet. It's been two days, and whatever forced him back to the city early still has his attention. He hasn't even come home to sleep. My phone continues its violent assault on the oak, and I reluctantly roll over to answer. Not bothering to look, I slide my finger across the screen and answer with a raspy hello.

"Still sleeping, princess?" His voice is distant, the wear of whatever he's dealing with clear in every word.

"I was. I'm not now. How much longer are you planning on sleeping at the office, Sebastian?"

"Hopefully, that was the last night." He sighs, exhaustion taking over him. "I think I've just about got things handled here."

"I miss you."

"I miss you too, princess. You have no idea how much."

"Then come home. I still have a few hours before I have to get ready for work."

"Danielle, if I could, you know I would. There's no place in the world I'd rather be right now than in your arms."

"Yeah..." I drift off, biting my lip to hold back the tears.

"Princess, I know you're hurt and I'm killing myself over that. I think about you lying awake at night staring at an empty spot in the bed next to you, and something inside of me goes hallow. I hate doing this to you. If there was any other way, I would take it, but—"

"I get it, Sebastian," I butt in, stopping him before I break. "Sometimes dating a powerhouse means having dinner alone, or waking up in an empty bed. You can't help it. No matter how much it hurts, it's something I'm going to have to get used to if I want to be with you. I'm trying..."

"So, you're not mad anymore?"

Pulling the blankets up around my shoulders, I sigh. "No, hotshot. I'm not mad anymore. I'll admit, I'm still not happy about you abandoning me on *your* family vacation, but I get it. You did what you had to do. I just wish you'd give yourself a break sometimes. Surely, everything won't fall apart if you take the extra time to have one dance with your girlfriend."

"I wish that were true," he replies, his voice cracking as a faint cough comes from the background. "Listen, I love you, but I gotta go."

"I love you too, Sebastian. *Please* try to come home tonight."

"I'll give it my best shot, princess."

My heart aching right out of my chest, I clutch my phone and stare up at the ceiling. The only good thing about this latest absence is that Sebastian's finally realizing the need to keep me in the know. Once I could finally stop fuming enough to decide what to do about being abandoned in the Hamptons, I called to let him know I was coming back to the city. He didn't answer, but sent me a text before I could even hang up the phone, letting me know that he'd call me later that night. Expecting him to keep me waiting, I packed my bags and got the hell out of Dodge. He did call, though, and he's checked in regularly since. It's hard to stay mad at him when that small action alone shows major progress. Still, I wish he'd come home.

Deciding there's no point in trying to go back to sleep, I grab my robe and walk through the dark hall toward the kitchen. I'm greeted by the outline of Cyrus Rhodes sitting on the couch as I round the corner to the living room. Heart hammering against my rib cage, I jump.

"Jesus!" I toss my hand against my chest and bend over to catch my breath. "Make some noise or something, would you? This shadow man routine's really creeping me the hell out!"

"Sorry, Ms. Stevens. I didn't know you were up."

"Well, I am," I reply, pulling at my robe to make sure I'm still covered. "Do you ever sleep?"

"Not when I'm on duty."

"You've been 'on duty' for the last thirty-six hours, Cyrus. You're telling me you haven't had a single wink during that time?"

"Before going civ, I had longer missions with less sleep." He shrugs. "I'll make it."

Realizing I'll never understand the expectations the military places on our brave men and women, I shake my head. "Well, if you're not sleeping, can I at least interest you in some coffee?"

"Coffee would be great." He stands, his body stiff and rigid as he follows me to the kitchen. "What's on the agenda for the day?"

"Just work," I answer, ignoring the miserable feeling in my gut at the thought of being face to face with Piper and Paul for the first time since things blew up the other night. "You could squeeze a nap in during those boring eight hours if you'd like." I wink at him. "I promise not to tell."

"I'm fine," he says, his stony face giving away nothing in the way of emotion.

Pulling the array of K-cups from the cabinet and setting them in front of him, I ask, "You sure? They say lack of sleep kills you, ya know?"

"If I can survive having heavy artillery fire all around me, I think I can survive a few days without sleep."

"Even so, I think I'd prefer to have Benson drive if you don't mind. I'm not saying I'm great at it or anything, but I kind of like this living thing. I think I'd like to keep trying it out for a while."

**** 

Thankfully, Benson does drive, and we make it to the office, though I'm questioning my reason for coming in with each passing second. Piper's absence doesn't go unnoticed as I restlessly gnaw at my pen. Mind swarming with scenarios, I anxiously tap my heel against the floor.

"Dani, can I see you in my office for a minute?" Paul asks through the intercom, causing me to jump.

"You got it," I reply, my legs wrought with tension as I stand.

"Close the door please," he says, without looking up.

"Um… okay," I reply, unsure of his tone.

"Thanks. Have a seat."

Growing increasingly unsettled by his stiffness, I take the seat opposite his desk and cross my legs.

"Right," he begins, looking at me. "So, I know you have the meeting with Burden's Bared this afternoon, but I'm afraid I'm going to have to ask someone else to fill in."

Startled, I uncross my legs and lean forward. "May I ask why?"

Arms behind his head, he leans back against his chair. "When you've been here, you've been great. Unfortunately, you haven't been here as often as I expect my employees to be. You're constantly tardy or taking extended leaves of absence—"

"Those—"

"And then there's the issue of client-staff relations. You've broken that rule not only once, but twice now."

"You—"

"There's also the issue of your relationship with the rest of the team."

"My what?" I ask, dumbfounded.

"Kristine in reception, for starters. You walk past her daily, and she's mentioned that you've never acknowledged her once."

"You're joking, right? This is another one of your tests. Like the one you gave me when you practically threw me to the wolves on my first day?"

Sternly looking at me and resting his elbows on his desk, he says, "No, Danielle, this isn't a test. I built P.E.S. under the foundation that we are better together. From the very start, I hoped to have a team that was so much more than that. We are a family here. I had high hopes that you would be a long-term member of this family, but I'm afraid I was wrong. It was bound to happen, eventually. I made the wrong choice in hiring you."

"You made the wrong choice," I repeat, deflating.

"I'm afraid I'm going to have to terminate your position with the company, effective immediately. You can leave your keycard on your desk when you pack your belongings. Security is waiting outside to escort you out."

"You're firing me?" Taking a deep breath, I ask, "Because I don't get along with the receptionist?"

"I'm firing you for all the reasons listed above, the quarrel with Piper over the weekend, *and* for this," he says, sliding his tablet across the table to me.

I'm staring at a blog post of some sort, but I'm not sure what I'm looking at. It appears to be a picture of Piper and Paul in an embrace at the party on Friday night, but I'm not sure why it has anything to do with me. Nor am I sure why anyone would care enough about Paul to post it.

"Do you think I had something to do with this? That I'm plotting against you in some way?" I ask, handing the tablet back to him.

"I don't think you are. I know you are," he answers, flipping to another screen on the tablet. "We found this on your computer."

My head spinning, I scan through the email. "I've never seen this in my life."

"Then explain how it was sent from your email account and the encrypted file showing where it originated was found on your computer."

"Paul," I start, looking down at the words again, "this is crazy. Why would I out your relationship with Piper? For one thing, I don't think anyone would care. As long as you're doing a great job with their media presence — which you do for every client — your sex life doesn't matter. Second, I'm the one that encouraged Piper to seek more. Why would I try to destroy something I helped build?"

"Because you were angry with her for the things she said on Friday."

"Do you honestly think I'm that juvenile? The last thing I spend my time worrying about is what someone said about me in a jealous moment. Check the security cameras. I spent my Monday at home recovering, just like everyone else."

"That's easier said than done," he replies. "I'm afraid someone hacked the building's security cameras. The thing we can't figure out, though, is who. It was clearly someone with a lot of pull in this city. You wouldn't happen to know anyone like that, would you?"

The condescending nature of his voice makes every protective bone in my body ache.

"You think Sebastian had something to do with this? You're losing your mind. Sebastian couldn't give two cents about who you're dating. The only reason he's even still using this firm is because..."

Lifting his eyebrows, he finishes my sentence. "Because you're here. I'm not an idiot, Danielle. I realized long ago that Sebastian Black had run out of use for me. It was only a matter of time before he dropped us. And then you showed up and suddenly what I fully expected to be the last club launch I ever did for Black turns into a full calendar of his events."

"Then the news broke that you were involved, and everything became much clearer. After the threat I received, when I considered letting you go the first time around, I knew that if I wanted to keep Black, I had to keep you. You're competent enough. I figured a promotion would calm the ripples and give you the motivation not to screw up again. Then Marcum happened—"

"And you orchestrated that. You're the one who pushed me up on that stage and practically begged me to ride the wave until it got the band where they needed to go. You want me gone? Fine, I'll go." Standing, I walk to the door and look over my shoulder. "But don't pretend like I wasn't a good employee. I've busted my ass for this company from the moment you chose me as an intern. Despite all the personal drama I've been dealing with, I've still given this company everything I have. Late nights. Taking the office home. Staying through lunch to make up for time missed. I've done all of that. And don't you dare pretend that the thing with Kyle is on me. That, *Mister Princeton*, was all part of your endgame, and it worked. Quite well, I might add. My keycard will be on the desk. Thank you for the opportunity, and for the lesson."

The security guard watches, quietly, as I pack up my personal affects and place the key card on the table. I should be sad. Normal people are sad when they're fired. This was my dream job, after all. I'm surprisingly okay, however. Sebastian will be furious and maybe that's part of why I know I shouldn't be. If Paul wanted me out of his company, he had every right to get rid of me. I would like to know who fabricated that email, though.

"Three in just a few months," the guard says as we step into the elevator. "I was in this building when Princeton moved in. I've barely seen him let go of three in a year. Let alone in just a matter of months. He must be cracking the whip up there."

"Yeah. Guess so," I say, letting the number sink in.

There's the assistant whose place I took, me, and... the person who was fired for leaking the story of Sebastian dating a member of the firm. I wonder if it was them. Paul never told me who they were, and I was so new to the firm at the time that I didn't know anyone. It seems likely, though. They had a motive. I just need to find means. Sebastian could do that for me. Deciding to talk to him about it after Geoff's photo shoot tonight, I thank the security guard and step onto the sidewalk.

**** 

"You're doing great, Dani. Remind me again why you don't model professionally?"

"Funny," I say, tossing the red scarf over my shoulder dramatically.

"I'm serious," Geoff encourages. "You're a lot easier to work with than most of the people that grace the front of this fair lens."

"And she's a hell of a lot sexier," Kyle says, opening the heavy metal door.

Geoff's idea of studio space for the day is a warehouse in Brooklyn that's currently not in use. It's a red brick building that sits right below the iconic Brooklyn Bridge, and I've been promised we will migrate there for some shots. I realize I still haven't told Sebastian that Geoff asked Kyle to do the shoot with me, but we had so many other things threatening to spoil our weekend that I didn't want to add to it. The very mention of Kyle's name brings that fire to Sebastian's eyes that I'm learning to take as a warning sign. In truth, part of me is afraid of going there.

"You're late," I say, the attraction I've carried for him since my youth undeniably still there as my body sinks against his for a hug. Squeezing tighter, his scent wafts around me, a dangerous trip down memory lane I know I'll never be able to repeat, forming in the dark recesses of my mind as he leans down to kiss my cheek.

"Don't mess up the hair," Geoff warns. "We've already lost precious time. Your outfit's behind the curtain. Hurry up. We're approaching Golden Hour."

"Geez, cut me some slack. I just took an hour-long train ride to get here, and that's all after getting up at four in the morning to do a press run."

"Whine while you're getting dressed," Geoff demands, shoving him toward the curtain.

Kyle looks at me, his eyes pleading with me to give in to his cause.

"You heard the man," I say, pointing to the curtain.

"Tough crowd," he jokes, stepping into Geoff's makeshift dressing room. "I think I did better with the DJs. Where were you, anyway?"

Geoff lifts a curious brow at me.

"I was here helping G set up," I say, as innocently as I can.

"Really, I thought you were heading up the meeting after everything wrapped. It's not like you to bail on such a serious commitment."

"I didn't bail, exactly..."

"Then what happened?"

"It's nothing. Are you almost ready?" I ask, nervously trying to change the subject.

"Not so fast," Geoff corners me. "What's going on?"

"We can talk about it later," I reply.

"Or you could save us all the suspense and explain now," Kyle counters, joining us.

I've never seen him in a suit, and I'm not sure how to respond. There's something about the way it hugs his body that makes me feel a little unsteady. While Sebastian makes suits look like a second skin, Kyle looks out of place and uncomfortable. Staring expectantly at me, he fidgets with his tie, presumably not knowing how to tie it. I'm not sure what concept Geoff's going for, but given the edginess of my bright red dress, I expected Kyle's ensemble to be a bit more like... well, like him.

"Fine," I sigh, taking the tie from his hands and lifting his collar. "I got fired today."

"You what?" Geoff asks, dramatically.

"How could they possibly fire you?" Kyle finishes for him. "You're awesome at what you do."

"It's a long story, but basically I've had a few infractions against me, and Paul just thought it would be best to let me go. Anyway, we're losing light, aren't we?" I ask, directing the conversation back to Geoff.

"Yes, we are. So, let's go. I can't afford to screw this up. It's all I've got going for me right now. First..." he leans in and undoes Kyle's jacket, loosens the perfect knot I just tied in his tie, and unbuttons at least half the buttons on his shirt.

By the time he's finished, Kyle's look matches mine perfectly, and I'm starting to see where he's going with this.

"Let's do it then," I say, lifting his camera bag.

"Do you need anything?" Kyle asks, swooping in like the gallant soldier that he is and taking it from me.

"Just this," I shrug, "an afternoon with my friends to forget about it."

"You got it." He winks and tosses his arm over my shoulder, careful not to mess up my stiff curls as Geoff chastises him again.

**\*\*\*\***

"We're just about done, guys," Geoff yells over his shoulder as he replaces his memory card. "I have one last setup left."

"So," Kyle says, unable to keep himself from stroking his hand over my skin through the crisscrossed cutouts that stretch from my neck to the curve of my backside. "You sure you're okay?"

"Promise," I reply, shivering beneath his touch. "For the first time in a long time, I'm fine."

"Alright," Geoff says, bringing his duffle bag over. "We're going all in for this one."

Feeling excited to see what his big finale will be, I watch as he reaches in the bag and pulls out a handgun. The familiar tightening building in my chest, I struggle to breathe. Feeling as though everything around me is moving in a high-speed orbit, I lose my balance and fall to the ground. Kneeling beside me, Kyle tries to help me up, and I push him off.

"Shit, Dani," Geoff says, taking the gun from my hand. "I'm sorry. I was so busy working through my own mess that I didn't even consider yours."

"It's okay," I pant.

Stroking my hair with his hand, he says, "No, it isn't, baby girl. God, I hate this! I hate all of it."

"Me too." I blink, tears spilling over my eyes as I look up at him. "Just when there's joy in the world again, the ghost of what I've done comes back to haunt me and everyone around me. I'm so sorry, G."

He places his lips on my forehead. "I think we can make it without the last shot. Wanna go grab a drink or something?"

"You can't," I protest.

"Ugh," he growls. "What's the point of staying sober? Life is literally a bitch, Dani. Every fucking time we turn around, it's doing something else to drag us down. People like you and me... we don't get happily ever after. We might as well enjoy this cruel world while we can."

"Geoffrey Taylor!" I scream, my anger giving me the fuel I need to stabilize myself. "Drop the bullshit right now! Look at what you're doing to yourself. Look at what you just did to me! This isn't you, G. Do you honestly think he would be proud of you if he were here now? Who got you back on track after your last screw up?"

"Jon," he replies solemnly.

"Right! And do you want that to all be for nothing? I get it, hunny," I say, softening. "I really do. You had an infinite love. Infinite loves only come once in a lifetime, G, you have to honor that. Do everything you can to live the life he would've wanted you to. That's the reason I still get out of bed in the morning, even with everything I've done—"

"You haven't done anything," Kyle intercedes, pulling me against him and kissing the top of my ear. "Your psycho ex-stepfather proved how crazy he was, and now he's missing. Don't put this on yourself."

Sighing, I turn to him and say, "It's more complicated than that. You've never pushed me for details about Walt, and I appreciate you for that. But I'm going to have to ask you to do it again."

He studies me for a few moments, the concern he'll always carry for me locked in those beautiful baby blues. "Of course, but that doesn't mean I'm going to sit here and let you blame yourself, either."

"Kyle, *please*," I beg, needing him to give us a minute.

He looks from me to Geoff and reluctantly says, "I'll pack you up, but first listen to me, sexy. I don't have to know what you went through to know you. That was true eight years ago, and it's just as true today. I've seen your heart, and I've fallen in love with it. You're not a bad person, Dani. You're the brightest fucking star that lives in my otherwise dull sky. I know you, sexy. I know every part of you. I feel you even when you're miles away. Nothing — *nothing* — can ever make you a bad person. You're an angel — *my angel* — and I will not let you beat yourself up over the dirty shit some sadistic asshole did to break you."

"*Kyle*," I whisper, knowing I shouldn't find comfort in his truth. The hot sting of my betrayal burning through my veins at the very thought of being *his*, I fight to capture this moment forever.

Placing his calloused fingers to my lips, he whispers. "I love you, Dani. You don't have to feel the same. It's not going to change anything." Without giving me the chance to reply, he kisses me on the cheek and sets off to gather the props Geoff has efficiently scattered everywhere.

"That was..." Geoff trails off.

"I can't go there, G. There's nothing but heartache at the end of that road. His. Sebastian's. Mine. Kyle will always be a part of me, the white knight that rescued me from the darkness, and if I hadn't caught Addison topless on his couch that day, then maybe I could've loved him. None of that matters now, though. I'm with Sebastian, and that's exactly where I want to stay."

"I get that, but baby girl... you just chewed my ass and spit it back out, lecturing me on infinite love. All the while, yours has been waiting eight years for you to wake the fuck up."

"Kyle?" I lower my voice. "You think Kyle is my forever? You're ridiculous."

"I'm just saying... guys like Kyle could bag any babe they wanted, and yet..."

"And yet what?"

"He may not be Pete Wentz or anything, but the guy has a pretty chatty fanbase these days. If he was leaving a trail of broken hearts behind, someone would've mentioned it in the Burdens Bared fandom. Don't you think?"

I shake my head. "You're crazy. I made my choice, and he accepted it. The spotlight has gone out on our show and Kyle knows it."

"You sure?"

"Yes, I'm sure. And how'd we get on this topic anyway?"

He stands and helps me from the ground. "I don't know, but thank your white knight" for me, will ya? I didn't care much for the other one."

He tries to mask the pain in his eyes, but I know him too well. Squeezing his shoulder, I let the silent understanding pass between us. He's still working through the stages — we both are — when the time is right, we'll finally talk about it.

# Chapter 24

S ebastian

I'm sending yet another email to William Rush about this custody thing when Danielle comes into my office. I can tell she wants my attention, but making her work for it is half the fun. Not looking in her direction, I pick up my phone from the desk and respond to a few of my more urgent texts. Under normal circumstances, I would've never let work pile up like this, but the past few days have been anything but normal.

She hops onto the edge of my desk and slides my laptop away. Shaking my head, I look up at her. "Good evening to you too, princess. Did you enjoy your time with Geoff?"

"I guess." She shrugs; her eyes alight with an unexpected sadness. "I'm just glad you're actually home."

Sliding away from the desk, I pull her onto my lap and kiss her softly. The taste of her kiss is like honey, so sweet it always leaves me aching for more. Rolling my tongue past her lips, I attempt to chase whatever new demon has her down away. Resisting the heat building between us, she pushes away from me.

"I'm hungry, and we need to talk. Have you had dinner?"

"I was waiting for you," I snap, the sting of her rejection more evident than I'd like.

"Don't get like that. It's nothing bad. It's just been a long day."

"Indeed, it has." I pull her close, twirling her hair in my fingers and soaking in the coconut scent. "I gave Bernice the night off since I knew you would be late getting home. What are you in the mood for? I'll have Robin order in for us."

"Seriously, hotshot. You've got to respect that girl a little more. She just gave you at least forty-eight hours of her time. Let her have a little for herself. We're two capable adults. Surely, we can dial the phone and order from a menu without your assistant."

"We can, but it's a time-consuming task that I prefer not to focus on."

"Ugh," she growls, standing abruptly. "I'm calling for pizza. It's fast and filling."

Confused and exhausted, I follow her to the other side of the room. Lifting her chin, I force her to look into my eyes. I pluck her phone from her hands, cup my hand to the nape of her neck, and press my lips to hers. Sealing her mouth with mine, I lick into it relentlessly. Giving her all the shit I've dealt with for the last few days and taking hers in return. For a moment she goes limp, her body melting into mine as her hands thrust into my hair. Out of nowhere, she stops, pushes me away, and takes back her phone.

"I'm trying not to take it too personally, princess, but we haven't seen each other in two days. What am I doing wrong?"

She cuts her eyes at me, a glare searing through the emeralds that would stop any man. Sizing me up, she sighs and returns to the task of ordering our dinner. My fingers tease into her hair again as she lifts the phone to her ear. Annoyed, she slaps them away and walks out of the room. Thoughts of everything that could possibly have been brought to her attention within the last forty-eight hours running through my head at warp speed, I follow her.

She tosses her phone on the table, picks up the television remote, and lies back on the couch. Refusing to let the only good thing in my life — the only person who's ever saw my fuckedupness and given me her undying love anyway — slip through my fingers, I kneel next to her. Cupping her face in my hands, I stroke my thumb along the soft edge of her jaw.

"Talk to me, Danielle. Tell me what I did so I can fix it."

Closing her eyes, she exhales. I watch as she props herself onto her elbow, leveling her face to mine. Her stare cuts through me, my anxiety rising as I wait for her to speak. At last she sighs and says, "It's not you, hotshot. Like I said, it was just a long day. I skipped lunch and I'm starving. I'm just cranky. Sorry for taking it out on you."

I lift her up, taking a seat next to her and placing her head in my lap. Lightly pressing my fingers to her forehead, I rub her temples. The load of what she's carrying falls almost automatically, her muscles going lax as the tension leaves. A light moan escapes her lips and my cock surges to attention. Desperate for her body wrapped around mine, I lower my hands to her shoulders. Kneading the knots away, I lean forward and lay feather light kisses on her forehead.

"I know the weekend didn't go exactly as we planned, princess, but you have my full attention now. You said you wanted to talk."

"Mm... not now." She shakes her head. "I just need to feel your hands on me. I need your warmth, your gentle touches, and the love that only you can give me."

"I can do that," I reply, grinning like a teenager about to get laid for the first time. "I love nothing more than worshipping your body like the deity you are."

"No sex." She snaps, wiping the smile right off my face. Her eyes fling open, and she gives me the best serious face she can. "I really do have to talk to you, and if you sex me into submission, it'll never happen."

"Oh, princess," I lean forward and lick her neck, sucking the salty skin into my mouth, and releasing it again. My eyes automatically find her nipples, their perky buds telling me everything I need to hear. "I've been craving this pussy for two days, seeing its perfectly pink plushness when I close my eyes at night. Tasting the sweetness of your juices on my tongue, like a man trapped in the desert, tastes water. If you think for one second that I'm not fucking you tonight, you're sadly mistaken. I will, however, at least wait until we've had dinner."

****

"So, I've arranged for us to get into your apartment and get your things this weekend."

"Great," she says, without really committing.

"And I specially ordered the movers from Mars..."

"K."

"Afterwards, they'd really like to take you back, clone you, and create enough sex goddesses to go around."

"Sounds good."

Trying to stifle my laughter, I say, "Danielle, that pizza can't possibly be this interesting."

Wiping her hands with a napkin, she turns to me. "I'm sorry. What were we talking about?"

"Why don't you tell me what's on your mind?"

She pushes her plate away and sighs. "Okay. First, remember that you love me."

"I could never forget," I reply, taking her hands and bringing her knuckles to my lips.

She takes a deep breath and smiles. "Okay. Kyle was at the shoot today."

My stomach sinks, my muscles growing tight under the pressure of my rising anger. Tightening my grip on her, I say, "Go on..."

"Geoff needed a male model. I didn't find out about it until the Hamptons this past weekend, but with everything else crazy that happened, I thought I should wait until we got back to tell you. Then you left early, and you stayed gone, and before I knew it..."

I close my eyes and remind myself to remain calm. I have warned the guitarist to stay away from her. He's either stupid or he has a death wish. Either way, perhaps it's time to pay him another visit.

"I need you to get that look out of your eyes," she insists, drawing me back to our conversation. "It was purely platonic. Geoff was right there the entire time and Kyle didn't even try to push the envelope."

"Then why are you so distracted?"

"That would be because of the thing that happened before the photo shoot. Did you get an email from Paul today?"

"Not that I'm aware," I answer, pulling my phone from my pocket and double checking.

"That's odd. I thought you would be one of the first clients he emailed. Then again, it gives him time to map out his next move as far as you're concerned—"

"Princess, you're rambling."

"Right. Sorry. Paul fired me today," she says, abruptly.

"Fired you? What were his justifications?"

"Apparently, I'm not a team player, and the fight with Piper over the weekend just proved it."

Returning my phone to my pocket, I take her hand. "I see. Well, it's safe to say that he's lost my business. I'll have Robin contact him first thing in the morning. As for your unemployment, I think we can find something for you within my PR department."

She places her hands on my lap, squeezing my thighs just enough to stir a reaction. "I love you, Sebastian, but no."

"No?" I question, trailing her cheek with my thumb.

"No," she repeats. "I'm actually quite relieved that we won't have to mix the business with the personal anymore."

"Oh?"

She laughs, and replies, "Yeah. I mean, don't get me wrong, hotshot. I love it when you're the boss in the bedroom. In the boardroom, not so much."

Shaking my head, I lean forward and kiss her. She melts against me, welcoming the warmth. I wrap my arms around her, twisting her hair into my hands, and drawing her closer. Her kiss reverberates to the deepest depths of my soul, her passion an awakening for my emotional needs just as much as it is my physical ones. Lifting her hands into my hair, she slides from her stool. I grip her hips and tug her against me.

Breath heavy, she pulls away, a blaze of lust sparkling in her beautiful green eyes. Eyes that captured my very soul the moment I looked into them. Licking her lips, she runs her hands over my painfully stiff erection. The friction of her fingers over the fabric of my sweatpants only adding to the swell. Hand on the nape of her neck, I seal my lips over hers again. She gasps, matching my greed with her own.

Her skin igniting with heat, I stand and lift her onto the counter. "Hold on tight and don't let go unless I tell you to."

"Okay," she pants, clutching her fingers around the edges.

Ripping her blouse — buttons scattering across the counter and floor — I kiss her neck and clasp her nipples in my hands, rolling them tightly as I bring my lips across her shoulder, and down the flat of her stomach. Shivering, she cries out for my body to merge with hers. Needing her to heal me of the pain the last few days have caused I take my time, kissing, licking, and caressing every ounce of skin she'll expose to me. Encircling her navel with my tongue, I tear away her skirt. Her red lace G-string rests on her hips, her engorged pussy pushing against the fabric for release.

Growling, I lower my head and run my tongue over the packaging. Rewarded with the taste of her sweetness mixed with lace, I grab the thin band and break her free. Placing my hands on her hips, I lower my mouth to her cleft. The sweet aroma of her lust intoxicating me, I part her lips with my fingers. Her pussy glistens with her desire, forcing my mouth to water. Starting with her taint, I lick my way to her clit.

"Sebastian!" Her screams reward me.

Like a famished man finding food for the first time in days, I devour her. The sound of her heavy breath filling my ears, I suck her clit into my mouth. Watching her unravel, I place two fingers between her slickened folds, finding her G-spot and begging her to come for me.

"Sebastian, I'm gonna... I'm gonna... ah!"

She comes undone around me, her muscles contracting on my fingers so tightly they feel as though they'll break. Taking her for all she's got, I roll my tongue over her clit and dip it into the opening of her center. White knuckling the counter, she spasms uncontrollably. The beautiful sight of her head thrashing back and forth fueling my need for her.

Rising, I lower my sweats and position myself between her legs. She throbs in response, desperate for more of my attention.

"Greedy little princess," I mock.

"Only for you," she gasps as I press my thumb into her and massage in slow circles.

Grazing my lips over her parted mouth, I trail kisses down her body catching a protruding nipple with my teeth and tearing a hole in the lace of her bra.

"Sebastian, please, I need you," she breathes.

"Need me to what, princess?" I tease, going for the other nipple.

Tossing her head back, she wraps her hand in my hair. "Ah, I can't wait anymore, Sebastian, please!"

Smirk threatening my lips, I place a soft kiss on the corner of her mouth. Placing my hands on her knees and splaying her open against the counter, I roll my hips, bringing the tip of my cock to her. Greedily, she clutches at me, her body begging for more. Gritting my teeth, I slide the length of my cock inside her with ease. My girth stretching her to the perfect fit.

"Fuck! Danielle, your pussy was made for me. I just hope you know that. It's mine." I place my lips to hers, parting my tongue into her mouth as I dive deeper and bring myself out again. "Mine to fuck. To taste. You're my home, princess. The place where happy memories are made. My hurt, my healer. You're my everything."

She spasms against me, rocking her hips against mine as I fill her completely. On a deep thrust, she cries out my name. Stilling, I stare into her eyes, allowing her to back away from the edge before thrusting back again. Gasping, she digs her nails into my flesh. With a roar, I toss my head back and quicken my pace.

"Sebastian, I don't want to without you," she pleads, tears spilling over her eyes as she tries to hold back.

"Soon, princess," I whisper as she rocks against me.

We work together in perfect harmony, each of us desperate for climax. Moaning, she rides my cock from below, taking me to the brink of no return. "Now," I command, the first violent burst shooting from me before I can stop it.

Her body reacts on demand, her sex clenching uncontrollably as she screams louder and louder. Ramming into her with everything I have, I coax, "That's it, Danielle. Come for me."

There's no end in sight as I drive into her, rubbing my head over her rough G-spot. My cock gives a great lurch and I throw my head back, a low growl escaping my throat. Slickening her with my seed, I pump into her with ease as she comes once... twice... three times, taking everything I have. Burying my head against her neck, I fall on top of her. Sweat coated bodies sticking together, I pull her up.

"I lose all control with you, princess. You own me," I pant.

"You own me too," she agrees, her chest heaving for air.

****

Spent from rounds two, three, and four, we lay in bed, Danielle wrapped in my arms. Her fingertips lightly brushing over the well-earned ridges in my abs. This is what I've needed for the last two nights, my magic pill that makes everything seem to make sense again. Realizing we never really finished our conversation from earlier, I ask, "So what's your next move? I would be happy to make you a kept woman, but something tells me you wouldn't go for that."

She shoves my chest and rolls her eyes. "Not even a little bit. I don't know what my plan is. I'm still figuring it out, but I think I'd like to try some nonprofit work. I still want to stay on the public relations side of things, but honestly, all the club openings and random parties just aren't what they were once cracked up to be. I want to do something more meaningful."

"I'll make some calls."

"And," she sits up to look me directly in the eye, "I would still like to do it as Danielle Stevens, qualified applicant, not as Danielle Stevens, girlfriend to Sebastian Black."

"You're sure?"

"Completely."

"Oka," I reply, reluctantly. "But you'll let me know if you need my help?"

"Of course."

"Then I guess I'll leave it in your hands. *For now...*"

"Sebastian—"

"Besides…" One hand on her ass, I bring the other to her cheek and roll her to her back. "I have other ways to keep my hands occupied at the moment."

She giggles and replies, "Fiend."

# Chapter 25

Danielle

It's been four days since I was let go from P.E.S. Four days, and already I feel like I'm losing my mind. Everything I said to Sebastian was true. After Jon's death, I just don't see a point behind the frivolous parties and events we typically hosted at P.E.S. However, I didn't realize how much purpose my job gave me. Without it to distract me during the day, I'm growing antsier by the minute. Geoff and I sit in the living room of Sebastian's penthouse browsing classifieds online, and watching some daytime drama that makes my skin crawl.

"Found one!" He shouts. "PR rep needed for busy firm specializing in... oh, crap. Sorry."

"Specializing in?" I ask.

"Celebrity clientele..." He tilts his head at me. "Baby girl, are you dead set on this nonprofit thing? I mean, we've looked. There's nothing out there. I don't mind carrying your rent for a while or anything, but that won't solve the issue of student loans."

Placing my laptop on the table, I pull my hair into a sloppy ponytail and bring my feet up under me. "I've told you, G, I'm over that glitz and glamor scene. I want to do something meaningful. I need to make a difference."

"I get needing to make a change. It's something I've been thinking about a lot lately, but you need to be practical about these things too. What about Yasmin? I'm sure she knows someone here in the city that needs a good fashion publicist. Have you considered calling her?"

Closing my eyes, I lean my head onto the back of the couch. Yasmin owns Hardwire, the public relations firm I interned at throughout college. She deals primarily in public relations for designers. I'd be lying if I hadn't considered her as a backup. I was just hoping I wouldn't have to use her.

Exhaling, I lean forward and close my laptop. "If I haven't found something in a month, I'll call her."

"Good, because I wanna talk more about that rent thing."

"Umm... okay..." I know I was kidding myself to think that we'd never have to talk about me moving in with Sebastian. Now that everything is happening tomorrow, I should just say it. Still, I can't bring myself to do so.

"I found a few options. I was thinking we could check 'em out next week. Sound good?"

"I'm not sure. We'll see what all comes up between now and then," I reply, avoiding having to elaborate by walking into the kitchen.

Hot on my heels, Geoff takes the fondue pot from my hands and sets it on the counter. "Every time I bring up moving you either a. become evasive, b. change the subject, or c. walk out of the room. What the hell's going on, baby girl?"

"Nothing." I move about the kitchen, piling my arms full of strawberries, bananas, pretzels, marshmallows, and shortbread. "You gonna help, or are you just gonna stand there?"

Crossing his arms, he replies, "I'll help when you get real with me. I *know* something's up. *You* know something's up. Don't play dumb with me, baby girl. I know you better than you know yourself. What're you trying to hide from me?"

Placing everything on the counter with an ungraceful motion that spills some of the strawberries from the carton, I look him straight in the eye. "Okay... just don't freak out."

"Oh, God!" He sinks to a barstool, holding his head in his hands. "I hate it when people say things like that. If you're starting with a 'just don't freak out', that means there's clearly something to freak out about."

Reaching across the counter, I clasp his hands. "It's nothing bad. *I swear*. It's just a big change, and given the last few months..."

"I get it." He opens the bag of marshmallows and pops one in his mouth. "So..."

"I'm moving in with Sebastian," I blurt, turning to the fridge for the apples and grapes I bought earlier this morning.

"Really?" He causally tosses another marshmallow in his mouth.

"You're being awfully indifferent about this..."

Shrugging, he reaches for an apple slice. "Baby girl, with all the shit we've faced lately, this is the least horrible thing that could've happened."

"So, you're okay?" Turning on the fondue pot, I arrange the rest of the spread on the counter. "I mean, we won't be living together anymore. You'll be alone, and I'm gonna tell you the truth, G, that scares the living shit out of me."

"I'm sure." He takes my hand and encloses it between his. "I'm going to fuck up sometimes, but it's not your mess to clean up. If this is what you want, then so be it."

"Really? Because when I brought it up before..."

"Listen, I've been a head case for the last few weeks. I know that, but I'm good now. I promise. Do what makes you happy, baby girl. I'll be fine." Tossing a grape in his mouth, he comes around the bar and pulls me into a hug. "I love you, Dani. At the end of the day, what I want most is to see you happy. If you're good, then I'm good."

"Dani..." The sound of Lauren's voice calls from a distance.

"I'm not sure I believe you, but we have to end the discussion now, anyway. Come on. You'll love Lauren."

Lauren's sporting her school uniform and a backpack stuffed so full I almost fear it'll pull her down. Standing in the entryway, her gray eyes shine. Smiling, she pulls her hair into a ponytail. "Thomas picked me up and said I should just head straight up. Hope it's okay."

"Are you kidding? Of course, it's okay." I hug her and move to take the backpack off her hands. "This is my bestie, Geoff."

"Nice to meet you," she answers, shifting her backpack off and shaking his hand.

"I've heard great things," he replies.

"So, have I. You're the photographer, right?"

"I prefer highly skilled photo artist, but I guess photographer works too."

Rolling my eyes, I say, "Don't get him started. We were just in the kitchen fixing up some snacks. Hungry?"

"You're joking, right?" She glances at Geoff and back at me. "I'm a seventeen-year-old who just finished four hours of training for a swim meet. *I'm starving.*"

I laugh. "Glad to hear it. G, why don't you head into the kitchen and order a few pizzas while we drop this in Lauren's room for the night?"

"Sounds good to me, baby girl, veggie supreme, and Lauren, what would you like?"

"Pepperoni and sausage with extra cheese and bell peppers. Can you get some cheesy bread too? Extra sauce cups."

"Damn, I guess you weren't kidding about the hunger thing."

She shrugs. "You swim for four hours and tell me if you feel like your stomach is feeding on itself."

Wishing I had her natural ease, I turn toward the hall. "Let me help you get this gigantic backpack to your room."

Leading her to a spare room, I toss her bag on the bed and watch as she sits next to it and slips off her shoes. Her facial swelling has decreased, but there's still a light purple tinge to her cheek.

"Lauren," I say, softly. "I don't want to pressure you, and I certainly don't want to overstep, but if you ever wanna talk about, you know, what happened to you, I'm here. Like I said, I don't want to make you uncomfortable, but I just thought you should know I've been there. Someone I used to trust hurt me, too. I know Sebastian will destroy anyone who ever lays a finger on you, and I get that you have Alana to confide in, but I just wanted to offer my shoulder as well."

She smiles. "Thanks, I'll keep that in mind."

Nodding, I turn to the door. "I'll let you get settled. We'll be in the kitchen when you're ready to join us."

"Dani?"

"Yeah." I stop in the doorway and look over my shoulder.

"Thank you, really. You don't know how much this means to me. Not just your offer to talk, but this... being here. I've waited a long time to be a part of Sebastian's other life. What I mean is... he has his life with me and then he has his life without me. I feel like now, because of you, I'm finally getting to be a part of that other side of him. It's a small part, but it means more to me than you'll ever know."

"I know exactly what you mean, and there's no need to thank me. I wouldn't be doing any of it if I didn't want to."

****

"Chris or Liam Hemsworth?" Lauren asks, stuffing another bite of pepperoni and sausage in her mouth.

"Chris," I answer, certainly. "Liam's too pretty boy for me. Any man who takes longer to get ready than I do is a no go."

"I'd make a sandwich." The corner of Geoff's mouth turns up with his reply. "Hemsworth on rye with just a hint of me."

Unable to control my laughter, I toss a throw pillow at him. "That's not how the game goes, nympho! It's called would you, rather? Pick one."

"Oh, that's how we're playing it these days? Fine, this question's only for Dani. Sorry, Lauren, but you'll understand when I'm finished."

She shrugs in response, taking a large gulp of Coke.

"Alright, baby girl. Time to fess up. Would you rather… Kyle Marcum *or* Sebastian Black?"

"Oh, look at that," Lauren says, looking down at her glass. "I just ran out of Coke."

"You stay," I insist. "I'll get it."

"No. No." She stands. "Please, let me. As much fun as this is, I'd much rather not listen to you gush about how good my brother is or isn't in bed."

I laugh. "Fair enough."

Geoff waits for her to get out of earshot before rounding on me again. "So… who do you choose? Sebastian or Kyle? You're the last woman alive, and you can only choose one of them to save the species with. Who is it?"

"I'd like to know the answer to that myself," Sebastian says, his voice sending shutters of longing through my spine.

Turning, my gaze meets his. The smirk on his lips letting me know he feels everything I'm feeling and more.

"When did you get here, hotshot?" I ask, grabbing hold of the couch and pulling myself from the floor. I place my hands on his hips and smile. "I thought you were going to be late tonight."

"Avoiding the question, I see." He winks and smiles at me. "You're an apt student, Ms. Stevens."

"Nah, I just had a master teacher." He leans forward to kiss me and I push him away, gesturing to the face mask I'm wearing. "I don't want you to get gooped."

"That's what showers are for," he replies, grabbing my ponytail and sealing his lips over mine.

Gently pushing his tongue into my mouth, he envelops mine. His hands move to my hips, squeezing possessively, and sending shock waves of want through my body. No longer concerned with my facemask, I step onto my tiptoes, deepening our kiss. My hands find the silk strands of his hair, my fingers tangling around his locks and holding tight. Sliding his hands to my thighs, he grabs my knees. He lifts my legs around his waist, my body completely his for the taking. Slumber party be damned; I'm lost in him. Moaning against his lips, I give in to the heat, taking me over from head to toes. Nibbling my bottom lip, he slides his hand up my shirt, resting it on the arch of my back.

"Oh, God! I should've made a few more glasses," Lauren says.

Laughing, I pull away from Sebastian and turn to her. "Sorry."

"Hey, little sister. Having fun?" He sets me down, leans in close, and whispers. "I think that was all the proof he needed, don't you?"

Still overly heated from his touch, his hot breath on my neck causes goosebumps to devour my body.

"I was having a blast until you showed up," she jokes. "Now I think I'm scarred for life."

"Good. Maybe it'll turn you off boys for a while. I've yet to meet this latest one." He cuts his eyes in her direction, a threatening cloud changing them from gray to black.

"And you won't," she challenges. "At least not until I can trust you to drop your overprotective bullshit."

"Fat chance." I plop down on the couch. "Want some pizza, hotshot? We have plenty."

He looks at Lauren, up at the television, and back at me. "What is this nonsense and what's he doing to that pig?"

"Don't tell me you've never seen *Varsity Blues*."

"Can't say that I have, nor can I say that I want to. I grabbed dinner at the office. I'm just going to bury myself in work for a while. You three have fun."

"Did I piss him off?" Lauren asks, settling back on her pillow mountain.

"Nah... don't worry about it. He's been a little off for days. Honestly, the only time I've seen him is if..." Rethinking my sentence, I look up at her. "You know what, never mind. Just know it's not you. Things have been weird since he had that work crisis over the weekend."

"Oh, right... the work crisis," she replies, her face becoming even more sullen than it was before. "I think I'll head to bed. Thanks for tonight."

"You don't need to thank me, and you don't have to go to bed if you don't want. We'll probably be up for hours yet."

"Thanks for the offer," she gathers her plate and glass, "but I'm actually pretty tired. These extra hours of swimming are taking their toll. I'll see you in the morning."

Silence falls over us as we watch her disappear into the kitchen.

"What was that about?" Geoff asks.

Shrugging, I turn to him. "Not sure. She had her own things to get through over the weekend. Maybe she's just not done processing it yet."

"Could be." He pulls himself onto the couch and puts my feet on his lap. "Still... it seemed like she knows something you don't."

Trying not to focus on how right he is, I pick up the remote. "Suddenly, I'm not feeling big on James Van Der Beek. What do you say to a little *Mean Girls* instead?"

"I say *Mean Girls* is always on the table," he answers, silently accepting my need for a change of subject.

****

"So, Lauren, did you have a good time?" We're in the car dropping Lauren off so that we can meet the movers at the apartment that will cease to be mine and Geoff's after today.

"I had a great time." She looks up from her phone. "Thanks again for having me."

"Like I told you multiple times last night and again this morning, there's no need to thank me."

"Sorry." She turns her attention back to her texts.

"There's no need to apologize, either. I just wish you would've been able to spend a little more time with this guy as well." I squeeze Sebastian's hand. "You've been working so much lately."

I could be imagining things, but I'm almost positive I see a knowing glance exchanged between him and Lauren.

"You've got me for the entire day today, princess."

"Yeah. Packing... that's how every girl dreams of spending her boyfriend's one day off."

"It's not how I dreamed of spending my Saturday. That's for sure," Geoff replies, taking a sip from the travel mug I prepared for him. "There's this little-known fact... Saturdays are for beauty sleep. You should try it sometime."

"Are you saying I'm ugly, Geoffrey Taylor?" I've dealt with morning Geoff enough to know that the best way to get him out of his mood is to give him a hard time about it.

"You know I'd never say that. Don't twist my words and don't think you're getting off easily. You owe me big for this one. I'm moving my entire life with less that twenty-four hours' notice."

"Again, I'm sorry about that one."

"Like I said, you owe me big."

"Name your price, Taylor."

"Oh no, baby girl. I'm saving this one up. Who knows what the future will bring, but when the opportunity presents itself, you better have your ass ready."

"Go to sleep, pretty one. We'll wake you when we get there," I reply, patting him on the head.

Sinking into myself, I stare out the window. I knew this day would come, but facing it is a different story. Leave it to Walt to take what was once a happy home and reduce it down to nothing. A sickening pain stabs at my chest at the thought of everything we've lost, everything he's taken from us. It was one thing when he was a cancer on my life, but now his malice has infected those around me. Even in death, Walter has stolen life from us. No matter how we try to go on, his ghost remains to haunt us.

Lost in my own thoughts, I hardly notice when the car comes to a stop at the curb in front of our complex. Looking up, I see Lauren still sitting in the seat across from us. Confused, I turn to Sebastian. "I thought we were taking Lauren home."

"You did," she replies.

"Well... yeah... it's not that I don't want you with us or anything. It's just... a lot has happened here. I'm not sure it's the best place for you to be."

"No, Dani, you misunderstood me. *This* is home for me. I live in the penthouse."

"You... *oh*." Realization dawns as the distant memory of running into Sebastian on the stairwell fills my brain. Turning to him, I note the wry smile on his face. "So... that day you knocked me down on the stairs you were..."

"Visiting my sister? That's correct. As for me knocking you down, I believe it was *you* who ran into *me*. For a while, I wasn't sure you were safe to be around. I mean, first you tried to plow me over on the sidewalk, then you sought to bring me down on the stairs... one has to wonder who the hunter was and who was the hunted."

"Ha. Ha." I roll my eyes and exhale. "Why didn't you tell me?"

"I didn't see a reason to. When you and I started this, we agreed it would be a short-term thing. By the time we realized it was more and you met Lauren, you'd already agreed to move in with me. You knew Lauren had an apartment of her own here in the city. What difference did the location make?"

I don't have an answer for him. All I know is that it's one more half-truth, one more lie, to add to the pile of dishonesty between us, because of that it matters.

"I'll be seeing ya," Lauren says, stepping out onto the sidewalk. "Thanks again for having me over. Sebastian, my swim meet is at four on Tuesday. You'd better be there."

"It's in my calendar and my assistant's. I wouldn't miss it." He climbs from the car and places an arm over her shoulders. "Come on, I'll walk you up." Turning back to the car he adds, "I'll be back for you in just a second, princess."

"Just meet me up there," I reply. "I'll have Geoff."

"You're sure?"

I glance over to my still sleepy, but now panicked, best friend. "I'm sure. We need to do this together.

****

*Suffocating.*

That's the only word I know of to describe the way it feels to walk through the door of my soon to be old apartment. Memories of the champagne toast Geoff and I shared on the day we moved in mix with the darker ones of Walt standing in this very doorway with a distant gleam in his eyes. Shuddering, I step over the threshold and into the living room. Everything is the same, but there's a sense of foreboding in the air. It's as though even the building knows that things have changed forever, it has changed us forever, and there's no going back.

It takes three hours to pack my room, and another four to separate what's mine from what's Geoff's in the others. When, at last, the last box has been sealed, Sebastian walks down with the movers. Suddenly overrun with emotion, I plop onto the couch and look around. I hate this place now, but I can't deny the joy it once brought me. Things seemed so bright when Geoff and I moved to the city. A fresh start for a girl who definitely needed one. New York was supposed to be the opportunity of a lifetime. Now, I'm down one job and two friends, and I've gained a handful of traumatic experiences I'm not sure I'll ever recover from.

Throwing himself down beside me, Geoff says, "So, this is it."

Voice shaking, I reply, "I guess so."

"It's the end of an era."

"There's still time for you to change your mind and come with me, you know."

"Baby girl, I love you. When this wears off, I'll have a beautiful home waiting for you," he says, stubbornly.

"Geoffrey Taylor, you're a bitch, but you're my bitch," I reply, hugging him.

"I only call 'em like I see 'em. You two are moving this along at warp speed."

"Just last night, you were all for this. What's changed?"

"I had some time to think about it."

"And…"

Fussing with his hair, he looks at me. "Don't get pissed."

"Why would I get pissed?"

"Because I now see this for what it really is."

"And that would be?"

"Your latest stunt." He pulls at a thread on his jeans, refusing to make direct eye contact.

"My stunt?"

"Dani." He pauses and studies me carefully. "I've known you a long time. I know you cope by not coping. You act out in order to create smaller problems that will distract you from the big ones. It's your pattern. Right now, you have a lot of colossal problems to deal with, so you need a big screw up to keep you from thinking about it."

"Oh, go ahead, G, tell me how you really feel," I huff.

"I just meant—"

"No. You know what, save it! You would do well to worry a little less about my patterns, and a little more about your own. When was the last time you thought about hitting the bottle?"

"Okay." He stands and straightens his clothes. "I'm going to finish packing my shit before this becomes something neither of us can take back."

"I think it's a little late for that," I reply, rolling my eyes.

"I love you, Danielle. Good luck," he says, turning down the hall.

Fuming, I leave my key on the bar and slam the door.

# Chapter 26

*S*ebastian

"How goes the moving in?" William Rush's voice booms through my cell. The hint of amusement in his tone is anything but amusing.

"Fine. She's settling in now. I thought I'd take advantage of the time by catching up. You left a few messages..."

"Damn right I did. Where ya been? It's not like you to drop off the fucking planet."

"I had things to handle."

"Ah... tapping that sweet ass that's now shacking up with you. I get it."

My jaw gives way to the tightness as my teeth grind against each other. Fueled by my rage, I knock back the last of my scotch and clench my hands around the edge of my desk. "Make your fucking point, Rush, and leave Danielle out of it!"

"Whoa... someone's feeling touchy today. Do we need to head back into the sharing circle?"

"You have exactly thirty seconds to say whatever the hell it was you needed to. Don't test my limits. I'm not a patient man on a good day. Today is not a good day."

"Chill, bro. I can see this living together thing is going to do little to help with your bipolar disorder. Okay... so, I have the paperwork ready to go. All that's waiting is your signature. We're good to go on that other matter as well. All you have to do is say the word and I'll send our proposal over. Walter Smith has no notable family to speak of, so it shouldn't be a problem. I can fax that over for you as well if you'd like to double check

213

things first. I've also bought you back out of all your contracts with Princeton, but it ain't coming cheap. Wanna tell me what happened there?"

"No, I don't. Just get me the figures, and I'll pay. Send the proposal. Let's hold off on the other issue. I'm not sure now is the right time."

"What? We've been working on this for years. You finally have your opening and you want to postpone it! What the hell happened to you in the Hamptons?"

"That's neither here nor there. Just hold off. I need some time to think things over."

I can hear him growl, though he's quick to recover. "If you say so, man. Just don't take too long. I'm not sure when another opportunity like this will present itself."

"Send the proposal and I'll look it over," I reply, hanging up the phone. My head fogged over by the reality that something I've wanted so badly for the last ten years may never become a possibility for me, I pour another scotch. Sipping at the smooth amber liquid, I open my desk drawer and pull out the framed picture.

The smiling face of a little girl with red pigtails and bright gray eyes looks back at me. Longing to feel the warmth of that smile settle in over me as I watch her play on the playground or feel her hair tickle my nose as I pull her into the embraces I lacked as a child, I stroke my finger over the frame. I was so close, but I can't move forward now. Not when the woman who birthed me is so fucked up. One more thing Isabelle has taken from me. One more reason to hate her.

Another sip to stop the stabbing pain where my heart should be. Emotions a catastrophic mess for all the world to see, I stare down at the picture again. Ten years old. I remember Lauren at this age, the terror in her eyes when she saw Isabelle again for the first time in two years. The innocence in her voice when she'd asked me if our birth mother would be coming home with us. The confusion on her face as she watched me walk away from her toward my other family... my actual family.

Teagan has never had to deal with anything like that. *Teagan*. It's not the name I would've chosen, of course. I've had a lot of time to stare at this picture and decide on a name worthy of someone so beautiful. *Ava Grace Black*. That's what I would've named her, had I been given the chance. Ava was my neighbor at the little house. She'd save leftovers for me when she had them to spare and was always more than happy to take me in when Isabelle went missing for a few days. Grace is my mother, Emmalyn's middle name.

It's the perfect name for a perfect child, and I'm positive it's what I would've given her had I been given the chance. Teagan Alana Anderson, that's the name she got, and I didn't have a single say. Now I never will. Draining my glass, I pour another. The paperwork was supposed to be filed by her birthday. For once I was going to get to be a part of it, instead of having to live vicariously through photos sent to me by investigators, I hire to track Alana on her visits.

Of course, I could still go through with it. I could say screw the risks and file the paperwork, anyway. It's not like Teagan and Isabelle will ever come close to one another. For that matter, it's not as though they'll ever even know about each other. I could keep Teagan safe, and Isabelle somewhat sane, and I could still get to be the father I've always longed to be. That wouldn't change Alana's reaction, though. She's going to try and take me down when she finds out I've been working against her on this. That's a risk I can't take right now, not with Isabelle so unstable. A relapse from the pathetic woman who birthed me was certainly not in the cards when I began this process. Danielle was supposed to have replaced Alana in all things, but now it's just not possible.

Danielle places her hand on mine, lowering my glass, and sealing my lips with a kiss. Thankful for her perfect timing, I pull her onto my lap. "Almost settled in, princess?"

"Not even close. I'll probably have boxes in that spare room for days." She sighs. "I'm starving, though. Any idea what you'd like for dinner?"

"Hmm... you on a silver platter?"

She laughs. "Feed me well, play your cards right, and I'm sure we can make that happen, hotshot."

"Well, I'm almost done here. Why don't you go slip into something a lot less comfortable and we can go out to celebrate?"

Yawning, she twirls her fingers in my hair. "I'd love to celebrate, but I don't think I have the energy. Can't we just order Chinese and curl up on the couch?"

"Sure." I place the frame back in the drawer. "You go order and I'll be in, in a minute."

"What's this?" She asks, her hand closing on the frame. "Another picture of Lauren?"

I clasp my hand over hers before she has the chance to pull it from the drawer. "It's nothing, princess, just an old photo." Prying her fingers free, I lace our hands together and bend her arm behind her back.

"I wanna see."

"It's nothing special, really." My lips lightly brush against hers. "I thought you said you were hungry."

"Quit trying to distract me." She pulls free. "What's the big deal? It's just a picture, right?"

Exhaling, I close the drawer. "Please don't push this, princess."

Her tone matching mine, she replies, "I don't see anyway else to do it, Sebastian. I know I had a small overreaction about Lauren's apartment, but you must try to understand where I'm coming from. It doesn't take a genius to know that you've made a habit of hiding things from me. I know you're trying now, and I appreciate that. But... Sebastian, when you get so mysterious about things as small as an old photograph, how am I supposed to believe you when it comes to the bigger things?"

"Would it make you feel any better if I told you this was a big thing?"

"Truthfully, it might make it worse. I'm not sure how many more big secrets I can take, but it's better for you to tell me now than for me to find out on my own later. That's when it hurts the most, Sebastian. When I hear it from your family or God forbid Alana."

The irony of the moment isn't lost on me. Of the remaining skeletons in my closet, this is one that no one in Danielle's reach can expose and yet, it will do less damage than the ones those who can get near her keep. Faced with the decision to choose between them, I know it's better to tell her about my plans for Teagan and ease her mind some than to have her digging for information from my mother again... or worse, my father.

"Okay, I'll tell you. Let's get you a drink first." Lifting the photo frame from the drawer and taking Danielle's hand, I lead her from the room. Sitting her on the couch, I pour a glass of Grey Goose and hand it to her.

Trembling, she takes a sip and looks up at me. "You're scaring me a little, hotshot."

I clutch the photo in my hand and sit on the coffee table in front of her. "This is a photo of my daughter, Teagan."

She looks back at me as though she's a small animal staring into the headlights of a car. I watch as she takes another sip of premium vodka, wipes her mouth, and then guzzles the rest of the tumbler down.

Placing the picture on the couch, I run my hands over her knees. "I know you're shocked, but I need you to say something."

"Okay..." Her voice is breathy with the strain of trying to remain calm. Hesitating, she searches my face as though she's expecting me to blow it off as a joke. When I don't, she lifts the frame and studies it. I can see the realization peeking through the haze in her eyes as she takes in Teagan's features. "The eyes... that wasn't a photo of Lauren in the Hamptons, was it?"

"No."

"But you said it was."

"Yes. I know I lied to you, Danielle. I'm sorry that I had to, but I couldn't tell you the truth."

"So, when you said you've never had contact with her, that Alana was basically keeping you from her, that was a lie, too?"

"No, it wasn't. I know this makes little sense—"

"You're damned right it doesn't make sense, Sebastian." She jerks to her feet and pours herself another glass. "You have a child with Alana. I don't like how I found out about it, but I've accepted it. What I don't get is why you'd lie to me about having contact with her, or why you'd tell me that the photo in your beach house was of your sister when it was, in fact, your daughter. Why would you make me out to be an idiot? Does Alana not want me around her? Is that what this is?"

Carefully taking her in my arms, I reply, "No, princess. This has nothing to do with Alana, and I *don't* have any contact with Teagan. I didn't lie to you about the way it all went down. I did, however, refrain from telling you my plan for what comes next. That's the reason I embellished on your assumption in the Hamptons. It's the reason I didn't want you to see this picture tonight..."

"And what exactly comes next?" She asks, her emerald pools staring at me as though she's seeing a new man.

Wishing I could stop being a constant source of disappointment in her life, I run my fingers through her hair. "I had a petition drawn up for visitation rights, but I'm not sure I'm going to go through with it now."

"Huh," she places her hands on my chest and pushes away from me, "when did you decide to fight back?"

"It's something I've been considering for the past few years, but I only moved forward with it a few weeks ago."

"Why now?"

"There had never been a good time before. I thought the right opportunity had presented itself, but now I'm not so sure."

Sending her beverage sloshing over the rim of the glass, she falls back onto the couch. I watch the rise and fall of her chest as she tries to reign in her emotions. Steadying herself with another gulp of liquid courage, she looks up at me and asks, "What changed?"

"A lot of things. For starters, I have a lot going on at work and I'm just not sure petitioning for visitation when I can't prove that I'll be able to follow through with it is a good idea. There's also the matter of the police investigation. It's unwise of me to venture into court proceedings over rights to my child when there's a missing persons investigation out there with my name on it. And then there's Lauren... whether or not I like it, Alana's become somewhat of a role model to her. I'm not sure I can risk their relationship over this. Alana is nothing if not vindictive. You know this all too well."

There are, of course, still omissions to my story, but Danielle will never know the real reason I'm giving up hope on ever having a relationship with my child is because my psychotic, addict of a mother doesn't know how to keep her shit together long enough for the rest of us to lead normal lives. Not that I think my life will ever be normal again after she used me for a bargaining chip. *Fuck my son and give me a place to sleep, scar him for life and give me coke, pay me and he'll suck your dick.*

Biting my cheek to suppress my rage, I look up at her. "Do you understand why I didn't want to drag you into this?"

"I'm not sure that I do," she answers with a dramatic sigh. "Sebastian, this will never work if you can't learn to let me be a part of the team. If I'm going to live here, I need to be part of your decisions. I'm not saying you have to consult me on your every move, but if you've suddenly decided to have a relationship with your kid, that affects me. That's a big thing, hotshot, and it's going to change you. Not to mention, you're only opening the door for more lies by keeping me in dark. I mean, what'd you expect? Did you think I wouldn't be curious why you were flying across country two or three times a year around major holidays? Or maybe you were just hoping I'd be too stupid to piece the pattern together."

Taking her glass and setting it on the coffee table, I sit next to her and wrap my arms around her. Placing a light kiss on her head, I run my thumb over her cheek. "Danielle, I could never think you were stupid. Your intelligence is one of the things I love most about you. I just thought I'd figure it all out as it unfolded. I never intended to keep you in the dark forever. I just didn't want to mention anything when we already have so much to deal with. And I wasn't sure I'd even win. Plus, I didn't want to give Alana any more reason to attack you. There are just so many components. You understand, don't you?"

"Yeah." She sighs and I can hear the doubt in her voice. "I think you should do it, Sebastian. At least as far as my mess is concerned in your decision. I can handle Alana, and I refuse to let you lose anything else because of what happened to Walt. Don't let me be a factor in your decision. Every father should have the chance to know his child. I know it ripped my dad apart that the opportunity was taken away from him for so long."

"This isn't like what happened with your mother and father, Danielle. Teagan has a suitable home. I've had background checks run on her adoptive parents. I have a tail on Alana every time she heads to Colorado, and I have security that monitors her closely without interfering. I'm not worried about her safety. I just... *I just want to know her.* I want her to know me, and I want her to know that I had nothing to do with the decision to give her up."

She smiles and though it's the strained type of smile one gives when they're trying to hold in other emotions; I find it mildly comforting. "I understand. In the end, I know you'll do whatever you want to, but if my drama is really as big of a factor in the decision as you say, then I want you to know it shouldn't be."

"Okay."

"I think I'll take a bath. I'll see you in a little while."

"I'll order dinner, and then I'll join you," I offer.

"No, that's okay." She sits up and places a quick peck on my cheek. "I want to be alone for a bit."

Alone.

The word hangs in the air like a pendulum, counting the seconds of isolation I've caused her. Hating myself for the reality that I'll never be able to give my all to her, I pour another scotch and walk to the kitchen for the Chinese menu. There are some things Danielle will be better off for not knowing about. Isabelle is one of those things.

****

Two o'clock in the morning and I'm awake, cold, sweaty, and alone. I roll onto my side and look for light coming through the bathroom door. Nothing. Danielle is gone. Heart beating franticly, I untangle myself from the bedspread and grab my sweats from the floor. Another fucking nightmare. As long as she's not by my side, they'll never stop. The hall is dark, but when I reach the living room, I can see the dim glow of lights coming from the kitchen.

Nervous anticipation coursing through my body, I stare at her. She's sitting on the counter, her bare ass against the smooth tile. My t-shirt hangs loosely off her delicate shoulder. Her back is arched and her head hangs over something I can't quite see. I clear my throat and stifle my laughter as I watch her jump, sending Kung Pao Chicken flying in the air.

"I didn't mean to scare you, princess." I tear off a handful of paper towels and pass them to her. "Just checking on you."

"I'm fine." She runs the paper towel through her hair, wiping the chicken out of her mahogany strands. "Go back to bed."

"I'm happy to keep you company while you eat, princess. I'm surprised you went to sleep without dinner to begin with."

"Wasn't hungry anymore." Sliding off the counter, she places the Chinese cartons in the fridge and throws away the rest of her mess. "And I'm done, anyway. Go back to bed. I'm just going to watch some Netflix until my food settles."

"I'll watch with you." I place my hand on her wrist, feeling her pulse quicken in response.

"No!" Jerking away, she walks into the living room.

Disappointed, I follow. "Okay. Let me have it. You're pissed. Let's have the fight so we can move on to the much more enjoyable act of making up." I wrap my arms around her waist and kiss her neck.

Shivering against me, she says, "There's nothing to fight about, Sebastian, and I'm not pissed. Just go to bed."

"Is this your version of giving me a taste of my own medicine, princess?" Pulling away, I sit on the couch and cross my arms. "I shut down emotionally, so now you're going to show me how it feels."

Sighing, she slides into the chair and pulls her legs under her. "I'm not doing anything like that, Sebastian. I'm not mad. I'm just... I don't know, processing things, I guess."

"Processing..."

"Yeah."

"How long do you think it will take you to process?"

"I'm not sure. I mean, you were going after visitation rights with your kid and you kept that from me. I know it seems like I'm overreacting, but that's a big thing to keep from someone you love, hotshot. I just can't help but wonder if the secrets get bigger. So far in our relationship, it has been one bombshell after another. Is this the last one, or should I build a bunker now?"

Throat constricting, I swim in the emerald pools of her eyes. I know I should tell her. If anyone will understand, she will. I can't though. Call me a coward, call me whatever you want. Everything in me screams that Danielle knowing about Isabelle is a terrible idea. Slowly walking to her, I kneel before her and place my head in her lap.

"I've told you, princess. My life is messy. I'm trying to clean things up without them tarnishing you. You shouldn't have to live with the shitstorm of my past."

Running her fingers through my hair, she lifts my gaze to meet hers. "I want to, Sebastian. I love you — all of you — the man you are, the boy you were, and everything between. I want you and no one else but you forever. I just don't know how many more secrets I can take."

"You're not leaving me." My grip on her hips tightens to white knuckle force. "I'm not letting you go."

Loosening my grip, she replies, "Then stop pushing me away. Come on. Let's go back to bed."

I carry her to our room, placing her on the bed, and climbing in behind her. Wrapping my arms around her, I listen to the silence stirring between us. I can't give her Isabelle, but that doesn't mean I can't give her anything.

"Danielle..."

"Hmm..."

"I reopened the investigation into Piper's past."

Snorting, she replies. "Doesn't surprise me."

"I'll let you know what I find out."

"Only if it has something to do with me. You may be okay with digging through people's private lives, but I'm not on that level yet. I'm not sure I ever will be. Whatever skeletons she has can stay hidden unless they give us any sign as to why she was running my name through the mud on that phone call."

I nod. "Okay. There's one other thing."

"Go for it."

"Do you remember the conversation we had about your family's property in Napa?"

She turns to face me, looping her arm through mine and nuzzling against my chest. "Of course."

"I'm going after it. Walt's disappearance has left a hole in his company, and I'm taking advantage of it."

"I knew you would, but..."

"What is it, princess?"

"Just be careful. You've already done more than enough when it comes to taking my life back from Walt. I don't want you to risk it all for a company I didn't even know I was supposed to own; let alone one, I wouldn't know the first thing about running."

"I'm excellent at-risk management, princess. You can rest assured. I'm going up there on Tuesday after Lauren's swim meet. Would you like to come?"

"To the meet, yes. To Napa, no. I want nothing to do with that place. Too many memories, too many ghosts."

"I understand," my lips graze over her temple, "more than you know. I can delay my arrival until Wednesday. We could head to L.A. Tuesday night, and you could spend some time with your family. Then we can fly to Vegas for Katie on Friday."

Hesitating, she considers the option carefully. "That sounds great, actually. I may even try to schedule a few meetings while I'm there. If I don't find a job soon, I'm going to go crazy."

"A job? In Los Angeles? Our life is here, Danielle. If you can't find a job in Manhattan, I'll find one for you."

Exaggerated sigh escaping her, she rolls over. "If I've told you once, I've told you a thousand times. I don't want you to do this for me. It's something I have to do on my own. I have a few contacts back home from when I interned in college. It's just a safety net."

"You're not leaving me, Danielle," I whisper again, my words catching in my throat.

# Chapter 27

Danielle

Tuesday comes without a single job prospect in sight, which means my meeting with Yasmin tomorrow is even more important. I just hope the tension between Sebastian and I doesn't distract me too much. Since I found out about his plans for his daughter, things have remained strained, to say the least. It's not even about the fact that he's considering filing for visitation rights. I can fully support him in that. It's that he insisted on hiding it from me, and I know he's hiding something much larger.

We sit together as the car rolls through the busy afternoon streets of Manhattan, but I can't help feeling as though we're miles apart. He aimlessly strokes my hand with his thumb as he replies to the seemingly never-ending stream of text messages coming through his phone. Watching him, I can't help but wonder if he'll ever let me in.

Sebastian's spent a lifetime thinking he wasn't worthy of love, yet he loves as ferociously as anyone can. Still, it's not enough. My stomach aches with the nagging thought that there are parts of Sebastian I'll never be able to reach, parts that impact him at the very core of who he is. I'd thought therapy would help, but as it turns out, we're both so psychotic that our therapist wants to continue getting to know us separately before treating us together.

I haven't missed a session, but I can't say the same thing for him. Whatever went down on Labor Day weekend has him so distracted that he can barely see anything else. Relief flooding over me as the car rolls to a stop, I exhale. We just have to make it through the afternoon with Lauren and we'll be in the air, headed west. A weekend at home with my family will do wonders for my mood, and I'm hoping a slight break away from me will improve his.

Storing his phone in his pocket, he squeezes my hand. "I'm sorry."

Surprised, I stare at him. His face is worn with worry, the handsome set of his chiseled jaw is rough with a five o'clock shadow. Smiling despite the agony I feel, I run my hand over the stubble. "You should've made time to shave. Lauren's friends are going to think you've been on a binger."

Shaking his head, he laughs the first laugh I've heard from him in days. Overwhelmed by the joy I feel, I throw my arms around his neck and pull him close. Returning my embrace, he buries his nose in my hair and whispers, "I'd be lost without you."

"I've been lost without you," I reply.

Scanning my face with his eyes, he takes my hands in his and kisses each one. "I suppose I haven't been much fun lately, have I?"

"I'm trying not to complain."

"There's a lot going on, and I guess I've just been distracted. I'll make it up to you, though, I promise."

"Just so you know, I don't need grand gestures, Sebastian. I just need you."

"Who said anything about grand gestures?" He asks, raising his eyebrows. "I was thinking more along the line of an introduction to the mile-high club."

I smack his shoulder playfully. "Once again, you're assuming sex can fix all the problems."

"Not at all," he responds, helping me from the car. "But it's certainly a start."

Hiding my smile, I follow him up the stairs

****

My ears pop as we ascend into the clouds. Popping a piece of gum in my mouth, I lean back against the couch and watch as Sebastian pours vodka into a crystal tumbler and hands it to me. "You're gonna need this."

"Oh really? Why's that?"

"Because…" he tips the glass to my lips, forcing me to swallow a large gulp. "I need you to do something for me."

"Hmm…" I glance at the bedroom. "Will I like this something?"

Smirking, he follows my gaze. "Probably not as much as I will, but I like where your head's at."

I follow him to the bedroom, my heart rate increasing with every step. The room is just big enough to hold a king-sized bed and small dresser. Feeling the black satin sheets with my palm, I sit on the bed and watch as Sebastian opens the door to the tiny bathroom. Opening the cabinet, he places his shaving kit on the counter and turns to me, causing the familiar crackle of chemistry to charge in the air between us.

"Not that I don't love the view, princess," he says, walking to me with the precision of a skilled hunter tracking its prey, "but I need you in there."

Bending low, he tucks his hand on the small of my back, lifting me into his chest. His other hand placed on my cheek, he kisses me. Sighing, I wrap my arms around him as his tongue licks into my mouth. Lowering my hands to his belt, I work on his buckle. He catches my wrists, feeling the rush of my pulse with his thumb.

"What about that mile-high club promise?" I ask, nipping at his earlobe.

Grabbing my ass, he lifts my legs over his hips and turns to the bathroom. "I've been doing some thinking, and I'm not sure you could handle it."

"Ass." I swat at him playfully.

"Yours is delicious if I remember correctly," he teases.

"Damn you, Sebastian Black. Sexual prowess is one of my super powers. It's not fair that you're better at it."

"Ah, am I?" He places me on the counter and opens the shaving kit.

"Look at you, you're about to shave on an airplane, for Christ's sake! Meanwhile, I'm over here with so many hormones rushing through my veins, I can barely control myself."

The devious smirk he wears so well returning to his face, he takes my hand and runs it over his dangerously hard cock. "Just because I'm better at hiding it doesn't mean you don't drive me crazy. I just know the pleasure of delayed gratification is well worth the wait." Winking, he returns his attention to the counter. "And I'm not planning on shaving anything, Danielle. You're going to do it for me."

Mouth agape, I stare at him, silently begging him to laugh. Instead, he disappears into the bedroom and starts rustling through the dresser. Returning with a bundle of red rope.

"You lost me at the blade, hotshot. What the hell is all of this?"

"This," he unties the bundle, revealing it to be several silk ropes bound by a single knot, "is going to be the thrill of your lifetime."

"You've lost your mind if I think I'm shaving your face with that thing. Let alone on an airplane that can hit *turbulence* at any minute!"

"You'll shave me with this razor, because it gets the best shave." His hand cups the back of my neck, pulling me closer to him. His heated breath brushing against the sensitive skin of my ear, he whispers, "You'll do it now, because I *trust* you."

Trust.

It's difficult for the average person. For people like Sebastian and me, it's damned near impossible. Running my hands over the curved muscles of his arms, I take a moment to look at him. Lips curling into a smile, he places a gentle kiss on my forehead.

"I love you, Danielle, but we can't keep pretending there isn't a wall between us. I know it's not on you. My past is threatening to destroy this just as much as yours. We're stronger than all of that, though. Maybe not alone, but together we are. I think I've found a way to make it happen, but you have to trust me, too."

"Depends. Are you going to finally tell me the truth — the whole truth — about what's been going on with you? There's more to it than the visitation rights, more than the investigation. It goes deeper than Lauren's troubles. I *know* you, Sebastian." Taking his hand between mine, I place it on my chest. "This heart beats for you, hotshot, but it breaks for you, too. *Your scars, my scars, our scars.* Remember that promise? It's a two-way road, Sebastian. You can't take on my burdens without giving me some of yours in return."

Sighing, he pulls his hand away. "I can't let you in on all my secrets. I wish I could, but I can't. It's the only way to keep you safe."

Stroking the lines from his brow with my thumb, I reply, "I *am* safe, Sebastian. As long as I'm with you, I'm safe."

Shaking his head, he runs his hands under my shirt and pulls it over my head. "And I plan to keep you that way."

Sliding his tongue into my mouth, his hands fall between my jeans and my hips. Stabilizing myself by holding his shoulders, I lift my hips from the counter. His lips find my collarbone, brushing softly over my skin. Arching my back, I try to protest, but the words won't come. Before I even know it's happening, my bra is on the floor.

"So, I believe we were about to give me the best shave of my life," he says, lifting the ropes from the counter.

"Hmm... is that what we were about to do? Your sexual politics won't distract me, Black. Eventually, you're going to have to tell me. Now, how am I supposed to give you 'the best shave of your life' when I'm all tied up?"

"Ahh... you're misunderstanding the purpose of Shibari, princess. You'll be tied up, yes, but you'll be restrained in ways unlike you've ever been bound before."

Sex clenching, I imagine the possibilities of his words. At his command, I stand. He runs his fingers through my hair and smiles.

"Have I told you how much this hair cut suits you, Danielle?"

"Actually, I don't think you've said much about it all."

"Well, it does. It also makes things a lot easier for me."

Intrigued, I look over my shoulder. "How is that?"

"You'll see," he replies with a wink. He glides his hands along my arms, positioning them out to the side. Trying not to think of how silly I must look, I wait for his instruction. "Just relax, princes, let me do all the work."

Holding the rope to my back with one hand, he uses the other to run the silk over the top of my breasts and around my back. There's a slight pull, and he's running it under my breast and repeating the process. Another pull and he's bringing the ropes over my shoulders. Pressing lightly, he indicates I can lower my arms. I feel the mild bite of the rope against my skin. Something familiar, yet foreign at the same time. The rope comes together to form a bra of sorts, only my breasts are fully exposed.

Before I have time to really evaluate it, he's back at it with another chord. This time, his finger expertly loops around the rope at my breastbone as he glides the other one through to connect them. Carefully he brings the silk chord around my waist, running it back through itself, and repeating the process in the other direction. When the rope seems to run out, he expertly ties another one on.

He's the artist, and I am the canvas. Pulse quickening, I imagine what I must look like to him. A glimpse of myself in the mirror reveals flushed cheeks and something else... something I didn't know it was possible to see within myself.

A warrior of sorts. Strong, confident, beautiful. The red ropes framing the bronze in my skin as though they were made to be there all along. Smiling, I run my hands over my breasts, feeling the ropes with my palms for the first time.

"Like what you see, princess?" Sebastian asks as he secures my newly fashioned harness with a tie.

"I can't believe I'm actually looking at myself." Running my hands down my stomach, I appreciate the intricate details of every loop and knot.

"I can." He kisses my neck, guiding my hands along the back so that I can explore the work he's done there. "This is the way you've always looked to me. I'm just glad you finally see it, too."

More aware of myself than I've ever been, I clench my thighs together, attempting to fight the flow of blood pooling in my sex.

"Don't fight it, princess."

His hands find my hips, and I realize I'm more aware of him, too. More in tune with where he's going now, knowing he'll stop before I have the chance to take his exploration any further. Turning my head, I offer him my lips. His fingers rolling over my panty-covered clit, he encases his mouth over mine. Weakened by the rush of sensations pulling me in a million directions at once, I moan and sink into him.

"I need to come, Sebastian," I whine breathlessly against his cheek.

"I know you do," he bites my lip, "and you will. First, you owe me a shave. When we land, we'll have dinner with your dad. Then I'll take you home and take you to bed."

"I'm wearing this through dinner?" I ask, suddenly feeling naked and exposed.

"Don't worry, princess. No one will know except for me and you." Lifting my legs over his, he places me back on the counter and hands me the straight edge. "Time for my closeup."

The razor shaking in my hand; I stare at him. "I can't do this, Sebastian. What if I hurt you? Oh, God! What if the plane jerks, I miss, and I hit your..." Tears clog my throat, taking the rest of my sentence with them. It's too risky. He's asking too much from me.

Wrapping his hand over my wrist, he steadies me. "You won't, Danielle. You're the strongest person I know. Just because you took one life doesn't mean you'll take another. I need you to know that. I need you to know that what you did to Walter was an extreme circumstance. It doesn't make you any less of the kindhearted woman I know. The only thing that can do that is you letting this consume you. It's time we tear down the wall, princess." His hands run over the rope corset. "Do you feel safe?"

"Yes."

"Protected?"

"I do."

"Loved?"

"Always," I say without hesitation.

"Good." Thumb and finger on my chin, he tilts my head so that we're eye to eye. "Make me feel those things too, Danielle. That blackness that you feel tugging at your soul? It stole mine a long time ago. Bring back the light, princess. Turn me into the man you deserve and more."

Glancing down at the knife, I ask, "This will do that for you?"

"I don't know, but it's a start. Danielle, I want you to do this for me. I need you to."

"Okay. Show me how."

Nodding, he warms a towel with hot water and instructs me to hold it over his face. I do so until he takes my hands away, and points to the shave cream. Lathering it in my hand, I use the small brush to run it along his face, taking care to cover the smooth contours of his jaw and trying to avoid getting it in his nose or mouth. Sebastian shows me how to hold the blade, so that my fingers are resting in all the best places for stability. Head tilted to the side, he signals that he's ready.

Praying that I'm steadier on the outside than I feel on the inside, I place my hand on his forehead and pull the skin of his jaw tight. Unflinching, his eyes lock on mine when the steel connects with his cheek. Gliding with ease, I scrape the first patch of hair free and wipe the blade clean with a towel. Heart thumping, I reclaim my position at his jaw. His eyes burn into me, soaking in the love I'm giving him and returning it. The ropes pinch just enough to remind me they're there as I twist for a better angle.

Gasping in response, I close my eyes and give into the rush of heat overtaking every inch of my skin. Thrumming with lust — mine or his, I can't tell — I run the razor over him again. Effortlessly, I give his right side a clean shave before repeating the process on his left and above his lip. The weight of the steel does all the work for me, allowing me to settle into a comfortable rhythm that I find surprisingly enjoyable.

Ears filled with the swishing sound of metal on stubble, I watch the hair fall from his face. The weight of my ropes ever present, reminding me that he owns me. The ease with which he offers himself up to me signaling that he is mine. Nipples budding at the thought of the power I have on him, I run my tongue over my lower lip.

Eyebrows lifted in response, his body just as tuned in to mine as mine is his, he asks, "Enjoying yourself, princess?"

"Mmm... very much," I purr, wiping the blade free.

"Good," closing the almost invisible gap between us, he grips my hips, "because this is the hard part."

Holding my calves, he wraps my legs around his waist and leans his head back. Breath hitched in my throat, I stare at the veins protruding from his delicate skin. With a squeeze, he returns his hands to my hips. Stomach lurching, I feel the warmth of his touch against my skin. *It'll be over before I know it. Slow and steady.* Cursing, I lift the steel to his chin.

Knowledgeable of the fact that all it takes is one wrong swipe and I've lost the love of my life forever, I slowly stroke down his neck. Grip tightened around my hips, he flinches. I wipe the blade free and exhale. *I can do this.* Trying to ignore the ringing in my ears, I repeat the process. My limbs feel heavy, my blood goes cold in my veins. Eyes trained on his pulse, I lift the blade to his neck once more. *One scrape.* Breathlessly, I wait for the unstoppable flow of blood. *Two scrapes.* Hot and cold at the same time, I wipe the sweat from my brow. *Three scrapes.*

Relief washing over me, I drop the blade on the floor and lunge at him. The tangy shaving cream burning my tongue, I force my way into his mouth. Locking my legs, I melt against him. He clutches my ass, lifting me and turning me against the wall. Fisting my hair, he holds me in place as he pecks his way down my neck and onto my shoulder. Taking my breast in his hand, he rolls his tongue over my nipple. So full of need I feel I might burst, I toss my head back. Ignoring the knock at the door, Sebastian carries me to the bed and sets me down. Starving for him, I watch as he pulls his cock free from his trousers.

"Sir, we're landing soon," Thomas says, knocking on the door once again.

"Dammit," Sebastian growls, running his hands through his hair in frustration. "Okay. We'll be out in a second." Pulling his pants back on, he walks to the bathroom and returns with my jeans and blouse. "Delayed gratification it is, princess."

Staring at him in disbelief, I put my top on. I'm not sure how much more build up I can take before exploding. Stopping me before I can pull my jeans on, Sebastian places a vibrating thong on the bed.

"You're wearing this to dinner as well. It completes the outfit, don't you think?"

Shifting my eyes from the red thong to him, I watch as he places the remote in his pocket and winks.

If I make it through dinner without ripping my clothes off and throwing myself on the table in front of him, it'll be a miracle.

****

The Spot is exactly as it's always been: bright, cheerful, and homey. The smell of cheeseburgers engulfing my nostrils, I try to play cool as I lead Sebastian to the crew's usual table. Although he claims no one will know I'm wearing the rope corset, I can feel the burn of the silk against my flesh. The knowledge of it only reminds me that in his pocket, Sebastian literally holds the key to what will undoubtedly bring down every inch of what little resolve I have left. Before I have time to put too much thought into how I'll maintain any sense of normalcy through this dinner, I'm sandwiched between Charlie Hammon and Elliot Brinkley.

"It's a Dani-sized sandwich! Who wants one?" They shout ritualistically.

"Don't you guys think I'm a little old for this?" I shout.

"Never," Elliot laughs, ruffling my hair.

"Knock it off guys," my dad says, pulling me into a hug. "Welcome home, mi bella," Thanks for getting her here safely, Sebastian."

"My pleasure." Sebastian shakes my father's hand and pulls my chair out for me. "I'm only sorry I won't be able to be around much. If it weren't for having to head north for a meeting tomorrow, I'd offer to take you and the lovely Bernadette to dinner."

"And risk the wrath of my mother?" Grinning, Daddy cuts his eyes at me. "Is he really that brave or just crazy?"

"Maybe just a tad of both." I laugh.

The words have barely left my mouth when my panties ignite with vibrations so extreme I gasp and jump. Sebastian's hand slips out of his pocket and the sweet torture stops.

"You okay?" my dad asks, stabilizing me.

"Fine." I cut my eyes to Sebastian. His public face is in full force, giving away no emotion. A storm of lust burning behind the dark gray of his pupils, his eyes tell a different story. Shivering under his gaze, I take my seat and turn back to my dad. "Just a chill."

"You're sure?"

"Absolutely, so have you told Nonna I'm home yet?"

"She wants us to come for dinner before I head to the base tomorrow."

"Works for me. I'll probably go when I get out of my meeting with Yasmin. I want to catch some sun at the beach, maybe squeeze in a little rollerblading."

Sebastian curls his finger in my hair. "Just be careful, princess."

Catching me rolling my eyes, he presses the magic button through his jeans. Gritting my teeth, I clutch my chair. "So, where's Bernadette?" I ask, trying to remain casual.

"I'm right here, sugar. Welcome home, Dani!" Order pad in hand, she smiles down at me. "I was 'round back when you guys came in. Has anyone taken your order yet?"

"You're on the night shift now?"

"Pulling a double."

Not caring about the grease stains on her uniform, my dad pulls her onto his knee and rubs her shoulders. Seeing him so happy melts something inside of me, and my cheeks ache from smiling so hard.

Winking at me, Daddy says, "Poor thing. She's been working doubles for a week now. They really could use an extra pair of hands around here if you know of anyone who needs the work."

"Well... at the rate I'm going, maybe I should put in an application," I reply glumly.

"Not going to happen," Sebastian says, sternly.

My dad only glances at him for a brief second before agreeing. "You're bright, talented, and young. No career worth having happens without a few setbacks. You'll get there, kid. Just don't give up."

"Trust me, sugar," Bernadette adds. "No matter how desperate you get; this is the last place you wanna be."

"She wouldn't have to be desperate if she'd let me intervene." Hiding his annoyance, Sebastian flips a menu open.

"Well, I personally think it's admirable to do this on your own, Dani," Charlie commends me. "I think I speak for the rest of the crew when I say we're proud of you for not using your connections."

"Absolutely," Elliot adds.

"Thanks guys." My smile warrants another jolt of vibrations to my clit, this one sending my knees to the table.

Catching his silverware, Daddy looks up at me. "Are you sure you're okay, mia bella ? You're acting awfully strange."

"I'm fine. Is there a draft?" I cut my eyes threateningly at Sebastian, who smiles behind his menu.

"Not that I can feel," Daddy replies. "Do you want my seat?"

"No, I'll be okay. Any chance you can take a break and have dinner with us, Bernadette?"

"Afraid not." She kisses my dad's cheek and stands, "I'm surprised they haven't already been over here for me. "What's everyone having? Extra fries if you make it quick and easy."

We order enough cheeseburgers, fries, and shakes to go around and pass back our menus. Leaning forward to check the ketchup bottle, I notice that my father's eyes are still focused on Bernadette even as she rounds the counter. Grateful that he has someone, I loop my arm through Sebastian's and place my head on his shoulder. He leans down and kisses the top of my head.

# Chapter 28

*Sebastian*

Poised on my bike, I watch Danielle say goodbye to her father and the rest of his crew. The sun shining through her black blouse offers just enough light to reveal the red of the ropes she's wearing. Cock twitching at the thought of what I have planned for her, I kick start the bike. Hugging her dad one last time, Danielle turns to me. Her smile hits me directly in the chest. *Fuck the plan. I'm devouring her as soon as I get a chance.*

"Ready to go, princess?"

"More than you know," she answers, climbing behind me and putting her helmet on.

"You're asking for it." Switching the remote in my pocket to on one last time, I pull from the curb. Squealing, she wraps her hands around me and digs her nails in my chest.

Coasting down the one-way street leading to my waterfront property, my excitement builds. Thoughts focused on how far I've come, I look at the sandstones. Hitting the button to open the garage, I park next to my DBS. Grip loosened, Danielle melts against me. Taking her hands, I help her off the bike and hold her trembling body up as I step off. Turning off her vibrating panties, I pull the helmet off her. Sweat coated hair sticks to her pink cheeks. Tears streaming down her face, she looks at me.

"I can't wait any longer, Sebastian."

"You don't have too, princess." Placing the helmet on the back of my bike, I hit the garage door button.

As it creaks to a close, I seal my mouth over hers, tasting her cherry lip gloss as my tongue rolls over her bottom lip. Her fingers fly to my hair, her grip demanding as she holds my head in place. Lifting her onto the hood of the Aston Martin, I undo the button on her jeans and help her wiggle out of them. Sending buttons flying around the garage, I rip her blouse open.

Hardened pink nipples begging for my attention, I cup her breasts in my hand. She arches her back at my kiss, her hands diving for my shirt. Shrugging my arms free of the sleeves, I lower her to her back. Desire fueled by the aroma of her, I pull the red triangle to the side. There's nothing the like the sight of Danielle's dripping wet pussy. Unable to control myself, I run my tongue along the length of her cleft. Gasping, she pulls my hair.

"You want more, princess?" I tease.

"I want it all," she begs.

"As you wish."

Kneeling, I wrap my arms under her sweet ass and bring my hands over her hips to hold her steady. Lips encasing the fleshy nub of her clit, I suckle her into my mouth. Writhing beneath me, she begs for more. Grip tightened, I hold her in place. The sweet silk of her orgasm on my taste buds, she convulses around me. Finger hooked on her G-spot, I coax her to finish. Cock throbbing, I stand and drop my pants to the ground.

"Please, Sebastian," she begs, tears leaking from her eyes.

"Move to the front of the car, Danielle."

Hungry eyes watching the entire time, she follows my command. Turning her around, I bend her over the hood, positioning one hand on each side until her chest rests flat against the metal. Parting her legs with my knees, I slip behind her. With one hand around her waist, I run the length of my cock between her slickened folds. Willingly surrendering, she tosses her head back against my chest. Wrapping my hand around her throat, I hold her there.

"Sebastian," she moans.

"I've got you, princess," I promise, kissing her temple.

The car shakes as I increase my tempo. My head rolls against her G-spot, causing her to scream. The roughness of her walls enveloping every inch I offer; I drive into her. Unable to contain her pleasure any longer, she quakes around me. Her fingers going white as she holds herself steady on the hood, she matches my rhythm. Cock swelling under the pressure of my release, I bring my fingers to her clit, massaging in fast circles.

"Fuck me!" She shouts, her body tensing as she floods my cock.

"Come for me, Danielle." I encourage, pressing harder.

She loses all control. Trembling from head to toe, she falls against the hood. Gripping her hips, I chase my orgasm. Barely coming down from her last high, she matches my pace again. Pussy clenching my cock like it's the last time I'll ever own her, she comes undone again. Cock throbbing, I follow suit, spilling everything I have into her. Breathless, I dig a knife from my pocket and cut her free of the corset, running my fingertips along the indentions in her skin.

"You have rope burn. Does it hurt?"

"Not too bad," she answers, turning to face me and wrapping her legs around mine. "Besides, it was worth it."

"Is that so?" Laughing, I place her on the hood of the car.

"Are you kidding? Hot sex on top of a hot car. What's not to love?"

"What would I do without you?" I ask, nuzzling into the nape of her neck.

She strokes her fingers through my damp hair. "Luckily, you'll never have to find out."

"I hope that's true," I whisper.

**\*\*\*\***

"It's official," Danielle says, placing her water glass on the nightstand and crawling back into bed. "We've had sex in every inch of this house."

"That sounds like a challenge to me," I tease, pulling her closer. "There are still the stairs, the pool, the living room fireplace—"

"Okay, smartass. I get your point." Locking her fingers with mine, she looks up at me. "Are you sure you have to do this thing tomorrow?"

"I'll be back before you know it."

"I wish that were true."

Kissing her head and moving her hair out of the way, I place her cheek on my shoulder. "Now I have a question for you?"

"I don't know if I'll see him or not, Sebastian. That's what you want to know, isn't it? If Kyle's on my agenda for the week?"

Swallowing, I weigh my words. "I know I can't keep you from him, Danielle. God knows I would if I could, but you're strong willed. If I push, you'll only pull away from me and fall back to him. I understand that now. So, I'm only going to say this once. If you find yourself in his bed, you can stay there. I won't fight him for you again. I love you and I want you to be happy, but I don't share what's mine."

Breaking free, she climbs on top of me and stares directly into my eyes. I can feel myself tensing beneath her touch and loathe washes over me. I hate being weak. Even for her, I can't handle the emotion. Gritting my teeth, I wait for her to speak.

"What would you say if I gave you the same threat regarding Alana?"

Leaning my head against the headboard, I reply, "I'd say you have nothing to worry about. Alana and I have been over for a long time. You fucked him just yesterday."

"It wasn't yesterday," she says, sadly.

"And yet the sting still feels just as fresh. I won't bring it up anymore, but I will be watching."

"Sebastian, look at me." She cups my face in her hands. "Really look at me. I can't let go of Kyle again. I won't. But I can promise you I'm yours." Gliding my hands over the mounds of her breast and down her flat torso, she continues, "Every inch of my skin longs for your touch. My lips ache for your kiss. You own me, hotshot. Even when I was with him, it was you I needed. Since the moment our eyes met in that boardroom, it's been you. Kyle knows how to cure my psychosis, but you know how to feed my soul." Her hips grind, driving her slickened pussy over my hardening cock. "Here in this bed with you is where I belong. This is where I matter most. This is where I feel complete. Everything in me belongs to you, Sebastian Black. Everything I have is yours. Take it."

Rolling her to her back, I wrap myself between her legs and sink into her, giving her all my fears and insecurities the best way I know how. By the time we've finished she's climaxed three times, and I choose to believe we're going to be okay. Cradling her close, I bury my nose in her hair and drift off to sleep.

# Chapter 29

Danielle

Standing on the patio, I let the smell of saltwater wash over me, bringing the most assured calm along with it. I could spend the rest of my days here. Maybe Sebastian could too. We could move Lauren out here and enroll her in a private school somewhere in the city. I could easily get a job here with the contacts I made while interning for Yasmin. We could start over; leave New York and all the trouble it's caused each of us behind.

Closing my eyes, I feel the rustle of the wind through my hair. My nipples peek through the fabric of Sebastian's button down as the coolness nips its way around my body. *It's a delightful dream.* Sighing, I carefully open the door and tiptoe into the bedroom. The perfection that is a sleeping Sebastian greets me. My sex humming with deeply rooted desire, I take in the sight of his exposed torso, the sheet resting just over his pelvis covering what I know to be a pleasure inducing cock endorsed by Aphrodite herself.

Unable to help myself, I crawl next to him, running my hands in his jet-black waves. Keeping his eyes closed, he pulls me tight against him. The feel of his heartbeat against mine controlling my thoughts, I crawl on top of him and nuzzle against his neck. His cock jolts in response, smacking against my ass and causing me to giggle.

"Don't go," I whisper.

"I have too." He brushes his lips over my ear. "It's the last piece to put you back together. I won't rest until it's finished."

"I'm as complete as I'll ever be. Right here. In this moment. With you."

Flipping me onto my back, he positions himself between my legs. Our eyes meeting, I can see the emotion swarming behind his charcoal irises. "If I knew how to suspend time, I would. We'd stay here forever — wrapped in each other — without a care in the world."

"Mm... sounds wonderful."

"It does," he kisses me gently, "but life doesn't work that way, princess. We can't wish the problems away, but I can fix them. Let me fix this, Danielle. Let me do the only thing I know how. I'll never be able to take away the pain or erase the scars, but this... *this* is what I was made for. If you don't want to run the company, it's fine. We'll sell it. Just let me win it back for you."

"Okay." Unable to say no when he's bearing his heart to me, I agree. "Just promise you'll be careful. If any red flags go up with the investigation, you'll stop and come right back to me."

"Detective West has no way of knowing anything about this. It's not exactly an on the books kind of meeting."

"That doesn't help ease my worry."

Goosebumps rising over my skin with his touch, I go lapse as he runs his hand down my body and cups the back of my knee. "Then let me fix that, too."

****

"Dani!" Yasmin beams, pulling me in for a hug. "It's been too long. I'm glad you called."

Leaving a cushion between us, I sit next to her on the couch. As usual, Yasmin looks immaculate in a white dress that shows her tiny waist and heels that only add to the length of her model thin legs. Pulling my sweater a little tighter over my full breasts, I turn to her. "It has been a while. I don't suppose you'd consider opening an office in Manhattan?"

"Are you kidding? I get enough of my fill of that garbage heap during fashion week. I need sunshine and fresh air."

"Even though you live in the smog capital of the United States?"

"Minor oversight," she laughs, taking her tea from her assistant. "How's the Big Apple treating you, anyway?"

"Terrible. That's why I'm here, actually."

"Oh?" I watch nervously as she places her teacup back on the saucer and sets it on the coffee table. Straightening her skirt, she slips off her shoes and pulls her feet under her. "What's the problem?"

"Paul fired me. He said I wasn't a team player."

"You? The girl who showed up to work thirty minutes early every day for two years with Starbucks in tow for the entire office?"

I nod. "It's a long story. Anyway, I can't say I was terribly sad to go. I mean, I learned a lot from P.E.S. and I'm thankful for that, but lately I've just been feeling like maybe there's more to all this."

"I'm not sure I follow."

"You know how I was volunteering at the UCLA Santa Monica Hospital before you brought me in here? The job was nothing more than copying flyers about various community outreach programs and distributing them around town, but it was a million times more rewarding than what I've been doing lately. All the club openings — the drunken girls stumbling out the door and barely missing my shoes when they puke — it's not for me. I want to do more. I want it to matter more."

"I see." Running her hand through the honey colored silk of her hair, she asks. "How can I help?"

"Well, even though your clientele is about seventy-five percent fashion, that other twenty-five percent is pro bono work you do for charities. That's the kind of job I want. I want to work more with accounts that matter. I'll start off at ground level again if I have to. I understand that I have to pay my dues. I just want to do something that makes a difference."

"Of course, I fully understand. That's why I started the pro bono work to begin with."

Focusing intently on her, I reply, "I'm glad you see where I'm coming from, because I was hoping you could put me in touch with one of your contacts in the city who might be looking for someone..."

"You want me to give you a leg up?" She laughs and takes a sip of her tea to recover. "I'm sorry. I just assumed that would be the last thing you'd need. I've been following your progress in New York, little prodigy. You're dating Sebastian Black now, correct? Couldn't he put you in touch with your pick of the litter? Why would you bother knocking on my door?"

Fighting past the annoyance settling in my cheeks, I answer. "I'd rather do this without him."

Her eyes flash with the kind of understanding only a powerful woman can give. "Ah. Well, at least I know everything I taught you is still in there. Never owe a man your career, otherwise, you'll owe him for the rest of your life."

"Exactly. Which is the last thing I want, so..."

"I wish I could help. I really do, but I don't know of anyone looking at the moment. Give me a few days, and I'll see what I can come up with. How's that sound?"

"It's the best offer I have," I joke.

Smiling, she puts her shoes back on. "Glad to hear it. You could always come back here, you know? I'd gladly find a place for you."

Thoughts turning to the sound of the waves crashing on the shore and the sight of the sun dancing across Sebastian's sleeping face, I allow myself to dream momentarily.

"I'd love to," I reply. "Really. I would, but my life's in New York now. I owe it to myself to stick around for a bit and see what happens next."

Another knowing flash in her eyes, she nods. "So, maybe you haven't held on to *everything* you learned from me. I'll check around and get back to you by Friday. How's that sound?"

"Sounds perfect! Thanks, Yasmin," I lean over and hug her, "and for the record, I remember every piece of wisdom you bestowed. Sebastian's not like Brian, though. He has nothing to gain by destroying my career, but I have everything to gain by giving him my heart."

Her face sullen, she stares at me for a few minutes. "For your sake, I hope that's true, Dani. I really do. Just promise me you'll watch out for yourself."

"Always. I'm going to make you proud, Yasmin. I can promise you that much."

"I don't doubt you for a second." She leads me to the door. "I'll be in touch."

****

A perfect sixty-three degrees and sunny afternoon in Venice Beach. Rolling to a stop, I sit on one of the concrete barriers separating the beach from the sidewalk. It's been years since I've rollerbladed the boardwalk. Sometime around my junior year in high school, I decided I was too cool to fight the hordes of tourists and gave it up. Still, everything about this day feels right. *Almost.*

Without giving it a second thought, I pull my phone from my back pocket and hit the speed dial. It only takes two rings before he answers in a rough, groggy voice. "Well, if it isn't Mick Jagger. Look who's suddenly not too busy to take my calls."

"Funny. When was the last time you called me, exactly?"

"Okay. So, you've got me there. What are you doing?"

"Recovering. How about you?"

"Same. I'm in Venice."

I can hear the squeaky springs of his mattress shifting beneath his weight. "Just couldn't stay away, could you?"

"What can I say? Your raw masculinity sucks me in every time." Despite trying hard not to, I burst into a fit of giggles.

"Seriously. Standup comedy. You should think about trying it."

"Don't be a dick. Are you coming out or not?"

Though I can hear him opening and closing his dresser drawers, he pretends to be affronted. "I don't remember being invited."

"I'll see you at our spot in say fifteen?"

"Make it thirty. I need to shave."

"Oh, come on, *Miss Priss*, since when have you ever cared about grooming?"

"Since that fucking publicist you used to work for made us see an image consultant."

"What?" Forgetting where I'm at, I jump to my feet in shock. The moment sets my rollerblades in motion, and I'm on my ass before I can even comprehend it. "Ouch! Dammit."

The usually crowded sidewalk is blessedly empty because of it being the middle of the day on a Wednesday, and I'm able to get back up before too many people notice.

"What the hell was that?" Kyle demands.

"Nothing. I lost my balance. Why is Paul forcing you to see a stylist? There's nothing wrong with your style. Devil may care works well for you, my friend. It always has."

Yelling over the sound of running water, he replies, "Since he convinced the guys we'd never make it mainstream unless we cleaned it up a little. On everything, sexy, if it were up to me, we'd drop him. He wasn't our first choice to begin with. I ran into your dad, who told me about your internship. The rest of the band wasn't thrilled about going with someone whose main portfolio was built on socialites and the nightclubs they frequent. It took a lot of begging and bribery to get them to agree to that first meeting."

"Kyle..." No amount of will can help me finish the rest of that sentence. He doesn't have to admit it. We both know the only reason he went through all that trouble was to reconnect with me.

"I'll see you soon, sexy."

Caught in a tangled web of my own emotions, I roll toward the frozen treats stand next to the skate park. It's here that I spent countless afternoons waiting for Kyle to finish work and catch a few waves with me. Ordering a Cherry Pineapple Big Stick, I settle at a picnic table and stare out onto the beach. The very grains of sand reek of memories. *Kyle and me getting our tattoos. When he kissed me under that palm tree and told me he loved me for the first time. The day my UCLA acceptance letter came, and Kyle brought me here to open it for me when I couldn't do it for myself.*

I don't want to hurt him, but at this point, it's inevitable. Sebastian's in the very blood that runs through my veins, the addiction I'll never be able to shake. As badly as I need Kyle, my ache for Sebastian is a thousand times more. In the end, I can only hope Kyle understands. Not wanting to deal with the trauma of my love life, I open the e-reader app on my phone and dive into the newest romance novel.

I'm just getting to the good part when a pair of calloused hands wrap around my face. Stunned, I scream.

"Calm down, sexy." Kyle laughs. "It's just me."

"You ass!" Slapping him, I close the app and lock my phone screen. "You nearly gave me a heart attack."

"Book porn that good? I've been standing behind you for at least five minutes."

Taking a gigantic slurp from my second Big Stick of the day, I feign ignorance. "Who says it was book porn?"

Clasping my hand in his, he guides my popsicle to his mouth, bites half of it off, and winks. "Ah... I just know you that well."

"Whatever, you don't know me as well as you think, Kyle Marcum." I rip my hand away from his and slurp my Popsicle once more. "The girl you knew is long gone."

"Oh really? Well, I'm willing to bet the woman you are would still love every last one of the dirty things I can do to you with that Big Stick just as much as that girl did."

Laughing despite myself, I watch him peel off his denim jacket. His tautly toned arms bulging from a white tank top as he clutches the edge of the table and sits across from me. "Maybe she would, but I can also guarantee she'd hate the yeast infection even more." I run my hand over his stubbly face. "I'm glad you didn't shave. I've always liked your scruff."

He shrugs, and I decide there's no point in pretending. Not with Kyle.

Head turned to the sky; I inhale the fragrance of the sea and turn my gaze back to him. "Why'd you come looking for me, Kyle?"

"Umm... you asked me to," he says, avoiding the actual heart of my question.

"You know what I mean."

"What can I say, sexy? I missed you."

"Have you ever asked yourself if we would've made it? I mean, even if I hadn't caught *her* on your couch that day... do you think we really could've had something?"

Stroking circles over my wrist with his thumb, he looks at me. "I think we still can."

I shake my head. "I'm with Sebastian, Kyle. Whatever we had or could've had. It's over. I love him. I live with him. It's him."

"You live with him, huh?"

Glancing out at the sun's reflection on the water, I say, "It's new."

"You don't say." He cups my chin in his hand and turns my head back toward him. "Dani, can you honestly say you don't feel anything when we're together?"

"Kyle—"

"No. No excuses or reasoning your way out of it. Do you feel anything at all when you're with me?"

"I feel a million things when I'm with you, Ky, but that doesn't matter. What I feel when I'm with him is so much more. You need to walk away from me before I destroy you."

"You don't get it, sexy. I've had my heart obliterated by you once before. I don't know if you can do any more damage or not, but I know you're the only one who can repair it."

"Ky, listen to me. I need you in my life. I didn't realize just how true that was until you were standing right in front of me again, but I do. I'm selfish. If I could have him and you, I would. It's not possible, though, and because of that; we can never be *DaniandKyle* again. You're not my guy, and I'm not your girl. Whatever we were, it's over. It's been over for a long time. Find some hot chick with a great personality and let yourself be treated the way you deserve."

Revealing a gorgeous dimple, he smiles and brings his hand to my cheek. "He's not the one for you, sexy. I know you think he is right now, but he's not. When you realize it — and one day you will — I'll be right here waiting for you. Until then, there's no reason for me to even think about finding someone else. I'd have nothing left to give her. You took it all ages ago and for the life of me, I've never been able to get it back."

Getting lost in his watery blue eyes, I sigh and push his hand away. "Dammit. Today wasn't supposed to be about this. Today was supposed to be about recovering. Isn't that what you said? Let's have some fun. What do you wanna do?"

"Oh, I think you already know what I want, but like I said, I'll wait. Did you bring shoes, or are you all blades?"

Forgetting I'm still in my rollerblades, I look down. "My shoes are in the car."

"So, let's go get 'em and see what kind of trouble we can get into."

# Chapter 30

*Sebastian*

"Was there any trouble?" I ask, the crisp evening air biting against my neck as I step from the car.

"None was reported," Thomas replies. "She met him at the boardwalk, they walked around for a while, and eventually played volleyball on the beach. Seemed innocent enough."

"Good. Maybe he's decided to take my warnings seriously. So, listen, I'm not sure exactly what we're walking into here. From what I gather, the Whitmores backed Walter on a few risky investments involving the orchard. Apparently, he didn't exactly come through. It would all be pretty standard if not for Jacob."

"Jacob Whitmore. The black sheep turned last living heir of the modern day Kennedyesque family. I went over the file you gave me. I'm ready for whatever he's got coming." Reassuring me, he pats the gun in the holster he wears under his jacket. "Just give me a clean shot and get the hell out of there as fast as you can."

We're met at the door by a butler who leads us to a large formal living room. Not unlike the home I grew up in, this house is filled with priceless antiques and family heirlooms. Sitting at a grand piano positioned prominently in the corner, Jacob Whitmore doesn't even acknowledge our presence. I can see the cords of his earbuds running down the sides of his face. His hands hover over keys that he seems almost afraid to touch. Bobbing his head to what appears to be a highly chaotic beat; he sways from left to right.

Mumbling to himself, the butler walks over to him and taps his shoulder. "Dammit, Nyles! What've I told you about fucking sneaking up on me like that?" He jumps to his feet, crashing the piano bench against the wall with his outburst. Animatedly waving his hands through the air, he grinds his teeth. "Do you want to die, Nyles? Is that what it is? Do you have a fucking death wish?"

"No, sir." His butler bows in a disgusting display of inferiority. "I'm sorry, sir. I only thought you should know your guests have arrived."

"Guests? What guests?"

"Mister Black and his associate, sir." Nyles motions in our direction. "You arranged to have them for dinner, sir. The cook is completing things now."

Jacob turns to us, his wild blonde hair whipping around his face in the haphazard way of someone who's too preoccupied for proper grooming. "Right. Of course." Approaching me, he extends his hand. "Sebastian Black. How could I've forgotten?"

"If this is a bad time, we can reschedule. I'll be in town for the next few days," I reply, annoyance threating to break my patience at any moment.

"Now's a fine time." He moves to the couch and kicks his feet onto the coffee table. "Have a seat."

Taking the seat opposite him, I begin, "I assume you know what this meeting's about, so I'll just cut to the chase. You want out of your investment with Walter Smith, and I want in. Tell me what it's going to take to make it happen."

"Slow down. Relax. We'll start with drinks. There's plenty of time for business. What'll you have?"

"Scotch on the rocks."

"Ah... you're one of those. Nyles, we'll have a scotch on the rocks and a rum and coke. Anything for your bodyguard?"

I glance at Thomas.

"Don't be so surprised, Sebastian. Is it okay if I call you Sebastian? I mean, we're in my home after all. It's only proper that the niceties be observed. Anyway, I pinned him for your body guard the second I saw him. It's all in the shoulders." He turns to Thomas. "You should really learn to loosen up a bit."

"Thomas is very good at what he does," I reply. "Surely, you can understand my need to have him accompany me. Your reputation precedes you, to say the least."

"As does yours." He takes his drink from the silver serving platter, and I follow suit. "To old money and new acquaintances."

Nodding, I raise my glass and take a careful sip. Despite having done my research, I think nothing could've prepared me for the oddity that is Jacob Whitmore, live and in living color.

"So, Sebastian," he sets his glass on the cherry wood coffee table and crosses his arms behind his head, "you've made quite a name for yourself in the entertainment world. But you started off in finance isn't that correct?"

"There are many subsidiaries within my corporation, as I'm sure you know. Finance wasn't my dream. It was my grandfather's. When my father declined his right to take over the company, they passed it to me. I wouldn't say I started there. True beginnings come from building from the ground up."

"And yet, it's the gift they gave you that brings you here today."

"I suppose you could say that." Not sure where he's going with this, I take another drink.

"We're a lot alike in that respect, Sebastian. I too was given a gift I never wanted. This universe of buttoned collars and business deals was supposed to be my brother's life. Not mine."

"From what I understand, the investigation into your brother's death was never solved."

"If you're good at hiding the evidence, you'll never get caught." The twinkle in his eye suggests he knows more about his brother's murder than he ever shared with the police. Beside me, I can feel Thomas tensing, his body ready to respond to anything this motherfucker is about to throw at us.

"Indeed."

"You know a thing or two about hiding the evidence. Don't you, Sebastian?"

Arching an eyebrow, I study him. "I'm not sure I know what you're referring to."

"Dinner is ready, sir," Niles interrupts.

"Ah, at last. Come. I find business is always better handled on a full stomach."

"Sir, I'm not sure you should go through with this," Thomas whispers in my ear as we follow Jacob into a large dining room with a low hanging chandelier positioned over a glass-topped table.

"I know I shouldn't, Thomas, but I have to. Danielle needs this, even if she doesn't know it. I'm determined to give it to her."

He nods and takes his place at the table across from me. Proving himself a master of ceremony, Jacob sets at the head of the table. He rings a bell to signal that we're ready to begin. Almost instantaneously, a maid approaches, struggling to balance three salads. By the time we've had dessert, my patience has grown impossibly thin.

"How about we finish up with a nightcap?" He asks as the maid takes our plates away.

"Actually, I think we should stick to the matter at hand. As I've said before, you want out and I want in. How much is it gonna take?"

"Before I give you a figure, why don't you tell me how this benefits you?"

"I'm not sure why that matters."

"Indulge me, Black. I'm only twenty-two, after all. I have a lot to learn from men like you. You wouldn't want to take over my investment unless it was beneficial to you. Tell me why I shouldn't just wait until whatever payoff you see comes through."

His naivety forces a snicker from my lips. "Believe me, my interests are purely personal. There's nothing profitable about the Stevens' holdings. You know it, and I know it."

"So, this is about the girl, then?"

"This is about righting a wrong that was done long ago by a man who neither I nor you want any further business with. I don't know where Walter Smith is," I lie, "but the best way to get what you want is to strike while the iron's hot. His entire company is going up in flames. Private companies tend to do that when the CEO goes missing. Truthfully, you're going to be hard pressed to find a better offer." I reach in my pocket and slide the envelope with my proposal in his direction. "I'm gonna level with you, Jacob. I know your situation. The best bet you have is me."

He opens the envelope and looks over the figures for a minute. "Surely you can do more..."

"What's your counter?"

"One night with your girl."

Fury bubbling in my gut, I'm on my feet before I even realize I'm pushing the chair back. Prepared for the worst, Thomas holds me back. Eyes bulging from his face, Jacob grins.

"I see I struck a nerve. My apologies. Please." He motions toward my vacant chair. "Sit. Let's start fresh."

I glare at him, my pulse thumping in my throat. "I'd prefer to stand. We have nothing left to discuss. That's my offer. You either take it or leave it. We're done here." Turning on my heel, I stride to toward the entryway.

"Sebastian," Jacob comes up behind me, "as you mentioned earlier, reputations have a way of preceding us. Yours has as well. I know things, Black. Things I'm sure you'd be willing to pay me a lot more to keep quiet."

"Kid, if you think you can blackmail me, you're greatly mistaken. You're not the first punk who thought he had what it takes to go up against me and you won't be the last. In the end, I'll get that property. Whether or not you stand to gain anything from the acquisition is up to you."

Unrelenting, I open the door and step out into the breezy night. Thomas is at my side in seconds. "Find out what he thinks he has on me," I order.

"I'll alert the team right away, sir." He opens the car door. "What's our next move?"

"I'm not leaving here without getting what I came for," I reply. "So, put a rush on things."

Already exhausted from dinner, I take my spot in the backseat and call my father. It's only been a few days since we got Isabelle settled back in at the clinic. Wishing I didn't have to play the role of her babysitter, I wait for him to answer. His hello sounds so tiresome that for a moment I grow nauseous as old anxieties come creeping below the surface.

"Hello, Father."

"Sebastian? You must be telepathic. I was just getting ready to call you."

"Should I have a drink ready for this?"

The sound of his laughter doing little to calm my nerves, he asks, "Why is it you always expect the worst?"

"You're the one that's been treating her for the past ten years. Why don't you tell me?"

"In her own way, she's trying."

"What'd you need?"

"Your mother and I had dinner with your sisters tonight. It's a shame you and Danielle couldn't make it."

"You know how things are in my line of work. It's part of why you refused the job."

"Very true," he chuckles. "How does Danielle feel about your constant travel?"

My head throbs with tension, and I rub my temples. "I don't mind having a casual conversation with you, Father, but I can tell this is a diversion tactic. You weren't thinking of me in the *you're my father and I'm your son* capacity. Whatever had me on your mind is related to Isabelle, so why don't you just tell me?"

"Sebastian, you're always on my mind. You're my son and I love you... but you're correct. I still think we need to try another family session."

"No."

His sigh showing the disappointment he feels, he softly says, "Lauren needs closure from what happened, Sebastian. Isabelle needs to release the guilt. This will be good for both of them, and you—"

"I can barely keep myself from snapping her neck when I think about what she did to Lauren. If you only knew everything I did to keep that girl safe." Refusing to let myself think of having to sell my soul for my little sister's safety, I pour myself a scotch. "My answer is no."

"Sebastian..."

"No, Father, that's my definitive answer."

The sound of ice cubes hitting crystal coming through the speakers, the silence stretches between us. After what feels like an eternity, he sighs. "At least think about it."

"It won't change my answer."

"But you'll consider it?"

Thumb stroking over my forehead, I answer, "Sure."

"Thank you, son," he replies, sounding relieved.

"I wouldn't thank me yet if I were you."

"I love you, son," he says, a sad undertone consuming his voice. "I'm only trying to help."

"I know," I reply, hating that I've once again disappointed him. "Maybe it's time that we both accept there's no help for someone like Isabelle."

"I certainly hope that's not the case. Otherwise, my life's work has been for not. I know you're busy. Your mother and I have a gala tomorrow night. It would work better if you could check in during office hours."

"Or maybe tomorrow will be the day I finally stop checking in all together."

"We both know that's not true, son. Try to get some rest tonight. You sound like you're running out of steam."

We hang up, and I watch the green hills roll by in the darkness as we follow the two-lane road. Needing to hear Danielle's voice, I drain my scotch and call her. Still unnerved from trials of the day, I tap my fingers on the seat as I impatiently wait for her to answer. "Hey, hotshot."

Tension instantly easing at the sound of her beautiful voice, I smile. "Hello, princess. Just thought I'd check in."

"Is that your way of saying you miss me, Sebastian Black?" She asks, her smile coming through the phone.

"Always. How's Nonna?"

"She's great, although I'm pretty sure you're in trouble the next time she sees you. She wasn't exactly thrilled that you skipped town without coming to see her first."

Picturing Danielle standing next to the old woman in her small kitchen, I loosen my tie. "Tell her I'll carve out time for a visit on my next trip."

"You better think twice before making her a promise, hotshot. She's not a fan of broken ones."

"Then I guess it's a good thing I don't make promises I can't keep. Although, I don't remember promising anything."

"Oh, believe me, she could not care less if you say the word or not. Nonna's a fan of taking people at their word. 'Speak what you mean and mean what you speak, Daniella.' Trust me, it took some getting used to coming from a house where I was expected to say nothing about anything that truly mattered. Anyway, how was the meeting?"

"If you're asking whether I'm holding the deed to your family's estate, the answer is no. I will get it for you, though."

"That's not what I was asking at all, actually, hotshot. I've already told you, I don't care about some long-lost inheritance. The only thing that matters to me is that you make it back here in one piece. Any chance you're able to wrap up early and fly back tonight?"

"You have no idea how tempting that offer is, Danielle. I'd love nothing more than to wash the sweet smell of tomato sauce from your skin and take you to bed."

"Sounds like a plan to me," she replies excitedly. "Call your pilot and tell him to gas up the jet."

Shaking my head at her persistence, I slump into the leather seat. "So, tell me about your day. Did you do anything *interesting*?"

"Are you asking if I saw Kyle? The answer's yes, and I'm catching his show at Whiskey Blue later tonight. He'll actually be here to pick me up in an hour."

"Hmm..." Hating myself for asking, I grip the armrest. "Just remember what I said. I love you, princess, but I'm not that guy."

"So, you keep reminding me. You have nothing to worry about. If it makes you feel any better, some of the other guys are riding with us, too."

"And where's the death trap you call a car?"

"She's parked in my grandparents' driveway. I had wine with dinner, so my dad and Nonno made me promise not to drive."

"Ah... another reason they've earned my respect. I could have a car come and pick you up, you know. Just because Thomas is with me doesn't mean the remaining members of your security team aren't competent motorists."

"Seriously, Sebastian. I'm going to be fine. I have no doubt that you'll have your goons following me around all evening — though I'm still not sure why they're necessary anymore — but I'm quite looking forward to the thirty-minute drive without their nagging presence."

Making a mental note to arrange transportation for anywhere she goes for the rest of the week, I reply, "This is the part of the conversation in which a good boyfriend would say something like have fun. I'm not sure I'm a good boyfriend, though, and if it means sharing you with Kyle Marcum, I'm not sure I want to be."

Her voice dropping to a tone much too seductive for someone standing in their grandparents' kitchen, she coos, "You're a great boyfriend, Sebastian, and I'm all yours. Bring your sexy, smirky, sulking ass back here, and I'll skip the concert to prove it."

The smooth cadence of her words reverberates in every fiber of my being, standing my cock at attention. "Careful what you wish for, princess. You may find you've bitten off more than you can chew."

"Hmm... while I'll admit it's quite a mouthful, I think I handle it masterfully."

"Indeed you do, princess. We're pulling up at the hotel now so I'll let you get back to your family. Be careful tonight."

"Learn to take your own advice. I love you, Sebastian."

"And I you, princess."

# Chapter 31

*D*<sup>anielle</sup>

*D* anielle

With a smile on my face, I hang up the phone and join the rest of my family on the back porch. Just like the thousands of times before this one, they are exactly where I expect them to be: my father in the wicker chair and my grandparents nuzzled closely on the swing. I take my place on the love seat, tossing my legs over the cushions and wrapping my arms around my knees.

"And how's Sebastian?" My dad asks.

Looking into their expectant faces, I laugh. "Am I that obvious?"

"I'll admit I'm not the guy's biggest fan, but I enjoy seeing that smile on your face, kid," Daddy says. "Plus, Mom was gushing all about it when she came out."

"I'm sure she was." Head shaking, I glance at my Nonna, who wears a bright smile on her face. "And I'm quite fond of this smile, too."

"Smiles like that should be reserved for marriage," my grandfather adds. "I go watch TV. Family Feud on in five minutes."

"I'm afraid I have to take my leave too," Daddy says, helping my grandfather to his feet. "Walk me out, angel-girl?"

"Gladly!"

"You'll come see me before you leave, Daniella?"

"I wouldn't have it any other way, Nonna. I'll be back once you've finished your prayers."

"Very good." She smiles and turns to my father. "Be careful out there tonight, Giovanni. The seasons are changing, and with them come new storms."

"I'm always careful, mamma," he says, kissing her forehead. "We'll talk tomorrow."

Arms linked, my father and I walk through the kitchen into the hallway, where my grandfather's shouts ring through the air.

"Socks. Underwear. Tie."

I look at my father, who shakes his head and calls, "What's the category, Pop?"

"Clothing items you buy without trying on. Shirt. Bra."

"Most women try on bras, Nonno. That's the reason the woman comes around with the measuring tape to assist you."

"Money. Driver's license. Credit card. Receipt."

"There's no reaching him now, angel-girl." Daddy laughs.

"I suppose not. Come on, old man. Let's get you to work."

"Hey now! Watch how you use the *o*-word around me."

Shaking my head, I hand him his jacket and step out onto the porch.

"You'll be careful tonight?" He asks.

"I will if you will."

"I'll be fine, kid. No need to worry about me." Giving me his concerned father look, he leans against the porch railing. "So, you're living with him now, huh?"

"I was wondering how long it was going to take for us to get to that."

"Were you? I'd say you calculated telling me at just the right time so that we wouldn't be able to. Nice touch; whispering it in my ear as you were leaving the diner last night, by the way."

"Oh, you liked that, did you?"

He tilts his head. "What do you think?"

Sweet smile plastered on my face, I reply, "I'm sorry, Daddy. It just happened so fast."

"Seems to be the way things go with you two. What's next? A shotgun wedding?"

"Don't even joke about that," I slug his shoulder playfully, "If anyone's in danger of a shotgun wedding it's you. Don't think I didn't notice Bernadette's car in the driveway when I dropped my luggage off this morning."

"Don't get ahead of yourself, angel-girl. Bernadette already knows I'd rather take it slow." Glancing at the lawn, he sighs. "After everything I went through with your mom, it's the only choice I have. Hearts get broken every day, but I'd rather mine not be one of them. I'd rather yours not be one either, which brings me back to Sebastian. Living together is serious business, Dani. Are you sure he's the right person for you to take that step with?"

Arms hugged across my chest, I watch a car drive by. "Daddy, I'm going to be honest with you. I don't know if Sebastian is *the one* or if there'll ever be a *one,* for that matter. After all I've been through, I could quite possibly be the most difficult person to love ever made. All I know is that not being with Sebastian feels like not having air in my lungs. Without him, I'm suffocating. I don't make it easy. Neither does he, but we make it work. I know you don't fully approve, but Sebastian's the one I need when I come home at night. He's the one that chases the ghosts away and shields me from the storm. If nothing else about him wins you over, at least appreciate that."

Smiling, he pulls me into a fatherly embrace. "I want to like him, angel-girl. I really do. There's just something about him I can't quite place. I'm trying to move past it. I promise."

"I know you are, Daddy. That's all I could ask of you."

I walk him to his truck, promising to call when I make it back from the concert, and walk back through the house to join Nonna on the back porch. When she hears the door creak open, she looks up and smiles. Holding her shawl open, she pats the seat next to her. Heart filled with love, I sit next to her and place my head on her shoulder.

"What's wrong, mia bella  Daniella?"

"Why would you think something's wrong?"

"You hardly speak through dinner. You look sad after saying goodbye to Giovani. You're sick of the heart, si?"

"Si," I sigh.

"Things not going so well with Sebastian?"

"No. Things are fine. He's just..." I look into her fading green eyes. "Nonna, was there ever a time in your relationship that you felt as though Nonno was hiding something from you? I don't mean something small, like the amount of cash in his wallet. I mean something bigger, like, something that could possibly change the course of both your lives forever."

"Aberto? No, he knows I'm no un pollo da spennare. He's too afraid of waking up to the tip of my knife."

Confused, I stare at her.

She chuckles. "I forget how little Italiano you know. I'm not someone you can easily take advantage of, Daniella, and neither are you. Don't let him do it."

"Oh." The sound of the wind blowing through the large palm tree to our left fills the air, and I exhale. "I don't think he's taking advantage of me. At least not intentionally. It's difficult for Sebastian to trust people."

"Ah, and you've only made it harder." Her eyes shine with wisdom. "What are you doing with Kyle? I thought that ended a long time ago."

Covering us with the afghan that's always readily hanging from the back of the swing, I reply, "So did I."

"Well..."

Careful to choose the right words, I close my eyes and lean back. "I don't know how to explain it. Something about him just pulls me in. I've tried to let him go, but I can't. Not completely, at least."

"Daniella, look at me." When my eyes meet hers, all I see is compassion. "You can't have them both. Who do you want most?"

"Sebastian," I answer without hesitation.

"Then give him what he wants. He needs you to distance yourself from Kyle, correct?"

"I'm trying, Nonna. I've been trying, but every time I picture myself never seeing his blue eyes, or making the dimple appear on his cheek again..." My words catch in my throat and I shake my head. "He means so much to me. It's just not enough."

"He loves you, Daniella. They both do. That's why you have to be fair to each of them. Concerts and days at the beach are just a good time for you. To Kyle, they're hope. And hope has the power to kill us faster than any bullet."

"Kyle knows how I feel about Sebastian. I've made it clear he's my choice."

"Tra il dire e il fare c'è di mezzo il mare, Daniella. Just remember that. It's cold. We go in now."

I help her to the door, letting her words run around in my mind. *Between saying and doing is the ocean, Danielle. Just remember that.*

****

Her words stick with me through the concert, and well into the rest of my week. Every time Cyrus picks me up to take me to the beach, or Sebastian calls to see what I'm up to, I hear her whisperings. When Kyle asks if I feel up to a trip to the Trapeze School, I'm haunted by the phrase. *Between saying and doing is the ocean, Danielle.*

All this time I've been confident that Kyle understood my stance, but what if Nonna's right? What if his persistence is more than just harmless flirtation? What if he really thinks I'll turn back to him at the first sign of trouble with Sebastian? How can I keep him without hurting him? How can I lose him without hurting myself?

By the time Friday comes around, I'm readier to fall into Sebastian's arms than I've ever been. Maybe it's selfish, maybe even a little unfair. All I know is that I need them both — in different ways — for many reasons. It's as simple as that. Right or wrong, we'll all just have to figure out a way to live with it.

Warmed by the sun's glow cascading around my small bedroom, I roll over and open my eyes. Through my haze, I see Sebastian unloading his pockets onto my dresser. Blankets thrown to the side, I lunge to my feet and throw my arms around him. His fingers lock on mine, and he pulls my hands to his chest.

"You have no idea how much I missed you, princess."

"Not half as much I as missed you. I thought you weren't getting back until this afternoon."

Eyes smoldering with lust, he turns to face me. His lips seal over mine, his tongue greedily possessing my mouth. Deepening the kiss, I wrap my hands in the silken strands of his hair and surrender. He wraps my legs around his waist and carries me to the bed, laying me down gently. Nose nuzzled in my neck, he whispers, "I love you, Danielle."

My legs entangled with his, I rest my head on his chest. Lifting his shirt, I trace my fingers across the ridges of his torso. "I love you too, Sebastian. Where's that kinky reunion you promised me?"

"Lost in the land of your father is in the next room." He laughs. "There'll be plenty of time for kink when we get to our suite later."

"Daddy's up? What time is it?"

"A little after ten."

"Crazy. He's usually in bed by now."

"He was just pulling up when I got here."

"He must've been at The Spot. He spends an ungodly amount of time there now."

Sebastian twirls his fingers in my hair. "He's in love, princess."

"Yeah, I guess." Studying his worry worn face, I ask, "So I take it you finally got your way?"

"Not just yet, but Thomas is wrapping things up for me. He'll meet us in Vegas this afternoon."

"And that's in his job description?"

"He's a jack of all trades." He skims my bottom lip with the pad of his thumb. "Besides, I flew back early to get you to stop worrying. How do you propose I do that?"

"My vote still goes to kinky reunion." Sitting up, I throw my legs over his waist and sit atop him.

A smirk spreading across his lips, he squeezes my hips and glides my pelvis over his stiffened cock. "I'm glad we're pulling for the same party, princess," he sits up, "but that doesn't change the fact that your father is in the next room. How about breakfast instead?"

"All we have in the way of breakfast food is Honey Bunches of Oats. Daddy's breakfasts at The Spot have apparently migrated to his off days, too."

"Get dressed. We'll go back to my place."

"Coffee and kink. It's all every woman dreams of."

Teeth grazing my nipple, he replies, "At least all the good ones."

Charged by the sexual tension growing between us, I bring my lips to his. He's flipping me on my back when my phone rings. "If that's the guitarist, I can't be held responsible for my actions," he says breathlessly.

I shove him off me and check. "It's Yasmin, the woman I had a meeting with the other day. I have to take it. She's checking on jobs for me in the city."

"Okay. I'll leave you to it. Just hurry. The faster we get to Malibu, the faster I can feed and fuck you. Not necessarily in that order."

Watching him walk away, I slide my finger over the talk button. "Good morning, Yasmin. How are you?"

"I'm great!" She exclaims. "And by the time you hang up this phone, you will be too."

"Really?" Excited tingles run through my body as I wait for her news.

"I promise. I've found two offers for you. One is great, and the other is pretty good."

Pulse racing, I reply, "Let's start with the great."

"I was hoping you'd say that. My assistant is leaving to be a stay at home mom. I know it's not much higher than where you're at now, but I have no doubt that you'd work through the ranks quickly. And I'm willing to let you bring in new accounts under my supervision while you're still a little green. What do you think?"

If Yasmin would've offered me this opportunity six months ago, I would've never left Los Angeles. I loved working for her. Everything I learned that got me the internship with P.E.S. came from late nights and early mornings at Yasmin's side. She took me under her wing and held me close. I always expected to eventually find my way onto her payroll, but when graduation came, there just wasn't a space open. So, I took the internship at Princeton Enterprise Solutions. And I moved across the country and started over. I found Sebastian. I can't turn my back on him and start over again.

"I'm sorry, Yasmin." Eyes closed, I hide from my reflection in the mirror attached to my dresser. "I would love to work for you again — it'd be a dream come true — but what I said in your office the other day still remains. I can't relocate."

"I was hoping a few days in the sun and sand would change your mind." The disappointed tone in her voice brings red flares of shame to my cheeks. "You're giving up a lot for this guy, Dani. Is he worth it?"

"I'm not giving up anything. I'm just re-prioritizing a few things. Did you know about the job opening when we met up?"

"I did, but I could tell you weren't ready to accept it. As I said, I'd hoped..."

"Yeah. I get it. Still no chance you'll open up an office in New York?"

"Never say never, but I'm sure you'll be off the market by then. I may have lied about the second offer. It's pretty great."

"And it's in Manhattan?"

Laughter fills her voice as she replies, "Yes. I still think you're making a mistake in building your career based on where your boyfriend's at, but I think you'll do well with this one. He actually has ties to Paul Princeton as well, and he's eager to meet with you."

"You're serious?"

"Apparently, the work you were doing there didn't go unnoticed. So, do you want the details?"

"Yes!" I nearly scream.

"Okay. His name is Jett Wilson, and he's opening a new firm in the city. He doesn't have much room for a crew at the moment, but he's looking to work with someone who isn't afraid to take risks. I gave you my highest recommendation, of course, but you'll still need to spend some time preparing yourself before you meet with him. I'm emailing you more information now. I think you and Jett together could take the world by storm, Dani. I really do."

"Oh my God! Thank you, Yasmin! Really, this sounds amazing. I can't wait to read over the details."

"You're welcome. Just promise me two things."

Recognizing the somber tone in her voice, I pull my pillow onto my lap and rest my elbows on it.

"One. When you make it big with this opportunity, you'll remember where you came from. I want to hear from you, and I'm always here to help if you need seasoned advice. Never forget that, okay?"

"I don't know how I could," I answer, honestly.

"Good. My number two is this... don't get so wrapped up in Sebastian that you lose Danielle. You've made it clear that this relationship means a great deal to you, but the girl who stormed into my office and demanded I give her an internship cared a great deal about her career. I loved that girl. I saw a lot of myself in her. Don't make the same mistakes I did. Your career will be what's left when he's gone."

Her words sting more than I'd like. I know she's projecting her own experiences onto me, but hearing the doubt in her voice fuels the insecurities that already live inside of me. The whole reason I didn't want Sebastian's help in finding another job is because I never want to look back on my success and only see him. Yasmin said this guy heard about what I did at P.E.S., but most of my work with the firm involved Sebastian's nightclubs. Does he only want to meet with me because I'm Sebastian Black's girlfriend, or is he really interested in Danielle Stevens?

"Dani?"

"I'm here, sorry. I was just taking it all in. Don't worry about me, Yasmin. I'm going to create a fire in the public relations world, just like I promised all those years ago."

"I'm counting on it. Listen, I've gotta run. Call me as soon as you've met with Jett. I can't wait to hear how it goes."

Thanking her, I hang up the phone and scroll to my email. Jett's offer is amazing. He's starting a company from the ground up, but he already has some great clients. One of which is an ethical standards company with the mission of bringing equal treatment to women in the workplace. His goal is to handle just enough of the glamor crap to pay the bills and focus on his genuine passion, the mission. Apparently, he isn't a fan of the constant parties and spoiled rich kids, either. Excitement boiling in my blood, I read over every word twice.

Confident that I can do everything the job requires and then some, I dial the number Yasmin provided. Unnerved, I chew my thumbnail as I wait for him to answer. My throat constricts when I hear him say hello.

Swallowing, I croak, "Hello is this Jett?"

"Yes. May I ask who this is?"

"My name's Danielle Stevens. I believe Yasmin spoke with you on behalf?"

"She did. Can you give me just a sec?"

"Sure."

The sounds of New York rush through my ears as I wait. I hear him mumble something to what I assume is a cabby and the sound of a car door slamming. There's a fair amount of shuffling and he's back. "Sorry. You caught me in the middle of a commute."

"Oh, if this is a bad time, I can call back, or you can call me. Either way."

His voice lightened with laughter, he replies, "Nonsense. You know business never sleeps in this city. So, I take it you've read the info I sent Yasmin?"

"I have, and it sounds amazing. When I return to the city next week, I would love to meet you. I'm available any time after Monday."

"Actually, I'm heading to Vegas for a week. Can we set something up for when I get back?"

"Of course. Or, you know what? I'll actually be in Vegas this weekend as well. I don't want to trump in on your vacation or anything, but I'd be willing to meet with you there if need be."

"Hmm..." Tension starts in my neck and spreads through my shoulders like flame as I wait for him to consider my offer. "I think we could make that work. What do you say to lunch tomorrow?"

"Sounds great!"

"Fantastic, I would say something professional like I'll have my assistant call you, but since I'm not equipped with one at the moment... is this a good number to reach you?"

"Yes," I reply, laughing.

"Fantastic. I'll see you tomorrow, Danielle. Have a safe flight."

"Thanks, you too."

Hanging up, I walk to my closet for something to wear. Selecting the jeans and gray off-shouldered top I packed for the flight, I make the decision to embrace this opportunity with everything I've got. There's no point in worrying about Jett's intentions until I've met with him. Besides, it's not like I have any other offers on the table.

# Chapter 32

*S*ebastian

Just after five, we land at Henderson Executive Airport and begin our thirty-mile drive into the heart of the Strip. Mesmerized, I watch Danielle apply pink lip gloss to her plush lips and contemplate ways to get out of this mandatory *guys' night* to spend time with her instead.

"He's your soon to be brother-in-law, hotshot." Stashing her gloss in her tote, she turns to me. "Bonding is good for you."

Eyes catching the cleavage spilling from the top of the tight lace dress she changed into, I pull her onto my lap. "I'd say we're about as bonded as we're going to get, princess. You and I, on the other hand..." My lips thin into a smirk, and I slide my hand under her short hemline. "I think we could use plenty more bonding time."

Rolling her eyes, she smacks my hand away playfully. "We *bonded* twice before breakfast, once this afternoon, and again on the plane. I'd dare to say we're effectively fused into the same person at this point."

"And yet..." I take her hand in mine and run it over the length of my expanding dick.

She shakes her head and snatches it away, planting a soft cherry flavored kiss on my lips. "Fiend."

"I thought you liked my sexual appetite?"

"Oh, I love your sexual appetite, hotshot. I also like spending time with your sisters. So, that means I'm not caving. Go to guys' night. I promise you can ravish me with your frustrations later."

Lips resting against the nape of her neck, I growl. "I'm going to take you up on that offer, Danielle. I suggest you prepare yourself."

We pull up to the valet in front of the Black Towers, one of four hotels I own along the Strip. The valet opens the door, smiling nervously when he sees my face. "Good evening, Mister Black."

"Our luggage is in the trunk. Have it brought to my suite." I take Danielle's hand and help her from the car. Eyes stinging from the countless camera flashes, I lead her from the entrance, through the lobby I paid too much to have decorated, and into the private glass elevator. Using my master key, I close the door behind us.

"I'm never going to get used to that." Bottom lip sucked between her teeth, she squeezes her trembling hand around mine

Hand resting against her face, I stroke my hand over her cheek. "It gets easier, princess. You get to the point where you don't even notice them, and then the story their after — in this case what happened on the night Jon died — loses its sizzle, and they move on to someone else."

Watery eyed, she looks up at me. "What if they don't move on, Sebastian? What if they find the truth?"

I pull her tight against me. Feeling her racing pulse, I cup her face in my hands. "There's nothing for them to find, princess. It was handled, masterfully, I might add."

"I'm just ready for all this to be over."

Pressing her head against my chest, I wrap my arms around her. Stroking my palms along her spine, I say, "I know."

The rest of the ride to the suite known as the *Chateau in the Sky* is silent. Stories below us, people busy themselves with showing tickets to tonight's show, securing tables at one of our in-house restaurants, or scampering about elsewhere. In a few hours, both nightclubs will be in full force, and I'll be somewhere on the casino floor while Danielle shakes her ass for others to see. Jaw clenched at the thought, I strengthen my embrace.

The doors open directly into the foyer of the massive suite I set Katie and Brad up in for the weekend. One of my sister's bridesmaid — bimbo number one I think — shrieks and welcomes us in as if I don't own the place. Placing her hands around my bicep, she leads us toward the dining room. Her head tilted toward me, she bats her eyelashes and asks something about my flight. Ignoring her, I break free, my grip tightening around Danielle's fingers.

"I think she has the hots for you," my princess whispers.

"There's not a woman in this room that could compare to the one I already have," I reply.

Bimbo announces our arrival to Katie, who jumps to her feet and sways a little unsteadily. "Sebastian!"

"How many have you had, sis?" I ask, catching her by the elbow.

Beaming, she throws her head back in a fit of laughter. "Relax, baby brother, this is a celebration."

I help her to her seat and shake Brad's hand while Danielle takes a place next to my baby sister, Julie. "Water with dinner *and* you're eating something with carbs."

"Carbs! I have a wedding dress to fit into next week."

"Carbs," I respond, definitively.

"See, I'm not the only one that thinks you should slow down," Brad says, stroking her cheek.

"Party pooper," Bimbo shouts.

I glare at her, and she stills in her seat. Satisfied, I hug Julie and sit next to Danielle.

"I'll watch out for her," she promises, leaning in so only I can hear.

"Thank you." I squeeze her shoulder affectionately. "How's school going, Jewels?"

"I missed classes this afternoon to get here. Mom and dad are probably going to kill me, but other than that, things are good."

"I'll deal with mother and father if need be. Just enjoy yourself... *within reason*."

She turns toward our sister. "Yeah, because I'd love to make an idiot of myself like that one."

"You guys should cut her some slack. It's her bachelorette party. She's supposed to get drunk, and be stupid, and regret it for the rest of her life."

"Oh, trust me," Jewels states, taking a sip of white wine. "She's going to regret it. I just didn't know the rest of the wedding party had their own plans for the weekend. Are you all set for our scavenger hunt?"

"I already told you, I want no part in that."

"Oh, come on, if I have to play, you have to play."

"Scavenger hunt?" I query.

"Your baby sister has the brilliant idea of making us all gallivant around town looking for guys with the best asses and taking pictures with police officers. You know the cliché Vegas bachelorette party experience."

"No." Hand cupped around her chin, I turn her head toward me. "Again, I say no."

She laughs, pulling away from me. "Settle down, brute. I don't think anyone's ass is better than yours—"

"Gag," Julie interrupts. "As I was saying, if I have to play, so does she. Suck it up, big brother. I'm sure Brad's buds have just as much debauchery planned for you."

"The last thing I'll be doing tonight is running around town making a fool of myself. I signed on for gambling. Period. Anything else will have to happen without me. Just as this little scavenger hunt will have to take place without the two of you."

"Hey, you're not hurting my feelings at all," Jewels replies. "The only reason I put any energy at all into it is because Katie asked for it. Do I look like the kind of girl who wants to run around town taking body shots off of random guys, and dancing on bars?"

"I thought things like this were only meant for the bride."

"Oh, they usually are, hotshot," Danielle explains. "Just another stipulation from your big sister. We all get a sheet. Each one has different activities on it. The first person to complete their sheet is the winner. Thank God for the no Instagram rule. The last thing I want are photos of this night circulating the web."

"That's the least of your worries, princess. Believe me." Hand possessively squeezing her thigh, I turn to the waiter and order a 14 oz. New York Sirloin and a glass of Macallan.

Beside me, Danielle orders the chicken masala and a glass of wine. Head resting on my shoulder, she checks her phone.

"He'll call. Stop worrying," I tell her.

"I'm not worried," she answers. "Just anxious. This is the first nibble I've had since I threw out my bait."

"If I remember correctly, I made you an offer the very day you were let go."

Head shaking, she peeks at me through her lashes. "No matter what happens with Jett, I won't work for you, Sebastian. I'll find something... *eventually*."

"Just imagine the fringe benefits." I slide my hand under the hem of her dress and stroke my finders over her lace covered clitoris.

With a gasp, she leans back. "I have, and that's exactly why I think it's a bad idea. Sebastian, I don't want to be your desk ornament. I want to do something, *become someone*. I can't do that if I don't take what I'm doing seriously, and let's face it," she catches my hand, bringing my fingers to a halt, "if we worked together and lived together, we'd either get nothing done, *or* we'd get so sick of being around each other that you'd end up sleeping at Windom every night."

"Do you honestly think I'd tire of you?"

"Yes." She laces her fingers through mine. "More importantly, I know I'd wear down from being with you so much. Don't take this the wrong way, but you're trying at best and your impatience is notorious. I, on the other hand, am stubborn and strong willed. We already fight more than your average couple. Let's not give ourselves one more way to break this. Life has already given us enough."

"Still," grinning, I slowly brush the hair from her neck and plant a kiss on her nape, "the fringe benefits."

"Fiend," she repeats, giving my thigh a squeeze and returning her attention to my sister.

# Chapter 33

*D*anielle

"Morning," Sebastian says, pouring a stream of steaming hot coffee into a cup and carrying it to the bed. "Coffee?"

"Yes," I croak, squinting through the pounding in my head. "How is it that you're already up and ready to take on the world?"

"I'm a superhuman, Danielle. Haven't you figured that out by now?" He winks and crawls into bed next to me.

Sitting up slowly, I take a sip from the porcelain cup. "Hilarious. Did you have fun last night?"

"I lost, which is ironic considering that I own the place, so any money taken out of my pocket is automatically going back in, in a sense. Blackjack isn't my game."

"You take too many risks," I taunt.

"I did pretty well on the roulette table, though. Seems dice is more my style." Storm brewing in his eyes, he takes my coffee cup and places it on the nightstand.

Blood bubbling with the heat of my desire for him, I lie back. "I seem to remember you being particularly gifted in that game."

"And I seem to remember promising you a ravishing."

Plush lips pressed against mine, he steadies himself over me. Legs wrapped around his, I press my palms to his back. Removing the tie from his robe, he tucks my wrists to my chest and secures my hands.

Moaning, I exhale and look up at him through hooded lids. "Indeed, you did, hotshot. And I seem to remember you telling me you never break a promise."

Heavy cock pressed against my thigh, he sinks his teeth into my neck. "Never."

****

The diner is a 1950s style with checkerboard floors and pale pink walls. Red vinyl booths line the walls and black stools sit at the counter, where servers wearing teal uniforms shout orders through the kitchen window. Feeling a bit like Sandy from *Grease*, I order a strawberry milkshake and skim through the selection in the mini jukebox on the table. "Here you go, Hun," a white-haired waitress with wisdom in her eyes says, handing me my shake.

"Thanks."

Foot tapping against the floor, I move my straw through the thick pink drink. Time seems to be at a standstill as I wait for Jett to arrive. Sweaty palmed, I pick up the menu and skim the long list of breakfast foods. The diner is open twenty-four hours every day, but you'll only find breakfast and ice cream. The oddity of it isn't lost on me as I decide on the buttermilk short stack.

"Johnnie B. Goode" blares through the jukebox on the table behind me, bringing me out of my own thoughts. Looking up, I watch an Elvis impersonator with gold studs on his suit walk through the door, followed by a nervous-looking guy in a cheap suit. He smiles a bit too wide when our eyes meet and quickly walks to my table. "Dani?"

"Yes, thanks for agreeing to meet me. I know you probably had better ways to spend your vacation," I gush, pink rising to my cheeks at my over enthusiasm. *I didn't even give him the chance to introduce himself.*

Having the grace not to notice, he slides into the vinyl seat across from me. "No, this works out perfectly. The sooner we seal the deal, the closer I'll be to having all my dreams come true."

"Oh, I wouldn't put that much faith in me. I *am* excited about the opportunity, though." I take my resume from my bag and slide it across the table. "I took the liberty of printing my resume last night just in case you wanted to have a look at it. As you'll see, I don't have a ton of experience independently working with accounts. I was just starting to take on a few at P.E.S. when I was terminated. I have a lot of clerical experience, though. And, I've worked closely with supervisors on many other projects. During my internship with Yasmin, I frequently worked at her right hand. I learned a lot from both her and Paul, and I can say with confidence that I'm ready to help you get things off the ground."

"That's all great, but what I'd really like to know is what's going to make you a suitable partner?"

Dumbfounded, I watch as he gives his order to the white-haired waitress. Turning back to me, his expression clouds and I see my own confusion mirrored in his eyes as I place my order.

Once she's gone, he says, "I'm sorry. What did you think this meeting was for?"

Squared shouldered, I straighten. "I thought it was a job interview. Yasmin said you were looking for an assistant." *Didn't she?*

"Uh-huh. Well... I'm not. At least not yet. Before I can even consider bringing on an assistant, I need a partner. The truth is, I've risen quite a bit of capital, but I need a lot more. Having someone on board to help with the financial load would be an enormous help, but I don't want to work with just anyone. Yasmin told me about your passion for the business and your desire to branch out and do something to make a difference. She also mentioned that bit about Princeton terminating you with what really seemed like no just cause."

"I know Princeton. I worked closely with him for an entire year. He spent the entire term of my internship grooming me. Telling me how much potential I had. How proud he was going to be to bring another male into the female driven world of public relations. Then, I confronted him about a client concept. Confrontation isn't really the right word, I guess. Anyway, my opinion and his didn't match. The client liked my pitch more, and he thanked me. The day my internship was scheduled to end, he called me into his office. I was fully expecting to be hired in permanently. What I got instead was a list of reasons why I wouldn't make it."

"No big deal, right? Things don't work out all the time. Except, every major and minor firm in the city also deemed me unemployable. If the sharks didn't want me, the minnows weren't sure why they would either. It's hard being a man in this business, but even harder when you've been blackballed. From what Yasmin said, the same thing is happening to you. So, I thought, who better to build with than someone who's been there?"

"Wow..." Lost for words, I take a sip of my now semi-melted milkshake and make room for the waitress to place our food on the table.

"So... I know this isn't what you were expecting, but what do you think?"

"Hmm... well," I pour maple syrup on my pancakes, "I think it's an interesting offer, but I'm not sure I want to be part of your revenge plot."

"Oh, no. God. No. I'm sorry. I didn't mean to make it sound like that at all. I've been dreaming of this for a long time. It's actually why I got into PR. I wanted the chance to shed light on the issues that weren't talked about as often. I just thought I'd have to spend several years working for *the man* before I actually got the chance. What Paul did was a blessing in disguise, really. It forced my hand and made me have to work toward the thing I wanted most. I don't want you because he burned you, too. I want you, because I've seen the work you do."

"I was at that Lickwid Leather and Lace event before everything went south. And before that, I was at the Naughty and Nice party. I know that wasn't Princeton. It was too edgy for him. Yasmin speaks highly of you and she's been nothing but honest with me. So, I trust her. Plus, your speech when I first sat down only solidified that you have the heart for this business. I want to work with someone who has that fire in them. I want to change the world, Dani, or at least I want to help give the people who really have the power to the edge they need to do it. You are the right person to help me with that."

Wiping my mouth with my napkin, I take in the sincerity of his words. "I'm flattered, Jett. I really am, but I don't think I'm in a position to invest in something right now. I'm barely out of college. My student loans are stacked to the ceiling, and my father doesn't exactly own a bank or anything. Given how much you seem to know about me, I'm willing to bet you know who I'm currently involved with. If you were expecting me to run to him with the opportunity, I'm sorry, but—"

"Dani," he swallows the bite of his omelet he's been chewing and looks at me, "I know you're dating Sebastian Black. I won't lie. The idea of having that kind of backing in our corner certainly is appealing, but I swear to you I never expected you to ask him for anything. In fact, Yasmin mentioned you were pretty adamant in doing this without him before I even had the chance to come up with the idea."

Elbow propped on the table, I reply, "Of course she did. Still... I'm just not sure I'm ready to make that leap."

"Understandable." Shoulders slumped, he leans against the booth. "Do me a favor?"

"Depends."

He laughs. "Fair enough. I'm going to email you my full prospectus when I get back to my room. I'll also send you all the info for my current investors and full summaries of my current clients. Take the week and think it over. When I get back to New York, have dinner with me and let me know what you think."

"Well... I'll consider it, but let's do drinks. Dinner's too long of an affair if I'm going to turn you down, and if I don't, drinks are more celebratory."

"See. That right there. It's why I need you in this with me."

Warmed by his words, I finish my shake. "Well, let's hope your prospectus makes me see why I should jump in."

****

"Oh my God! I'm never drinking again, you guys," Katie whines.

Julie and I have joined her alongside the private rooftop pool attached to her suite while we wait for the rest of her bridesmaids. It's a sunny day in Las Vegas, the desert air drying the water droplets on my skin. I adjust my sunglasses and turn to her. "I will remind you of that tonight. Although, I'm sure Sebastian will beat me to it."

"Ugh! What's his deal, anyway? Brad said he practically kept a waitress with scotch in hand waiting last night. How's he not hung over?"

"This is a question I've frequently asked myself. Trust me."

"I wonder how he's dealing with the groomsman golf game." Julie chuckles. "Remember when Daddy signed them up for that father-son charity game?"

"And Sebastian got so pissed he threw his driver at the caddy," Katie chimes in, squealing. "That was a long time ago, Jewels. He's not an edgy sixteen-year-old anymore. You were too young to remember it, but his mood swings were out-of-control back then."

"Oh, I remember more than you think. Then they got better, then Alana came and well... it's supposed to be a party, so I'll leave it there." Julie looks at me and smiles. "The important thing is, he has you now. You're the best thing that's ever happened to him, Dani, I swear."

"I think you give me too much credit."

"I don't," Katie cuts in. "I'm thrilled Sebastian's finally found someone, and as far as sisters go... I think we're pretty lucky ourselves."

"Oh definitely," Julie adds. "I mean, I I love you, Kate, but Dani can hook me up with rock stars."

"Well, sure, Dani can get you rock stars. However, I have old, bald dentists in my arsenal. Let's get real for a minute. Which would you truly prefer to wake up next to for the rest of your life?"

I listen to the sound of their laughter, wishing I could come up with something witty to add to the conversation. The only thing that hangs in my mind, though, is a single word. Sister. I hadn't realized it before Katie mentioned it, but I want to be their sister. Even with their faults, I'd love nothing more than to be a part of Sebastian's family. To be his for the rest of my life. We have so much ground to cover before we take that step, though.

# Chapter 34

S ebastian

"A toast," all eyes turn to me as I raise my glass in honor of my sister and the man she's chosen. I look over at her and feel warmed by the smile on her face. Katie's found love. It's an abstract I never believed in until Danielle. Now I know how real and enthralling it can be. "Forever is hard for me to grasp. For a long time, I didn't believe in infinities. Pledging your love to the same person for a lifetime seemed foolish. Then Katie met Brad. When I look at them, I know that sometimes a lifetime passes in no time at all."

"Being caught in the middle of Kathryn and Julie, I've seen a lot of boyfriends come and go. The day I met Bradley, I knew he was different. Suddenly, when I looked at my sister, infinity didn't seem so finite. Even though I didn't quite understand what love was at the time, I knew theirs was real. I watched her smile, and it was clear. If he could cause that smile every day for the rest of her life, she'd be okay. Some people might call me overprotective."

A few chuckles break through my speech, and I pause to give them a chance to die down.

"It's a fatal flaw. One I'm not ashamed of. When your sisters are as stunning as mine, how can you be anything else? Still, when Kate's with Brad, I know she's safe. I look at her now and see a smile just as bright as the one she wore when bringing him home to meet our family for the first time. I can only hope I'll still be saying the same thing an infinite number of years from now. Katie, I wish you a lifetime of joy and happiness. Brad, I've given you a lot of tests, and to my surprise, you passed them all. If you can survive me, I know you'll get her through whatever life throws at you. It's a pleasure to welcome you into our family. Cheers to your love."

The clinking of champagne glasses fills the air as I take my seat next to Danielle. Leaning in, she whispers, "I didn't know you had it in you, hotshot."

"Princess, you ain't seen nothing yet." I wink and take a sip of the sickeningly sweet champagne.

On cue, bright pink fireworks erupt from each of my properties along the strip. The sky illuminates with my message: *Congratulations Katie and Brad*. Another round fires, purple this time, casting light on the rooftop and turning every face a brilliant shade of violet. Mesmerized, Danielle places her head on my shoulder. Arm wrapped tightly around her, I plant my lips to her forehead. The show continues above us, purple fading to blue, then green and back to pink. Hearts, stars, streams of golden light. No holds were barred in this production, I made sure of it. Across from us, people flock to the windows of their rooms, oblivious as to what all the commotion is for.

Once it's all wrapped up, Katie gets up and pulls her arms around my neck. With my free hand, I reach up pat her shoulder. "Thanks, little brother. That was incredible. How'd you get away with launching fireworks?"

"Anything's possible if your pockets are deep enough. Besides, the fire department was on standby at each of the properties. It was all handled with care."

"How'd I get so lucky?" She asks. "Most girls get stuck with annoying dweebs for little brothers, and I got you."

"I'm the lucky one, Katie. Few sisters would've put up with all the shit you had to."

We stare at each other, letting the understanding pass between us.

"Well, I'm glad the two of you feel so lucky. Personally, I think I drew the short end of the stick on both accounts," Julie cuts in, lightening the mood. "I mean, this is supposed to be a celebration, and the two of you are acting like someone's dying. Honestly, I can't believe I chose this over studying."

"And just like that, *Baby Child Syndrome* rears its ugly head again," Kate says, rolling her eyes and turning to join Brad again.

"You really are amazing." Danielle pulls back and wraps her hand around mine. "Thanks for giving me this week. After the disaster that was the Hamptons, I needed the time away to detox."

"It doesn't have to be over yet."

"What do you mean?"

Brushing my lips over her knuckles, I ask, "How do you feel about Aspen?"

"Aspen?"

"I have a hotel there as well, princess."

"I don't have any clothes for the mountains," Danielle adds.

I laugh. "You have clothes, princess. They're at my suite waiting for you. I have some business to take care of because of the looming holiday season. It's been several months since I've set foot on the grounds. I need to make sure things are ready. I was planning on surprising you with the trip all along."

"I've never been on skis in my life."

"It's not really time for skiing," brushing the hair from her shoulder I kiss her collarbone, "but when the time comes we can go again, and I'll teach you just as I've taught you so many other things."

"Mm..." She strokes her hand over my thigh, leaning closer. "You do make an excellent professor."

"I could teach you a few things now if you feel up to a lesson." Jeans straining to contain my hard-on, I pull her from her seat.

"Where are you two lovebirds headed?" Jewels asks.

"I have business to close up, and there's no way I'm leaving Danielle alone with you lushes."

She rolls her eyes. "Seriously, that's lamest way of saying, 'we're off to fuck like bunnies' I've ever heard."

Danielle laughs and leans down to hug her. "Have a good night, Jewels."

****

Thirty-thousand feet over the air, I read the newest proposal from that punk kid, Jacob Whitmore. He's asking for stock in Black Industries and a substantial increase in the initial amount I've offered him. "He's a fucking psycho," I mutter.

"Huh?" Danielle looks up from her tablet.

"Nothing. Just work. What're you up to over there?"

Legs swinging off my lap, she sits up and holds her tablet out to me. "It's Jett's prospectus. Everything sounds amazing, but I just don't know if it's something I'm ready for. Do you mind looking at it?"

"Of course, I don't mind." I take the tablet from her and extend my arm out. Taking my cue, she crawls across the couch and rests her head on my chest. "I'm surprised you waited this long to ask me. This is what, the fifth time you've read over things now?"

"I had my reasons."

"In any case, let me see what you're working with."

I read through the executive summary and company profile. As far as jobs go, this one sounds like they plucked it straight from Danielle's dreams. The various analytic reports prove that Jett Wilson is more than competent enough to pull it off. The only thing that seems to be missing is capital, a problem I could easily solve. I know it, and she knows it. We also both know the last thing she wants is to address it with me.

"Sounds good to me, princess. What's the problem?"

"The problem is, I'm twenty-three, Sebastian. I'm not sure I'm up for the challenge of starting a company. I'm barely out of college. We won't even mention student loans. If — and let's face it, it's a big if — I were to find a lender who'd back me with a loan to buy into the opportunity, there's a very good chance this thing would sink. Then I'm stuck with so much debt, I'll never climb my way out of it."

"So, let's tackle your problems one at a time. You're twenty-three. I was younger than you when I took over my grandfather's company, and not much older when I opened my independent corporation."

"Yeah," she smiles, "but you're *you*. There's a big difference there."

"Don't sell yourself short, Danielle. I've seen what you're capable of. Every business — including the ones I venture into — can fail. It's a risk we all take."

"I guess that's true." Her chest rising and falling with her exhale, she says, "Still... I think you have too much confidence in me."

"And I could argue that you don't have enough in yourself. You'd be great at this, princess. Can I tell you what I really think?"

"Like I'd ever be able to stop you."

"I think you've spent most of your life with limited options. You never pictured yourself starting your own firm, because you never saw it as an opportunity. Now, here it is, knocking on your door and you're scared. And there's nothing wrong with that, but I also think if you don't do it, you'll regret it for the rest of your life."

Gaze trained on the tablet, she closes her eyes. I can tell by the practiced rhythm of her breath that she's pondering my words. "So, you're saying I should do it?"

"I think you already know you should do it."

"You're right. It's an amazing opportunity, and I'd be an idiot to not at least *try*. I guess I'll start looking into loans when we get back to the city."

"Yeah, about that..."

"Sebastian—"

"Just hear me out, princess. I know you don't want my help, but you need financial backing, right? I'm only offering to do what you're going to ask others to do. You don't want my name attached to your success story. I appreciate you for that. I've spent my entire life being used by people, Danielle. That you look at me and just see me, not my bank account, means the world. The truth remains, though, that my name carries a fair amount of weight with it. You need weight. Jett is no more experienced in this than you are. I can tell he's done the legwork, but when it comes to clout, the two of you just don't have what takes to pack a powerful punch. Let me be your boxing glove, princess. I'll be a silent partner. You and Jett will have complete control. The only thing I'm asking is that you'll let me attend the meeting with him next week."

"If you're only interested in a silent partnership, why do you need to attend any meetings? Is this going to turn into another one of your explosive jealousy bits?"

With her faced cupped in my hand, I look directly at her. The apprehension in her sparkling emeralds owning me, I stroke my thumb over her cheek. "Is there a reason for it to, princess?"

"None. I've already done the sleeping with a client thing. I think I'll skip the cliché sleeping with the boss part of the story."

"Ah, but he wouldn't be your boss. He'd be your business partner," I counter, playfully.

"Minor details." She sweeps her hand through the air to gesture her indifference. "So, if it's not about jealousy, then what's it about?"

"Business."

Eyebrows arched, she tilts her head and looks up at me skeptically.

"It's business, Danielle. You said it yourself. You don't know the right questions to ask. I want to make sure that this is just as beneficial for you as it him."

Eyes lightening, she throws her arms over my shoulders and pulls herself onto of my lap. "In that case, I'd love for you to join us." Fingers locked in my hair, she brushes her lips against mine. "Thank you."

"For?"

"Loving me," she smiles.

"You didn't give me any other choice, princess."

\*\*\*\*

"It's beautiful here," Danielle says, watching the orange and yellow hillsides roll by as the BMW X5 climbs toward the Black Grand Aspen. "It reminds me a little of Napa, but in a good way."

"Oh really? How's that?"

"It's stupid, really." Cheeks tinged pink, she looks at me. "My mom and I used to go for hikes a lot when she was still alive. Our house sat on forty-plus acres, so there was plenty of room for exploring. We'd start at the vines. I'd pick grapes and eat them as we went. Walt would've blown a gasket had he known." I watch the clouds roll over her at the memory of her stepfather. Brushing them off, she pulls her knees into the seat and spins toward me. "Anyway, it was pretty there in the fall. Everything was red and gold. Just like it is here. The closest I've been to it before now has been my runs through Central Park lately."

"I'm sorry." I place my arm over her shoulders and pull her close. "I know what it's like to have wonderful memories destroyed by the bad ones."

She shrugs. "Nothing we can do about. Although..."

"Why do I feel like I'm not going to like the sound of this?"

"Well... I shared a story about my mom. I'd love it if you shared one about your birth mother. I know you said you hardly remember her, but you found Lauren, so I know you have to know more than you claim."

Stiffening, I scroll through my Isabelle databank. *Memories of her passed out in her own vomit. Images of her returning home after disappearing for days, her skin dirty and clothes unkempt. The most recent memory of Isabelle curled up on a dirty floor in a ran down house in the outer boroughs.* These aren't things I plan on tainting Danielle with.

"You already have one."

"Lauren doesn't count. That story's more about how you met her than anything to do with your beginnings."

"I wasn't talking about Lauren." Grip tightening around her, I exhale. "Movies in the Park."

She allows an uncomfortable silence to build between us as she takes it all in. "I thought you meant Emmalyn."

"And I allowed you to, for reasons I'm sure you can understand."

She nods. "So, how'd the tradition start?"

Running my shaky hand through my hair, I take a few calming breaths. "We were living on the street... *again*. It was so hot outside. You've lived in Manhattan in June. You know what that's like. Anyway, my stomach was growling so badly I kept thinking I was going to be sick. Is — my birth mom — saw the notice for the movie on a corkboard a few blocks away from the park. I didn't feel like walking anymore. I sat on the ground and threw a tantrum."

"She was determined, though. She promised me we'd have fun. I didn't believe her. I'd gotten used to her broken promises, but then she told me if I stopped crying and came along, she'd buy me a hotdog. I was too hungry not to do what she said. When we got to The Square, the first thing we did was sit on the fountain. I didn't understand why we weren't going for my hot dog, but she looked at me, smiled, and said, "Wanna go swimming?" It was so hot I couldn't resist.

"She helped me in the fountain and told me whenever I saw a shiny coin to bend over and pick it up. I nearly choked to death the first time I tried, but after a while I got the hang of holding my nose shut with my fingers. I gave every cent I found to her. When we had enough for a hot dog, she helped me out of the fountain and bought one for me with the works: mustard, ketchup, relish, and onions. After that, we found a spot in the shade and waited for the movie to start. *The Land Before Time*. I'd never seen it before, and it fascinated me. After that, it kind of became a thing to do. The movies weren't always targeted at kids, but I never really cared. When you're sleeping under the shelter of bus stops and store awnings, you kind of learn to be thankful for anything that feels normal. And for a couple of hours every few days, Movies in the Park let me be just that. *Normal*."

"Sebastian," wet lashed, she laces her fingers through mine and crawls onto my lap, "I won't pity you. I know the last thing you want is another person looking at you with that look in their eye. Just know that I appreciate you telling me that. It helps to know more about where you came from."

Taking my strength from her, I pull her close. The rest of the ride up the mountain passes in silence. We stop in front of the hotel, and Thomas opens the door for us, leaning close when I step out to keep Danielle from hearing. "When you have a moment to spare, we need a meeting."

I nod my head and take Danielle's hand. "Ready for an adventure, princess?"

"Always."

She follows me through the glass doors, into the rustic lobby with its giant brick fireplace and softly lit chandeliers. In summer there's no fire to greet the guests, but during the busy season the warmth explodes through the lobby instantly, making you feel at home here. I lead her to the desk where I inform the clerk we'll be staying in my suite and instruct him to have his manager phone within the hour.

My suite comes equipped with a full kitchen, dining room, living area, two bedrooms, and two baths. I watch as Danielle moves along, running her fingers over the marble countertops and brick fireplaces. Wanting her to experience everything about this place that makes it special, I walk to the window and open the curtains to expose the panoramic view of the Rockies. Now, they're full of oranges, reds, and golds. When we return in the winter with my family, there'll be a snow-covered wonderland awaiting us.

"How are you feeling, princess? Sometimes the altitude can be too much to handle."

"I'm great," she yawns, "still a little tired from all the weekend excitement. I think."

"Were you tired when you woke up this morning?"

"No. Not really."

"It's the altitude. Come on." I lead her into the bedroom and help her onto the bed, curling up behind her. "Better?"

"A little. I hadn't realized I was dizzy until we started walking."

"It comes on quickly. We'll rest here for a few minutes and see how you are once you've had time to adjust."

"Okay."

Palm brushing against her hair, I cradle her in my arms until I hear her breathing slow. Slipping my arm from beneath her, I walk to the closet and kick off my shoes. Sighing, I walk to the bathroom and turn on the shower. The hot water pelts down on my face, dripping off my chin and running down my abdomen. I'll have to stay closer to the room than I'd originally planned to keep an eye on her, but thankfully I have plenty of extra hands to get the jobs done. While she naps, I'll meet with Thomas and the team. Then I'll discuss tomorrow's staff meeting with whatever manager happens to be on duty now. The last and most important thing I'll take care of is the treehouse. One way or another, Danielle will recover from the altitude sickness and everything will unfold as I've planned.

# Chapter 35

*D*<sup>anielle</sup>

I awaken with a start, honey-comb yellow sun blazing in my eyes. Squinting, I look around the unfamiliar bedroom. Sebastian's lying next to me, one arm slung over his face, the other resting on his abs. Smile spreading across my face, I graze my lips over his.

Hand lifting to brush the hair from my face, he opens his eyes and smiles. "Good morning, princess. Feeling better?"

"Much. Thanks for taking care of me."

He presses on the back of my head, lowering my lips to his. "No need to thank me. I'll always take care of you, Danielle. So, I'm guessing you're starving?"

"Yes!" I rock back onto my heels and place a hand over my stomach. "How long was I out?"

"About a day."

"That explains the headache."

"It could, or it could be part of the altitude sickness. I'll have some Tylenol sent up for you."

"Thanks. I'm gonna hit the shower. That should help some, too."

"Sounds like a good idea. I'd join you, but I have a few things to take care of."

Eyes focused on the alarm clock, I reply, "It's six o'clock in the morning, hotshot. What can you possibly have to take care of at six in the morning?"

"The things I was supposed to take care of when I turned my alarm off at four and went back to sleep with you."

"Has anyone ever told you that you're going to suffer from exhaustion one of these days?"

"Several people, but I don't believe them."

"Right," I roll my eyes, "you have super powers. How silly of me to have forgotten?"

I attempt to stand, but he grabs my arm and pulls me back down. "Before this day's over with, you'll know just how *super* I can be."

\*\*\*\*

Sebastian has breakfast with me, crepes and fresh fruit, and heads down to his staff meeting. Now I'm left alone in the colossal luxury suite. Hand gripped around my phone, I think of Geoff. It's been over a week since our fight and I haven't heard one word from him. That's the problem with having a best friend who's just as stubborn as you. One of you eventually must cave or else pride will be the downfall of one of the most important relationships in your life. Our general rule is that it'll be the person who caused the most damage. I guess Geoff's forgotten that he was the one who started the whole thing.

Teeth clenched, I bring the phone to my ear. The ringing echoes in the cloudy remnants of my altitude-altered brain. I'm not even sure why the fight escalated, or what it even started over, for that matter. The only thing I am sure of is that it had nothing to do with me moving in with Sebastian, and everything to do with tensions already being high. For that, we can both be forgiven.

"Hey, baby girl," he answers, his voice tired.

"Hey, asshole."

"I'm the asshole? You're the one who hasn't called to apologize," he snips.

"Pot calling the kettle black."

"Ugh, you drive me crazy!" He growls.

"Back at you," I snap.

For a few minutes we just sit in silence, his breath sounding in my ear and mine in his.

"So, how's the moving going?" He asks at last, his tone dramatically lighter.

Sinking against the chair, I breathe a sigh of relief. "It's going. There are still boxes everywhere. We spent most of last week in California, we spent the weekend in Vegas, and now we're in Aspen."

"What the hell are you doing in Aspen?"

"Why wouldn't I be in Aspen?"

He laughs. "Because you hate cold, you've never skied in your life, and you believe the Yeti is real."

"Hey, the Yeti is totally real!" My stomach shakes with my laughter.

"Whatever you say, baby girl. I'm glad you called. I've missed you."

"I've missed you too. More than you know. Wanna come over and hang out when I get back? I'm sure you could use a break from your parents by now?"

"Actually, I'm not with my parents anymore. I took that apartment in The Village. I've been here since Thursday."

"Wow! That was fast."

"Yeah," I can picture him shrugging as he continues, "once you weren't a factor anymore, I just went with it. It's the right place for me. My only issue so far's been the five-floor walkup. You don't know how much I hate lugging my camera and equipment up and down the stairs every day."

"I can imagine." Hand on my ankle, I draw my leg under me. "Speaking of work, have you heard anything about the fashion show yet?"

"Yeah. I got it."

"What? Oh my God, G, that's great!"

"Thanks. It gives me a way to keep pushing forward, at least. So, can I count on you to be my assistant for the night now that you're unemployed?"

"Well, that all depends, actually. I might be starting my own firm. Well... not really *my* own firm. I'd be joining in as a partner in someone else's firm, but it's still a very real opportunity."

"What? When did this happen?"

Mind turned back to the meeting I had in that 50s diner, I answer, "Last week. I haven't officially accepted, but I'm meeting with Jett — the guy I'll be going into business with — next week to finalize everything."

"Whoa."

"I'd like to think that was a happy whoa, but I know you better than that. What's on your mind?"

I hear wind rustling through the speaker and Geoff saying hello to someone in passing, then he's back. "Sorry, you caught me in the middle of getting ready for work. What was I saying?"

"I believe the exact word was 'whoa'."

"Right. It's not that it's bad, necessarily. Just, you know, it's only been a week and already you've traveled the country at Mister Big's side, practically started a new job, and done God only knows what else. Meanwhile, I've moved into a new place, and received what's possibly the biggest break of my career. A lot's happening. Don't you find it strange that neither of us thought to call the other one to tell them about it?"

"I was pissed at you. You knew I wasn't going to call. What's your excuse?"

"Embarrassed, I guess. I unloaded a lot of shit onto you that really had nothing to do with you moving in with Sebastian and everything to do with me. Every time I think I'm over it, there's just one more reminder. I found one of the suitcases he brought to New York that weekend when we were packing. It was just sitting there when I opened the door, haunting me with its presence. I didn't even know he took it to the apartment. We were staying at Sebastian's with you. I just assumed all the reminders of that weekend were with the stuff you brought to Mom and Dad's."

Heart bursting, I wipe the tears from my eyes. "Want me to help you go through it?"

"No. At least not right now. Eventually, I'll have the strength it takes to open it up. And when that day comes, yes, I'd love to have you beside me. For now, it's sitting in the closet of the spare room at my new place. I just need to leave it there."

"I understand." The sound of the door snapping shut in the foyer lets me know Sebastian's back from his meeting. Head turned, I see him standing in the entryway. "Listen, G, Sebastian's back. We're having dinner as soon as I get back, though. Your place. I'll christen the new kitchen."

"Sounds great to me, baby girl. Beware the Yeti."

"Oh, you're hilarious. I love you."

"Love your crazy ass, too. See you when you get back."

Phone placed in the back pocket of my jeans, I walk to Sebastian and wrap my arms around his waist. "How was the meeting, hotshot?"

"About as boring as to be expected. How was your morning? I see you found the clothes I left for you."

"I did. I do not understand why I need the sweater, though. You said it's going to be like seventy degrees today."

"You'll be thankful for the sweater, trust me." He leads me to a chair close to the fireplace and pulls me onto his lap. "So, that was Geoffrey you were talking to?"

"Yep. All's good now."

"I'm glad," he brushes his lips across mine and nuzzles his nose into my hair, "So you're feeling better? The headache's gone?"

"Completely."

"And you're in a good mood since you just patched things up with Geoff?"

I laugh. "Are you trying to say I'm moody, hotshot?"

"I'm smart enough not to get into that argument." He winks and tucks my hair behind my ear. "I'm all done here. Ready to go?"

"Depends," I arch my eyebrow at him, curiously, "where are we going? Belize? Zimbabwe? Some private island you have stashed away somewhere? "

His eyes alight with laughter, he answers, "It's an adventure, princess. You don't get to know any details."

****

"A hot-air balloon? That's your big adventure?" Ears filled with the whooshing of the balloon filling, I look over at him.

"It's only the beginning," he takes my hand in his, leading me toward our pilot, "you're not afraid of heights, are you? I just realized, I never thought to ask."

Something in his stare tells me he knows more about my experiences with heights than he's leading on, but I also know there's no point in fishing for details. "Nope. No tree was tall enough for me as a kid."

"Good."

The basket rises off the ground, and we're instructed to jump in. Sebastian picks me up, lifts me over, and then pulls himself in after. Enthralled, I hang on to the edge and stare out at the clear blue sky as we slowly climb higher and higher. Arms protectively placed on either side of mine, Sebastian leans over me.

"This is incredible!" I shout, leaning my head back against his chest.

"I thought you'd enjoy it. Just wait."

Before I know it, the ground has faded into a grid of resort rooftops and tree lined mountains. The reds, golds, and greens creating a mesmerizing canvas of color unlike any I've seen before. The roar of fire filling our ears, we ascend higher still. The sun peeks over the mountains, bouncing off the ice-covered caps and radiating the landscape with its luminance. I gasp at the beauty of it all, and Sebastian wraps his arms around me. Wind whipping through my hair, I turn my head and kiss his cheek. "Thank you for this."

287

We drift through the clouds at a peaceful pace, drifting over the little hills and valleys that make up this enchanting getaway. As we approach a field edged by a dense forest, our pilot brings us back toward the ground. The plummet is less calm than the takeoff, and my body jars against Sebastian's. He clamps his hands around my waist, holding me steady. On the ground below, I see two men in blue shirts directing us. We hover close enough for them to grab the basket, and they bring us back to Earth with a soft thud. Once everything's squared away, Sebastian hands our pilot a few hundred-dollar bills and helps me down from the basket.

"How do you feel?"

"Are you kidding me? I'd go again right now if you'd let me," I gush.

He places an arm over my shoulder and leads me to a blanket with a small picnic set up. "Now, aren't you glad I made you wear the sweater?"

"If you're waiting for me to say you were right, it's never gonna happen," I smart, easing my way onto the blanket.

Sebastian reaches into the picnic basket and pulls out a bottle of champagne, expertly pouring two glasses.

"Always the romantic," I tease, taking one from him.

"For you, I make the exception."

"That's where you're wrong, hotshot. For me, you are the exception. No one has ever put so much thought into all the details before. You always keep me guessing."

Amused, he prods, "And that's a good thing?"

"It's a great thing. Name a woman who tells you she doesn't enjoy being surprised, and I'll show you a liar."

Propped on his elbow, he looks up at me. "So, what are your guesses now?"

"Honestly? I don't have any. I have no idea what you're up to. Whatever it is, it's going to have to be pretty big to top that balloon ride."

"Oh, I think I'm up to the challenge." He winks and raises his glass in the air. "To guesses and second chances."

Tilting my glass against his, I take a sip and lie next to him. "So, do I get any hints?"

"Hints you say?" He reaches into the basket and unpacks our lunch. "No hints. You get olives al forno, margherita pizza, and an artesian cheese board."

"Not as good as a hint," He holds a piece of crusty bread with cheese spread across it out for me to taste. I sink my teeth into it, allowing the richness to coat my tongue, "but delicious none the less."

Extending a plate in front of me, he glances at the mountain behind us. "Good, you'll need every ounce of strength it gives you. Mangia." *Eat up.*

"Hmm... I love it when you talk of me needing my strength." I laugh and take a bite of the acidic tomato and basil pizza.

"Just remember that when you're hiking up that trail." I glance at the trail leading into the forest behind us. "Hiking? We're going in there?"

"Yep. Like I said, it's an adventure." He laughs at my expression. "Why do you look so shocked?"

"Don't take this the wrong way, but you just don't strike me as the rugged outdoorsy type."

He shrugs. "I'm not, but in this case, the view's worth it. Now eat. I want to get there before the sun goes down."

"The sun doesn't set for hours, Sebastian."

"Trust me. The sooner we leave, the better."

****

Panting for breath, I stare at the house in the clearing. Like something out of a dream, the log cabin sets on stilts with two adjoining cabins next to it. Wooden bridges lead from the ground up and connect the three.

"This is what we walked all that way for?" I ask, bending low to catch my breath. "No offense, hotshot, but the view from the hotel was better."

"I wouldn't be so sure about that. Here." He pulls a bottle of water from his backpack and hands it to me. "Catch your breath and we'll go up."

I sit on the ground and take several gulps. Leaving me to it, Sebastian disappears into the house. A few seconds later, lights twinkle on, illuminating the bridges. Sealing the cap on the now empty water bottle, I stand and follow the stone trail to the first ladder.

"Are you sure this thing's safe?" I call up.

"I thought you weren't afraid of heights."

"I'm not, but that doesn't mean I'm for plummeting to my death, either. It's a tree-house after all."

"It's probably sturdier than our penthouse," he calls back.

"I doubt that," I mutter, following the path the rest of the way to him.

He greets me at the door with a smile. "What do you think?"

"Is this one of those living out your childhood fantasies things you men are notorious for?"

"No. Well, yes, it started out as that, but it became something more. This is where I do some of my best thinking."

"Up here... alone... in the woods... with no shower?"

"There's a fully loaded cabin attached, but you have to come through the house to get to it."

"So, I have to go up, just to go back down?"

The devious smirk he's famous for spreads across his lips. "You don't have to, but I love it when you do."

Shoving against his chest, I laugh. "Whatever you say, hotshot. So, what do we do now?"

"Come on." Lacing my fingers through his, he leads me through a small kitchen — with no appliances, I note — and to the door leading to one of the other bridges. "Close your eyes."

"Okay, but you better not be hiding the Yeti out there."

He laughs and raises his eyebrow at me. "The Yeti?"

"It's nothing. I used to have an irrational fear of the Abominable Snowman when I was little. Geoff brought it up when we talked this afternoon."

"Ah... well, I can promise there are no snowmen, abominable or otherwise. Now, close your eyes or I'll blindfold, bind, and gag you like the sexy slave you are."

"Mm... yes, master."

Doing as he commands, I listen to the door creak open. Sebastian takes my hands in his once more and leads me out onto the bridge. Hands firmly planted on my shoulders, he turns me toward the railing and places his chin on my shoulder.

"I've never shared this place with anyone, Danielle. My family and I come here every year for Christmas and not even they know I have this land. Alana's never seen it, none of my *others* could've even imagined it. I live so much of my life for everyone else. I didn't want to share this. Not until now. Not until you. You can open your eyes now."

Blinking, I open my eyes and stare out at the town below us. It looks like a postcard from this distance, the sun setting below the mountains and casting shadows across the resorts below. Pink sky meets purple mountains, orange and red leaves rustle with the light breeze. The air is crisp and clean, like no air I've breathed before. Lights glowing from the hotels and cabins, the only sign of life beyond Sebastian and me.

"Okay. You win. This view *is* worth it."

Palms resting on my stomach, he pulls my back against his chest. "Told you."

Our bodies flushed as one, we stand there watching the stillness of it all until the sky goes black. Chilled, I run my hands over my arms and shiver.

"Cold?" Sebastian asks, breaking the silence.

"A little."

"Still want that shower?"

I turn to him. "More than you'll ever know."

"Okay, come with me."

He leads me through another one of the treehouse's towers. This one is set up like a bedroom, complete with a dresser and matching nightstands.

"You sleep up here?"

"Sometimes."

Shaking my head, I follow him through the door and onto another bridge, which is concealed by tree limbs. Carefully placed lanterns as our guide, we follow it down to the deck of a much larger cabin. The deck hangs right over the edge of the mountain. Pausing, I look over and see the field we picnicked on below.

"I'm on top of the world, *literally*."

"I'm glad you're enjoying yourself, princess." He pulls me toward a sliding glass door. "The shower's this way."

"How'd you ever manage to keep this place a secret?"

"It's easier than you might think. No one else in my life feels the need to ask as many questions as you do." He winks and leads me into the living room, flipping a light switch.

A gorgeous chandelier comes to life, casting light across the wooden interior, accented with leather sofas, a corner fireplace, and a large flat screen television. We move through the room, carefully skirting around the coffee table, and pause briefly at the kitchen where Sebastian deposits his backpack on the counter.

True to form, Sebastian has left no detail unnoticed. I run my fingers over the granite countertops and make note of the state-of-the-art appliances. He empties the water into the fridge and turns to me.

"So, there's a loft up those stairs," he nods toward a hand carved wooden staircase. "A dining room just through there and an office across from it."

"Of course." I roll my eyes. "Do you ever stop working?"

Ignoring me, he continues, "The bedroom is through this door. Come on."

I follow him into a bedroom with a king-sized bed, its own gas fireplace, and French doors leading out onto a private balcony. Sprawled carefully across the bed is an elegant red laced dress, with a black underlay. Matching Christian Louboutins rest in the box beside it.

"Um... Sebastian?"

"Yes."

"When'd you have time to bring a dress here?"

"It's been here since last night. Under my supervision, Thomas arranged everything we need."

"So, when you said no one knew about this place?"

"Danielle, you should assume Thomas knows everything there is to know about me. For security reasons, he has to."

I'm glad one of us does.

He strokes his thumb over my cheek, melting away any doubt I had. "He keeps his distance. There's another small cabin on the other side of the treehouse. When I'm here, you can find him there. The first time he came into the main house was when I had him do so on Sunday. I initially planned on doing all this myself, but then the altitude sickness hit..."

I nod. "It means just as much, regardless."

"Let's get you in the shower."

Fingertips skimming my flesh, he presses his lips to mine. Breathlessly, I sink against him. He runs his hands under my shirt, the heat of his palms igniting a fire on my skin. Undoing the button on my jeans, he glides his hands along my sides and lowers to a squat in front of me. He pulls my jeans free, his fingertips moving over my thighs and down my legs, leaving a trail of goosebumps as they go. Sucking on my thigh, he kisses his way over my hip bone and sucks at my tattoo before moving up my torso. Sighing, I watch as he curls his fingers under the hem of my shirt. Heart beating out of my chest, I raise my arms, allowing him to pull it over my head.

Fingers smoothing my hair, he kisses me again. His lips tease their way to my ear as he takes my bra clasps between his fingers and unhooks me. Teeth grazing across my nipple, he wraps my legs around his waist and carries me to the bathroom. I sit on the counter while he turns the hot water on. Surrounded by steam, I watch as he pulls his shirt over his head. The lined ridges of his biceps and torso bulging with the movement.

Clenched thighs, I fight my growing anticipation as he undoes his jeans. Wearing nothing but his boxers, he takes my hand and helps me from the counter. One knee on the floor, he encases my hipbones with his hands. In an instant, he hooks his thumbs under the waistband of my panties and strips me bare. Gasping, I step into the shower.

Eyes closed, I allow the warmth of the water to consume me. Stepping behind me, Sebastian wraps one arm over my breasts and pulls me against him. He finds my clit with the fingers of his free hand and begins massaging me in rushed circles. Needy, I toss my head back and moan. His girth expands against my butt, fueling my arousal. I grind against him and a low, guttural growl escapes his lips.

"Turn around," he demands.

Chest heaving, I turn and face him. Smoldering eyes locking onto mine, our mouths collide. He shoves my back against the wall; the water splashing down on us as his tongue devours mine. Reaching beside me, he grabs a towel and a bottle of body wash. Leaving me breathless, he pulls away and works up a generous lather. Stiff cock pressed against my hipbone, he runs the towel over my skin.

Brazen, I pour a generous amount of body wash in my palm and gently glide my hands over his back and torso. Cock jerking, he spins me around and clamps his soapy palms around my breasts, kneading at them. Moaning, I toss my head back and wrap my hand around his girth.

Teeth gritted, he growls into my ear and brings one hand to my clit. Wrapped in him, I tighten my grip and quicken my strokes. Not to be outdone, he hooks his fingers inside of me, pulling at my G-spot and sending a jolt to my stomach. Panting, I press my free hand against the wall to steady myself.

Breath hitched between his teeth, he grabs and pulls it behind my back bending me over. Ready for him, I spread my legs. Heavy laden, the tip of his head brushes against the opening of my core. Desperate to be filled with him, I push my hips back. Roaring in response, he pulls away and starts the torment again. Swollen clit brushing over the length of his cock, I plead, "Please, Sebastian. Fuck me. Now!"

"Are you sure you're ready?" He asks. "I don't plan on being gentle."

"I'm ready," I promise.

Hand on my hip, he wraps the other in my hair and yanks. Pleasure filled moan responding to the sting, I snap my head back. Shoving himself inside of me, he stretches me to a snug fit.

"I love this tight little pussy, princess. I want to bury myself inside you, and never return."

"Please," I cry.

Balls slapping against my thighs, his pace quickens. Shaking legs barely able to hold me upright, I rock in time with him. Freeing my hair, he catches my other hip in his hand to stabilize me. Fireworks exploding in my head, I come undone around him. The heated rush of my orgasm making it easier for him to maneuver, he lies on the floor and positions me on top of him.

Shower stream running in my face, I grind against him. Shoulders lifted from the ground, he places one hand on my back and runs the fingers of the other along my clit. Second orgasm building from where the first left off, I arch my back and place my hands on his hips.

"Fuck!" He growls, his head rolling across my G-spot as I slide down on him.

Body convulsing, I feel his cock twitch under me. Greedy for his come, I increase the intensity of my rhythm. Hand gripped on my wrist, he explodes within me. Brought to my undoing by his pleasure, I cry out. Sex clenching around him, I drink him in until he has nothing left to give. Spent, I roll off him and curl beside him.

Cold water flooding on the shower floor around us, Sebastian stands and shuts off the tap. Shaking, I take his hand and lift from the floor. He grabs a towel off the rack and wraps me in it, kissing my forehead. "I'll leave you to it, princess. Take all the time you need. I have a lot to do."

"Haven't we already discovered that I don't care for getting ready when I don't know what I'm getting ready for?"

"Well, we're in a cabin in the middle of nowhere, so..."

"And yet," I turn my head to the bathroom door, "there's a fabulous red dress lying on the bed..."

"I'm confident you'll figure something out," he says, winking and walking out of the room.

"Most infuriating man ever," I mutter, smiling into the mirror and opening drawers in search of a hairdryer. Like always, Sebastian covered it all. Anything I could ever need is right at my fingertips.

****

Eyes locked on my reflection, I remind myself to breathe. Nervous energy pulsing through my veins, I examine my *look* one last time. The lace hugs my body in all the right places, the black under red giving me a sultry advantage. As per usual, when Geoff's not around, I've pulled my hair into a sleek ponytail. My eyes are lined in black to give them a dramatic edge, and I painted my lips a dark red. Slipping into the stiff new shoes, I walk across the room and open the door. "Magic" by Coldplay playing softly in the living room takes me by surprise. It's not Sebastian's usual genre by any means.

Smiling at his attention to detail, I follow the votive-lit trail to the dining room. The table is aglow with groups of votive candles surrounding the place settings and a bowl filled with pink-colored water, rose petals, and floating candles rests in the middle. On the floor lining the walls are more votives, and carefully positioned around the table are pairs of candelabras, dimly lit with tapers. A bouquet of lilies is propped in one of the chairs.

Butterflies in my stomach, I pluck the card loose and smell them. *Baiser Vole Cartier perfume and my mother*. I don't remember ever telling Sebastian that they were my favorite flower, but I know for certain I never mentioned the significance of their scent and my mother's favorite perfume or the fact that she took her namesake from them. Teary-eyed at the unexpected memory, I turn my attention to the card.

*When I see you, you see me.*

*All my love,*

*Sebastian*

Holding the card against my chest, I walk to the kitchen. Busy with something I can't see, Sebastian's back is turned to me. Dressed in a tailored dark gray suit, he looks like a dirty dream brought to life. Trying to keep my hormones at bay, I say, "Subtly isn't your strong suit. Is it hotshot?"

I can tell by his posture that he's smirking, but when he turns around and hits me with it, I feel myself melting where I stand. "You look pleasantly sinful," he says, taking my face in his hands for a kiss.

Pulling away, I run my hand over the silk of my favorite red tie. "You don't look half bad yourself." I lift the card in the air and smile. "Thank you for the flowers. I love you too."

"And that makes me lucky," he winks at the play on his safe word, "ready for dinner?"

"Depends. Is it edible?" I ask. "You've made it clear your kitchen skills aren't quite up to par. No worries, though. We all have to be bad at something."

"What I wouldn't give to still have the power to spank you," he threatens, smiling. "It's from the hotel."

Leading me back into the dining room, he pulls out my chair for me and takes the seat across from mine. Pulling his phone from his interior pocket, he sends a quick text and turns it on silent. "It's not off, but it will be less distracting this way."

"Silent works. Trust me, Sebastian, after all this I can compromise with silent. So, are you planning on serving me this meal you promised, or is making food magically appear one of your super powers?"

"Good evening, Miss Stevens," Thomas says.

I look up to see him wearing an equally handsome suit and carrying a bucket of ice and a bottle of champagne. Shaking my head at Sebastian, I thank him and wait patiently as he pours a glass for each of us.

"So now he's a driver, security detail, contract negotiator, and butler..."

Sebastian smiles, and my heart stops beating. "I told you, princess," he takes my hand in his, "he's a man of many talents. If it makes you feel any better, though, this is a job he actually volunteered for."

"Hmm... now I'm even more intrigued."

"What was that you said earlier?" Eyes alight with mischief, he pauses and stares at me. "Oh yeah, 'I always keep you guessing'. I'm just trying to live up to my reputation."

"I'd say the reputation has been far exceeded at this point."

Thomas returns, placing a quinoa Caesar salad in front of each of us. It's as delicious as it sounds and followed by equally appetizing tomato walnut basil pasta. Sebastian and I eat, laugh, and chat playfully through each course. By the time we've finished our dessert, chocolate cake with raspberry lime salsa, I don't think there's any way I could eat another bite. "Silhouette" by Active Child and Ellie Goulding plays, and I'm swaying in my chair before I even realize it.

"I love this song."

Sebastian makes his way around the table and holds a hand out to me. "I've noticed. Dance with me?"

"Always," I reply, placing my napkin on the table and my hand in his.

He leads me to the living room and places his hands on the small of my back. I rest mine around his neck, the purely masculine scent of his skin intoxicating me as he sways us in time with the music. Alone with him, I feel at home. It's a feeling I never want to lose. My pulse races as his warm breath teases the sensitive skin of my neck.

"Have I told you how delicious you taste?" He asks, gently kissing my collar bone.

I giggle. "Not today, no."

"Shame on me," he says, winking. "Are you happy, Danielle?"

"I'm as happy as I can be, all things considered," I reply honestly.

"That's all I can ask for, I suppose. Has the past week been a pleasant break for you?"

"I haven't forgotten it all, but it's done a lot of good to get out of the city. Thank you for bringing me here, by the way. It's so peaceful."

"I'm glad you're enjoying it."

His palms pressing on the skin exposed by the cutout in the back of my dress, he holds me close. We finish the song in silence, my head resting on his shoulder and his atop mine.

"Thank you for the dance," I say.

"The pleasure was all mine, Miss Stevens." I can't help but smile at the memory of when we first met. "Will you follow me to one more stop on our adventure?"

"I'd follow you anywhere, hotshot."

Hand-in-hand, we walk onto the deck, now illuminated with twinkling fairy lights, and across the bridge leading up to the tree house. Sebastian opens the curtained door, and the room comes to life with candlelight. Floor covered with wall to wall rose petals. It's like something out of a fairytale.

"Sebastian," I whisper, lost for words.

"Come with me."

We follow the trail of flowers and candles through the other door, across the second bridge, and into the equally breathtaking main room. Sebastian leaves me standing in the middle while he goes to the kitchen area and opens a drawer. Ignoring the fire hazard, I stare at the heart-shaped candle display on the floor. White icicle lights hang from the rafters. The sweet smell of jasmine fills the air. Stomach a ball of nerves, I watch Sebastian walk back to where I stand with a blindfold in hand.

"You have to wear this for the next part."

Hand shaking, I hold my ponytail up and allow him to place the blindfold over my head. Blindly following him, I listen for clues as to what to expect next. The creaking of boards beneath our feet tells me we're on the last bridge — the one he didn't take me on before. Guiding me, Sebastian places my hand on the railing and instructs me to hold on. The somewhat distant sound of a door opening echoes through my ears, followed closely by the sound of "Never Stop" by SafetySuit.

Returning, Sebastian turns me around so that I'm facing him. His hands hold on to my face, his kiss gentle but intentional. Sighing against his lips, I release the bar and fist my hand into his hair. He pulls away, taking my hand and guiding me into the other room. The song starts again, and I hear the door close. Moving me to the center of the room, Sebastian takes the blindfold off.

Eyes threatened with tears, I look around. This room is also decorated with candlelight and flower petals. To my left is an iPod dock, playing the song on repeat. Behind me, a small table holds a projector and a laptop. Directly in front of me is the blank screen it's intended to play on. Sebastian turns me to face him, his eyes wet.

"I love you, Danielle," he says, his voice catching. "You have no idea how much."

Terrified, I watch him trying to reel in his emotions. He swallows and takes several deep breaths. Then, ever so slowly, lowers to the one knee.

"Oh my God!" I gasp, my hands shaking uncontrollably as I cover my mouth. "Sebastian..."

Smiling up at me, he pulls me down onto his knee. "I like control. I crave it like some crave water. Yet, when you come around, I lose all hope of it. We're messy, and broken, and so imperfect that we somehow find a way to make all of that make sense. Before I met you, I thought I was as complete as I was ever going to get. I was content to live in my darkness as long as no one had to live there with me. You changed that, Danielle."

Eyelashes clumped with tears, I stare down at his blurry outline.

Smiling, he continues, "You changed me. You brought light into my world. You showed me what I was missing. I thought I had it all planned out. Now the only thing I can know for certain is that without you, it's meaningless. I love you, princess, and that's why..."

Giving me a gentle push, he slides me off his lap and stands behind me as the screen comes to life. Gasping for breath, I stare at the image of my mother's grave. The headstone and surrounding earth are covered in pink lilies. Her favorite. Just like mine. The camera is only focused on the granite tombstone for a few seconds, but I spend them reading the words to myself once more.

*Lillian Nichole Stevens-Smith*

*Beloved wife, devoted mother, and friend to her community.*

Sebastian pulls me in a little tighter as the camera rotates to show his face on the screen.

"You told me you couldn't come back here, but I wanted to bring you at least once," the him on camera whispers. "I already got your dad's blessing, but I know how important it would've been for you to have hers. You're not your mother, Danielle, and I am not Walter. I've been having a nice long chat with her, and she agrees with me. There's no point in waiting until we've been together longer. You know me. Inside and out. You've been exposed to the darkest pieces of me, and you stayed anyway. We can't fail, because we already know everything we're facing. So—"

Feeling weightless, I stare at the screen, wondering what comes next. My knees wobble with nerves, and I have to ball my fingernails into my hands to control my shaking. I'm unaware that Sebastian has stopped holding onto me until he reaches his hand up onto my thigh and says, "Turn around, princess."

The first thing I see is Sebastian smiling up at me. The second is the ring. A massive princess-cut black diamond held in place with two rows of crisscrossing white diamonds holding it in place on either side, all set in a black gold band.

"Marry me," he demands, true to his nature.

*Never a question, always an answer.*

"Sebastian, I—"

"No thinking," he says. "Just feel."

Slowly exhaling, I close my eyes. I want to marry this man. Everything in my heart is screaming yes, but logically I know it's crazy. We've barely been together for four months, and during that time we've already broken up once. Plus, there's the added factor of the secrets he's still intent on keeping. How can I marry him when I don't know what else is hiding behind the storm in his eyes? *How can I not?* There's never going to be another man in my life like Sebastian. No one will ever understand me like he does.

*When I see you, you see me.*

The beautifully scripted words of his card flash through my mind. Conflicted, I open my eyes and look down at him. The brightness of his joy has faded to worry. Lines wrinkle his forehead, and his lips are cast downward in a frown."

"I love you, Sebastian," I whisper, falling to my knees in front of him.

"I love you too, Danielle. So, marry me." He places the ring in my hand. "I know we have a lot of work to do, but it doesn't matter if we do it now or later. We're going to end up here either way. Marry me, princess. Make me complete."

"I never knew I wanted marriage," I answer. "Not until you, but now I know it's the only way I want our story to end."

"Why do I feel like there's another but to that sentence?" He takes my hand in his and squeezes as though I'm his lifeline.

"I can't say yes, Sebastian." A wave of nausea hits at the disappointment on his face. "I'm not saying no either. I'm saying... *maybe*."

"Maybe?" He stands and dusts his pants legs.

"Yes. Maybe," I reply, following him. I cup his face in my hands and stare into his eyes. "I want to marry you, Sebastian. If I didn't have an ounce of logic in me at all, I'd say yes in a heartbeat. I just can't right now. Not like this. Your proposal was perfect. It's everything most girls would ever dream of and then some. Please let my answer be perfect as well. Can you give me some time to think things through?"

He runs his hand over his face and looks back at me. "I guess that's fair."

Exhaling, I loop my hands around his waist. "Thank you, Sebastian."

# Chapter 36

*S*ebastian

"Jacob Whitmore on hold for you," Robin's voice rings through my intercom.

"Send him through." Ready for battle, I settle into my chair. Jacob Whitmore tried to wage a war. He didn't realize he was going against the fucking general. Tie loosened, I press the blinking button and bring the handset to my ear. "Jacob. How nice of you to return my call."

"I assume this is about the investment. I've made my terms clear, Black. Tag on another zero and give me a stake in your company. That's the only way we have a deal."

"Oh, I'm well aware of your terms. Before this conversation goes any further, I need to ask, are you on a secure line, Jacob?"

"What the fuck does that mean?"

"I'm only trying to protect you," I drum my fingers on my desk, "there are things we need to discuss that require a bit of discretion."

"Unless you're offering what I asked for, we have nothing left to discuss."

Eyes trained on the black and white surveillance footage, I lean forward and rest my elbows on my desk. "Very well. I think you'll change your mind soon, Jacob. Do you remember visiting a club named Vivid over the weekend?"

"So, I blew off a little steam. Anyone dealing with you would've done the same."

"I have no doubt many people would agree with you. However, what you failed to realize is that Vivid is a holding of Black, Inc. You were doing business with me without even realizing it. Apparently, you didn't do your research as thoroughly as you believed."

"Still not seeing your point," he replies, sounding bored.

"Right. I don't like to beat around the bush either. You met with a young girl while you were there. Pretty. Blonde hair. Great ass. Remember her?"

"Is getting your dick sucked in the bathroom a crime these days?"

"No. Not exactly. I'm sure it could qualify as a public indecency misdemeanor, but we both know a slap on the wrist means nothing to you. How many times have you been brought in on DUIs now? Eleven if I'm not mistaken. That's some lawyer you have, Jacob. I may have to reconsider my own representation. Anyway, it was a Saturday night. You wanted to have a good time. I get it. What I don't understand is why that pretty girl has been reported missing. Apparently, the last time anyone saw her was on Saturday when she told her friends she was going home with 'the hot guy she met at the bar'. We both know that's not the last time she was seen. Don't we, Jacob?"

"Make your point, Black."

"My point, Whitmore, is this… Blair Cooper was just another girl. Just another notch in your belt. But to her parents and friends, she was much more. She was an athlete, and a straight-A student. At nineteen years old, she was supposed to have her whole life ahead of her. Then she met you. Blair didn't make it home with the guy from the bar — *you* — that night, did she, Jacob? She made it as far as the parking lot before passing out from what I can only assume was alcohol poisoning." Stomach churning, I press the play button and watch the images on screen come to life. "It's what happened next that truly fascinates me. At first you thought it was a joke. You laughed and tried to help her up. Then the realization hit."

"For a minute, it looked like you were going to help her. Maybe it was when you were taking those last few paces between your car and the door that she took her last breath. Regardless, you waited too long. What gets me the most is that once the realization hit, you seemed to calm down completely. I'd dare say that most people who witnessed the event would say you handled it like a professional." Bile rising in my throat, I watch him toss the dead girl over his shoulder and throw her into his car. *Lauren's only a few years younger than this girl.* Chasing away the thought, I stop the footage. "The thing I can't figure out is where you disposed of the body."

"Body?" He asks, his voice raising a few octaves. "What body? I took that girl home and fucked her brains out. When I woke up the next morning, she was gone. Whatever happened between my house and hers has nothing to do with me."

"Maybe that's true. I could've misinterpreted the video. Perhaps the local police can do a better job with their copy."

"Video?"

"The security footage from the club. They were, of course, contacted as part of the investigation. I own the property, so naturally I was notified. I'm looking at the footage now."

"Your bullshitting. Your henchman already told you I don't have any dirt on you. You're just using the same scare tactic I tried during our first meeting."

"Am I? Maybe so. Either way, I would give that brilliant lawyer of yours a call. Something tells me you're going to need him."

Voice shaking, he asks, "What do you want from me?"

"You already know what I want."

"And then you'll make the evidence go away?"

"Of course," I pull the drive from my desktop and twirl it in my fingers, "the contract's in your inbox now. Just sign it, send it my way, and this will all be over."

"You'll have it in ten minutes."

"Oh and, Jacob, the price has been reduced. I'm sure you can understand."

He mumbles something that sounds a lot like "*motherfucker*" and hangs up. Energy spent, I lean back in my chair and run my fingers through my hair. I want nothing more than to wipe my hands clean of the situation and be done with this sick little bastard once and for all. Shifting gears, I press the intercom and tell Robin to send Thomas in. Straightening my suit, I walk to the bar and pour two glasses of scotch.

"I take it things went as planned," Thomas asks, taking one.

"Here's to five 'o'clock," I reply, lifting my glass toward him. "He asked for ten minutes."

The sound from my desktop lets me know it's done. "That's probably him now."

I open the attachment and scan over all the lines. Noting that all the electronic signatures are there, I turn to Thomas. "Send the footage."

"You're sure?"

I toss back the rest of my drink and nod. "I already have two murders on my conscious. I won't have another one. Not this one, at least. Those men were monsters. This girl was innocent. She was just a kid, and there are people out there mourning her. Send the footage, wait a few days, and then make sure her family gets my check. It won't end their pain, but the little shit met her at one of my clubs. The least I can do is step up and help them give their daughter the burial she deserves."

"Consider it handled. I also have the report you asked for." He pulls a flash drive from his pocket. "Everything we've found about the girl so far is in there."

"Ah... Piper. Just one more fire I get to put out on behalf of Danielle. The tap is still working?"

"We'll be aware of every conversation."

"Good work, Thomas. Keep me updated."

He nods. "As for the other thing... everyone's in place. When Alana arrives in Colorado next week, we'll be ready."

Spinning my empty glass across my desktop, I lean back in my chair and stare at the ceiling. Alana's semi-annual visit with Teagan. I can't believe it's only been six months since I had to deal with the agony that she was hugging our daughter when I couldn't. I think of the flash drive holding the video surveillance from their last visit. It's locked in my safe at home with all the others. Perhaps it's time for me to revisit them.

"Thanks for the update."

"It's what you pay me for."

"Have you confirmed Danielle's agenda for the night?"

"She's meeting Geoffrey Taylor in The Village for dinner at eight. I'm driving her."

"Make sure she suspects nothing."

"Can I speak freely, sir?"

"I'm not your C.O., Thomas. You've been with me long enough to know yours is one of the few opinions I value."

Age shown by the lines around his eyes, he smiles. "I'm not sure that's the case on this one, but I appreciate it nonetheless. I think it's time you tell Ms. Stevens about Isabelle. She's the canyon standing in the way of where you are now, and Danielle accepting your proposal. Isabelle has already stolen a lot from you. I've watched her do it. Don't let her take Ms. Stevens, too."

"That's exactly why I'm not telling Danielle."

Disapproval briefly flashing in his eyes, he sets his empty glass on the table and fastens his lapels. "I'll give you a full report once I've sent over the footage."

I don't have to excuse him. We both know we're done here. It's bad enough that my father used Lauren to guilt me into this family session with our birth mother. I will not make it worse by having Danielle thrown in the middle of it all.

**** 

"She said maybe. *Maybe.* Who the fuck says maybe?"

"*Lauren...*"

"Don't *Lauren* me like that. There are way more important things for us to discuss than my use of the f-word. Besides, I'm not a child anymore *and* I dealt with enough during my childhood to have earned the right to say fuck whenever I fucking want." The corner of my sister's lips turn upward into a sneer as she turns her head in my direction.

"Well, I hate to point out how wrong you are. Especially when you're feeling particularly indignant at the moment, but I wasn't about to lecture you on your language. My issue is your quick judgement of Danielle. Put yourself in her position."

"Hmm..." She puts a finger to her lips. "Let me think for a minute... a rich, eligible, and *somewhat* attractive man," smile spread wide, she looks at me over the rim of her sunglasses, "pledges his undying love to me, and gives me a rock the size of one of Jupiter's moons. What to do? What to do?"

Peddle pressed to the floor, I switch lanes. "It's not as easy as you're making it. *I'm* not as easy as you're making me. Danielle has every right to have concerns. For starters, she comes from a different background than either of us. Danielle's seen what a difficult marriage can do to someone. Then, there's the added factor of the baggage she carries around from her childhood. You and I both know what it's like to have someone steal what should've been the happiest years of your life from you. Which brings me to the fact that I'll never be able to let Danielle into every part of my world. Isabelle is a nuclear weapon on a good day. I will not have Danielle anywhere near her when the blast finally goes off."

"But you *love* each other, Sebastian," she whines. "That should be enough. Every romantic comedy I've ever watched says so."

"You're too wise to believe in fairytales. We both know it."

"Of course I am. Cinderella's prince would've taken one look at those rags and ran screaming, because she would've wrecked his public image. Sleeping Beauty would've woken up from that coma not even knowing who the random guy sucking her face was.

And don't even get me started on The Little Mermaid. That's what makes my point even stronger. I *need* to believe in your fairytale, Sebastian. I *want* to see things work out for you, because unlike those losers in the storybooks, you deserve a happy ending. We *all* do."

Hand gripped tightly around the steering wheel, I risk looking at her. Tears spill from beneath her shades, and I can only picture the helpless look in her eyes. She tries to hide her pain by smiling, but I know just how deep that knife cuts. I gave up on *hope* a long time ago, but my beautiful little sister can't seem to let it go. Ever the innocent one, despite how much experience life has thrown at her. My experiences taught me to take my emotions, lock them up tight, and forget they ever existed. Lauren wears her heart on her sleeve. She's a lot like Danielle in that way.

"I'm not giving up on her just yet," I reply. "Danielle asked for time. I'm giving it to, but my result will be the same as I've always planned. I will marry Danielle Stevens. There's no force in nature that can stop me."

"I'm glad to hear it." She leans her head back against the leather seat. "Maybe I could talk to her?"

"No."

"But—"

"The answer to your every argument is no."

"Fine." Arms crossed, she looks back at me. "Let's have a new argument, then. When am I getting my own Lamborghini?"

"When hell freezes over."

"Haven't you heard, big brother?" She points to the exit sign leading to my father's clinic. "It already has."

"Truer words were never spoken." I cut my eyes to her once again. "I'm only doing this for you. The second it gets to be too much, say the word. We'll be out of here faster than Isabelle's head can spin."

"Don't talk about her like that, Sebastian. She may be a train wreck, but she's still our mother."

White knuckled force keeping my hands on the wheel, I stare straight ahead. Isabelle gave birth to me, but she's not my mother. I never knew exactly what having a mother was supposed to feel like until I woke up in the hospital with Emmalyn holding my hand. Our family — the Black family — has certainly had its share of problems, but we support each other through them. When I went looking for Isabelle all those years ago, I was hoping to use my newfound understanding of family to help her.

What happened instead was that I found Lauren. I thought I was doing the best thing for her by getting custody. Listening to the desperation in her voice as she outlines her hopes for this therapy session, however, I can't help but wonder if she would've been better off getting a family of her own. *A proper family.* Patient souls like Richard and Emmalyn, who would give her the space she needed, but also hold her close before she even realized that was the answer.

She deserves that from life. Instead, she got a dysfunctional older brother who locked her away with a nanny. How can I even be considering trying to make Teagan a part of my life, when Lauren's been here all along and I've still kept her a secret from so many people who matter most to me?

Ears filled with the echo of our footsteps, I lead Lauren to my father's office. Though I say I'm here for her, the truth is Lauren's just as steadying for me. She needs this and I need to give it to her. Shaking hand wrapped around the doorknob, I nod in her direction. Responding with a thumbs up, she smiles. Here goes nothing.

"Ah, I was wondering how much longer you'd be," my father says, looking up from his laptop. "Did you run into traffic, son?"

"Some. Nothing unusual. Lauren was a little late getting out of school."

"Understandable." Twinkling eyes studying me, he gives me a hug and turns to Lauren to do the same. "Make yourselves comfortable. I'll be right back with Isabelle."

"Wait!" Lauren screeches, grabbing for my arm.

My father and I both turn our complete attention to her. Face ghostly white, she drives her fingernails into my forearm. Hand on her elbow, I attempt to ease her shaking. Her eyes dart from left to right, studying mine. Heavy breaths coming from her mouth, she struggles to find her words. "I don't... I don't think I can do this. The last time I saw her was when she... when she..." A stream of tears flows from her eyes.

Helpless, I pull her against my chest, cradling the back of her head in my hand. Father closes the door and carefully walks toward us. "What you're feeling is perfectly normal, Lauren. I want you to know you're not alone in this. The hurt that addicts cause..." He glances up at me, and I know he's reliving the sleepless nights consumed by my nightmares. "Well, it's not an easy one to erase. That's why I felt it was important to do this session. Isabelle needs to face what she's done," his eyes dart up to mine again, "to both of you."

"She won't care," Lauren sniffles. "She's never cared. My whole life, I've been second to Sebastian. Before I even knew him, she raved about how amazing our lives would be when he came back. I've been here for her every weekend for years. When she gets released, I'm the one who visits Black House daily to check on her. Still, nothing I do will ever make me him. She'll never love us both, she can't."

Like ice on the skin amid a hot summer's day, her words cut straight through me. I promised long ago that nothing would ever bring Lauren any harm, and I've been doing it all along without realizing it. Breaking free, I sink into one of the tan chairs facing my father's desk. Head cradled in my hands, I stare at the floor in front of me.

"It's not your fault," she continues, squatting beside me. "You've always done the best you can for all of us. You're my big brother, and I love you. I'd literally be lost without you. Who knows where I would've ended up if you wouldn't have taken her to court? It's just that..." Hands gripping the chair so hard it creaks, she looks up at me.

"What? Tell me what I'm doing wrong, and I'll fix it."

"You don't love her, Sebastian. You tolerate her, because you feel you have to for me, but you don't love her. *I do*. She's my mother. I'll always love her, but she's never loved me. It's not your fault. It just hurts. That's all." She shrugs, laughs, and looks up at my dad. "Sorry, Doctor B. I guess this therapy thing really is all it's cracked up to be. You haven't even brought my mom into the room yet, and I'm already acting like a crazy person."

He smiles at her. "You're not crazy, Lauren. You're a young girl who carries around an unspeakable amount of pain. That makes you brave, not broken, and it certainly doesn't put you in the category of crazy — not that there is such a thing."

"Thanks," she answers.

"There's no need to thank me." Optimistic gaze turned on me, he adds, "Sebastian, do you have anything you'd like to contribute to the conversation?"

"I..." Throat constricted, I look from one desperate face to the other. I know they want me to have some form of a remarkable epiphany, like the one my sister just expressed. I just can't. Vulnerability opens the window for others to destroy you. Frankly, I've had all the destruction I'm willing to tolerate for this lifetime. "No."

Frowning, he straightens and returns his attention to Lauren. "It's your call. We can end this session now, and you can walk away. I think Isabelle needs to hear what you have to say, though. If not today, okay, but eventually you're going to have to talk about the problems you have with her behavior." He directs his gaze at me again. "It's the only way you'll ever free yourself from the pain."

"We're already here," she exhales, taking a seat on one of the plush couches. "We might as well get it out of the way."

"You're sure?"

She nods.

"And, Sebastian?"

Fumbling with the buttons of my jacket, I answer, "I'm here for Lauren. If she says go, we go."

Switching from therapist to father, his gaze puts me in the hot seat. Well-practiced at not giving myself away, I glare back at him. Chest heaving, he sighs and runs a hand through his hair. "Okay then, I'll be back in a minute."

I wait for my father to leave before finding my way to the empty cushion beside Lauren. Smile weakened, she looks over at me. I scan her face for a few uncertain minutes and sigh. "I'm sorry, Lauren. I didn't know."

"How could you?"

"I should have."

Head shaking, she grabs my hand. "No, Sebastian. You shouldn't. You have your own issues with Isabelle. I'm not clueless. Something happened between the two of you. I don't even try to imagine it. You have your secrets, and I respect that. Some things — especially the things Isabelle is capable of — are too painful to talk about." She pulls the hem of her school uniform over the scar on her knee. Just another reminder of Isabelle's negligence. "You made it easy for me. I could only talk about that night on the subway, because of you. I know I can't do the same for you. You'd never let me. I also know you think you're protecting me, and I guess maybe in some ways you are. If I knew what she did to you, then maybe I could hate her, too. Sometimes I think hating her would make it all easier, but then I look at you. No matter how much loving her hurts, it's pretty obvious to me that hating her is worse."

"She does love you." I clutch her hands. "Isabelle did something for you she could never do for me. She came back for you. Trust me, in Isabelle's world, that's love."

"Bashie!" The shrillness of my birth mother's voice cuts through the silence of the moment, griping my insides and choking the air from my lungs.

Fist clenched, I look over at her. Skin grayed from the years of sniffing away her pain, she wears a baggy sweater and jeans that hang from her scrawny hips. Cracked lips parted into a smile that shows her brittle teeth. She looks at me, string bean hair covering the clouded gray eyes she shares with each of us. She walks into the room. I can tell by the redness of her hands that she's been scratching through her withdrawals.

"Isabelle, why don't you have a seat here?" My father leads her to a seat directly across the coffee table from Lauren and me and takes the empty chair next to hers. "I'll sit right here for support. Sound good?"

"Thank you," her voice is lower now, shaken. Wide-eyed, she looks at Lauren. "How are you?"

"I'm fine, Momma." Palms slickened with sweat, she holds my hand a little tighter. "How are you?"

"Are you here to take me home, Bashie?" She asks, ignoring the question.

"Isabelle," my dad gently begins. "Sebastian and Lauren are here for our family session. Remember? We discussed this."

"*Our* family," she looks at him longingly, "I like the sound of that."

Clearing his throat, he loosens his tie. "Right, well... let's begin."

I shift my focus from him to her and back. *What hasn't he told me?*

"Lauren, why don't we begin with you? The last time you saw your mom, things didn't go so well. Is there anything you'd like to share about that experience?"

Spots of blood shown on the lip pressed between her teeth, she looks over at me. I nod and give her hand a gentle squeeze. Exhaling, she turns her attention back to Isabelle. "I'm sorry I upset you."

"You didn't upset me. Bashie, are you going to take me home soon?"

Stone faced, I glare at her. Picking up on my rage, my father turns the conversation back to Lauren. "Isabelle, Lauren's trying to talk to you right now. Why don't we focus on her? Lauren, you were saying..."

"I want you to get better, Momma." The delicate features of her youthful face soften as she watches Isabelle rub the sleeve of her sweater. "We both do, Sebastian and me. Do you remember the last time you saw me?"

"Of course, we had dinner at my apartment. You bought me pizza."

Blinking, Lauren tries to hide her tears. "That was weeks ago, Momma. I've been to see you at least six times since then."

"You have?"

Lauren nods.

"I guess I forgot."

"It's okay. You've had a lot of other things to focus on."

"You had a rough night, Isabelle," my father interjects. "Detoxing is a lengthy process. Under ordinary circumstances, we'd wait until you were further down the road before trying a session like this. Your case is special to me, though." He smiles. "We've tried several methods of helping you over the last few years, so I thought it was time we get a little unconventional."

"You think I'm special?" She asks, shoving her sweaty hair behind her ear and revealing the dark circles under her eyes.

"Yes, Isabelle. I think you're very special," he answers. "Can you do something for me?"

"I want to."

"Good. I need you to stop scratching," he moves her fingers away from her now raw wrist, "and I want you to close your eyes." Eyes closed, she leans her head back. "Good. Now, this will not be easy, but let's try. I want you to push past everything that's happened in the last two weeks. I know they haven't been easy. You're sick and we all want you to get better. That's what we're here for. For you to do that, though, we're going to have to work past how bad you feel right now. Think about what happened before you got sick, Isabelle. Do you remember? You were at your apartment with Lauren, and then you started feeling bad. You kept feeling bad for a few days, and then Sebastian came. What happened when he came?"

"He brought me here," she answers, trembling.

"Very good. And then you got very sick. Almost as sick as you are right now, but not quite. Right?"

"Then I got better and Lauren came."

"Very good," he coaxes. "What happened after that?"

"She... I..." Isabelle's eyes hurl open. "I don't want to do this anymore."

Too shaky to stand on her own, she lifts from her chair and falls back down again. Tears run down her cheeks, and she stares at Lauren's shoes. My father places a hand on her elbow, his thumb stroking over her sweater to soothe her. Drawing into a ball, she pulls away from him.

"I didn't mean to," she whimpers.

Jaw clenched, I pull my hand away from Lauren's and ball my fist into the couch. Head throbbing with the beating of my pulse, I direct my gaze to the coffee table.

"No one here thinks you did." I refuse to meet his eyes as he coddles her. "That doesn't change the fact that it happened. Lauren's come today, because she wants to talk to you about it. Can you let her do that?"

"I think I'm going to throw up," Isabelle replies.

My father sets his tablet on the coffee table and helps Isabelle to her feet. "Let me get her to the nurse. Give me a sec."

Isabelle's legs barely support her as she leans on my father and walks toward the hall. Mouth dry, I try to think of anything other than the scotch waiting for me at home. Beside me, Lauren shifts in her seat.

Turning toward her, I notice she's crying. "You okay?"

"This is horrible, Sebastian."

Weakened by the pain in her voice, I pull her head onto my shoulder. "I know. We can leave. I'll text my father from the car. It's up to you."

Leaning against the back of the couch, she quietly stares at the door. Her leg bounces up and down, and she keeps clenching and unclenching her fists. "No. If she's well enough to continue when they get back, then we'll continue. I need to know."

We sit there in silence; her lost in her thoughts and me in mine. The seconds tick away on the miniature grandfather clock my father keeps on his bookcase. Absently, I watch the pendulum swing back and forth. Once again, I picture myself walking away from Isabelle and never looking back. Still, I sit frozen to the soft cushion. He could be gone for minutes; it could be days. Either way, I don't notice his return. His hand grips my shoulder and I spin to see him standing over me. Worried eyes fixated on me, Lauren sits beside me, holding a crumpled tissue in her hands.

"Where'd you go, son?" He asks, gently.

"Nowhere. How is she?"

Inching onto the coffee table, he sighs. "Isabelle is doing what she's done hundreds of times before. The sad truth is, the process doesn't get easier, it only gets harder. Honestly, I don't know how many more times she can put her body through this before it shuts down completely."

Lauren tries to stop it, but a sob forces its way from her chest. "Why is she like this, Doctor B?"

"I wish I could answer that for you," his sympathetic eyes meet mine before darting back to her, "I really do. Doctor-patient confidentiality laws prevent it. What I can say is this, your mother has her own battle scars. I don't think she ever meant to let you down. I just don't think she knew how to be any other way."

"I didn't," Isabelle replies feebly, clinging to the nurse who's helping her.

"The shower was a success. If she has anymore issues, you know where to find me," the nurse says to my father.

"Thank you," he takes Isabelle's arm and helps her back to her chair. "Welcome back, Isabelle. Feeling better?"

"Yes." Not even glancing in Lauren and my direction, she pulls her sweater sleeves over her hands and brings her knobby knees up to her chest.

I can't help but notice these clothes are hanging off her too, which means it's already time to buy new ones. I make a mental note to have Robin handle it and turn away. Half an hour of back and forth between my father, Lauren, and Isabelle passes with no incidents. At last, my father's timer goes off and he closes the case on his tablet. "Lauren and Isabelle, you did great today. I think we've established a good starting point. Isabelle, it's time for dinner. I can have a tray brought to your room and a companion can come sit with you, or if you're feeling up to it, you can head down to the cafeteria."

"I'll eat in my room. Can Bashie take me?"

My father cuts me with a reprimanding stare. "Actually, I still have a few things I need to talk to him about. Lauren, why don't you walk Isabelle down to the nurse? They'll know what to do from there."

"Okay. Come on, Momma." Lauren takes Isabelle's shaking hand and helps her from the chair.

Waiting until the door closes once again, my father rounds on me. "You didn't even try, son."

"I'm too old for lectures, Father. I told you from the beginning, I'm here for Lauren. That's it. Beyond that, Isabelle and I don't need a relationship."

"She's the woman who gave birth to you, Sebastian."

Unable to stop the growl in my throat, I stand and shove my hands in my pockets.

"Just listen, son," he looks up at me, "Emmalyn and I have loved being your parents. No matter what happens between you and Isabelle, the relationship you have with us won't change. You gave me one too many headaches for me to forget the years I spent raising you anytime soon."

"You think that's what I'm afraid of?" I snort. "I wish it were as simple as that."

"If it's not about hurting us, then what is it? Why won't you let me help you work past your issues with your birth mother?"

"Because she's a fucking lunatic!" I bellow. "Do you not understand that? Dad, you've won awards for this shit. How can you not see that she's a hopeless cause?"

"Because I see her desperation, son. I see that she's a mother who really believed she was doing her best. It doesn't change that she got it wrong. You think it's easy for me to treat her? To you I hold her hand, coddle her, and forget that she's the same woman who left *my son* abandoned on the street. I do it for you, Sebastian. I push this issue for *you*. Just like you do it for Lauren, and will one day do something just as difficult for your own kids."

Stomach twisted in a knot, I grab a bottle of water from his fridge. "Tell Lauren I'll be in the car waiting."

"Sebastian, don't leave. Son, we have to figure out a way to get you past this."

Ignoring him, I open the door and walk out.

# Chapter 37

*D*<sup>anielle</sup>

"Wow! This place is great, G. I'll admit when you said The Village, I was expecting a crappy studio like a true starving artist," I say, hugging him as soon as he opens the door.

"Oh, come on now, baby girl! You know I'm too fabulous for that."

He leads me through the small entry where he's set up a gallery of his work and into the open floor plan of the rest of his new space. The couch we once shared is set alongside a new coffee table with the television mounted on the adjacent wall. Our old dining room table now sits atop a brand-new rug. His kitchen is certainly smaller than our old one, but he's managed to fit our old appliances in there.

"So, the bedrooms are through those doors," he says, pointing to a door and handing me a glass of sparkling water. "Each has its own bathroom."

I set the grocery bag I've been carrying on the counter. "Nice. Have you started searching for roommates yet?"

"Nope. I'm not sure I'm going to get a roomie. It just wouldn't be the same without you. And let's face it. I'm too neurotic to make a good living companion for most people."

"True story. So, are you starving," I pull my semi-engagement ring from my pocket and drop it on the counter, "or do you want to sit and chat first?"

"What... the... fuck?" Wide eyed, he stares at my solid black rock, and slowly turns his head back up at me. "Cook and chat. Time for some multi-tasking, baby girl. Start from the beginning."

By the time I finish recounting the entire thing, I've prepared and plate Geoff's favorite meal: balsamic vinegar and rosemary chicken, potatoes au gratin, glazed carrots, and rolls. We carry our plates to the table in silence as he processes everything. Foot tapping, I watch as he takes a glazed carrot between his teeth and sinks into it. "This is great, baby girl. Thanks."

"Oh my God! Are we just not going to discuss it?"

"What's there to discuss?"

"Umm... hello! I may be getting married. *Me!* That's not exactly a small thing. What the hell do I know about marriage?"

"Dani, your grandparents have been married since the first humans inhabited the Earth. You know a lot about marriage. That's not your hang up."

"So, what is?" Eyes locked on him, I tear a chunk from my roll and slather it with butter.

"Sebastian."

"Sebastian?"

Knife and fork in hand, he shrugs. "I don't want to cause another World War so I'm shutting up. Great chicken, by the way."

"Geoffrey Taylor, don't you dare start holding back on me now. I came to you first, because I *know* you'll tell me the truth regardless of if I want to hear it or not."

Placing his utensils on the table, he leans against the chair and crosses his arms. "Okay. Just don't forget you asked for it. First, it's completely crazy that the *proposee* is expected to immediately respond to the proposal. The *proposer* gets a while to think about these things. Second, Mister Big is not a normal guy. You want nothing more than to be a normal girl. You're afraid that marrying him will mean you never can be, although in my honest opinion you threw that chance away the day you agreed to move in with him. Last, what'd you move out here for?"

"To kick start my career."

"And now everywhere you turn you're going to get a leg up, because you're *Sebastian Black's wife.* That's assuming he even still lets you work after you're married. You want me to be real? You had every right to say maybe. Hell, you had every right to say no. You've known the guy what? Ninety days? How are you supposed to pledge the rest of your life to him?"

"In all fairness, my Nonna and Nonno only knew each other six weeks before he proposed."

"Oh please! Your grandparents, as beautiful as their love story is, are not the norm. For that matter, they were going through all this during the married at fifteen with a baby on each hip and one at your feet by the time you're twenty era. It was different time, baby girl."

Swallowing a mouthful of potatoes, I take a drink of water and look back at him. "So, you're saying I should decline?"

"I can't make that choice for you, baby girl, and that's what you're really afraid of. This is one of those moments that no matter how much advice you get from anyone else, you're the only one who knows. Are you going to tell your dad about it?"

"He already knows. At least that's what Sebastian said on the video. I'm not sure if he knew he was going to do it so soon, but apparently Daddy gave his blessing."

"So, find out why. Your dad wouldn't sign off on it just because. His biggest fear in this world is losing you. If he said yes, there's a reason for it."

"I guess you're right. Anyway, let's talk about something else. Tell me all about the fashion show."

We don't discuss the engagement again for the rest of the night, and I'm thankful for it. Before I know it, it's almost midnight and I still must get back to my side of the city. Geoff walks me down to the street, kisses my cheek, and promises we'll get together again next week. The entire way back to the penthouse, I think about his words.

*If he said yes, there's a reason for it.*

I hadn't really paid much attention to that detail before now, but it's absolutely true. My dad would've never given his consent if there wasn't something to this whole thing he saw that I'm not. Still, it doesn't really make any sense given our conversation last week. Making a mental note to call him as soon as I get the chance, I lean my head against the window and watch the city die down.

****

*I'm definitely overdressed.*

I stand in front of the mirror wearing a sleeveless mint green dress with an embellished neckline. We have drinks with Jett in half an hour, and from there we're off to the Black

317

Connecticut Compound for Katie's wedding rehersal. Stomach a ball of nerves, I grab my bag from the bed and take the elevator to the parking garage. Punctual as always, Sean already has the town car pulled up and waiting for me.

"Music today, Dani?"

"Actually, Sean, I think I'll just sit alone with my thoughts for a while."

"As you wish."

Thumbnail between my teeth, I watch the pedestrians rushing about on the sidewalk. I'm still not sure I'm doing the best thing in starting this partnership, but Sebastian says there's always a risk in business and he'd know. I just wish there was someone to give me the answers I need in my personal life. Mind-fucked, I pull the black diamond ring from my purse. It's heavy in my hand, but even heavier is the decision weighing on my mind. Remembering my conversation with Geoff last night, I secure the ring back in the box and toss it back in my purse. My dad answers his phone before it can give a complete ring. "I've been waiting for your call."

Ease washing over me like the sea, I sink into the leather seat and laugh. "Are you at work?"

"Nope. I'm having a quick dinner at The Spot."

"Seriously, move in there already," I snort. "Do you have time to talk?"

"I always have time for you, angel-girl. Nothing's going to change that. What's up?"

"Not a lot. I'm on my way to drinks with that Jett guy. I decided to accept his proposal."

"Good for you. It's a great opportunity."

"Yeah." I close my eyes and sigh. "I'm still a little, okay a lot, nervous about it all."

"You'll be great, mia bella . Even better, you can build an office here and move home."

Tension leaving my stomach, I burst into a fit of laughter. "When are you and Nonna going to give up on that pipe dream?"

"As soon as it becomes a reality." I can hear the ringing of the door behind him, and my heart plunges into the bottom of my stomach. In truth, it becomes harder to fight them every time they mention it. "So, any other proposals on the table you'd like to discuss?"

Careful not to mess up my hair too badly, I twirl my finger in my ponytail. "How do you always do that?"

"Do what?"

"See past my bullshit and get to the real problem."

"Because I'm your father and it's my job. So, I'm taking it things didn't go over so well."

"Did you know about this when we talked at Nonna's?"

"He asked my permission when I was in New York a few months ago, and again when you were here for the funeral. I didn't know he had the actual plan in place until he came back from his business trip."

Cheeks flaming, I try to fight the annoyance I'm feeling. *Sebastian's been planning this for weeks and no one thought they should tell me.* "So, why'd you say yes? I mean, when we talked, it didn't seem like you were ready for me to take such a big step."

"You want the truth?"

"Have I ever asked you for anything else?"

"Bernadette convinced me."

"She what? Since when does your girlfriend have a say in my personal life?" Body tense, I grab a bottle of water from the mini fridge and take a few sips.

"She was there when he asked the third time. Truthfully, she felt awkward giving her opinion, but I asked for it. I thought you liked her."

Imagining his disappointment, I sigh and begin peeling the label from the green glass. "Of course, I do. I'm sorry, I just... he went to mom's grave. Did you know that? I haven't been there since we put her in the ground, but he went."

"Bernadette's not trying to replace your mother, angel-girl," he says, softly.

"I know." Eyes filled with tears, I take another shaky sip. "It's ridiculous, really. I mean, mom never even saw me in a relationship, and still here I am finding it hard to not have her advice on this."

"What do you think she'd say?"

"Mom? The woman who gave up love for money? She'd tell me to be glad Sebastian can offer me both and accept the ring."

Sadness overcoming him, he replies, "You're probably correct about that one. So, what's stopping you?"

"Ugh. I don't know. I love Sebastian, but it's like I told you... I'm just not sure marriage is a thing in my life."

"I hope that's not true."

Fiddling with the engagement ring I wear that was meant for my mother, I ask, "I need to know why you said yes. I mean besides Bernadette. You wouldn't have said yes if you didn't believe somewhere in there that this would be good for me."

The sound of his breath rushes through my ear with his exhale. "It was your smile."

"My smile?"

"At Mom's house. You were on the phone with Sebastian, and when you came out, you were smiling like I've never seen you smile before. When he was in front of me, smiling almost as big as I may add, explaining everything he had planned, I thought about that smile. He loves you, angel-girl, even though I have reservations about him. I didn't see it at first, or rather, I didn't want to. I'm still not sure I'm ready to let you go, but if he makes you that happy, he can't be all bad. So, if you decide this is what you want, I'll support you every step of the way."

Throat filled with a lump of emotion, I process his words as Thomas parallel parks the car in front of the lounge. "What do you think I should do?"

"Even if I could tell you that, you wouldn't listen. I thought you should never move to New York to begin with, if I remember correctly. I for damn sure went on record with saying you shouldn't give him a second glance. If you didn't listen then, why would I even waste my breath now?"

"Hilarious."

He chuckles. "All jokes aside? I think you need to do what makes you happy, kiddo. You've spent your whole life trapped in the purgatory of the girl you used to be and the woman you want to be. If marrying Sebastian is part of the dream for you, then do it. If it's not, don't. I'll be here for you, and I'll continue to love you either way."

"You might not always feel like it, but you really are the best dad in the world. Just remember, if I go through with this, you have to wear a penguin coat and dance with me in front of the masses."

"On second thought, forget everything I just said," he jokes.

I laugh. "I love you, Daddy."

"Ti amo, angel-girl. Good luck with your meeting *and* everything else. I'll be here if you need me."

Sean opens the door and I step onto the sidewalk. Hugging myself, I walk through the door and scan the low-lit tables for Jett. He's sitting on a white sofa with a rectangular wooden coffee table in front. Across from the coffee table are two black leather chairs. Polite smile shining across my face, I make my way to him. He shakes my hand and offers me a seat next to him. I take a chair and order a vodka and cranberry for myself and a scotch for Sebastian.

"Is this a good sign?" Jett asks, asking for his own vodka soda to be refreshed.

"Let's just wait until Sebastian gets here."

"Well, can I at least say I read over the suggestions you sent? I knew you were the right choice."

"Not starting without me, I hope," Sebastian says, arriving in time with the waitress and leaning down to kiss my cheek.

"Nope, I just got here."

"I'm glad I'm not late." He leans forward and extends his hand to Jett. "I'm Sebastian—"

"Sebastian Black. Of course, I know who you are. Jett Wilson."

"It's nice to meet you, Jett," Sebastian replies, taking his scotch from the waitress and handing me my drink. "I don't mean to intrude. I just wanted to obverse and maybe offer a small suggestion or two. I trust Danielle has already mentioned I'd like to come on as a silent partner."

"I read something about that in her email. How much of a percentage would we be talking about?"

"Actually," I cut in. "That's the beauty of our arrangement. Sebastian doesn't want any ownership. He would essentially be a lender, only he's acting as a silent investor. I'll give him one percent of my fifty percent share. Any equity he earns will go toward paying back his initial loan. If once his initial loan is paid in full, we haven't needed him to invest anymore capital, Sebastian will sell his one percent back to me. If we need additional capital, the same terms apply once we've paid off any debt we owe him."

Jett takes a drink from his glass and allows his eyes to skim over Sebastian. "And this is legit? I mean, you won't try to change the terms on us later or anything?"

"I want the best for Danielle," Sebastian says. "I do have one slight change I'd like to discuss now that we're all together."

Alarm bells ringing, I turn my head toward him. He gives me his business smile and pulls a pen from the interior pocket of his jacket. Grabbing a cocktail napkin from the table, he jots down a number and slides it to Jett. "I'm prepared to put down this much as an initial investment. In exchange, you'll agree to split this partnership fifty-one to forty-nine in Danielle's favor. She'll use the extra one percent to repay my investment, and I'll never be listed on any official documentation as anything other than an investor. The two of you will maintain all legal rights to the company, and I'll simply be a bank."

Jett stares at the napkin in disbelief. Meanwhile, my attention remains focused on Sebastian. Glass brought to his lips, he places a hand on my knee and strokes my skin with his thumb. Flesh flushed with heat, I part my lips and watch him. Lust spreads through my veins, mixing with my fury. I want to slap him and tear his clothes off all at the same time. Jett takes another sip of his vodka soda. Hand shaking slightly, he places the glass on the table and asks, "What happens after we have paid the loan in full?"

"That would be for you and Danielle to decide."

"We'd split the partnership equally," I say, cutting my eyes at Sebastian. "Jett, I don't want to take this company from you. It's your dream, your baby. I'm just someone who shares the same vision."

"Have you seen these numbers?" He asks.

"I haven't, but I don't need to. It doesn't affect my decision. I want to jump on board with you. Sebastian offered to be my backer. I didn't want to agree at first, but I'd be lying if I pretended to have another option. If you're not comfortable with this agreement, I understand. If you want to renegotiate any part of the terms he's given you, you're well within your right. I want you to be comfortable. For this partnership to work, we have to take the other person's feelings, thoughts, and opinions into account."

"Dani, there's enough money here to start three companies." Eyes wide, he finishes his drink. "If you're in, I'm in. There's nothing left for me to think about."

"Really?" I all but squeal.

"Really." He stands and reaches over the table.

Following suit, I place my hand in his for a shake and stumble slightly when he pulls me in for a hug. Sebastian's quick to launch to his feet behind me. Grabbing my arm and pulling me back to his side, he extends his hand in Jett's direction. "I'll send a contract first thing on Monday. I can understand you needing to have a lawyer look first."

"Of course," he shakes Sebastian's hand enthusiastically, "I kind of wish I still had something to toast with."

Sebastian laughs, his stiff public laugh, and reclaims his hand to signal the waitress. "Well, let's change that."

We toast and spend the next half hour discussing business. All the time in the back of my mind, I wonder if this is what life will be like if I say yes. We'll have a discussion, come to an agreement, and Sebastian will do whatever he wants in the end. Mind spinning toward my mother's marriage to an alpha-male, I finish off my cocktail. We must discuss this at some point. I'm going to drive myself crazy if we don't.

.

# Chapter 38

*Sebastian*

"Ready for this?" I ask, sliding into the car beside Danielle.

"I know we have to be there for Katie, and I want to. I'm just not sure I'm in the mood for your grandparents."

The silk strands of her hair move about my fingers with ease as I loop my hand through them. "I thought you'd be elated. You just officially became the head of your own public relations firm."

"Yeah, it's exciting. I'm just thinking."

Using the tiny tongs, I place ice in two glasses and prepare our drinks. "About?"

She reaches out and takes the vodka from my hand. Using all the restraint I have, I watch as she swirls the glass and brings it to her cotton candy painted lips. Time freezes as she takes a long drink and stares into the glass. Fingers seeking the warmth of her skin, I glide my hand under the hem of her dress.

Leaning her head back, she brings her legs over mine and sighs. "Is this what being married is going to feel like?"

"Care to elaborate?" I remove her shoe and massage her heel.

Fires of Oz burning in her eyes, she fixes her stare on me. "We'll discuss something behind closed doors, but when it comes down to it, you'll do whatever you want? I mean, I know that's the way it's always been, but what you're asking from me... marriage... it's about partnership. The only way it's ever going to work is if you truly treat me like a partner."

"The only way it *will* work. Are you saying yes, princess?" My heart leaping against my ribs, I squeeze her foot.

Grimacing, she pulls away. "*Ouch!* Believe it or not, I do still have nerve endings in there."

"Sorry," I straighten my pants legs and look over at her, "I didn't realize I was squeezing so tight." I capture her ankle and pull her foot back onto my lap. "You still didn't answer my question."

"Because it doesn't require an answer," she sulks. "When I say yes — *if* I say yes — you will definitely know it. Now, why don't *you* answer my question?"

"What's this about?"

"Did you really think I'd be completely okay with you changing the terms of the loan?"

Reeling with a new sense of understanding, I smile. "So, you're upset about the new conditions. I was only trying to help."

"You humiliated me!" She spins in her seat, drawing her feet under her. "You sat there letting me think I was in control of our side of things, and then you just completely took over and blindsided me. God, Sebastian! I have to work with this man! He has to trust in my decisions and you.... *you*... ugh!" Full wrath of her temper directed at me, she throws her arms in the air. "I'm not my mother, Sebastian. You said it yourself. I'm not one of those trophy wives who will sit, lie, and roll over whenever they're commanded."

Capturing her wrist in my hand, I stroke my thumb over her pulse. "I think I can prove you wrong about that last statement."

Softening, she smiles and pulls her wrist free. "I'm serious, Sebastian. We both know I can't be that girl. Please don't ask me to be."

"I'm not, Danielle. I thought I was helping. If you're not happy with the arrangement, we can go back to the one we'd previously discussed."

"It's not that easy. Jett's amped about this. I can't just change things on him. That's not how *partnerships* work."

"I won't beg you, but I can promise you that a marriage to me will be everything you expect it to be. You know who I am. This is going to be messy, princess. Both of us will screw up more times than we think we will ever be able to. We'll scream and break things. We'll even break each other on more than one occasion." Noticing the subtle shake of her shoulders, I grip her hands in mine. "We will, Danielle, but we'll fix each other, too. This will never be *Cinderella*. That's the one thing on this fucking planet I can't give you, but that doesn't mean I'll stop trying. Just marry me, Danielle. Stop delaying what we both already know we need."

"I'm just not ready yet, Sebastian." She looks away. "I promise I'll give you an answer soon. I just need to know this won't go up in flames if I say yes."

Hand on her cheek, I turn her face toward mine again. Sealing my lips over hers, I thrust my tongue into her mouth. She resists, forcing me to spill all my desperation into her. Wrapping my arms around her, I press her body against me. Nipples hardening through her dress, she moans against my mouth. Shameless, I cast her panties to the side and encircle her clit with my thumb. Knuckle white grip forcing the leather to squeak, she slams her hand onto the seat and tosses her head back.

"Sebastian," she pants.

The breathless sound of my name coming from her lips fueling my hunger, I adjust my throbbing dick. "Burn with me, Danielle," I whisper, kissing the spot between her neck and earlobe. "If we go up in flames, stand in the heat and burn with me. That's all I ask of you."

Chest rising and falling in time with her heated breath, she digs her nails into my arm. "And what happens when we both go down in ashes?"

Needing her to understand the distances I'm willing to go for her, I place both hands on her face and stare into the eyes that captured my very soul. "Like the phoenix, we will rise again. I'll never give up on us, Danielle." The car rolls to a stop and I look up to see that we're in my parents' driveway. Searching her one last time, I pull free and straighten her clothes.

She grabs my arm as I reach up to adjust my tie. "I'll never give up on us either, Sebastian. I just..."

"Get out of the car already! What the hell are you waiting for?" Julie screams, ripping the door open. "I need a cover. I was supposed to be here two hours ago to help Katie with a few final touches, and I got stuck at school. She'll be easier on me if I have you as a buffer."

Heartbroken by the look in Danielle's eyes, I turn to my sister. "I doubt that. She's left me no less than ten messages today, reminding me that, as one of Brad's groomsmen, it's my duty to be at this rehearsal." I step out and clasp Danielle's hand in mine. She squeezes in response, giving me her strength and taking some of mine.

I risk looking back at her. Her hair is pulled into one of her signature ponytails, her makeup bringing out the sparkling gems of her eyes. She focuses on me as she steps from the car, her eyes never leaving mine. Leaning into me, she whispers, "I love you. Of that, I'm absolutely sure."

Small smile on the corner of my lips, I place my arm around her and nod my head. "Shall we, ladies?"

**** 

"Do you have to get that?" Danielle asks, lifting her head from my chest.

Retrieving my phone from the interior pocket of my jacket, I check the caller id. Mouth gone dry, I nod and leave the dance floor.

"Hello." I snap, bringing the phone to my ear.

"Sebastian Black?"

"You already know it's me."

"Right. I'm just making sure. Wouldn't want any *confidential* information getting loose," the sneering voice of Detective West taunts.

"What can I do for you tonight, Detective? I'm kind of in the middle of something." I turn to see Danielle talking to Jewels at the edge of the dance floor. The song changes to one more up tempo, and they find their way to the center of the parquet. Turning my back on them, I edge my way out of the tent.

"I just wanted to see if you had any information you'd like to share with us."

"I've already told you everything I know. I thought I made that perfectly clear the last time we discussed this matter."

"If you could see what I have on my desk, I think you'd reconsider. When she goes down, just remember I gave you a chance."

"West, if you fucking threaten her again, I'll have your head!" I snarl.

"Oh, we're feeling touchy tonight. I always enjoyed getting a rise out of you," he says, his grin evident in his voice. "I'll see you soon."

"I mean it, West. Stay the fuck away from her."

"It's you or her, Black. The clock's ticking."

The click of his phone rings in my ear like fireworks through the sky. Lump in my throat, I loosen my tie and turn my attention to the tent. Katie, Julie, and Danielle light up the party, their smiles bright as they laugh and dance in a huddle. Stomach lurching, I let his threat sink in. Retrieving my phone again, I send a text to Thomas.

*What do the police have?*

*I'm checking on that now. What do you know?*

*West just made contact.*

*I'll have an answer within the hour.*

Hand trembling, I place the phone back in my pocket and run my fingers through my hair. A deep inhale returning oxygen to my blood, I watch my girls. Nothing will hurt them. Not a single hair on either of their heads will ever be damaged. Especially not Danielle, my princess, my savior. She's been to hell, faced the devil himself, and somehow, she survived. She may've had to face Walter Smith alone, but I'm here now. This isn't her problem anymore, it's mine.

It all comes down to the plan. Iron fisted, I've spent the last few weeks preparing for this. I have alerted everyone on my team. Thomas is just waiting for my word to act. We'll protect her. I'm confident about that. Assured by my proactive tactics, I walk to the bar and order a fresh round of drinks for Danielle and me.

"Gran's in rare form tonight, if I say so myself," Katie says, coming up behind me.

"Isn't she always?" I take my drinks from the bartender in exchange for a healthy tip.

"An hour. We were in there for an hour and didn't even rehearse anything. We just sat there taking her shit and listening to her opinion of how *my* wedding should be."

"Katie, I promise you, you're going to have the wedding of your dreams."

She hugs me, and I pat the back of her head. "How can you make that promise? You know what *they're* like."

"Let's just say they aren't the only Blacks with a few tricks up their sleeves. I heard mother mentioning something about a tranquilizer."

Danielle's at my side before Kathryn has a chance to stifle her laughter. Arm wrapped around my waist, she takes her drink. Hand brushing the silk strands of her hair, I pull her closer.

Smiling in Katie's direction, she says, "I'm glad you're finally enjoying yourself."

"Yeah, this night's been a massive nightmare. As soon as this party clears out, I'm heading upstairs and crashing. You guys staying over?"

"Actually, I think we'll head home. I just got a call that was rather pressing." I take Danielle's glass and set it on the bar.

"Little brother, if you're late to my wedding, I will sever your head from your shoulders and sell it on eBay."

"Look at Bridezilla showing her claws." I laugh, leaning in to kiss her cheek. "Relax, Kate. I'll be the first one here."

"That's kind of hard to do when everyone else is sleeping here!" She yells as Danielle and I make our way through the crowd.

"So, I'm pretty sure Katie's going to kill you," Danielle says, leaning in close as the night air swarms us.

"She'll understand once the entire ordeal is over. I've never been much for a full house. It's one thing when it's just the family, but they're planning for all the bridesmaids and groomsmen, plus various others. It's all a bit too crowded for me."

"You don't have to lie to me." She winks, sliding into the car. "I know your true motives."

"Oh?" Brow raised, I slide in next to her. "What are they?"

"Why, to get me home and in bed where you'll proceed to fuck me into an oblivion, of course."

Caging her body to mine, I kiss her and whisper, "If that were my intention, I wouldn't wait until we got home. I'd just take full advantage of you right here."

"Well," she unzips her dress and slides it from her shoulders, "we both know how much I enjoy that tie."

Nipping my teeth across her nipple, I loosen my tie. "I love you, Danielle Rose Stevens. No matter what happens, promise me you'll remember that."

Feather soft fingertips, running over my jaw, she looks deep into my eyes. "I could *never* forget, Sebastian."

I tie her arms to the door, but I'm not aggressive. Not tonight. The uncertainty of it all fills me with an overwhelming need to savor every second we have left. Kissing, caressing, and licking my way over every golden inch of her skin, I make love to her the entire ride back to the city. When we've finished, I lay entangled in her with tears crowning my eyes. The plan may've been in place for a month, but I hoped it would've never come to this.

**\*\*\*\***

Brought back to a conscious state by the chirping of my phone, I stare at the city lights pouring through my window. With one arm still under Danielle, I roll to my back and focus on the ceiling tiles above us. For once, I'd love to just let it wait. Thinking of Isabelle, I slide my hand over the talk button and bring the phone to my ear.

"Sorry to wake you, sir," Thomas says.

"What is it?" I growl, feeling Danielle stir beside me.

"*He's* here."

"Coming up the elevator now, sir," he answers.

"Stall him for as long as you can," I reply, moving from the bed and pulling on my boxers.

"Sebastian?" Danielle mumbles.

Turning on the lamp, I sit next to her and run my hand over her silky, chestnut colored locks. "Open your eyes, princess. I need you to listen to me."

"What's wrong?" She asks, alarm written on her face as she stares up at me.

"Things are about to blow up, but I need you to trust me. It's all going to be okay. I promise. Just trust me."

Wide eyed, she sits up. "Sebastian—"

"Do you have a warrant?" Thomas's voice comes from the hallway.

"Is that?" She asks, her breath quickening as she pieces the puzzle together.

Finger on my lips, I signal for her to be quiet, take her hand, and drag her to the closet.

"What the hell is going on?" She hisses.

Memorizing her every pore, I stare at her. Her eyes are dilated, and her chest heaves as she tries to steady herself. Lifting my hands to her face, I swipe my thumbs over her cheeks and kiss her softly. She melts under my touch, and I'm surprised by the feeling in my gut. I hate doing this to her, but I have no choice.

"Detective West is here to arrest me, princess-"

"But—"

"Shh..." I say, handing her a robe. "Just put this on and trust me. Can you do that?"

"Do I have a choice?"

"No." There's a loud knock on the door, and I grip her shoulders firmly. "We don't have time to argue about this, Danielle. I've been planning for this for quite some time. Just do everything Thomas tells you to. That includes playing nice with Alana."

"Sebastian, I'm scared."

"I know," I reply, pulling her into my chest as another booming knock sounds through the room. "I'm sorry. This too will pass, princess. I promise. Just play along for as long as it takes."

"Okay," she breathes, trying to repress the tears pooling in her eyes.

I pull on a pair of sweats and a t-shirt, and then take her hand in mine again. "I'll hold on for as long as I can, but once that door opens…"

"Wait!" she exclaims.

Pulling my hand free of the doorknob, I turn to her. She lunges at me. Attacking me with her lips, her kiss so electric that I feel its shock waves in every nerve I have. Needing her like a thirsting man needs water, I pull her flush against me, grabbing her legs and lifting her from the ground. She wraps herself around me, her body trembling as she caresses my tongue with hers. I hold her for as long as I can until we're once again interrupted by the threatening knock from outside. Pulling away, I try to speak but find I have no words.

"I know," she says, nodding and lowering herself to the ground again.

She clasps her hand in mine as I twist the lock and pull the door open. "Detective West, it's a little late for house calls, isn't it?"

"Sebastian Black," his disgusting voice says, proudly, as he pulls my arm behind my back. "You have the right to remain silent."

Danielle holds my hand as tightly as she can, pleading for my touch to not leave her skin. I see an officer stepping toward her and let go. My wrists sting from the bite of the cuffs into my flesh, but it's nothing compared to the pains in my chest caused by the desperate look in her eyes.

"Sebastian," she breathes, tears spilling onto her cheeks.

Straining, I fight against him to get to her.

"Anything you say or do can and will be used against you in a court of law," he continues.

Helplessly, she comes toward me. I watch in dismay as the other officer steps between us, holding her back.

"I love you, princess," I say, not giving a damn about Miranda Rights. "It's going to be okay."

Thomas comes to her rescue as Detective West continues reading me my rights. The feel of his slimy hands on my skin brings a rush of nausea with it.

"Do you understand these rights as I have explained them to you?" He asks at last.

Refusing to take my eyes off Danielle, I nod my head.

He leads me through the hall and into the foyer. I look for her as we wait for the elevator. Her shoulders shake as the tears stream down her face. "I love you," she mouths. Feeling the sting of tears behind my eyes, I look away.

*Thomas will take care of her. It's all in his hands now.*

Even though it's three o'clock in the morning, photographers surrounded my building. The flashing of their cameras cutting through the night like a knife. As if my PR team didn't already have enough mess to clean up from Walter Smith's untimely presence in my life, now I'm giving them this. It will be worth it, though, if it keeps Danielle safe.

His fingers discreetly running through my hair, Detective West places his hand on my head and lowers me into the cop car. Stomach lurching, I buck away from him as best I can. The door closes with a heavy thud, and my chest tightens. *I'll be alone in a cell where he'll have constant access to me.* The thought should've occurred to me before, but it's only now that I fully understand the ramifications of what I'm doing.

Closing my eyes, I grind my wrists against the metal of the handcuffs. Heartbeat echoing in my ears, I try to reassure myself that I'll be safe. Throat clenched, I stare at the back of his greasy head. *I'm not that little boy anymore.*

"Looks like I finally got you, boy," he snarls, turning in his seat. "Wait until I tell the others. The mighty Sebastian Black has finally fallen."

# Chapter 39

*D*anielle

The elevator closes, and the bottom falls out. Lunging at the wall, I slam my hand on the button. Chest constrained, I barely give the doors time to fully open before running inside. Somewhere through the haze of my mind, I can hear Sean telling me to stay in the apartment. He throws his hands between the doors before they can close.

"Unless you drag me back, I'm going to him," I say firmly.

"I'll allow you to go as far as the sidewalk. After that, we have to discuss a few things."

"What's there to discuss? We're going to the police station."

"Ms. Stevens."

"Dammit, Sean! My name is Dani, and regardless of what Sebastian told you, I'm not made of porcelain. He's not going down for something I did." Impatiently, I press the button for the lobby again. "Doesn't this fucking elevator go any faster?"

Eyes trained on the door, Sean doesn't allow himself to be phased by my outburst. Head throbbing, I cross my arms over my chest and squeeze my eyes shut to keep the tears from falling. *He asked me to marry him. Why did I wait?* It's just one more thing I'll fix during all this mess. Jarred by the noise of the doors opening, I open my eyes.

The lobby seems foreign. Apart from my move-in day, Sebastian and I have always used the entrance from the garage below. Ignoring the curious glance from the desk clerk, I charge through the glass doors. Blinded by hundreds of lights flashing at once, I fight my way through the sea of paparazzi. This is going to be a public relations nightmare. I'll fix it too.

Skin rubbed raw by the chilly night air, I stare at the street. Three police cars are lined in a row, their red and blue lights flashing in an uneasy sequence. Knotted stomach, I watch as Detective West guides Sebastian into the middle car. Taste of salty tears on my lips, I run toward them. Sean catches me around the middle, my legs dangling from the ground as I scream Sebastian's name. Kicking and punching, I fight against his hold. Sebastian turns his head toward the window as the car begins to pull away.

"I love you," he mouths.

"No!" I scream, breaking free and running for the car.

Sean catches me again, my body going lapse against his hold. Supporting us both, he turns me back toward the lobby. A gust of wind grips my ankle and I remember for the first time that I'm barefoot and wearing only a robe. Not caring, I turn toward the stairs leading down to the parking garage.

"Dani, listen to me," he says, gripping my shoulders. "We have a plan. *He* has a plan. Do you trust him?"

"With my life," I whisper, wiping my nose clean with my sleeve.

"Then do exactly as I say. We need to get you back into the apartment. I have a few calls to make."

Numb, I nod and follow him to the elevator.

****

Relentless ticking of the wall clock ringing through my ears, I stare at the window. Tapping my fingers against the ceramic mug, I notice for the first time my coffee's gone cold. I set it on the sofa table and pull the blanket tighter around my shoulders. Soft orange light creeps through the living room, and I'm suddenly aware it's dawn. Sebastian's been in police custody for hours and I'm sitting here like a brainless twit, unable to do anything to help him.

Dinging elevator sounding through the silence, I toss my blanket aside and leap from the couch. Alana steps into the foyer, dressed to the nines in a fitted dress cropped at the knee and boots. She undoes the buttons on her coat and hangs it from a hook on the rack by the door.

"Where's Thomas?"

Blood boiling, I glare at her. "Go away, Alana."

Ignoring me, she storms to the living room. "Your defiance is shocking, I would've expected you to listen for once given the seriousness of the matter."

"Listen you inbred bitch! No one has time for your shit today. Shut your fucking mouth, or I'll shut it for you."

Momentarily startled, she steps back and studies me. "Humph." Turning her back, she strides down the hallway shouting, "Thomas."

Seeing red, I chase after her. Auburn hair entangled around my knuckles, I pull her back.

"Are you crazy?" She screams. "Get off me!"

Ridden with rage, I slap her across the face. "I've hated you since the moment I met you," I roar. "You're a lying, manipulative, self-entitled bitch who thinks she can do whatever she wants to whomever she wants if it serves her end game. You disgust me. You have no business here. Get out of my house!"

"Ms. Stevens, please!" Sean yells, pulling me away. "Control yourself. I understand how difficult this must be for you, but you're only making it worse."

"If you only knew just how much *business* I had here!" Alana shouts, smoothing her hair. "I may be a bitch, but at least I'm not a *whore*!"

"That's enough, Ms. Sinclair!" Sean snaps. "Bernice, if you could please see Ms. Sinclair to Mister Black's office. I'll be with her in a minute. Ms. Stevens come with me."

Chastised, I follow him down the hall. Sebastian asked me to be civil. It was one of his last requests, and still I lost my cool. Worse, I exploded with violence. What's happening to me?

Sean opens the door to my bedroom, and escorts me through. "Get some rest. Have a shower. I'll have Bernice bring you some food. There's nothing for you to do until time for the wedding."

"I'm not hungry. And if you think you can keep me in here until Katie's wedding, you're crazier than she is. I'm going to that police station. One way or another. I've been patient long enough."

"Dani?"

Head snapping toward the door, I meet a pair of watery gray eyes. Softening, I half run, half walk to Sebastian's sister. Lauren throws her arms around me, and sobs. "I saw it on the news. My nanny was watching. Dani, what happened? Where's Sebastian? Is he okay?"

"You know Sebastian. I'm sure he's in control of the situation, even now," I lie, running my hand over her head and looping my arm through hers. I lead her to the living room, and ask, "Have you had breakfast?"

"No. I threw on the first jeans I could find and rushed over here."

"Okay." Clutching my phone, I arrange the blanket over us both. "What would you like? I'll have Bernice make something."

"I don't think I can eat a thing if I tried. I feel like I'm gonna puke."

"Yeah. Me too," I answer, honestly. "But, I know Sebastian would kill me if I didn't at least try and get you to eat something. How about green smoothies?"

"Why aren't you with him?"

"He apparently doesn't want me there. I've tried. *Believe me*. Every time I make a move, someone on the staff pulls me away. They claim I can see him when the timing is right."

****

"You'll call me when you know something?" Lauren asks.

We stand on the stairs outside of her school. Dressed in her school uniform, the innocence of her years shows. Unable to help myself, I tuck her hair behind her ear and pull her into a hug. "I promise. Try and have a good day."

"Fat chance."

Head dropped, she walks up the old steps. Heartbroken, I look after her until she's through the doors. *Sebastian's all she has.* I must make sure he makes it out for her. Determined to seize the chance while I've got it, I turn and scan the street. Cyrus is leaned against the car watching my every move. *There's no way out.*

Reluctantly, I walk back to the town car and take my place in the backseat. Sullen, I stare out the window trying to decide how to get to him. My phone vibrates in my jacket pocket, startling me back to attention. Fumbling to get it out, I push the talk button and bring it to my ear.

"Dani. It's Emmalyn, Sebastian's mother." Raging panic in her voice, she tries to stay calm. "How are you, darling?"

"Hello, Emmalyn. I'm assuming you've seen the news." Head in my hand, I struggle to come up with a way to explain the situation to Sebastian's mother. "I'm sorry. I don't really know very much."

"I'm in the city. Can you meet me?"

"Where?"

"Are you home? I'm on my way now."

"Um..." *How am I going to explain the current chaos at Sebastian and my apartment? Furthermore, what will Emmalyn think when she sees Alana.*

"Don't worry about tidying up, darling. The last thing I'm worried about is whether there are magazines on the end table. I'll see you soon."

Mind on the verge of exploding, I tuck my phone back in my pocket and exhale. The buildings become a blur of limestone as Benson weaves us in and out of traffic. The ride back to the apartment seems to take half the time it should. Quaking, I take the elevator to the penthouse. Emmalyn's already seated in the living room when I walk through the foyer. As always, her hair is perfectly groomed. Not a single strand out of place.

Blinding white teeth shining at me, she smiles. "I hope it's okay that I let myself in. Your housekeeper said I should wait for you here. She makes an excellent tea, by the way. I'm sure she'd be happy to help with some of these boxes."

"Yeah." Exhausted, I fall onto the couch and bring my knees to my chest. "I'm sure she would. I'm just not big on the idea of having someone else do my dirty work."

"Of course. I'm sorry. I'm not good at making small talk when I'm this nervous." She sets her tea cup on the table and reaches for my hand. "This is all coming out of left field for us but judging from the footage on the news you weren't exactly expecting it either."

Clueless, I stare at her.

Thumb rubbing over my knuckles, she clarifies, "The bathrobe."

"Great. On top of everything, my ass is plastered on national television."

"I can only imagine how rough this has been for you. What exactly happened?"

"Mrs. Black, I don't mean to be disrespectful. I'm apologizing now if it seems that way, but I'm exhausted. I'm just wondering why you aren't in Hartford getting things ready for the wedding? Doesn't Katie need you?"

"The wedding? That's the reason I'm here. Kathryn's threatened to call the whole thing off if Sebastian can't be there."

Sickened, I pull the sleeves of my sweater over my hands. *Now my mess is ruining Katie's day too.* "I'm sorry."

"Oh, hunny, it's not your fault." Emmalyn pulls me into a hug. "What do you say we get some answers?"

"I've been told he isn't allowed visitors. Only legal counsel."

"Well, I'm a lawyer, aren't I?"

Realization dawning, I jump from the couch. "Can you sit tight for just a sec?"

"Uh... sure. Okay."

Pulse racing, I jet to Sebastian's office. Thomas and Alana are both gone. Teeth clenched, I chew on my jaw. *Screw this plan of Sebastian's.* I want to play along, but it's nearly impossible when no one wants to clue me in on what exactly that means. Turning on my heel, I march back into the living room.

"Okay, let's do it!"

# Chapter 40

*S*ebastian

Fist balled, I fight the prickles running through my skin and stare straight ahead through the bars. If the piece of shit comes for me, I'll be ready for him this time. Knuckles twisted in a ball on my lap, I shake my head free of the tormented memories threatening to escape. Muscles contracting at the sound of the buzzer, I grit my teeth and wait. Practiced breaths keeping the beat of my heart steady, I stand.

Tobacco-stained teeth bared in a cocky smile; he pushes the oily hair from his face and comes to a stop in front of my cell. "Doing okay in there, *Bashie*?"

"Is my lawyer here?" I snap.

"You seem a little tense, *boy*. I'd be happy to work the kinks out for you."

Jarred by his words, I rub the pads of my finger and thumb together. "I have nothing to say to you without legal counsel present."

"Pity, and here I thought we'd have a little fun." He pulls a key from his pocket and unlocks the door. "Come on, boy. You have a visitor."

Reptilian touch encasing my wrist, he places the cuffs on me and leads me from my cell. Even the feel of his hand on my elbow makes me feel sick. Nostrils flared, I exhale and force myself to think about anything else. My heart sinks as I remember the look on Danielle's face as the squad car pulled away, the helplessness as she fought against Thomas to get to me. I'd give anything to see her now.

The interrogation room they lead me to is severely bright compared to the shadowy cell I've been sitting in over the last few hours. Eyes squinted, I see Thomas sitting at the table Detective West first occupied upon our arrival. Taking the one opposite him, I cut my eyes to West as he unhooks one cuff and secures me to the table.

"You've got fifteen minutes," he pipes.

Click of the door confirming he's officially gone, I sink against the chair. "How's Danielle?"

"She's not making things easy, but I think we've finally got her calmed down a bit."

"Is she cooperating with Alana?"

He clears his throat, and instantly I know I've asked too much of her. "I'd say that's been the hardest part of the process."

Tired eyes burning, I run my free hand over my face. "Make her understand how vitally important it is that she does exactly what you say, especially where Alana's concerned."

"I'll give it my best shot, sir, but we both know Ms. Stevens is nothing if not rebellious."

Smiling for the first time since I got his phone call this morning, I nod my head. "Truer words have never been spoken, Thomas. How's everything else getting on?"

"Plan B."

Jaw clenched, I drop my head. "When'd she find out?"

"She was at the building nearly as soon as the sun came up. Ms. Stevens got her to school alright, and I've got people on her."

"And what about the rest?"

"Your mother is in the city. She arrived as soon as the news cycles began as well. Last I checked, she was at the penthouse with Ms. Stevens."

"Fuck," I mumble. "This is turning into a veritable nightmare."

"You prepared for all these scenarios and more, sir. Don't worry. We've got you covered. Our time's almost over, so before I go, do you have any more instructions?"

"Find Rush. I called him hours ago."

"We're on top of that as well, sir. He was in the country with his in laws. He should be here soon enough."

"And Isabelle's still under watch?"

He nods. "Mister Black actually took care of that one for us. He instructed the staff to keep her out of the dayroom. She won't have access to a television for the rest of the day."

"Good. Last thing. Did Alana get it?"

"She's working on it, sir."

Relief settling into my chest, I straighten. "Excellent. Good work, Thomas."

"Time's up," West interrupts.

"I've got everything under control, sir," Thomas assures, gripping the doorknob.

I nod and watch him walk away, pulse quickening at the realization that I'm now alone with the detective. His thumb strokes over my pulse as he resituates my cuffs. Blood thickening, I jerk away from him.

"Mm…" He moans. "Glad to see you're feeling feisty again. Careful, boy, you wouldn't want to get too carried away. I'd hate to call in for a *psychological evaluation*. I know just the doctor to do it."

The smell of his sweat ensnaring my nostrils, I resist the temptation to drive my elbow into his nose. I'm doing this for my princess. For her, I'll play by the book. Once her name's clear, however, I'm bringing this fucking jail down on his perverted head.

"You sit *tight* now," he mocks, releasing me. "Real tight. You know how I prefer it."

Throat clogged with bile, I wait for his footsteps to fade before sitting on the dingy bed. Elbows rested on my knees, I hang my head in my hands and stare at the gray floor. *Danielle*. The sparkle in her eyes, the way her hair blows in the wind. "Be my strength, princess. It's the only way I'm going to be able to be yours," I whisper.

****

Time passes slowly when you're sitting in a box with nothing but iron and cement surrounding you. It feels like hours have passed since Detective West left me standing here, but the reality is it has only been minutes. Heightened awareness, I walk with him back to the interrogation room. All the while thinking of the decrease in pay coming Rush's way after taking so long.

Eyes adjusted to the light, I grow warm all over. Danielle looks up at me, sad smile caressing her lips. West goes through the unnecessary ritual of cuffing me to the table. Fingers twitching, she watches. Her longing wraps around me like a warm blanket. Mesmerized, I skim my eyes over the tear stains on her cheeks. She's beautiful, even now.

"What are you—?"

"Everyone has the right to legal counsel, Mister Black," my mother interrupts, winking at me. "I'm sorry it took us so long."

Head tilted in Detective West's direction, I wait for him to close the door. Danielle lunges from her seat toward me, but my mother places a hand on her shoulder and nods her head in the camera's direction.

"Sorry," my princess responds. "I'm just so glad you're safe. What the hell happened?"

"Thomas will explain everything when the times right, princess." I nudge the tips of my fingers against hers. "*You* just have to calm down and trust him."

"And who is going to explain things to me?" My mother questions.

"Mother—"

"No, son. This time you'll let me talk. I reviewed the file when we got here. You're being charged with murder! They have a body, for Christ's sake!"

Danielle's shoulders go rigid. Eyes bulged from their sockets, she stares at me expectantly. No longer caring what the police have to say about it, I wrap my hand around her wrist and stroke my thumb over her racing pulse.

Hot breath rushing through my nostrils, I exhale and turn to my mother. "It's nothing to worry about, Mother. Everything's being handled."

"Sebastian, you're my son. No matter what you've done, I'll always love you. Just let me get you some competent help."

"Rush is handling things, Mother. He should be here any minute."

"Your frat brother? You think he's enough to get you out of this? You need *real* criminal counsel. Someone with experience."

"I *trust* Rush enough to let him handle this. That should be enough for you."

Arms crossed, she presses her lips into a firm line and exhales. Unable to bear the disappointment in her eyes, I fold my hand over Danielle's. "You understand, don't you, princess?"

Licking a salty tear from her lips, she keeps her eyes trained on mine. The anguish I see in her worried green irises sends the building crashing down around me. Swallowing, I silently plea for her to agree with me. Chest heaving, she nods.

I squeeze her hand. "Thank you."

Shoulder's squared my mother crosses one leg over the other. Eye's turned to slits, she glares at me. "I will not let my only son go to jail for something he didn't do. Sebastian, I know you're capable of a lot of things, but murder isn't one of them."

Feeling as though someone's punched me in the gut, I once again push down the urge to confess the truth of that night all those years ago. "Mother, as always it's your faith in me that gives me the confidence to know I'll win."

Softening, she reaches her hand to my cuffed arm. "At least let me sit co-chair."

"I'll be out in time for Kate's wedding. Go home. Make sure it's everything she's expecting and more."

"Don't do that," Danielle says, her voice shaking. "Don't give me false hope."

Signaling for her to lean closer, I pull her arm. Hand against her wet cheek, I place a stray strand of hair behind her ear. "I love you, princess. Save the first dance for me. I promise I'll be there."

# Chapter 41

*D*anielle

"Thanks for riding back with me," Emmalyn says, her voice careful.

"Honestly, I should be thanking you. I'm getting beyond tired of body guards and secrets."

Eyes darting to her rearview mirror, she laughs. "I don't think you're escaping them anytime soon."

Refusing to give Cyrus and the rest of Sebastian's hired goons the satisfaction of looking back, I flip the lid down and check my makeup. It's easy to tell I've been crying, but I don't even care.

"Don't worry about the puffiness, darling. My makeup artist can work miracles."

"Thank you," I reply, softly. "Especially for lying so that I could see him."

"I didn't lie, sweetheart. I'm an officer of the court. I'm not allowed to lie. You were my assistant, just as I said. For those four hours at least." She winks and grips the wheel a little tighter. "Do you believe what he said?"

Heartbeat pounding against my ribs, I close the visor and look out the window. "About what?"

"Getting out in time for the wedding. Have you met this Rush kid? Because I have, as a courtesy to Sebastian, I hired him as an intern for a summer."

"No, I haven't met him," I lie. My one encounter with Sebastian's lawyer was when I was brought to the police station for question weeks ago. "What's he like?"

344

"He's an incompetent tool," she snorts.

"Really?"

Allowing herself some time to think about how to respond, she pulls into the garage of her massive Connecticut home. "I'm probably exaggerating. Richard's always saying I need to learn how to be a little less particular about things, especially when it comes to things at my office. Anyway, let's get you inside. The girls will certainly be happy to see you."

"Emmalyn," I place my hand on hers, "as far as Sebastian making it to the wedding, he promised me he would. He's never broken a promise to me thus far, but this time..."

"Yeah," she sighs. "I'm afraid of the same thing."

****

Not able to handle any more of the giggling from Katie's bridesmaids, I excuse myself and wonder aimlessly around the house until I find Richard's study. Relieved to find the door still unlocked, I pour myself a vodka on the rocks and sit on the black leather couch. Mind whirling, I pull the engagement ring from my pocket and twirl it in my fingertips. I'm not sure what makes me place it on my hand, but once it's there, nothing in me will allow it to come off. Lost in thought, I jump at the feel of the heavy hand on my shoulder.

"Day drinking, are we?" Richard asks. "Mind if I join you?"

"Be my guest," I answer. "It's your alcohol, after all."

"You raise an excellent point. I presume my office is the place to get away to today."

I fold my legs to give him room to sit. "Sorry, I wasn't meaning to end up here. It just sort of happened. Then I saw the liquor cart, and now here I am."

"It's fine, Dani. I'm happy to have the company, even if it was a surprise. Wanna talk about it?"

Pondering my options, I study him carefully. I'm not fully sure I should reveal my secrets to Richard, and I know it will piss Sebastian off if I do. Still, if I don't tell someone, I won't make it out of this day.

"You're a therapist, correct?"

"Technically, I'm a psychiatrist—"

"But you do therapy sessions as well, right?" I cut him off.

"Yes. Where's this going?"

Slamming back the rest of my drink, I shove my hand in my pocket and pull out all the cash I have on me. "Here's fifty bucks," I say, walking back to the drink cart. "I'd like a session."

"Danielle," he follows me, "when I asked if you'd like to talk, I meant free of charge."

Throat burning from the crisp vodka, I fall back on the couch. "I know, but trust me. Once I've said what I need to say, you'll be glad you took the cash."

Pouring another glass for himself as well, he stares down at the wrinkled bills. "Dani, does this have anything to do with Sebastian?"

"I can't confirm or deny that until you tell me that anything I say is now covered under doctor-patient confidentiality."

"Assuming you're not about to reveal any plans to harm yourself or others, and assuming you're not going to confess any harm done by you to a minor, then yes. I'll consider this conversation with you as a formal session."

"If you need more money to make things legit, I'm fine with that. I'll pay whatever the bill is. That's just all I had on me."

"Why don't you say what you need to? We'll figure out the rest later. For now, I'm more than happy to consider this," he pulls a five-dollar bill from the pile and returns the rest to me, "as a proper fee for my services."

Exhaling, I lean back against the leather and drain the rest of my liquid courage from the glass. "Okay. Sebastian didn't kill Walter Smith."

Never flinching, he strides to the door and turns the lock. "How do you know this?"

"Because I know who did," I reply, my gaze meeting his blue eyes.

He sits at his desk, clasps his hands together, and carefully asks, "What do you mean, you know who did?"

"I mean, I am the only person on the planet who can tell the police exactly what went down on the night Walter Smith disappeared."

"I see... and you're not offering this information because..."

"That's the part I can't tell you. What I can say is that I have a distinct feeling that the body the police have isn't Walt's. I can also say that I'm pretty sure Detective West knows this."

Running his hand over his brow in a way that's so like Sebastian's it makes my heart ache, he replies, "Dani, you have to know how this sounds."

"I know I sound like a lunatic." I stand and pace the room. "Believe me, I've spent the entire day feeling like one. I wouldn't be telling you any of this, I *shouldn't* be telling you any of this, but the thing is, Richard, I'm desperate. I know desperation is one of the worst emotions, but in my experience, it can also lead to great clarity. This is one of those times in which I see everything clearly. *Almost*."

"Why'd you add the 'almost'?"

"I know Sebastian's being set up. I know he knows it too, but he won't do anything to change it because he thinks he's protecting me—"

"Wait, protecting you. Protecting you from what?"

"I can't answer that, Doctor Black," I reply cautiously.

"You don't mean. Dani, are you telling me *you* killed this Walter Smith person? Is that why my son's in jail?" Forgetting his training, he flies from his seat, sending it crashing into the bookcase behind him.

Startled, I make a dash for the door. "Maybe this was a mistake. I'm sorry, forget I said anything."

"No," he polishes off the rest of his scotch and runs a hand through his blonde hair. Catching his breath, he returns to his chair. "No. I'm sorry. I agreed to treat this as I would any other session, and I will from this point forward. I need to let you know that this is a gray area for me, though. If you're confessing to murder—"

"I'm not confessing to anything," I interrupt. "Hypothetically, if I killed someone, I wouldn't be dumb enough to confess it to anyone, therapist or not."

"Right, and *hypothetically,* I think you would also know that confessing something like that to me would put me in a tight spot. It would mean that any action I took with that knowledge would start a war with my son. The last thing I'm looking to do is give him more reason to place a wedge between us."

"More reason?"

"It's nothing. I shouldn't have mentioned it."

Moistening my lips, I nod. "So, it's safe to assume we both have our secrets where your son's concerned."

"It looks that way, doesn't it? The question becomes, would you like to continue this session knowing what we know about each other?"

Easing back onto the couch, I cross my legs. I must tell someone else about this theory of mine, someone who won't tell me to "just go with the plan". Decision made, I nod.

"Okay then. You mentioned you believe Sebastian is going along with some form of set up to protect you. What leads you to believe it's a setup?"

"For starters, Walter Smith is, was, my stepfather." I can see him piecing the puzzle together, but I'm no longer worried that he's going to take the information he knows and use it against me. "If the police had really found his body, they would've asked me to identify it."

"Why are you so certain that you would've been the one they called?"

"Because Walt doesn't have anyone else *and* because he was stalking me prior to his death."

"He was stalking you?"

"Yes, and that's something I will absolutely not be talking about. What it's important for you to know is that Detective West knew about my history with Walt. There was an incident a few weeks ago in which an associate ended up calling the police. When Walt went missing, Detective West not only dug into those records, but also records from when I lived with Walter in California."

"Mm hmm. So, let's assume for a second that he would've contacted you had he found the body. You still haven't told me why you think this officer would have it out for my son."

"That's because I don't know. Call it woman's intuition if you need to, but there's more to the story of Sebastian Black and the Detective. I've known it since the first time we encountered him. I'm not sure, but I think it goes back to his time on the street. You know, when he was still with his birth mother. Do you know anything that would give us a clue?"

"I don't..." He drifts away and I know he's hiding something. "But I may know someone who does."

Grabbing ahold of the tiny ray of hope with everything in me, I clasp my hands together. "And you can get in touch with this person."

"I'm one of few who can," he replies.

"How soon?"

"After the wedding. We can make the trip together if you'd like. I know for a fact they've wanted to meet you."

Feeling chilled by the oddity of hi statement, I stare at him.

"You have nothing to be afraid of, Danielle," he says, genuinely. "I might, but I can promise you don't."

"Well, in that case, I guess I should go meet up with the girls and finish getting ready. If Sebastian can't be here for this, I'll do my best to make sure Katie knows he's here in spirit."

****

"Time to line up, ladies," Katie's wedding planner calls.

"Well, that's my cue," I say, setting my half empty glass of champagne on the coffee table in the church's bridal suite.

"Dani," Katie grabs my hand, "thank you for being here. I know you have more important things to do in the city."

I pull her in for a quick hug. "I think we both know Sebastian doesn't want my help. You look beautiful, by the way. I'll see you out there."

Sebastian's parents invited me to sit with them in the front row, which means all eyes are on me as I walk down the aisle. Trying hard not to think about the fact that most of these people saw my bare ass on their morning news, I keep my head down and focus on the pew. Richard Sr. and Virginia pretend not to notice my existence as I approach. Hoping I remember enough etiquette from my childhood to get through the event without Sebastian's guidance, I sit on the hard cushion and cross one leg over the other.

A talented tenor starts the processional by singing "La Vie en Rose" by Andrea Bocelli. In unison, we all turn our heads toward the back of the room. Wearing a bright smile and a navy chiffon dress, Emmalyn owns the aisle. The second she's seated beside me, I feel my tension releasing. She smiles and pulls a tissue from her purse to dab the already forming tears from her eyes. Brad's mother follows, trailed closely behind by two of his groomsmen.

The song switches to one I don't recognize, sang by the undeniably beautiful female vocalist, and the processional continues. Another groomsman, then another, and then... the moment I see him, the rest of the church fades away. Dressed in his tux, a red rose sticking from his lapel, he puts on his public face smile and commands the attention of everyone in the room. *Sebastian.* Drawn to him by the unseen force that connects us, I fight the urge to rush from my seat and run to him.

349

Shaking, Emmalyn reaches over and grabs my hand. I cling to hers with just as much desperation. *If this is a dream, we're both sharing the same one.* Meeting my eyes out of the corner of his, his smile momentarily changes to the private one reserved only for me. He takes his position at the altar, his attention remaining focused on me. For a moment, I forget where I am.

Then the bridesmaids come, each trying hard not to make a scene when they see him. Julie, Katie's maid of honor, has the hardest time. Eyes finding Sebastian, she stumbles up the step to the altar. Brad reaches forward to catch her, and she slowly makes her way to her official place. Confused, she looks toward our pew and back at Sebastian. Unable to contain her smile, she stares at him for a moment and redirects her attention to the aisle where the flower girl and ring bearer are coming our way.

The music changes to the traditional wedding march, and I force myself to stand and look at Katie. Wedding photographers stepping forward from both ends of the aisle, she stands in the entry just long enough to compose herself. Twitching hand, I fight the urge to look at Sebastian. At last, Richard and Katie are standing in front of us.

She should look at Brad, but her attention is on her little brother. Breaking free of Richard's grasp, she runs up the steps and nearly knocks him down with her embrace. Sobbing, she remembers what today's about and turns back to Brad. Confused expression on his face, Richard meets her there. As soon as the clergy asks who gives this woman, he joins us on our pew.

"How'd he make it happen?" he whispers.

"I don't know," Emmalyn replies.

"He promised me he would," I answer, blinking through the tears as I stare up at him.

Catching my eye from his peripheral, he winks and slightly nods his head in Katie and Brad's direction. Breathless laugh escaping me, I shake my head and force myself to focus my attention where it should be.

# Chapter 42

*S*ebastian

Weddings have never had much effect on me, but tonight feels different. *Another flash from the bright light on the photographer's camera.* Eyes focusing, I stare at the pew that's now empty except for her. I love my sister, but if she doesn't wrap this shit up soon, I'm likely to snap. Stretching the tension out of my neck, I force myself to smile for another stupid photograph that probably won't even get ordered. My mother has a knack for making people pose for pictures until we have achieved the *perfect* shot.

"I think that's it for the group shots," the overly priced man says at last.

"Sebastian, wait!" My mother calls after me as I dart down the steps.

"Later, Mother," I reply, yanking Danielle up by the hand and racing toward the door.

"Happy to see me, hotshot?" Her laughter is like the sweetest music to my ears.

Pinning her against the ancient bricks, I fold her mouth into mine. Her kiss is pure ecstasy, the delicate stroke of her tongue my ultimate aphrodisiac. Disregarding the reporters, I run my hand down her body and pull her leg over mine. Moan released from her lips, she thaws against me.

Ears filled with the murmuring of reporters, I pull away and hand her a pair of designer shades. "Put these on and take my hand."

I lead her through the swarm, dodging the mics and tape recorders being thrown in my face. I can't believe these vultures couldn't even find the decency to respect my sister's wedding. Opening the door to my Spider, I shield her as best I can as she climbs inside.

Elbowing my way through the herd, I take my place behind the wheel and pull onto the street.

"Are they going to follow us to your parents' house?" she sobs.

Pulling her shaking hand to my lips, I answer, "I'd like to see them try. The security team is ready."

"Why weren't they at the church?"

I link our fingers together and switch gears. "Because I have them stationed at points within a fifteen-mile radius of the house. This is the only thing I wasn't prepared for. I didn't expect anything to go down this weekend."

"But you were expecting it?"

"Yes," I sigh. "I'm sorry, princess. I know what you're thinking, but this isn't like that. There was a plan. I was pretty sure it'd work, but not one hundred percent certain. Until I knew I didn't want you to worry, or to get your hopes up, for that matter."

Finally, free of the hounds, she sinks against the leather seat. "I'm too exhausted to be pissed, Sebastian. I'm just glad you're okay."

"I am," I stroke her leg through the slit in her dress, "now that I'm with you, I'm perfect."

"How are you here?"

"What do you mean?" Turning the corner wide, I glance at her.

She takes the sunglasses off and allows me to see the seriousness in her eyes. "Don't play games with me, Sebastian. Not tonight. Just answer the question."

Knuckles white from the grip I have on the steering wheel, I sort through the facts for the version of the truth that will upset her least. "There was a hidden piece of evidence. I had it. Once the police got it, they had no choice but to let me go."

"So, you framed someone else?"

"I didn't say that, did I? It's exactly what I said. I had something that proved it wasn't me."

"What evidence?"

"At this time, it's best that you don't know the answer to that. I doubt West is ready to drop this just yet."

Turning her head toward the window, she shuts me out for the rest of the ride. When I pull up to the valet, she finally looks over at me. "Was it Walt's body?"

"No."

"You're sure?"

Hands cupped around her face, I stare directly into her eyes. "I'm completely positive, Danielle. This wasn't your fault." I look back at the parking attendant waiting for me to open the door. "Listen, the story is too long for me to get into here, but I will explain everything. Do you trust me?"

"Will you promise?"

"Yes, I promise." I place my lips on hers. "Can you wait until the time is right?"

She sighs. "I'll try."

Feet on the ground, I hand my keys off to the parking attendant and help Danielle from the car. Hands linked, we walk through the front door and into the sitting room. Stopping short of the French doors leading to my sister's reception, I turn her to face me. Chest tight, I scan her face, allowing ample time to take in the soft lines of her cheekbones and roundness of her nose.

"What is it?" She asks, eyes brightened by her smile.

Eyes closed, I exhale. "I have a question for you."

"Sebastian, you're freaking me out. Can you at least open your eyes while you ask it? I'm not sure I can handle anymore drama today."

Mouth dry, I lift her left hand into her line of sight. "Does this mean you're saying yes?"

Smile fading, she looks down at the black stone and back up at me. Bottom lip quivering, she runs her tongue along the seam and takes a deep breath. My stomach dropping, I clutch onto her.

She looks back down at the ring one time and smiles. "Yes, Sebastian! I'll marry you. I'll marry you right now if you want me to."

Relief rushes out of me with my breath. I take her in my arms and spin her around. "You scared the shit out of me, princess."

She laughs. "Really? After everything you've dealt with today, I'm the one that scared you."

"You're the only part of the day that mattered." Still holding her off the floor, I wrap one hand in her hair and press her lips to mine.

****

*Danielle*

His kiss burning a hole through my core, I clench my thighs together and bend my knees to build a barrier for the flood pooling between my legs. Pouring all I have into him,

I wrap my arms around his neck and squeeze. *I love this man with every fiber of my being.* Nothing on Earth could keep me from marrying him. *Not now.* Not after everything we've been through today.

"Oh, my!" Emmalyn's voice cuts through the air. "Are we interrupting something?"

Gray eyes shining, Sebastian pulls away with a smile and sets me back down. Fingers twisted in mine, he closes the gap between us, his parents, and Julie. Body tingling all over, I look at each of their expectant faces.

"Sorry for the scene," he begins, smiling down at me. "I forgot where we were for a moment."

"You what?" Julie teases. "You're the king of calculation. What in the world could've possibly gotten you so swept up?"

Lips thinned into his infamous smirk, he raises his eyebrows at her. "The fact that I'm the lucky man who gets to marry this amazing woman." He turns to me and kisses my forehead.

Squealing, Emmalyn and Julie both throw their arms around us. Giddy, I place a palm on Emmalyn's back. I don't know when the change occurred, but somehow, I became one of them.

Emmalyn pulls away, and pries Julie off Sebastian. "You're serious about this? It's not some kind of get out of jail free card or something, right?"

"I asked her last week, Mother."

"And you kept it a secret this long," Julie slaps him. "When did you do it? Was it when we were in Vegas? Oh my God! Was it after the fireworks show? I'm going to kill you for not letting us all be a part of it."

"Slow down, Jewels," he laughs.

Focusing on her, I reply, "It was in Colorado. And we weren't keeping it a secret. He asked, but I didn't accept until now. That's what you walked in on."

"Oh!" Eyes filled with tears, Emmalyn claps her hands. "Oh, Richard! Tonight's turning out to be perfect. Wouldn't you say it's perfect?"

"Hmm... perfect indeed," he answers, a little less enthusiastically than I'd hoped.

Looking at him for the first time since the excitement began, I notice the apprehension in his eyes. "I know I probably wasn't your first choice, but I love your son."

"Danielle—"

"No, son. I'll speak for myself, thank you," Richard interrupts. "Dani, I wouldn't choose anyone other than you for my son. I've made that mistake. It taught me well. It's just been a long day. A lot has happened. A lot of *confessions* were made. I'm just processing."

Humbled by the dawn of new understanding, I nod.

"Forget him," Emmalyn says, waving her arms through the air excitedly and hugging us again. "He'll pipe up after a glass of champagne. Katie and Brad will be here any minute, but we have to make plans to celebrate! Dani, name your time and place. We'll handle everything else."

"What are we celebrating?" Alana's voice rings through the air, turning my blood cold.

Wicked smile on her face, Emmalyn spins on her heel. "Sebastian and Dani are engaged."

"What!" Sweeping past the rest of the crowd, she marches up to us and takes a tight hold on my left hand. "No," she says, snidely. "You can't do this!"

"I believe it's already done," I reply, ripping my hand from hers. "Face it, Alana. *You lost.*"

Ignoring me, she looks up at Sebastian. "You can't do this, and you know why."

"Why is that, Alana?" I find the courage to say the things I've been dying to for months. "Because I'm the lowly paramedic's daughter? Because Sebastian didn't love you and it's easier for you to believe that the reason for that was because he can't love anyone? Because you need to have control over him, and you know you'll never have it so long as he's marrying me—"

"Shut up," she interrupts. "Sebastian, the only way for you to marry her is if—"

"That's correct," Sebastian interrupts.

"I won't go through with it," she snarls. "I'm not signing a damned thing."

The hair on the back of my neck stands on edge. A sudden chill washing over me, I turn to him. "Sebastian? What's she talking about?" I ask, my voice raspy.

Smiling a cruel smile that lets me know there's more to this than jealousy, Alana says, "Does she not know? I thought you had no more secrets between you, Sebastian. I guess you still couldn't bring yourself to tell her *everything*, though, could you? Some secrets are just too much for poor, sweet, damaged little Dani to handle. Aren't they, darling?"

She runs her fingertips along his jawline, and I feel as though I'll lose my lunch.

"Don't do this here, Alana," Sebastian warns.

Eyes twinkling, she looks around the room. "Oh, I think this is the perfect place to do this," she says, focusing her sights on me once again. "Dani, Sebastian can't marry you—"

"Enough," he growls, grabbing her elbow and pulling her toward the French doors leading to the backyard.

"Because he's already married to me," she finishes.

Everything happens at warp speed. I can't make out one voice from the next as his family breaks out into hysterics. Blood rushing from my face, I look into his eyes. Using my stare to plead with him, I beg him to tell me it isn't true. The regret etched into the lines on his face tells me everything I need to know. Pulling his ring from my finger, I drop it on the floor. He steps toward me, and I turn away. Running from the room, I make my way down the hall and onto the lawn.

*I knew it was too good to be true.*

# Also Available

**Run Series**

Run from You

Run With You

# Coming Soon

The Final Installment in the Run Series
Run All the Way

# Acknowledgements

As always, I'm nothing without God. I don't say this with the intention of trying to "convert" you to some religion. I write it, because I have always personally believed that there's a force bigger than myself driving the wheel to this life. When I wake up each morning and look at all I've been given, it's impossible for me not to know deep inside of myself that there is someone out there who found me worthy enough to bless me with this life. It's a simple truth for me. If it's not a truth for you, I don't hold it against you in any way.

Next in line is my husband. Maurice, you and I have certainly had our ups and downs. In this life there've been times when we've both wanted to throw in the towel. Much like Dani and Sebastian, our love is real and filled with imperfections. We've broken each other, fixed each other, and protected each other more times than I'm able to count. Still, through every storm, every heartbreak, every sleepless night; you are the glue that holds me together. The anchor that keeps me from drifting away. If there's one thing I know about the future, it's that it's incomplete without you in it. Thank you for loving me like you do. Thank you for believing in me when I'm not strong enough to believe in myself. Thank you for carrying me when I'm too weak to walk. Above everything, thank you for the sacrifices you've made along this journey to my dream. There've been many, yet you never complain.

My darling children. You're my driving force. Everything I do in this life, I do it for your future. I know you've had your own sacrifices to make along this journey. Mostly, in the amount of time I've had to spend working to build my platform or market the books. Despite everything, I hope you know how much I love you. To my daughter, we've literally grown up together. I'm the woman I am today, because I became your mother when I was the girl I was then. The most difficult thing I've ever had to face was in reliving the pain of what he did to me while I watched those lines become two. His sins are not yours to carry, my princess. The love I have for you is completely independent of the anger I had for him. You saved me. As you come into your own even more, I hope that is the truth you cling to. You're a light in this world and I hope you never stop shining.

To my boys, it's your energy and love that gets me out of bed most mornings. I was afraid of being a mom to boys. I didn't think I'd know how to do the job. In my mind, you'd take one look at me and know that I was a fraud. Yet, the minute I held either of you in my arms you awakened something inside of me that I didn't know existed. I may never be the mom who plays in the dirt with you, but I will always love you. One of the greatest joys I have in this life is in knowing that I'll forever be the first woman to hold your hearts. While you're definitely different in some ways, you're just as alike in others. I can't wait to see the men you'll grow to be.

Even in the indie world, it literally takes a village to produce a book. I wish I had the space to devote a paragraph or more to every single person who contributes to the "behind the scenes" of this journey. Sadly, I do not. However, there are a few people that it would be remiss of me not to recognize.

For starters, Maria, you've been with me in this journey from the beginning. I honestly wouldn't have made it this far without you. From teasers to blog tours, you've been the one handling all of that so that I can focus on the important part of my job, writing. You've been a sounding board for new ideas, a shoulder to cry my frustrations to, and a constant source of encouragement. Most of all, you've grown into a dear friend. Thank you for responding to that request for beta readers what seems likes years ago. I truly believe you are an angel sent to me in human form. There are not enough ways to say thank you for everything you do, but that doesn't make me appreciate it any less.

Wendy Darling, you have been one of the true wonders of this book world. You came into my life a reviewer and have grown into one of the truest of friends. Thanks for sharing parts of your life with me, and for accepting bits of mine in return. Your love for Sebastian and Dani's story will not soon be forgotten.

Chloe, you have also been there since the start. Thank you for inspiring a belief in my writing that I never would've had. Our late-night chats are one of my cherished treasures. Get ready, there's a whole 'nother book for you to get me through.

To all of my Kittens, our little family has saved me in many ways. For the majority of my life, I've been a wonder. I've searched high and low for my place in this world, and with you at my side I've found it. You may never truly understand just how much your love means to me, but that will never stop it from touching the deepest, darkest layers of my heart.

To all of the amazing beta readers who gave this book their time and attention, I owe you much more than I'll ever be able to repay. Thank you for your countless hours and for always being willing to let me pick your brain just a little more.

To all of the bloggers who supported this process through reviews, blog tours, blog hops, spotlights, and so much more; thank you for all your hard work. The indie community is what it's grown to be because of your dedication. Your time and energy is greatly appreciated, not just by me, but by hundreds like me.

Lastly, to you dear reader, thank you for once again taking a chance on me and my writing. As always, I hope you find it worthy. I cannot express how much your willingness to spend your hard-earned buck on my words means to me. A simple thank you just doesn't suffice, however, for now that's what I have. So, thank you! From the bottom of my heart, I appreciate every single one of you. Xo

# Author Bio

K andice is a serial lover of all things pink, chocolate enthusiast, homeschooling mother, and wannabe yogi.

Kandi's love of storytelling can be traced back to her fourth-grade year, when a history lesson on Native Americans became too unimaginative for her liking. She took it upon herself to liven things up by creating a story that was based on half-truths about a self-named Indian Princess.

Kandice is in fact of Native American heritage (her great-grandmother was a full-blooded Cherokee) and in her own mind a princess, so you can see where her inspiration came from. Her story was a huge hit with friends, and an author was born.

Kandice was born and raised in rural Arkansas, where she currently lives with her husband and three children. Though, if you ask her she'll confirm that her soul is lost somewhere on the west coast waiting for the day that her body can rejoin it.

Printed in Great Britain
by Amazon

37676501R00205